John Stoughton

Howard, the Philanthropist, and His Friends

John Stoughton

Howard, the Philanthropist, and His Friends

ISBN/EAN: 9783337013462

Printed in Europe, USA, Canada, Australia, Japan

Cover: Foto ©Andreas Hilbeck / pixelio.de

More available books at **www.hansebooks.com**

HOWARD'S HOUSE AT CARDINGTON

HOWARD

THE PHILANTHROPIST

AND HIS FRIENDS.

BY

JOHN STOUGHTON, D.D.

Author of "William Penn," "History of Religion in England," etc.

London:

HODDER AND STOUGHTON,

27, PATERNOSTER ROW.

MDCCCLXXXIV.

TO

SAMUEL WHITBREAD, ESQ.,

M.P. FOR BEDFORD,

A DISTINGUISHED DESCENDANT OF

HOWARD'S HONOURED FRIEND AND RELATIVE,

THIS VOLUME

IS DEDICATED, WITH PROFOUND RESPECT,

AND IN GRATEFUL ACKNOWLEDGMENT

OF ASSISTANCE IN PREPARING IT

KINDLY RENDERED

BY THE WHITBREAD FAMILY.

IN the home of my childhood there hung an engraving of John Howard, visiting a prison cell and relieving the miserable inmates. Underneath were Burke's memorable words, "This Gentleman has visited all Europe, not to survey the sumptuousness of palaces or the stateliness of temples, but to dive into the depths of dungeons, to plunge into the infection of hospitals, to take the gauge and dimensions of misery, to remember the forgotten, to attend to the neglected." The picture and the words made an indelible impression on my mind, and the sight of them recently, after the lapse of more than sixty years, renewed it in all its vividness. Howard was chief amongst the heroes of my boyhood. I never cared for warriors or sages as I did for him; and stories of his prison visits were to me a great delight.

About thirty years since I was requested by my friend, the late Rev. William Alliott, of Bedford, to prepare a memorial of the philanthropist, to be delivered at an anniversary of Howard Chapel. Relics were shown and traditions were related on the occasion. They revived the image of my early favourite, and led to a new examination of his works and of his ways. It struck me, that though eulogies in abundance had been pronounced on his achievements, full justice had not been done to his religious peculiarities, his ecclesiastical relations, and certain aspects of his personal character. A few years ago, when released from pastoral engagements, I resumed these studies, arranging illustrations I had gathered and recording conclusions I had reached. The MS. was laid aside for reasons I need not relate; but during the past year my publishers urged me to resume the task, as former Lives of Howard were most of them out of print and failed to meet the increasing taste for biographical literature.

What I have written is based upon an examination of original authorities, including Howard's own works, which are really biographical; a view of his "Character and Public Services," published by Dr. Aiken; and Funeral Sermons preached by ministers who were his personal friends. In periodical literature soon after his death, and in the industrious collection of what could be gathered respecting him at the time by Dr. James Baldwin Brown, in Memoirs originally published in 1818, may be found all the leading facts of the philanthropist's history; but an important addition to the number of his letters was made by the Rev. J. Field, in a small book entitled " Correspondence of Howard, 1855," now out of print and difficult to be obtained.

Popular Lives of varied merit have been written by Dixon, Field, and Taylor; and views of Howard's services are furnished by Mr. Bellows and Dr. Guy.

Howard's friends and followers deserve to have their names associated with his, and therefore brief notices respecting them are incorporated in this volume. His friends, for the most part, are little known; but I have had the good fortune to gain information respecting those of them who were ministers of religion, from a large collection of Funeral Sermons in the library of New College. Of Mr. Whitbread, Howard's great friend, I have learned much from Lady Isabella Whitbread, who most kindly placed before me at Southill, family documents, throwing light on his beautiful character and also upon matters relating to Howard himself and his unhappy son.

For much interesting information relative to Howard's connection with Bedford, I am indebted to the late Rev. W. Alliott, and also to the Rev. John Brown, the present minister of Bunyan Meeting in that town.

My descriptions of Howard's homes and haunts are derived from visits to them at different periods; and my best thanks are due to General Mills and Miss Whitbread for their courteous assistance when I was last at Cardington. From descendants of Mr. Prole, Howard's servant, I learned much when rambling about the neighbourhood in 1852.

I make no apology for connecting personal reminiscences of foreign travel with the records of Howard's journeys; as, with the exception of Northern Europe, almost all the places referred to in his books and letters it has been my privilege to visit—several of them repeatedly.

CONTENTS.

CHAPTER I.

BOYHOOD.

1726–1742.

MOST persons, when standing under the dome of St. Paul's Cathedral, are attracted by a conspicuous statue to the left, as they enter the choir. Attired in Roman costume, with sandaled feet, a key in one hand, a scroll in the other,—broken chains lying on the top of a pedestal—the figure would scarcely, even with the latter device, suggest the man it is intended to represent, were it not for the inscribed name, JOHN HOWARD. His real appearance strangely differed from such a classic ideal. His character did not rest on the study of Roman or Greek literature, he felt no admiration for its philosophers or poets, and was utterly devoid of sympathy with its triumphant warriors. His simplicity and naturalness presented a contrast to the guise and attitude assigned by the sculptor.

An epitaph, composed by his friend, Samuel Whitbread, M.P., informs us that Howard was born at Hackney, in the County of Middlesex in the year 1726. It may be presumed that he had authority for this statement; yet successive biographers give different accounts as to the place and date of the philanthropist's birth. According to an unsupported tradition, he first saw the light at Cardington. His earliest

Biographer,[1] who was on terms of intimate acquaintance, informs us that his father had a house, first at
Enfield, and afterwards at Hackney; adding—"It
was, *I believe*, at the former of these places, that Mr.
Howard was born." With this statement agrees the
testimony of a second witness "well acquainted with
him." On the other hand, writers, soon after his
death, speak of him as born at Clapton; within the
parish of Hackney; one of them cites Howard's
authority to that effect. This, I think, in connection
with the inscription in St. Paul's, sufficiently settles
the point. The years 1724 and 1727 have been
assigned as the period of his birth; but the date 1726
on the monument is confirmed by the words of a
person, who stated that Howard told him in 1787, he
was then sixty-one years of age.

John Stowe, in his "Survey of London," remarks:
"On the north side of the priory of St. Bartholomew
is a lane truly called Long, which reacheth from
Smithfield to Aldersgate Street; built on both sides
with tenements for brokers, tipplers, and such-like."
After Stowe's time, the brokers predominated; and
an annotator upon Strype describes Long Lane as
"a place of note for the sale of apparel, linen, *uphol-
sterers'* goods, both second-hand and new, but chiefly
old." It is more than probable, many a thrifty tradesman in that neighbourhood made a decent fortune;
but no gains were ever turned to such a use as those
acquired by one citizen, who lived there in the first
quarter of the last century. For John Howard's
father was partner in a firm that had "a very considerable upholstery and carpet business" somewhere

[1] Dr. Aiken.

about the corner of Long Lane ; and he so prospered that he was fined for refusing to serve as Sheriff in 1739, when the son had reached the age of thirteen. A fortune inherited from his parent mainly contributed to the resources on which he drew so largely in his memorable career.

The elder Howard was a decidedly pious man. "He maintained," we are informed, "great order and regularity in his house ; and to his constant observance of the Sabbath, and of the duty of family prayer, his son, perhaps, was indebted for that piety which ever after formed a distinguished feature in his character." Whether the worthy upholsterer retired from business before or after his son's birth, is not clear ; but if the conclusion adopted as to the birth-place of the latter be correct, it would seem likely that the family at the time were living, not in the city, but amidst Clapton green fields. In a still more rustic locality however he spent his earliest years, for he turned out a sickly child ; and after his mother's death,—of whom we can gather nothing except that her maiden name was Cholmley, and that she died soon after his birth, —he was taken to Cardington, where his father held some property. Nursed there by the wife of John Prole, of whom I shall have much to say hereafter, he derived benefit from country breezes and wholesome diet; this village, three miles from Bedford, became the scene of his early boyhood, whilst the old trees, the older church, and the winding Ouse older still, formed the background of his earliest recollections.

When of sufficient age, he was sent to the town of Hertford, and placed under the tuition of a school-

master named Worsley. This person is said by some
to have been a "good Greek scholar;" but, whether
through the master's fault or the pupil's inaptitude,
or, it might be, through directions from the parent,
who did not wish him to be classically drilled, the
lad learned little ; for it is reported by Dr. Aiken,
that in later life, he declared, "with more indignation
than he commonly expressed, how, after a continuance
of seven years at this school, he left it, not fairly
taught one thing." [1]

The elder Howard dwelt in the parish of Hackney,
celebrated as the residence of Dr. Bates ; of Matthew
Henry after he left Chester; and of other Nonconformist celebrities. His principles,—for he was an Independent,—would be strengthened by the traditions
and social atmosphere of the neighbourhood ; and it
was a natural thing for him to entrust his son's education to a member of his own communion. Dr. Aiken
speaks of this schoolmaster, as "extremely deficient
in qualifications requisite for such an office," and of
opulent Dissenters amongst Independents as peculiarly liable to misplace confidence in defective
teachers. We can imagine the pupil at Hertford as
thin and fragile, with a benevolent countenance,
prominent nose, bright eyes, and thin lips, the last
showing he had a will of his own ; hair cut short in
front, and curled behind, his clothes like a court dress
in miniature—they complete the boy's portrait.

The next step in his education requires more ex-
planation than it has received from his biographers.
The Act of Uniformity in 1662 excluded Noncon-

---

[1] A View of the Characer and Public Services of the late John
Howard, Esq., LL.D., F.R.S. By John Aiken, M.D.

formists from the national seats of learning; and therefore they had to provide for the further instruction of their sons, after leaving ordinary schools, as best they could. Hence arose *Academies*, as they were called—not like our boys' schools, not like colleges of the present day; but of an intermediate kind, generally, if not always, so conducted as to include ministerial and lay pupils. Several Institutions of this kind existed in the country; those of the first period were, with two exceptions, under the care of Puritan clergymen ejected from the Establishment. Those of the second period, down to the middle of the eighteenth century, had presiding over them ministers educated in Scotch and other Universities, or trained in private for the office they fulfilled. Academies had no Councils or Committees to support them, though help might be afforded by affluent friends. It is a misnomer to dignify the instructors with modern titles. In some cases there was only one tutor; in others, there were not more than two.

Misapprehensions of their nature are followed by defective notions of the education they could afford. Theology was by no means an exclusive study. Greek, Latin, and mathematics came within the curriculum. At Kibworth, where Dr. Doddridge was educated, a liberal course was pursued. "The Greek poets," says that accomplished scholar, "which gave us the most employment, were Theocritus, Homer, and Pindar."

More than one of these Academies existed in London, and that which is connected with the history of Howard, was for a time under the care of Thomas Rowe, of Newington Green, son of John Rowe, one of the ministers at Westminster Abbey during the Commonwealth. Among Thomas Rowe's pupils was Dr. Watts. Rowe's successors included Dr. Ridgley, with whom was associated, as tutor in philosophy and languages, John Eames. He is described as Howard's tutor. Eames was a man of singular ability and of unusual attainments. After passing through Merchant Taylors' school, he prepared for the ministry, but did not enter a pulpit more than once : nervousness, coupled with defective utterance, produced an utter failure on the occasion. He consequently gave up all idea of being a preacher. His talents and attainments, however, fitting him for educational work, he assisted, and then succeeded, Dr. Ridgley, who died in 1734. He continued tutor until his death, in 1744. He distinguished himself in scientific pursuits ; and being favoured with the acquaintance of Sir Isaac Newton, that philosopher introduced him to the Royal Society, of which he was elected member. So great was his scholarship, that Dr. Watts said to one of his students, " Your tutor is the most learned man I ever knew." He numbered amongst his pupils, Dr. Furneaux, Dr. Savage, and Dr. Price; and he is said also, at one time, to have had under his care Thomas Secker, afterwards Archbishop of Canterbury.

Certainly Howard was placed for a short time under the tuition of Mr. Eames ; but whether as private pupil or as one in common with others under his care, I cannot say.[1] Dr. Price, one of the theological stu-

---

[1] Dr. Brown has confounded the Institution presided over by Mr. Eames, with the Academy supported by Mr. Coward, a London Merchant. Howard did not study there.

dents, is known to have been his companion; and companionship between them ripened into friendship. What exactly were Mr. Eames' opinions I cannot ascertain, but he is described as of "a candid and liberal disposition, and a friend to free inquiry, which exposed him to much opposition and uneasiness from some narrow-minded persons." His piety, however, is attested by Dr. Watts, in a singular remark, after his friend's death,—"What a change did Mr. Eames experience, but a few hours between his lecturing to his pupils, and his hearing the lectures of angels." Nevertheless, I question whether this excellent man had quite the same cast of religious sentiment as we shall find strongly expressed in the correspondence of his distinguished pupil.

What Mr. Eames did for Howard's education, I am at a loss to determine; for Dr. Aiken says, "he was never able to speak or write his native language with grammatical correctness, and that his acquaintance with other languages—the French perhaps excepted—was slight and superficial." On the other hand, Dr. Stennett, on whose ministry Howard attended when in London, affirmed that his understanding and judgment "were enriched and improved by a variety of useful knowledge. And, as he had a taste for polite literature, so he was well versed in most of the modern languages, which he took no small pains to acquire, that he might be the better enabled to carry his benevolent purposes into effect."[1] What Aiken says respecting Howard's mode of writing English is per-

[1] "A Sermon occasioned by the death of John Howard, Esq." What opportunities the two authors had of forming these opinions, will appear hereafter.

fectly correct ; but I feel some doubt, as to what he tells us about Howard's acquaintance with languages, since Dr. Stennett, who knew him intimately, gives a different account ; surely Howard must have known much of other tongues besides his own, or he could never have conversed with foreigners in the way he did. Instances of such conversation we shall meet with in future chapters. Moreover, I should infer from Stennett's statement, that Howard must in early life have laid the foundation of subsequent attainments. My impression is, when the two testimonies are balanced, that his education was not so imperfect as appears from the one, nor so complete as we might conclude from the other. Perhaps he was one of those who, with plenty of mental vigour in other directions, have a natural incapacity for acquiring much " school learning," but who nevertheless learn enough to form the basis of subsequent acquirements.

The school-boy was bound apprentice to Alderman Newnham, a grocer in Watling Street ; and hence, to other memories which pleasantly haunt the streets of London, we may add this of the grocer's apprentice passing along that thoroughfare. The old city near London Bridge, has become familiar through engravings and descriptions ; and we are at no loss to picture the apprentice looking about him and making his observations, as he rambled under the shadow of the Monument and past the Boar's Head in Eastcheap.

CHAPTER II.

SELF-EDUCATION.

1742–1751.

HOWARD'S father died in September, 1742; and being left without parents, with no relation near enough to exercise a strong personal influence over him, the son to a great extent became his own master. He was entitled to a fair fortune for those days—seven thousand pounds in money, with plate and furniture falling to his share. That sum was to be paid when he came of age; and being residuary legatee of his father's property, after payment of eight thousand pounds to his only sister, he had the prospect of temporal prosperity. The executors were Lawrence Channing, husband to the testator's sister; Ive Whitbread of Cardington, related to the deceased; and Lewin Cholmley, a friend and connection of Howard's mother. These gentlemen had so much confidence in the youth, then only seventeen years old, that they gave him considerable power over the management of his possessions.

He was now his own master—a perilous position for most young men of his age; but it is evident that those who knew him‑ best were convinced he would not abuse the freedom they entrusted in his hands. It would seem as if he had been well schooled in filial obedience, if not in other things, for he had submitted to commercial drudgery, with no liking for scales and ledgers, for hogsheads of sugar and chests of tea; and we find him, when he could do as he pleased, obtaining release from his indentures. At once he attended to the preservation and improvement of his patrimony.

The Clapton house, left by old Mr. Howard, came into his possession. It is described in 1790 as "a venerable mansion, though decayed and disfigured;" situated on the western side of the village street; soon after that date it was pulled down. It stood in need of repair when the young man first called it his own; and he did not fail to do with it what was necessary in the way of repairs.

A story is handed down,—one of several traditions which will appear in this volume,—exhibiting a curious combination of benevolence and eccentricity in Howard's character. A gardener, whose Christian name was Henry, liked to tell, when he was ninety years old and John Howard had won a world-wide fame, how his old master's son might be seen close to a buttress of the garden wall, waiting for the baker as he drove by in his little cart. When the youth had bought a loaf of the man, he would fling it over the wall, and, with a laugh, call out to the servant, " Harry, see if there be not something for you among the cabbages." The frolicsomeness of the lad bore a kindly stamp; and the regularity of his appearance, exactly when the cart came up, indicated his ingrained punctuality.. Generosity, order, and a spice of fun were elements in the philanthropist from beginning to end.

He did not make the Clapton house his home;

that was let, and before he fixed on a residence, he underwent an important process, which it is necessary carefully to detail, as it prepared him for the work of his after life. It was a process of *self-education*, not carried on with any consciousness of what would follow, but making up for school deficiencies.

> " The world was all before him, where to choose
> A place of rest, and Providence his guide."

Providence *was* his guide, and he was led into a noble "rest," a rest of conscience and of soul, in doing a great work appointed by God, and never to be accomplished without His help and blessing. "The way of man is not in himself, and it is not in man that walketh to direct his path." The true picture of life, with a human being in the fore front, fulfilling a destiny, requires a grand background, with a Divine presence and guardianship throwing a shadow across the path, and guiding the traveller step by step; as Murillo, in his charming picture by the door of Seville Cathedral, represents an Angel leading a child in a way he knows not. So I think of Howard at that critical era of his life.

We find him, soon after his emancipation from business, starting on a Continental tour. No mention is made of this in some early biographical sketches; but, as Dr. Aiken speaks of the circumstance in a decided tone, there exists no room for doubt on the subject. Delicate health had probably something to do with the motives which prompted this journey. As repeatedly, in notices of his early life, there are references indicating that he was far from robust, a change of air might be thought beneficial; but besides that,

I think he must early have been fond of travelling, as we have records of four Continental journeys before he entered upon his memorable prison tours. He evidently liked the change and excitement of travel. It seems to have been almost the only recreation in which he indulged ; that it was, in some instances at least, to him a delightful recreation, is obvious, notwithstanding the unselfish and heroic ends which he proposed to himself in his later expeditions. If in those days great difficulty existed in moving from place to place, there also prevailed an idea, that to visit distant capitals, and learn their manners and customs, was desirable, if not indispensable, for a gentleman's education. It is possible even that young Howard might regard a Continental tour as adapted to make up for educational defects, and to improve his knowledge of languages—French in particular. He was fond of change, and had that innate love of novelty which often grows stronger as years advance.

At all events, this is plain, that he started for France and Italy when he was between eighteen and twenty years old. How he travelled, whether alone or in company, we are not informed.

As a defective education is attributed to him, so he is considered to have been wanting in artistic taste. Burke's eulogium may be regarded by some as countenancing the idea. Here, again, conclusions are drawn too hastily. He is known to have had a collection of pictures in his house at Cardington. His house at Cardington, it is said by some one, " was better filled with paintings and drawings than any other on a small scale that he ever saw."[1] We shall

[1] Robt. Hall's Works, iv. 17.

meet hereafter with several indications that, in his benevolent tours he was not blind to the charms of Art, though he would not allow them to have supremacy over his mind. Some have thought he bought pictures on this first journey, which is quite possible ; it is also possible that he procured them afterwards, when he had more ample means at his disposal.

On his return to England, he went to live at Stoke Newington, not much improved in health, but with sufficient strength to enable him to pursue a course of study which helped to make up for lost time. If not a scholar, he was fond of books. Unable to construe with ease either Greek or Latin, he liked to read English ; and he availed himself of leisure for that purpose. Also he had a decided taste for science, which the example and attainments of his master, John Eames, would tend to stimulate. Natural philosophy, in its more popular branches, and even the practice of medicine, occupied a considerable amount of his attention ; the latter became of essential service on many occasions in his benevolent career. Howard had considerable powers of observation, and by the accumulation of natural facts, and the watchful notice of men and things, he educated himself more efficiently than many do who have won honours at a University.

At Stoke Newington he suffered from nervous fever, and only through prescribed diet of a simple kind, and the utmost self-discipline, did he overcome perils which beset his early days. Horse exercise, it is said, was added to other means of improving health ; and around this simple circumstance stories have gathered to the effect, that he rode in the morning to a common a few miles off, with some book in his pocket, and that, sitting down to read, he would leave the animal to graze on the surrounding herbage. Much mythical history grows around illustrious names, and our hero did not escape the common fate; yet this not improbable story points to the fact, that he was fond of reading, and liked it better than joining a shooting party, or following the hounds.

At the time he lived in Newington he was thought to be consumptive; and his "rigorous regimen" is reported to have produced extraordinary habits of abstinence ever afterwards. He suffered from nervous fever, and on that account visited Bristol Hot Wells, and after drinking the waters would walk under the rocks by the side of the Avon, and wander about the breezy Downs.

But Newington was his home till about 1755. It does not appear in what spiritual state of mind he was at that period. There are decisive proofs of evangelical convictions in his letters and journals; but whether by a sudden change he reached them, or whether he resembled a child, "who cannot tell when he first began to love his father," it is impossible to determine; it is likely, however, that parental influence contributed to fix that decision of character which continued to the end of his days.

Stoke Newington, like Hackney, was noted for Dissenters; the "Green," still retaining tints of its early social colour, used to be called "the favourite seat of Dissenting Muses," for there Theophilus Gale and Charles Morton educated young men; and amongst them were Samuel Wesley, father of John and Charles, and another celebrity of a different class—Daniel de Foe. Dr. Price, at a later time, preached at a Presbyterian Meeting House on the same green; and in the old street to the north stood an Independent place of worship, of which I have a recollection as it appeared fifty years ago. It had a small pulpit surmounted by a large sounding board; tall-backed pews and a heavy gallery even then told of earlier days. The exterior presented blank walls pierced by ugly windows and an ugly door, whilst a high-pitched roof stamped the whole with a barn-like look. The original edifice had been taken down to make way for the new mansion of Sir Thomas Abney, and the place just referred to was erected about 1700. In that building Howard worshipped, and of the Church there he became a member.

During the period of Howard's residence in Newington, Abney House, which occupied part of the ground now enclosed within Abney Park Cemetery, was in its perfection—an old fashioned edifice, with a brick front, within high garden walls, faced by a quaint iron gate, redolent of the reign of William III. and Queen Anne. Inside, it was full of cumbrous furniture, and from the windows could be seen a wide-spreading garden, with noble trees and trimly-cut shrubs, tulips, roses, and manifold English flowers. There lived Dame Abney, relict of the famous Lord Mayor, Sir Thomas Abney, with her daughter Sarah, both pious women, addicted to works of benevolence. There also resided the poet, philosopher, and divine— Isaac Watts. One day the Countess of Huntingdon called on him. "Madam," said he, "your Ladyship is come to see me on a very remarkable day." "Why

so remarkable?" she asked. " This day, thirty years
since, I came hither to the house of my good friend,
Sir Thomas Abney, intending to spend but one single
week under his friendly roof, and I have extended
my visit to the length of exactly thirty years." "Sir,"
added the hostess, "what you have termed a long
thirty years' visit, I consider as the shortest visit my
family ever received." The family were members of
Dr. Watts' Church, at Bury Street. But probably
.the Doctor with his hostess and her daughter sometimes worshipped in the neighbouring Meeting House,
which seems to have been connected with the Abney
estate. A young person like Howard living near, for
a few years before the death of Watts, and a longer
space before the death of Dame Abney, could not
fail to become acquainted with so distinguished a
circle. It was inevitable that they should be thrown
into each others' society; for then Dissenters were
much more clannish than they are now. Persecution
in former days had brought them together. And in
the middle of the last century they recalled stories
of sufferers for conscience sake, who, in that very
neighbourhood, had been imprisoned, or mulcted in
heavy fines, under Charles II. and his brother James.
Though comparatively halcyon days had dawned
after the Revolution, the clouds had returned after
the rain, under Queen Anne. Memories of trouble
were bonds of union ; they bound together the Dissenters in Newington, as members of the same
religious family.

Watts could not but be a centre of attraction, and
he brought to Newington many a visitor. We learn
much respecting his home and his friendships, and

more a great deal would be known by young Howard when in that vicinity. Watts had a study much talked of—with lines from Horace over the door; and the mantlepiece and shelves laden with books of every kind. Thither came Dr. Doddridge, younger than Watts, but not destined to survive him more than three years. The two Divines grew into each others' hearts; and I have heard from the lips of a son to the gentleman who witnessed the incident, how the venerable bard, oppressed by infirmities, rose from his chair to take leave of Doddridge for the last time, whilst the latter stretched out his arms, as if, like Elisha, he was endeavouring to catch the mantle of an ascending prophet. There too was often seen Dr. Gibbons, then a youthful pastor at Haberdashers' Hall. And others outside the circle of Nonconformity were visitants, especially Mr. Speaker Onslow, who went down in his coach with a few others, to take leave of Watts just before his death. Some of these notabilities Howard would personally know, and of them all he certainly heard. Influence proceeding from these associations contributed to form the religious character which to the end of life he exemplified, and that is the reason for my specifying them here.

I like to think of the young man coming in contact with one who had made his mark on English Literature; of the two talking about Sir Thomas Abney,—whom Howard's father, a Dissenting nominee for the shrievalty of London, must have known; and of his receiving the venerable sage's advice, as they took a turn together down shady avenues in the garden and the park.

It is not certain by whom the religious society, worshipping in the meeting house described, was originally formed. The earliest pastor was Joseph Cawthorne, ejected from Stamford; but in 1752, Meredith Townshend became pastor, and remained with the Church in that capacity until, from age and infirmity, he felt compelled to resign his charge in 1789, a year before the death of Howard. He had been an assistant for a short time to Dr. Watts at Bury Street; and his religious sentiments, we are told, "proceeded much upon *the plan*" of that Divine. We learn further, that he faithfully preached the Gospel "in a practical way;" that his sermons were plain, serious, and earnest; that his addresses at the Lord's Supper were pathetic; that he took an affectionate interest in young people; that his habits were unassuming and his conversation was instructive. In consequence of his prudence and peaceableness, "he had not an enemy living or dying." His death is said to have been in accordance with his life. Often had he been heard to exclaim, "Oh that it might please God to permit me quietly to slip away without any noise or bustle!" It did so please God. The good man was heard one morning praying at intervals till four o'clock; soon afterwards his daughter found "his eyes closed and his breath departed." He expired at Bath in 1801, aged 87.

These particulars are interesting in connection with our biography, because between Meredith and Howard an affectionate friendship sprung up, and we shall find Meredith visiting Howard after he left Newington. He was likely to win the love and confidence of the young gentleman who attended his ministry, and who was by him received into Church fellowship soon after 1752. Howard's connection with the Newington congregation remained until he died ; for it used to be common amongst Dissenters to have their names retained on the roll where they were first inscribed. When people moved from place to place, they were unwilling, they said, to " forsake their first love." In all his wanderings he regarded that unattractive meeting house as his spiritual home. Sympathies, in his case, however, were not contracted within local limits, for in different' ways he largely assisted benevolent objects in the neighbourhood and elsewhere.

The period between seventeen and twenty-five, especially in the life of a young man left in the world his own master, cannot but be a critical era, owing to temptations which surround his path. The present chapter covers that period ; and if ever eight years occurred, full of more than ordinary danger to one in Howard's circumstances, they came between 1742 and 1750. To say nothing of its being a time of political unsettlement, when English rule was shaken to its foundations,—for in 1745 nobody knew whether the House of Hanover or the Stuart Dynasty was to occupy the throne,—it must be remembered that just then the controversy between Deism and Christianity was rife ; publications denying the claims of the Gospel and the Resurrection of our Saviour were issuing from the press ; and with these were coupled others of a specious description, which, whilst paying compliments in one way, were in other ways digging up the corner stones of our holy faith. Gambling and duelling were common amongst the upper classes.

Works of fiction made people familiar with scenes and incidents thoroughly immoral. The stage produced spectacles unfriendly to domestic virtue. Dissipated young men ran to uncommon excesses of vice and riot, and lay in wait to catch others within their fatal toils. London abounded in besetments of this sort; and to them it is plain enough that Howard, with his independent fortune, living near the metropolis where he had been born and bred, was particularly exposed.

The period was one, not only of danger, but of self-education, which happily brought him safely through. Defects in the tuition of earlier years were, to a considerable extent, supplied; but more than that, intellectual, moral, and religious habits were formed, which proved, not only safeguards, but forces productive of a grand character in himself, and of immense benefits to mankind. Travel, study, friendship, were the main methods of this successful culture. He became a *traveller*, almost as soon as he ceased to be an apprentice. Something of the Ulysses bent—something of a mood in which discoverers fulfil their mission, striving to break ice round the pole, or to reach the source of African rivers, is visible in the Howard of later years; and in these early times we see him making an experimental trip, which must have involved discipline very useful to him in after expeditions. He was fond of reading, of studying nature, and of making experiments, the consequence of which will presently appear; and in intercourse afforded him in the Newington suburb, he discovered further means of personal improvement, which he was not slow to appropriate and apply. Above all, in this momentous course of self-education, when we find him giving himself to the service of God, and making public profession of faith in the Saviour, the leaves of life become stamped with a Divine signature, which prepares for words of truth and deeds of sacrifice, such as cover and illuminate the record, page after page, to the melancholy yet glorious end.

CHAPTER III.

HIS FIRST MARRIAGE.

1751-1756.

BIOGRAPHERS of Howard are much puzzled about dates. What space intervened between his return to England and the next important event of his life, cannot be decided. But when he was about the age of twenty-five he married ; and that marriage has given rise to much remark. The circumstances which led to it certainly were uncommon.

Lodgings which he first occupied in the village of Stoke Newington not proving convenient, and the attention shown by his landlady not meeting his wants or his wishes, he removed to apartments in the house of Mrs. Sarah Loidore (or Lardeau), a widow residing in Church Street, who seems to have taken much interest in her lodger ; and, as his delicate health required, nursed him with extraordinary care. She thus won unbounded thankfulness, which he expressed in an extraordinary way. The widow had reached the mature age of fifty-two, and Howard was scarcely half as old ; but as he had some strange notions, which, when they took the shape of duty, became irresistible, he considered he could not justly repay his hostess by anything short of an offer of marriage. Evidently a conscientious sense of obligation led him to take this singular step. He who from a calm principle of benevolence afterwards consecrated himself to the reformation of a village, and then to the reformation of the prison world, now from a calm principle of gratitude resolved to employ himself for *her* welfare who had promoted *his*. It is amusing to find in a pamphlet entitled, "The Life of the late John Howard, Esq., with a Review of his Travels," the following statement, in which the writer, one would think, must have largely drawn upon imagination : "On the first opportunity, he expressed his sentiments to her in the strongest terms of affection, assuring her that if she rejected his proposal, he would become an exile for ever to his family and friends. The lady was upwards of forty, in fact upwards of fifty, and therefore urged the disagreement of their years, as well as their circumstances ; but after allowing her twenty-four hours for a final reply, his eloquence surmounted all her obstacles, and she consented to a union wherein gratitude was to supply the deficiency of passion." This story of an ardent lover and his mistress would no doubt have amazed and displeased the persons to whom it referred ; but it was not made public until 1790, when both of them were in their graves. Then the idea of it, in the history of so illustrious a man as the great philanthropist, attracted general attention and created no little amusement.

It is, however, certain that the match proved a happy one ; and when the lady suffered from illness, her husband did everything in his power to promote her comfort. The same enthusiastic chronicler from whom we have now quoted, proceeds to inform us that Howard uniformly behaved to his wife with the greatest tenderness, and had been often heard to say, "that he would freely part with a hundred pounds to give her one good night's rest." The small independent property which she possessed, he, with characteristic disinterestedness, settled on her sister. Mrs. Howard is described as "a woman of excellent character, amiable in her disposition, sincere in her piety, endowed with a good mental capacity, and forward in exercising its powers in every good word and work." And though she belonged to the Communion of the Church of England, a difference in ecclesiastical opinions threw no shadow over their wedded life, for the strongest of bonds existed in their spiritual sympathies and their common love to God and Christ.

The union did not last long. She died on the 10th of November, 1755, aged 54, "in hopes of a joyful resurrection through the merits of Jesus Christ"; as appeared from an inscription on her tombstone in the churchyard of St. Mary's, Whitechapel. The same writer who describes the courtship, informs us that after her death Howard more than once declared that were he to marry again, he would prefer just such another person and mind as hers, to all the charms of youth and beauty. Nay, more, he tells us that as "a remembrance of her, he ever after carried about with him, and when alone always used a dessert spoon that had belonged to her." Dr. Brown, in his memoirs gravely states, "The servants of Mr. Howard inform me, that they never saw the spoon, or heard anything of it, which could not have been the case, had he used it so constantly as he is represented to have done." The assertion and the denial are equally amusing.

Howard broke up housekeeping at Stoke Newington after his first wife's death, and distributed amongst the poorer housekeepers of the neighbourhood, such parts of his furniture as he did not want in apartments he took for a temporary residence in St. Paul's Churchyard. The old gardener, to whom he used to throw loaves over the wall, gratefully remembered to the day of his death, that upon his master's removal he had for his dividend, as he was wont to call it, a bedstead and bedding complete, a table, half a dozen chairs, and a new scythe, besides receiving a guinea for a single day's work, spent probably in assisting the removal of furniture which his master reserved for his own use.

Howard's love of travel soon revived. He determined to visit Portugal, devasted by the earthquake of 1755, which occurred shortly before his wife's death. The motive for his expedition has been thus interpreted : " Howard, attracted by reports of the sufferings of the survivors, no sooner found himself at his own disposal, than he determined to hasten with the utmost speed to their assistance." Whatever might be his object, it was certainly frustrated— The high seas were then far from safe—privateers were scouring the deep in quest of spoil. This circumstance, according to a not very trustworthy account published in 1790, was urged by " a Dissenting minister," Howard's " intimate friend " as a reason for his stopping at home. It was " tempting Providence," said this "intimate friend," "to run such a risk of being taken by some of the ships of France, then at war with this country." At all events, the young widower did not reach Portugal.

In the first section of his work, on "The State of Prisons," he described what happened at the time. "How they"—the French—"treat English prisoners of war, I knew by experience in 1756; when a Lisbon packet (the *Hanover*) in which I went passenger, in order to make the tour of Portugal, was taken by a French privateer. Before we reached Brest, I suffered the extremity of thirst, not having for above forty hours one drop of water; nor hardly a morsel of food. In the castle at Brest, I lay six nights upon straw: and observing how cruelly my countrymen were used there, and at Morlaix, whither I was carried next; during the two months I was at Carhaix upon parole, I corresponded with the English prisoners at Brest, Morlaix, and Dinan. At the last of those towns were several of our ship's crew, and my servant. I had sufficient evidence of their being treated with such barbarity, that many hundreds had perished; and that thirty-six were buried in a hole at Dinan in one day."

As this is the first occasion for introducing a quotation from Howard's correspondence, and as I shall have to employ extracts hereafter, it may be well, once for all, to make a remark respecting the manner in which his letters are written. Handwriting has been of late years much studied as a key to character. His penmanship was in accordance with his firmness, decision, and boldness of spirit. Nobody can look on what he wrote without seeing that he had a strong will, and that he knew how to carry it into effect. But his style of expression indicates great carelessness; and his manner of spelling words is certainly of a very unique description. Orthography must have been strangely neglected a century earlier, when a nobleman wrote about his clothes as of an " ash culler ;" and a lady of title wrote the word " go " with two additional vowels—*"gooe."* But orthography in every-day communications received more attention in Howard's time, though nothing like the correctness aimed at in our elementary schools was either attained or attempted. Howard's spelling must be estimated, not by our standard, but by that of his own day ; yet, judged by this rule, it is plain he had never troubled himself much with the use of a dictionary. As to his method of writing the names of foreign towns, one is often puzzled to know what he means. It would be unsightly as well as worthless, to print literal transcripts from his diary and correspondence, and therefore the passages I employ for the illustration of his life are presented in modern spelling, and I have not scrupled occasionally to correct small grammatical errors.

Some further particulars of Howard's captivity are supplied by the Rev. Samuel Palmer, in the *Universal Magazine* for 1790. After being kept at Brest for some time without food, " a joint of mutton was thrown into the filthy dungeon, which the prisoners were obliged to tear to pieces and gnaw like dogs." At Carhaix, Howard was allowed liberty on parole, upon which he went into lodgings, where the master of the house, though an utter stranger, supplied him with clothes and money, as he had been deprived, at Brest, of all he had. This kind-hearted person supported the stranger on the faith of being paid for it when he should reach England. He was allowed to return on condition of his coming back to France, if the Government at home refused to exchange him for a French naval officer. When his friends congratulated him on his escape, he desired them to postpone their expressions of joy until he had fulfilled his obligations. Like Regulus, he was ready to resume his captivity, if he could not obtain freedom on the terms to which he was pledged. His word was his bond.

His sufferings abroad have been attributed to his having "behaved with so much hauteur, so much *à l'Anglais*, to the captain of the privateer." The author of this suggestion in the *Gentleman's Magazine* for 1790 is not to be depended on; but it is quite possible that the high-minded prisoner—whatever prudence might have dictated—was in no mood to treat with much consideration a man whom he looked upon as not better than a pirate. Howard was not apt to conceal his feelings, and, throughout life, it was a habit with him calmly to speak his mind.

He thought more of others than himself. "When I came to England, still on parole," he says, " I made known to the Commissioners of Sick and Wounded Seamen, the various particulars (already related), which gained their attention and thanks. Remonstrance was made to the French Court ; our sailors had redress ; and those that were in the three prisons mentioned above " (Brest, Morlaix, and Carhaix) "were brought home in the first cartel ships. A lady from Ireland, who married in France, had bequeathed, in trust with the magistrates of St. Malo, sundry charities, one of which was a penny a day to every English prisoner of war in Dinan. This was duly paid, and saved the lives of many brave and useful men. Perhaps what I suffered on this occasion increased my sympathy with the unhappy people whose case is the subject of this book." Such a passage at the opening of his work on "The State of Prisons," indicates plainly enough that even at that early period he had feelings which contributed to a long career of self-sacrifice.

It was in 1756, according to his own statement, that he was taken prisoner and returned to England. In the same year he was admitted a member of the Royal Society. That Society, from the year 1710 till 1782, held its meetings in Crane Court—" a very handsome open place with freestone pavement and graced with good buildings, the front house being larger than the rest," and built by Sir Christopher Wren. Within that house the members assembled in Howard's time—where sat the president "at the middle of the table in an elbow chair—holding a little wooden mace in his hand, with which he would strike the table when he would command silence." There sits the new member, thin and spare, with large eyes, bold Roman nose, and lips expressive of strength of character—his face crowned with a tie wig and double curls. The circumstances of Howard's election as member of this Society, though it would be unreasonable to rank him amongst English philosophers, proves that, at least, he had some taste for science, and was anxious to increase his information. We have seen already that, at an early age, he was wont to amuse himself with the study of medicine, and probably other branches of knowledge. Express mention is made of his "great taste for meteorological observations, which he followed up with much assiduity."

All that he ever contributed to the Transactions of the Royal Society, were papers on the degree of cold observed at Cardington in the winter of 1763, when Bird's thermometer was as low as 10½ ; on the heat of the waters at Bath ; and on the heat of the ground on Mount Vesuvius. He also experimented on " the union of the primary colours in different proportions, in which he employed himself with some assiduity."[1] Such slight achievements give him no title to be ranked amongst scientific men ; and Dr. Aiken admits the honour of Fellowship was not conferred upon him in consequence of any extraordinary proficiency in science, "but rather in conformity to the laudable practice of that Society, of attracting gentlemen of fortune and leisure to the interests of knowledge."[2]

A fondness for the country, which presented advantages for the investigation of natural objects, and a desire to improve his estate at Cardington, led him, soon after his return to England, to take up his abode in that Bedfordshire village, which during the rest of life remained his principal home.

We are at this point in a better position than ever fully to understand his self-education. Now, as before, he was forming habits which prepared him for the after-business of life. We witness a habit of singular independence acting under a conviction of duty in all affairs, and making his own conscience, not the opinion of others, the guide of conduct, as appears in the instance of his marriage, when he set criticism at nought and would go his own way. But for a spirit of independence gradually growing up, and strengthening itself by acts small and great, he

---

[1] Aiken, p. 23.   [2] Ibid., p. 21.

never could have accomplished the tasks he afterwards undertook amidst the doubts of friends and
the opposition of foes. Next to that, we notice more
manifest than before a spirit of enterprise. His first
tour, lost in obscurity, no doubt involved, as I have
said, discipline useful in after-life; but his purpose
in visiting Portugal is still more of a piece with his
later travellings; and what he saw and endured in
a French prison unmistakably educated him for that
which afterwards made him celebrated.

Inquisitiveness, penetrating and persevering when
not profound, challenges our notice as we read of his
studying medicine, and of early scientific experiments, which fitted him to be a Fellow of the Royal
Society. And as we see him beginning to collect and
marshal facts, to set them down in order for a purpose then not much thought of, he really comes out
as a statist before statistics had been established and
reduced to a system.

CHAPTER IV.

SECOND MARRIAGE.

1756–1770.

ABOUT two years after his admission to the Royal Society, he married a second time. In the "Life of Howard" by Dr. Brown, there is the portrait of a lady, whose maiden name was Henrietta Leeds, daughter of Edward Leeds, of Croxton, in Cambridgeshire, Sergeant-at-law. She appears with an ample forehead, arched brows, eyes expressive of intelligence and affection, and the rest of her features moulded well and finely set. Her smoothly dressed hair, thrown back according to the fashion of the day, is surmounted by a white coiffure, having a central ornament of jewelled stars ; a lace kerchief covers her bust with embroidered folds. Looking into her face, one can hardly help seeing under it a thoughtful mind, a loving soul, a meek and gentle spirit. Nobody has pried into the secrets of the courtship ; certainly no one has revealed them, though they must have been more tempting than in the former instance. We only know that on the 25th of April, 1758, they were united, and that their chosen home was Cardington.

Cardington, described by Lysons as "a neat village," lies about three miles south-east of Bedford ; and along the northern side of the parish runs the river Ouse. The church, dedicated to St. Mary, is not remarkable for its architecture ; but it possesses monuments belonging to the Gascoignes, Harveys, and other families to be afterwards noticed. Close to it stands the house in which Howard lived. It came into his possession from his father, and to this he added other property obtained by purchase.

It is interesting to notice that Cardington lay near Elstow, where John Bunyan was born. Within a walk of two or three miles is the church where the "glorious dreamer," when a youth, rang the bells ; and the green where, after plunging into village sports, he passed through religious experiences which he graphically describes. These spots, together with the cottage where he first saw the light, must have been familiar to John Howard, though I do not remember any allusion to them in his published works, or in his printed correspondence. With Bunyan he must have felt a strong religious sympathy, for their piety in some respects was of the same character ; and certain outbursts of fervid devotion I shall hereafter describe, bear a marked resemblance to passages found in Bunyan's writings.

It is a singular coincidence, that as Howard's first wife was a Churchwoman, so was his second ; and in each case spiritual sympathy prevented ecclesiastical collision. They both united traits of character often deemed incompatible—conscientiously attached to their own denominations, they were not unwilling to worship with other communions. She, like her husband, was decidedly evangelical in sentiment ; and, according to a custom prevalent in former days amongst Puritans, and not unknown amongst Anglo-

Catholics,—though in their case it took a different form,—she wrote with her own hand, "a surrender and dedication of herself to her God and her Saviour;" and this document Howard is said to have carried with him on his journeys. According to the testimony of a lady who had known her well, Howard, soon after marriage, "sold some jewels his wife had no longer any inclination to wear, and put the money into a purse, called by herself and her husband, *the charity purse.*" And it is further related, that when they were in London, soon after her marriage, he took his wife to the Pantheon, in order " to ascertain what effect such a scene would have upon her mind. As they mingled with the throng, and walked the round, she appeared lost in thought. "Now, Harriet," he said, "I must insist on your telling me what you have been thinking about." "Well," she replied, "if I must tell you, I have been thinking of Mr. ——'s sermon last Sunday." [1] The strange test which he characteristically applied was met to his satisfaction.

In the course of this narrative there are many proofs of his strong will, indeed his love of mastery. He had a nature made to rule, and he seems to have been conscious of it. "He had a high idea," we are told, "of the authority of the head of a family. And he thought it right, because most convenient, to maintain it for the sake of avoiding the unhappy consequences of domestic disputes. On this principle," says a friend, "I have more than once heard him pleasantly relate the agreement he made with the last Mrs. Howard, previous to their marriage, that to

---

[1] Brown's Memoirs of Howard. Second edition, p. 25.

prevent altercations about those little matters which he had observed to be the chief grounds of uneasiness in families, he should always decide. To this the amiable lady readily consented, and ever adhered. Nor did she ever regret the agreement, which she found to be attended with the happiest effects."[1] Had she not been "an amiable lady," the result would have been far otherwise.

Agreeing with him in matters of taste, she busied herself in the Cardington improvements; and we see her light form tripping over the grass to train some wayward flowers, while her husband discusses with the gardener, matters touching the management of trees and the laying out of walks. As she united with him in the institution of the charity purse, and put into it what had been obtained by the sale of her jewels, so also, once, when striking the yearly balance of accounts, he found a surplus, and purposed that they should expend it in a trip to London, for her gratification; she outstripped the philanthropist, and replied, as she thought of new tenements they were erecting for their peasant neighbours; "What a pretty cottage it would build." So the money went for that. Care for the cottagers was a ruling passion in this remarkable couple; they gave employment whilst they bestowed charity; and, it is said, that most of the linen for the household was spun by villagers, under Mrs. Howard's direction. At a later period, he increased the stock, and thus furnished industrial employment for people who could earn a living in no other way. Aided by his wife, he is seen

---

[1] Dr. Brown (p. 55), on the authority of the Rev. S. Palmer.

at Cardington in the character of a village reformer. In that capacity, he opened his benevolent mission; by these humbler offices, he trained himself for subsequent wider usefulness, and when he had won, without seeking, a renown which filled the civilized world, he persevered in the discharge of his rural duties. If only the monarch can boast of transforming into marble a metropolis of brick, it is within the power of most landed proprietors to reduce their domains to order, and to clothe them with neatness. Howard felt he had such power. The tenements on his estate were, like others of that day, badly constructed, badly ventilated, badly drained. He pulled them down, and built new ones after an improved method, securing light, air, and cleanliness; adding ornament to convenience, and consulting taste, while he attained utility. Behind the palings which enclosed the trim little garden, stocked with useful vegetables, and decked with gay and fragrant flowers, rose white-fronted cottages, with weather-tight roofs. The occupants, as they sat by the door on a summer evening, rejoiced in the contrast which their new abodes presented to former wretched dwellings on the spot, and felt the thanks they could only imperfectly express. The beneficent landlord sometimes came and sat down by their side, eating an apple, we are told, to give familiarity to the interview, and gently patting the heads of boys and girls, as he gave them halfpence. Habits of cleanliness, in which he excelled, he sought to promote amongst his tenantry, by personal inspection of their houses, and by strict injunctions to wash well the floors. His alterations provided employment. The village became a scene of busy industry; and while he employed men in building, ditching, and draining, he set the women to work in making linen for household purposes. No one knew better than he did, that man has a body as well as a soul, and that we attempt the work of intellectual elevation at fearful odds, when the objects of our philanthropy are victims of filth, disease, and hunger. Having cared for the temporal needs of the poor, this country gentleman thought of the mind, and paid attention to their highest interests. He founded schools, when schools were not popular as at present, opening them to the children of all sects, and imposing no condition which could touch the consciences of parents. The young folks were required on a Sunday to attend a place of worship; but neither church nor meeting house was prescribed. He made a similar stipulation with his tenantry, and had one cottage fitted up as a place for preaching.

The change which he wrought in the village was very great, aided, as we shall see hereafter, by a distinguished neighbour and friend.[1] When recently driving from Bedford to Cardington, I was struck with the dull, tame, scenery for a couple of miles, and with the contrast which opened, when approaching Howard's village. Noble trees, forming an avenue, rise on either side the road. Hedgerows and cottages, neatly kept, speak of careful husbandry and pleasant homes; the road to Howard's house, under the shadow of the church, indicates an approach to one of those unpretending gentlemen's houses, so characteristic of our rural neighbourhoods. A touch of

[1] Mr. Whitbread.

Howard's taste, with that of his co-operator, were visible every step I took.

The story just told is simple enough ; some may deem it scarcely worth telling. Hundreds of land-owners are doing the same now. But what is a matter of course at present, was, a century and a half since, a rare exception. We have only to visit some villages, in which dwellings a hundred and fifty years old remain unaltered, to understand the miserable provision made for farm labourers at that period. Schools,—Board, National, or British,—are plentiful up and down the country ; but recollections which run over not more than fifty years, are sufficient to prove what an immense educational revolution has taken place within that time. Industry, universally inculcated, is also, in unnumbered instances, well exemplified ; but when Howard lived, an opposite state of things obtained. That cleanliness is next to godliness, has become a motto ; pure water is counted a precious blessing ; and a fountain by the wayside furnishes it abundantly to man and beast ; ideas, estimates, and provisions of such kinds rarely existed when some men now living were little boys.

Howard really exhibited *originality* in his benevolence, in this as well as in his prison enterprise. The latter has overshadowed and dwarfed the former ; yet the former is enough to elevate its author to a niche in the temple of benevolence. Improvement of dwellings for the poor ; elementary education for all classes ; encouragement of individual industry on the principle that people must help themselves ; and a plentiful supply of good water—these are conditions of social well-being which Howard worked into his schemes for Cardington improvement. It has been said by an American orator: "Considering the time, more than a century ago, and the general prejudices which then prevailed against the possibility or the desirableness of raising the rural population above an abject condition, I am not certain that Howard's plan for elevating the tenantry on his own estate was not a more remarkable evidence of his characteristic independence of public sentiment, and a bolder display of self-reliance, than even his attack on the prison system. It was, however, in the same line, and only a first wave of the tide that from his heart was to sweep over Europe."[1]   The mental independence which appears in this and other divisions of his career is noteworthy. He did not wait for examples. He did not sit with folded arms till committees woke him up by sending an importunate circular. He did not simply retail other folks' ideas; he did not execute patronized plans. He thought and acted for himself. Only one Observer he noticed. He ever lived as in his great " Taskmaster's eye."

It is interesting to notice that about the same time in which Howard engaged in improving his Cardington property, his neighbour, Francis, Duke of Bedford, who had landed possessions, according to Mr. Burke, " more extensive than the territory of many of the Grecian republics," set himself to effect a vast revolution in his princely estate. Bedfordshire had been, as to two-thirds of it, a mere common field, cultivated and used in humble fashion by poor tenants under

[1] John Howard, his Life, Character, and Services. By H. W. Bellows, an Address delivered before the International Prison Congress in London, July, 1873.

the Manorial lord.   Undrained water often destroyed crops where there were any ; sheep died of rot by scores and scores; and implements of husbandry were as rude as those we now see in Spain.   The Duke wrought a marvellous change.   He effected on a large scale what Howard could only accomplish on a small one.   And it may be added that a like spirit of enter- prise went on all over the Bedford Level as it was called.   Lands were more and more drained, and tracts once studded with reeds, the refuge of wild ducks, yielded crops of corn.   " Since the drainage of the Fens, numerous villages have sprung up where previously was nothing but a watery waste, without house or inhabitant, and several of the bordering towns have doubled their population." [1]   In such im- provements Howard would rejoice.

Soon after the commencement of these village reforms, Mrs. Howard's health began to give her hus- band uneasiness ; he thought a milder climate might be of advantage.   He accordingly fixed upon the New Forest, in Hampshire, which, with its woodland scenery and its green glades, afforded a striking con- trast to the landscapes of the Bedford Level ; its warmer atmosphere promised relief and improvement to the beloved invalid.   The spot selected was Wat- combe, near Lymington, where, within a few miles' drive, delightful visits could be paid to the ivy-covered ruins of Beaulieu Abbey, the Roman camp at Buck- land Rings, Boldre Church with its tree-girdled churchyard, and Shirley and Sway Commons, where there is "one vast stretch of heather, which late in the

[1] Journal of Royal Agricultural Society, vol. xii., p. 259. Quoted by Charles Knight, Hist. of England, vol. vii., p. 15.

summer covers the ground with its crimson and ame-
thyst."[1]   There was a house and small estate at Watcombe belonging to Captain Blake of the East India
Company, who had managed by a display of Eastern
assumption to alienate the friendly regard of his
neighbours. This property was purchased by Howard,
who by his benevolent demeanour speedily wrought
a revolution in the village. Blake, a sportsman, had
employed "all the contrivances of engines and guns"
in order to preserve himself "from the depredations
and hostilities of the rustic population; but Howard,"
says Dr. Brown, was "no sportsman, no executor of
the game laws, and in no respects an encroacher on
the rights and advantages of others."[2] So now things
went on smoothly and pleasantly. The squire and
his lady were kind to the people, and the people were
respectful to the squire and his lady. For three or
four years they remained in this sylvan retreat, and
during that period his old nurse, living at Cardington,
excited his sympathy and attracted his attention, for
she was getting near her last home, and suffered from
the infirmities of advanced age. He had been accustomed to pay her visits, and provide a good stock of
coal for her in cold weather ; now, when he heard that
the candle of life was burning down to the socket,
he would write to Cardington, directing a supply
of comforts for the sufferer ; and on her death "he
ordered her to be buried, at his expense, in her native
village."[3]

This residence of the philanthropist at Watcombe
has almost entirely disappeared. Only a small part,

<hr>

[1] Wise's New Forest, p. 81.   [2] Brown's Memoirs, p. 27.
[3] Brown, p. 28.

originally occupied by servants, now remains. It is used as a farmhouse, and stands on the edge of Brockenhurst Park, belonging to Mr. Morant, who has built a stately mansion in the midst of his beautiful domain. Magnificent oaks give a special charm to the rich sylvan scenery, and a ramble in the woods is full of enjoyment. The village church is not far off, with an early Norman doorway and a Purbeck marble font of the same period. An enormous oak, and a yew-tree with a hollow trunk, ivy-covered, are the chief objects attracting general notice in the churchyard, and must have interested Howard, distinguished as he was by rural tastes. Standing there two summers since, I could picture him in his cocked hat, on the way to Sunday worship ; and the memory of the good man pleasantly haunts the neighbourhood when visited by persons acquainted with his history. But though I found references to him in guide books, I was very curious to know whether traces of his living there lingered in the present generation. Upon inquiry, I discovered that those I spoke to were not only ignorant of his having lived at Watcombe, but did not even know his name. "Was he a bee-keeper?" asked one of the villagers, across whose mind I imagine there passed thoughts of a neighbour of some such name. The person who now resides in the fragment of Howard's house had never heard of its illustrious occupant. Curious, that one who has filled the world with his fame should be forgotten in the place where he lived for two or three years !

The situation of Watcombe did not fulfil its promise. It did not agree with Mrs. Howard ; and in addition to this strong reason for a removal, it is said that vapours in the neighbourhood were unfavourable to her husband's astronomical observations. He therefore resolved to return to Cardington. There he resumed the execution of reformatory plans, and proceeded to enlarge and improve his dwelling, to take in a field of three acres for the enlargement of pleasure grounds, to form a shrubbery, to lay down a lawn, and to arrange a walk skirted by firs. With satisfaction he reported what he was doing. "We have lately got the workmen clear of the house for this year, and hope to complete my small habitation. We find it more comfortable and suitable to our small family than Watcombe, and I hope we are fixed for what time Providence shall allot us. I have my books and instruments comfortably about me, and I hope for more time to enjoy them."[1]

Howard's gardener, when ninety years old, would proudly point out a tree planted by his mistress, which remained precious in his master's eyes, and a particular description is preserved of the "root house," at the end of the pleasure grounds. It was made of gnarled roots and ancient trunks, and was furnished with corresponding rustic simplicity—peat "cut out of a moss at Ampthill," and rude benches serving for seats. Trifling ornaments and relics were added from time to time; and particular mention is made of a bookcase containing the works of Baxter, Flavel, Hervey, and other Evangelical divines, favourites with the master of the place, together with poems of Milton, Watts, Young, and Thomson. Other works lined the shelves, including travels and

[1] Cardington, Oct. 27th, 1762. Samuel Whitbread, Esq., Chiswell Street, London.

books on science, proper for a Fellow of the Royal
Society.   The Bible which the philanthropist used
in his travels, was at a later date added to the collection.   An inscription was fixed opposite the door,
consisting of the following lines :—

> " O solitude, bless'd state of life below,
>   Friend to our thought and balm to all our woe ;
>   Far from thronged cities my abode remove,
>   To realms of innocence, and peace, and love.
>
> " That when the sable shades of night appear,
>   And life's fair light no more these eyes shall cheer ;
>   Its work may be fulfilled, its progress won,
>   By virtue measured, not a lengthened sun."

The lines are given in Brown's Memoirs of Howard,
and he tells us he copied them from Mrs. Howard's
handwriting.   The tradition is, that she composed
them ; but, so far as the first stanza is concerned, this
seems to be a mistake, for that occurs, it is said, in
Brown's Essay on the Universe, from which she
copied them.

It may be added, that in connection with the root
house a bath was contrived, which Howard used
every morning, summer and winter.

A memorial was erected after Howard's death,
bearing these words :—

" This garden was formed, the root house built, and
the trees which overshadow and adorn them were
planted in the year 1762, by John Howard, the
philanthropist, who lived for many years in this retirement, before his virtuous energies were called into
action, and he quitted it to become the benefactor of
mankind.

"To this spot he eagerly returned to pass the interval between those labours which ended in his death, and have insured to him a guiltless and imperishable fame.

"Joseph Crockford, whose hand put the seedlings into the earth under his master's eye, has spent the intervening years in watching and assisting their growth; exhibiting, in his narrow circle, a model of sobriety, industry, and neatness.

"He still lives, in his eightieth year; faithful to his duties, and strong to fulfil them; contented in his station, pleased with his charge, and full of the remembrance of his beloved master."[1]

When Dr. Brown visited the place, an aged servant conducted him to the monument. "Never," said poor old Joshua Crockford, as he stood by the simple memorial, which Mr. Whitbread had erected on the lawn by the side of the house, to record the faithful attachment of an old servant to the best of masters, —his voice faltering, and a tear standing in his eyes as he spoke—"Never shall I see two such men again."

The house belonging to Howard, and left by him to the Whitbreads, is now occupied by General Mills, who married into the family; and there very recently it was my privilege to pay a visit, when I was favoured with the intelligent and sympathetic ciceroneship of Miss Whitbread, who pointed out alterations made in the grounds. Howard's residence remains almost intact—the front plain and unpretentious, but pleasantly covered with foliage trained on lattice work; the interior containing rooms he

---

[1] This was composed by Samuel Whitbread, Esq., M.P. He will be noticed hereafter.

occupied. But to the sides of the original dwelling are now attached additional buildings, with spacious and lofty apartments, making the whole much larger than it was in the philanthropist's time. Relics of him are carefully preserved. They include large pieces of wood-carving which decorated the root-house, an owl carved in stone, an hour-glass, a pruning-knife, and five books, one belonging to his wife, Henrietta Leeds. A characteristic likeness of him hangs in the hall. The lawn and shrubberies are much as they were. There remains a fine tree opposite the house, which bears the original master's name, and another, I was informed, once stood corresponding with it, called after John Bunyan—a circumstance which brings together the two most memorable men that ever lived in Bedfordshire.

Hidden amidst the shrubbery growths are divers small stone figures, one of a fox, which once carried in its mouth some sort of prey, another a figure of sportsmanlike appearance carrying a gun. Under these and other forms General Mills thinks there are covert meanings, illustrative of that turn for humour which, with very different endowments, undoubtedly marked Howard's character. A large crowbar is shown which he was accustomed to use industriously; for when alterations went on, he was wont to be foremost amongst the workmen.

I may add here that at Southill, the seat of Samuel Whitbread, Esq., M.P., I saw a catalogue of Howard's Library and an inventory of his furniture—made after his death. The volumes numbered about 800 at a rough calculation. A parchment rent-roll account book, kept in exact order, indicates his prevalent habit. Scientific studies were not neglected by the Fellow of the Royal Society after his return to Cardington ; and in the Philosophical Transactions we have the following record, already noticed :—

"Sir, I would beg leave to acquaint you of a degree of cold that I observed at Cardington, in Bedfordshire, the 22nd of November last, just before sunrise; Fahrenheit's scale, by one of Bird's thermometers, being so low as ten and a half. If it should throw any light on the locality of cold, or you think it worth the Society's observation, I would leave to your better judgment. I remain, with great esteem, Sir, Your obedient Servant,

"Read April 12th, 1764." "JOHN HOWARD."

In connection with this meteorological report may be inserted the legend related in the sixteenth volume of *The Gentleman's Magazine*, "That in whatever Mr. H. engaged, it was *summis viribus*," and "that on the frost setting in, he used, during the continuance, to leave his bed at two every morning, for the purpose of observing the state of a thermometer which was placed in his garden at some distance from his house."

Within a year and a half after the observation had been sent to Crane Court, death darkened the writer's dwelling. Henrietta gave birth to a son on the 27th of March, 1765. All seemed going on well. On Sunday morning, the 31st, her husband attended church; on his return violent symptoms appeared, and in a little time the lady expired in his arms. No one can tell what he felt at that moment; but in the gospel of Christ he possessed an effectual remedy for the sorrows of bereavement.

It is related that Howard, like Bishop Wilberforce, regularly kept the anniversary of his wife's death, and, so far also resembling Dr. Johnson, he spent the day in fasting, meditation, and prayer. " I recollect his telling me," says one of his friends, "just before he set out on one of his foreign excursions, as he was with his son "—the boy born four days before his mother died—" walking round some plantations he was making at Cardington, and pointing out to him further improvements which he had in contemplation, ' These, however, Jack ' (I think he called him), 'in case I should not come back, you will pursue or not, as you may think proper ; but remember, this walk was planted by your mother, and if you ever touch a twig of it, may my blessing never rest upon you.' " [1] Her domestics fondly cherished her memory. Howard gave the lady's-maid, Mrs. Prole, the miniature from which Henrietta's well-known portrait was engraved ; and when large offers of money were made to her, that she might part with it, " No," she said, " I will never part with anything that was my excellent master's and mistress's till I want a piece of bread. My master gave me this picture because he knew I should value it, and I will keep it to the day of my death."   These and other things I saw thirty years ago, when in the possession of Mrs. Prole's son ; what now remains of the Howard relics in the Proles' family were shown me very recently:—The miniature just mentioned, a pair of clogs which Mrs. Howard wore in the garden, a knife, and, above all, a little copper kettle which Howard carried with him on his travels.   These are carefully preserved, together with

[1] *Gentleman's Mag.* vol. lx., p. 288.   The sentence is confused.

two or three autograph letters written to the old servant.

One of the first things noticeable after the death of Mrs. Howard, is the baptism of her child, a rite which was administered by Meredith Townshend, pastor at Stoke Newington. The child was both a solace and a care. The bereaved parent loved him for his mother's sake as well as his own, and watched his growth with deep delight. Entrusted to a faithful nurse, the boy throve, but before he became a. year old, the father shared with the nurse in the management of him. It may seem needless to notice this, but for reasons which will hereafter appear.

According to Howard's ideas, "education had a place from the dawn of life." Regarding children as being "without reason and experience," he said they were "marked out as the subjects of absolute authority"; believing this, the father, when the child began to cry, would lay him quietly on his lap until he became perfectly still; he never "humoured" the little one, but insisted on entire submission; and after persevering in this course, he said "he believed his son would have put his finger into the fire if he had commanded him."[1]

In philosophizing upon the nursery Howard was an adept; and in his theory of bringing up children he had perfect confidence. On the sincerity of his affection there cannot rest a shadow of doubt, but as to the wisdom of his plans there will be a diversity of opinion. The enforcement of obedience to parental authority he carried to an extraordinary extent; and a lady writes, "When I was with some friends on a

[1] Aiken, p. 43.

E

visit to Mr. Howard, he took us into the garden, and as we were walking, he bid the child put off his shoe, which he did, and walked as well as he could upon the ground for a short time, till his father bid him put it on again."[1]   Discipline of this kind was well meant, and might bend or break a stubborn will; but it is certain to do harm as well as good.   Had the mother's tenderness tempered the father's authority, domestic rule probably would have been modified, though one cannot forget the law laid down before the nuptials.   At all events the child was an immense loser by his mother's death.   More of this hereafter.

Time is a merciful healer; yet, after more than a year's seclusion, grief continued to prey on the widower, so as to injure health never robust; and in the months of November and December, 1766, we find him visiting the town of Bath, then in the zenith of its fame, a fresh lustre having been given to its popularity by the discovery of Roman baths there in 1755.   Beau Nash's reign of idle vanity was over, but numbers of the fashionable and the fair still rushed to the city on a hill to search for pleasure, if not health, in the crowded pump-room.   To say that Howard had no taste for such scenes, is language too mild; they were his positive aversion; perhaps no gentleman in England disliked them more.   But travelling was to him a relief, and the medicinal waters promised benefit to his much-tried physical constitution.   He also endeavoured to amuse himself with his favourite observations; and in January, 1767, a letter was received by Dr. Watson, respecting the

---

[1] Brown, p. 62.

heat of the Bath waters, and read to the Royal Society in the month of April following. In the same winter he went to London, and there enjoyed the society of literary and scientific friends, amongst others, that of the eminent physician to whom the letter just mentioned was addressed.

In the spring he determined on making an excursion to Holland, and invited as his companion one who afterwards distinguished himself in literature as editor of "Camden's Britannia," and as the author of topographical and antiquarian works. This was Richard Gough, son of a gentleman who lived in a handsome mansion on his own estate at Enfield. His father was dead at this time, and he was living with his widowed mother, in the enjoyment of the paternal domain. When he was only about seventeen his archæological taste was in full bloom; and one who became imbued with a similar spirit long afterwards, describes him in the following terms:—

"The mouldering turret and the crumbling arch, the moss-covered stone and the obliterated inscription, served to excite in his mind the most ardent sensations, and to kindle that fire of antiquarian research which afterwards never knew decay, which burnt with undiminished lustre at the close of his existence, and which prompted him, when in the full enjoyment of his bodily faculties, to explore long-deserted castles and mansions, to tread long-neglected bye-ways, and to snatch from impending oblivion many a precious relic and many a venerable ancestry! He is the Camden of modern times."[1]

---

[1] Dibdin, quoted by Nichols, vol. vi., p. 306.

Mr. Gough, thirty years of age in 1767, was on the February of that year admitted Fellow of the Royal Society; and perhaps in Crane Court he attracted Howard's notice, or perhaps their acquaintance arose from some common connection with Dissenting friends ; for though Gough was a Churchman, he had been educated by a Nonconformist minister before he went to Cambridge, and in later life visited another of the same profession in Dorsetshire.[1]   However that might be, Howard wished for Gough's company in his projected tour.   The language of the letter is such as to indicate Howard's acquaintance with the family at Enfield ; and his promise to the mother of taking care of a man already thirty years old, is rather amusing.

" *To Richard Gough, Esq., Winchester Street.*

" DEAR SIR,—Having fixed with my brother Leeds the tour through Holland, about the week after next, I seem desirous, if I could, to persuade you to take the journey with us for about a month, as I am certain you will be highly entertained with the excessive pleasantness of Holland.   In the spring of the year all is a neat beautiful garden, and not wanting in antiquities to entertain a gentleman who has a turn that way ; expense of travelling is less there than in England, and dress not more regarded ; care of a young voyager permit me to assure Mrs. Gough shall not be wanting.   I am sure, on the review, it will be a pleasing jaunt to my friend ; as such, I could

---

[1] Nichols' Anecdotes, vol. vi., p. 265.

not go without giving you a line, being with much esteem,

" Dear sir,

"Your most humble servant,

" JOHN HOWARD."

"*Cardington, near Bedford,*
   "*May* 5, 1767."

But the invitation was politely declined, and so Howard started with Mr. Leeds, his brother-in-law, as a companion. Of incidents connected with this Dutch excursion I can find no account. It was most likely short and rapid, as he spoke in his letter to Mr. Gough of being absent "about a month."

Two years afterwards a similar invitation reached Mr. Gough.

"DEAR SIR,—I have heard you express a desire of seeing Italy. I could not go abroad without saying how much your company would add to my pleasure, as our thoughts relative to the gay and expensive schemes are similar. My boy is going from me to school. I intend, about the 21st of September, crossing the water for Calais, so to the southern part of France to Geneva, or going in a Leghorn or Naples ship by sea, as would afford greater variety, and not be so fatiguing or expensive as by land both ways; the accommodation aboard these ships being far more preferable to any of the packets. Shall probably be at Geneva about Christmas, where I intend fixing my winter quarters. I am sure I should be very happy if the scheme was agreeable to you, as I intend it to be a frugal one, and shall appear as

an English gentleman without glare or show. The
passage, with a genty (*sic*) table, always fresh meat or
fowls, twenty guineas. You will favour me the first
opportunity with a line.

"I am, Sir,

"Your friend and servant,

"J. HOWARD."

" *Cardington, August 30th,* 1769.

"Would beg my best compliments to our friend
Mr. Bush and Mrs. Gough."

This invitation met with the same fate as the one
before. Here Mr. Gough passes out of the circle of
Howard's biography; but before we lose sight of
him altogether, it should be said that he was well
worthy of the philanthropist's regards on account of
his own philanthropic character. To the poor and
the afflicted "he was at all times a father, a protector,
and a benefactor." [1]

Settled down once more at Cardington, Howard
remained there until the Autumn of 1769. To this
period belong several anecdotes in connection with
his son, which, for reasons to be seen hereafter, are
very important.

One incident led to a base misrepresentation.
The report ran, that he had been cruel to the boy—
that "he once locked him up for several hours in
a solitary place, having soon after gone to Bedford
with the key in his pocket and did not return till
night." Some people increased the terrors of the
story by saying the child was put upon a high shelf,
from which a fall might have been fatal. The real

---

[1] Nichols' Anecdotes, vol. vi., p. 311.

fact, as taken from Howard's own lips, is thus related by his friend, Meredith Townshend, in *The Universal Magazine* for 1796.

"It was Mr. Howard's constant practice to walk out with his child in the garden while the servants were at dinner. In one of these little excursions, with Master Howard in his hand (who was then about three years old) the father being much entertained with the innocent prattle of his son, they went on till they came to the root-house or hermitage, in a retired part of the garden, with which the young gentleman was familiarly acquainted, and were there for some time, diverting one another. During this the servant came in great haste to inform his master that a gentleman on horseback was at the door, and desired to speak with Mr. Howard immediately upon business of some importance; and as he wished to be with him as soon as possible, he said to his son, 'Jack, be a good boy, and keep quiet, and I shall come very soon to you again.' And so, locking the door to prevent the child from going out and prowling about the garden by himself, to the hazard of getting into some mischief, he put the key in his pocket and ran to the person in waiting as fast as he could. The conversation between them lasted much longer than he expected, and put the thought of the child out of his mind. Upon the gentleman's departure, he asked the servant where Jack was, and received for answer that he supposed him to be in the root-house where he had left him. And then instantly recollecting the incident he flew to set him at liberty, and found him quietly asleep on the matting of the floor; and when he was waked could not perceive that the confinement had made any disagreeable impression upon his mind." [1]

Dr. Brown has accumulated proofs, that, notwithstanding the theory of education which Howard adopted, he was in many respects a kind and even indulgent father. He would take out the boy in his chaise for a drive, and carry toys for his amusement. They were numerous, and those for the garden included "tiny carts and wheelbarrows, spades and rakes," and other contrivances for juvenile amusement. Friends related how with natural fondness his father would "show him off" to admiring visitors. I well remember that, when visiting Bedford thirty years ago, people pointed out the pew where Howard sat at meeting, and told me that he would stand up with his arm round his son's waist, holding a hymn-book before his eyes, and helping him to spell out easy words of Divine praise. The child would stroke his father's shoulder with his little hands and play with the buttons of his coat.

About Michaelmas, 1769, Howard placed him under the care of a lady who kept a boarding-school at Cheshunt in Hertfordshire, where he was treated with kindness; and the father, being now free from the immediate charge of the child, permitted himself once more to indulge in foreign travel, now choosing the fair scenes of Italy as his destination.

As he intended to be away for a long period, he broke up his Cardington establishment, leaving, as bailiff John Prole, his coachman, who had married Mrs. Howard's lady's maid. Not succeeding in a second

---

[1] The Rev. S. Palmer endorsed this letter.

effort to secure Mr. Gough as a companion, he started alone for Calais, and travelled through France to Geneva, where he tarried a few weeks by the charming lake before crossing the Alps to Lombardy. During this journey he kept a diary, and by help of it we are enabled to follow him from place to place.

Judging from passages which have been published, we might infer, and many have inferred, that there was in Howard's mind an utter absence of that taste for natural scenery which is now so common in the case of travellers. Passing over the Alps on the way to Italy, he indulges in no description of mountains, valleys, rocks, waterfalls, pine forests, vineyards, and other views, which break on a tourist's eye as he descends from hills in Savoy to plains in Lombardy. Though it may seem strange to us now, this state of mind was not uncommon in the last century. The poet Gray, indeed, in his letters to Mr. West, does break forth into a few warm exclamations as he alludes to the descent from Mount Cenis ; but, if I remember right, in the account Bishop Burnet gives of his foreign travels, more of terror is manifested at the sight of steep precipices than admiration on beholding a valley rich in vineyards and gardens. A wide-spread taste for natural beauties is of recent growth, and results from mental cultivation promoted by modern authors, especially Walter Scott.

Howard's first entry is dated Nov. 26, 1769, and seems to have been written at Turin. In it he reckons up eighty Italian holidays, and laments the Sabbath-breaking which he witnessed. The shock he received from what he saw of Roman Catholic worship, plainly indicates his Puritan sentiments. " What curtseys, bowings, and ceremonies have I seen at Turin,—how is a sacred Sabbath called a feast day, not for holy but unholy things—operas, ballad-singing, concerts ; one hundred and thirty-eight lights at the altar for a feast of St. Anthony; what dressing and undressing of the Archbishop, what parade before the Cardinal at Milan !"

That which was uppermost in the traveller's mind at this moment, appears from an entry he made at Turin in his Journal on the 30th of November, 1769.

" My return without seeing the southern parts of Italy was after much deliberation. I feared a misimprovement of a talent spent for mere curiosity at the loss of many Sabbaths ; and as many donations must be suspended for my pleasure, which would have been, as I hope, contrary to the general conduct of my life ; and which, on a retrospective view on a death-bed, would cause pain, as unbecoming a disciple of Christ, whose mind should be formed in my soul. These thoughts, with distance from my dear boy, determine me to check my curiosity." " Why should vanity and folly, pictures and baubles, or even the stupendous mountains, beautiful hills, or rich valleys—which ere long will all be consumed—engross the thoughts of a candidate for an eternal everlasting kingdom ? Is a worm ever to crawl on earth, whom God has raised to the hope of glory, which ere long will be revealed to them who are washed and sanctified by faith in the blood of the Divine Redeemer ? Look forward, O my soul. How low, how mean, how little is everything but what has a view to that glorious world of light, life, and love ! The preparation of the heart is of God. Prepare the heart, O God, of Thy unworthy creature; and unto Thee be all the glory through the boundless ages of eternity."[1]

These sentences express a state of mind above the common order of experience; they indicate what Dr. Chalmers calls "the expulsive power of a new affection."

As this is the first explicit revelation which we have of Howard's spiritual experience, it is impossible to tell whether the feelings thus expressed had long been habitual, or whether a change had come over him, lifting up his faith and love to a higher level than before. It is surprising to discover, that a man so self-controlled, so calmly methodical, so simple and practical in his common ways, should have had such deep religious sensibility; yet the qualities just enumerated are by no means incompatible with profound emotion. A steady understanding and a strong will are not weakened by affections of the kind just indicated ; they are often found united in Christian people. Though expressions of the nature cited will often occur in this narrative, showing that they were habitual in later life, it is likely that an impulse had been given to such spiritual emotions by the trial through which he had passed, and the consolations he had received from the Gospel of Christ.

In seasons of deep affliction, or when past griefs acutely touch the mind, it is not uncommon for an unsympathetic feeling to come over a spirit of impassioned piety. Dark clouds spread over the sky and dim the fairest scenes. What, at other times, would interest and delight, lose their charm ; even the

[1] Brown, p. 78.

bright sunshine provokes a feeling of irritation, and it is thought wrong to indulge in earthly pleasure. The shadow of the tomb where some loved one lies, and which we are soon ourselves to enter, falls solemnly over our life-path, each step we take. Eternity for the moment swallows up time. So it was with Howard as he turned his back on Italy.

In his travels at this period, we see that he re-crossed the Alps, returned to Geneva, and spent about ten days in Paris, which he calls "a dirty city" —no doubt a just appellation in the middle of the eighteenth century. He proceeded to Abbeville, and there, on the 4th of January, 1770, wrote a letter to the Rev. Joshua Symonds, giving a general description of his tour up to that time.

"Having an opportunity by an Italian gentleman, with whom I have travelled, I thought a few lines would not be unacceptable. After I landed in France, my first object was Geneva, where I spent some time before I went into Italy. The luxury and wickedness of the inhabitants would ever give a thinking mind pain, amidst the richest country, abounding with the noblest productions of human power and skill. I was seven days recrossing the Alps. The weather was very cold—the thermometer eleven degrees below the freezing point. The quick descent by sledges on the snow, and other particulars, may perhaps afford some little entertainment on a winter's evening. I returned· to Geneva. There, are some exemplary persons; yet the principles of one of the vilest of men (Voltaire), with the corruptions of the French, who are within one mile of the city, have greatly debased its ancient purity and splendour. I spent about ten

days at the dirty city of Paris. The streets are so
narrow, and no footpaths, that there is no stirring
out, but in a coach ; and as to their hackney coaches,
they are abominable. There were but few English
in Paris. I dined with about twenty at our ambassador's, Lord Harcourt. I am now on my route to
Holland, a favourite country of mine ; the only one,
except our own, where propriety and elegance are
mixed. Above all, I esteem it for its religious liberty.

"Thus, dear sir, I am travelling from one country
to another, and, I trust, with some good hope, through
abundant grace, to a yet better. My knowledge of
human nature should be enlarged by seeing more
of the tempers, tastes, and dispositions of different
people ; but shudder, my soul, at the glimpse of a
thought of its dignity and excellence, for how is the
gold become dross. I bless God I am well. I have
a calm and easy flow of spirits. I am preserved and
supported through not a little fatigue. My thoughts
are often with you on the Sabbath-day. I always
loved my Cardington and Bedford friends; but I think
distance makes me love them more."[1]

Leaving France, Howard bent his way to Holland.
He had expressed a wish to visit it, in the invitation
sent to Mr. Gough to become his companion ; and he
had spoken of the country in a way which indicated
that he thought it according to his taste, though he
had not seen it. I find no description of what he
now witnessed in the land of old cities, crowded shipping, busy quays, pleasant canals, fertile meadows,
browsing cattle, comfortable homesteads, and toy-like

[1] Brown, p. 81. Howard's religious feeling at this time was
peculiarly intense.

tenements. But we can imagine objects of that class
had charms for the gentleman farmer from Cardington, with memories of Bedfordshire scenes. Howard
felt himself at home amongst Dutch landscapes,
Dutch people, and Dutch industry.

However congenial with his tastes Holland might
be, there was one subject above everything which
interested his mind. Spending a Sunday evening [1]
in the quaint and courtly Hague, he poured out his
soul in the pages of his Journal. He writes : " I
would record the goodness of God to the un-
worthiest of His creatures. I have had for some days
past an habitual serious frame, relenting for my sin
and folly, applying to the blood of Jesus Christ,
solemnly surrendering myself and babe to Him,
begging the conduct of His Holy Spirit ; and I hope
I have a more tender conscience by the greater fear of
offending God, a temper more abstracted from this
world, more resigned to death or life, thirsting for
union and communion with God as *my* Lord and *my*
God. Oh, the wonders of redeeming love ! Some faint
hope have even I,—through redeeming mercy, the
perfect righteousness, and the full atoning Sacrifice
—that I shall ere long be made the monument of the
rich free grace and mercy of God through the Divine
Redeemer. Oh, shout my soul—grace ! grace ! free
sovereign, rich, unbounded grace ! Not I, not I, an
ill-deserving, a hell-deserving creature ! But where
sin has abounded, I trust grace superabounds. Some
hope I have—what joy in that hope—that nothing
shall separate my soul from the love of God in Christ

[1] February 11th, 1770.

Jesus. And, my soul, as such a frame is thy delight, pray frequently, and fervently, to the father of spirits, to bless His word, and your retired moments, to your serious conduct in life."

Such language may be scarcely intelligible to some; yet, making allowance for conventional expressions, it really points to tides of emotion which have swept through Christian minds in all ages and in all Churches. The tone is intensely devout, such as we find in the letters of Whitefield and Rutherford. It indicates ecstasies of which we have traces in the lives of Doddridge, Flavel, and Howe; and again, when we listen to mediæval saints such as Buonaventura and Bernard, we catch strains in a similar key; going further back, we meet with them in the Confessions of Augustine.[1]

A similar outburst occurs in an entry made at Lyons, whither he made his way after leaving Holland—for he was an erratic tourist. "Blessed be the name of the Lord! Endeavour, O my soul, to cultivate and maintain a thankful, serious, humble, and resigned frame and temper of mind. May it be thy chief desire that the honour of God, the spreading of the Redeemer's name and Gospel may be promoted. Consider the everlasting worth of spiritual and divine enjoyments; then thou wilt see the vanity and nothingness of worldly pleasures. Remember, O my soul, St. Paul, who was determined to know nothing in comparison of Jesus Christ and Him crucified. A tenderness of conscience I would ever cultivate, no step would I take without acknowledging God."

---

[1] The great Latin Father is not less impassioned.

From Holland, in his strangely zigzag course, Howard made his way to Italy; and proceeding through France he reached the Papal City of Avignon on the olive-clothed banks of the river Rhone, and passed on to the flourishing port of Marseilles. Then he passed Toulon, where he noticed "flowering shrubs in the hedges, and, in most gardens, oranges and lemons." Next we see him at the beautiful Antibes. Cannes was of no importance then; and indeed no part of the Riviera had attained its present fame. Taking a felucca, he swept along the coast to Nice and Monaco. Then he speaks of going over the Apennines into Italy. "Those mountains," he remarks, " are three or four days in passing, for many many miles there is hardly a three-foot road, with precipices into the sea, I should guess three times the height of St. Paul's ; but the mules are so sure-footed there is nothing to fear, though the road is also very bad. Through the mercy of God, I travel pleasantly on."

By this description he must have meant that part of the Mediterranean shore which we now know as the Corniche road, which generally throws the tourist into raptures. He does not seem to have felt them ; yet on reaching " Geneva the superb," with its magnificent harbour, its streets full of palaces, its striped Duomo, and its charming situation, he appears to have been moved ; for "the stateliness of the city," he goes on to say, " is not exceeded by any I have seen."

He mentions Leghorn, then Pisa, then Florence, Oddly enough, he says of the Duomo in the second of these cities, " It is remarkable for its elegant church, the gates of which were brought from Jerusalem." Of the third, he remarks, " Florence being the seat of the arts, I visited the gallery many days." This indicates his taste for pictures; and we can follow him in imagination examining the Raphaels in the Uffizi and the Pitti palace, and also gazing with interest on the Ghiberti gates of the Baptistery, the graceful campanile by Giotto, and the solemn aisles of the Duomo.

Reaching Rome, he was evidently impressed, for he says, " The amazing ruins of temples, palaces, and aqueducts give some faint idea of its amazing grandeur, but it is comparatively now a desert. The description of them, as also of St. Peter's Church and the Vatican, I must defer till I have the pleasure of seeing you." [1] Rome was then under the rule of Clement XIII., a pontiff distinguished more by his virtues than his policy. He struggled to uphold the prerogatives of his see, and found it hard work to maintain the cause of the Jesuits. He disliked change, and resisted reform. Howard saw him in the streets riding in his state coach as popes then were wont to do. " The Pope passed very close by me yesterday; he waved his hand to bless me. I bowed, but not kneeling, some of the Cardinals were displeased. But I never can nor will to any human creature, or invention, as I should tremble at the thought of the adoration I have seen paid to him and the wafer. My temper is too open for this country; yet an important bit of news of this court " (he cautiously writes, " expuls - - n of the J-s-ites ") " that

---

[1] Letter to the Rev. Joshua Symonds, dated Rome, May 22nd, 1770.

I now know I durst not commit to writing. That cruelest of all inventions, the Inquisition, stops all mouths."

The Palazzo del S.S. Uffizio—where the tribunal was established in 1536—is in a street near the famous colonnade of St. Peter's. As the old tribunal was abolished in 1849, this building was afterwards used as a barrack for French soldiers—the new tribunal, established by Pio Nono, now holds its meetings in the Vatican. The Dominican convent of Sopra Minerva, close to the Pantheon, was connected with the Inquisition ; there Galileo was tried ; but the convent is now suppressed, and its halls, library, and MSS. are appropriated to public uses. Howard wished to see the interior of the Inquisition, but he informs us " The chambers of this silent and melancholy abode were quite inaccessible to me ; and yet I spent near two hours about the court and the private apartments, till my continuance there began to raise suspicion."[1] This, I conclude, refers to the Office by the Vatican, not that of Sopra Minerva.

From Rome he posted to Naples, saying, " As I return to see the great procession on the 15th of June, I intend staying about a fortnight." But whilst he took a great interest in the antiquities as well as the prisons of the " eternal city," his thoughts were ever recurring to another eternal city.

" Thus," my dear friend, he writes to Mr. Symonds, " am I travelling over desolate places of ancient grandeur, and felt it to overpower that selfish and

---

[1] This was written at a later period, perhaps. Comp. Brown p. 255, and Field, p. 253.

vain principle that is rooted in my constitution and that humbles the pride of one's heart! And when at other times I view in statues, paintings, architecture, etc., the utmost stretch of human skill, how should one's thoughts be raised to that glorious world, that heavenly city, the city of the living God—where sin, sorrow, and every imperfection will be done away! Oh! the free, sovereign, unbounded grace of our Lord Jesus Christ! How thankful should we Protestants be for this glorious Gospel which we have in our hands. The happiness we are exulting in, millions in this country are denied."

Arrived at Naples, he would not be insensible to the charming sweep of the Mediterranean shore, the blue waters, the blue sky, and the buildings which climb up the hill towards the castle of St. Elmo. He ascended Vesuvius, as we shall see, for meteorological researches, and tested the degree of heat at the highest point of the mountain. He laid himself down on the lava, which was intolerably hot, and immersed his thermometer in the liquid at the volcano's mouth. The results he transmitted to the Royal Society, and they were published in the " Philosophical Transactions."

In Puritan times, and at later periods, as hinted already, devout people had been accustomed to make a covenant with the Almighty in a written form, dedicating themselves to His service, and praying for Divine grace to keep their vows. Howard adopted this practice, and committed to paper the following expressions of holy desire amongst many others of a similar kind :—

"O my soul, keep close to Him in the amiable

light of redeeming love, and amidst the snares thou
art particularly exposed to in a country of such
wickedness and folly. Stand thou in awe and sin
not ; see what progress thou makest in thy religious
journey. Art thou nearer the Heavenly Canaan?
A little while, and thy journey will be ended ; be
thou faithful unto death. Lord, I believe, help my
unbelief. O compassionate and Divine Redeemer,
save me from the dreadful guilt and power of sin,
and accept of my solemn, free, and, I trust, unre-
served surrender of my soul and of my dear child, all
I am and have into Thy hands. Thus, O Lord, my
God, even a worm is humbly bold to covenant with
Thee. Do Thou ratify and confirm it, and make me
the everlasting monument of Thy unbounded mercy.
Amen, Amen, Amen.

" Hoping my heart deceives me not, and trusting
in His mercy for restraining and preventing grace,
though rejoicing in returning what I have received of
Him into His hands, yet with fear and trembling, I
sign my unworthy name,

" JOHN HOWARD."

"Naples, 27th of May, 1770."

This solemn covenant, it seems, he was accustomed
to review, for in 1789, at Moscow, just before his
death, he wrote a renewal of it.

On his return to Rome he sent the following
letter to Lady Whitbread [1] :—

---

[1] For these and other letters to the Whitbread family, I am
indebted to the " Howard Correspondence," published by the
Rev. Mr. Field—a book now out of print. He was permitted
to copy them from originals in the possession of a descendant
from Mr. Whitbread.

" *Rome, June* 13, 1770.

" MADAM,—

"I have just received a very obliging letter on my return from Naples. When ladies condemn, we must plead guilty, and hope our judges are merciful : so I enter not on my defence. Since I had the pleasure of writing to Mr. Whitbread from Geneva, I have visited Leghorn, Pisa, and Florence. In those places, as indeed both in Rome and Naples, I often see paintings of the first and second class, leaving all the inferior ones. I confess that I had seen nothing before I came to Rome. I had often read of the Laocoon, the Apollo, the Gladiator, the Pantheon and Coliseum, the paintings of Raphael, Titian, and Guido; yet the description fell far short, as it does also of the magnificence and elegance of St. Peter's. To that church and the Vatican I go most evenings, the views from the latter being inexpressibly fine. The Pope I have often seen. The worthy good man dispenses with my kneeling. I should tremble to pay that homage to any human creature that I have seen paid to him.

" The Pretender passed close by me yesterday, and I had a full strong view of him. He has the look of a mere sot, very stupid, dull, and bending double ; quite altered to what I saw him twenty years ago in France.

" The situation of Naples is fine. As I have the best *cartes*,[1] it may afford your ladyship some pleasure to see them. I ascended Mount Vesuvius, and when I was up three parts of the hill, the earth was, by my thermometer, somewhat warmer than the

---

[1] Views.

atmosphere. I then took the temperature every five minutes, till I got to the top. The heat was continually increasing. After I had stood the smoke a quarter of an hour, I breathed freely ; so with three men I descended so far as they would go with me, where the earth or brimstone was so heated that, in frequent experiments, it raised my thermometer to 240°, which is near 30° hotter than boiling water, and in some places it fired some paper I put in. As these experiments have never before been made, I thought the account of them might afford your ladyship some entertainment.

"We begin to have hot weather here, so I shall make my pilgrimage in the night to Loretto, and from thence to Venice, where I shall stay about a fortnight, when, I think, I shall take my route through Germany to my favourite country, Holland. When at Rotterdam I shall hope to be favoured with a letter, though I believe I shall hardly be there till the middle or latter end of September, as I seldom fix any route or time in any place. This uncertainty prevents my hearing so often from my friends as I could wish. Permit me to say I am with much esteem,

" Your ladyship's obliged and
" Most humble servant,
" JOHN HOWARD."

In the streets of Rome he met with the *Confraternità della Misericordia*—a brotherhood of Charity known by the singular garb they wear when on duty. He describes the cemetery where criminals are interred :—

"I was in Rome on the 29th of August, the only day in the year when the burial-place is open to the public. Adjoining an elegant church is a chapel. In the portico and on one side are marble squares, in which are circular apertures for the interments of those who are executed. Round these stones is inscribed "Domine, cum veneris judicare, noli nos condemnare."

He visited Civita Vecchia to inspect the Pope's galleys. Prisoners condemned for life were chained two and two, and if guilty of forgery, they had to wear an iron glove. Punished for limited terms, they were fastened by a single chain; but after the lapse of two years a ring only was attached to the leg, and this was lessened as the expiration of imprisonment approached. "None are sent to the galleys," he says, "under the age of twenty; criminals of a younger age are kept at the Hospital of St. Michele in Rome till they are of age."[1] Of the prison at Civita Vecchia, containing 1364 prisoners, he gives a horrible account. He saw a low vaulted room with only gleams of light, where men were chained heavily, and fastened down, and the noise they made was "such as may be imagined at the entrance of hell." Amongst them were 700 murderers and bandits. "They were a ghastly crew, haggard, ferocious, reckless assassins."

"What are you here for?" Howard said to a heavy-looking fellow lying on his back. The man would not answer, but a companion said, "He is here for stabbing." "Why is he in this part of the prison?"

[1] Foreign Prisons, p. 96.

"Because he is incorrigible." "What are you con-demned for?" he inquired of another. "For murder."

On his way, again and again, at Naples and Rome, and afterwards when travelling homewards, he re-corded in his Journal and in letters, self-abasing lamentations. Though on a mission of mercy, and everywhere behaving with the utmost circumspection, he confesses, in language like that of Augustine, not in style but in spirit, his utter sinfulness, wrestling with God for mercy and forgiveness.

It appears from the following letter, that passing from Italy, he visited Stuttgart, the capital of Wurtemberg, pleasantly situated, with long, wide streets, and a Royal palace.

" Stuttgart, July 26th, 1770.

"MY LADY,—I received a very kind letter at Venice; accept a very poor return,—my thanks,—also for your obliging visit to my boy. When I left Rome, I steered my course to Loretto. The immense riches that are there locked up are as surprising as the folly of the votaries. The superstition, folly, and nonsense that one hears and sees, must give any thinking mind pain, and that such a gross imposition should be car-ried on such a number of years. They say the Virgin's chamber was brought over the Venetian Gulf, A.D. 1290; and they told me it was brought by a miracle, and supported from falling by a miracle, though enclosed by a marble case, and many iron bars to prevent its falling in. I could not help saying, in their *holy* chamber, it would be another miracle to make me believe either one or the other.

"I went from thence to Bologna, and spent a few days there. The city is no otherwise remarkable than for the piazzas (as in Covent Garden) to every house. There are some fine pictures, and one rich Monastery of the Olivetano, from whence is one of the finest views in Italy. Thence I came to Venice, the situation of which amidst many, as it were floating islands, is surprising ; yet when I saw the Rialto, St. Mark's Place, etc., I was much disappointed ; prints had raised my expectation, but they—the realities—fell short. The streets are all alleys—in many places two persons cannot pass. The houses are all dirty, the canals quite offensive, so that it required some patience to stay eight or ten days. And I was not singular, as an English family there told me they never were so tired of a place in a week's time."[1]

The course he took next is uncertain, except that we find him at Heidelberg in July. Afterwards he reached Rotterdam ; and he sat down one Sunday night to express his sentiments in the following strain :—

"This morning, on the review of the temper of my mind, how humbled I ought to be before God. I have an evil and wicked heart, ever ready to depart from Him, starting aside like a deceitful bow, mourning yet trusting in my Lord and my God, when by calm, retired thoughts, I would hope I am one step forward on my Christian journey. Yet, alas ! in company how many steps backward ! God give me wisdom !"

"I desire, with profound veneration, to bless and praise God for His merciful preservation of me in my long journey. No danger, no accident, has befallen me ; but I am among the living, I trust, ever to praise

---

[1] Addressed to Lady Whitbread. Howard Correspondence.

Him. And as to my soul, among all its weakness and folly, yet I have some hope it has not lost ground this year of travelling. I am very desirous of returning with a right spirit, not only wiser, but better, with a cheerful humility, a more general love, and benevolence towards my fellow-creatures, watchful of my thoughts, my words, my actions, and resigned to the will of God, that I may walk with God, and lead a more useful and honourable life in this world."[1]

From the Hague, that favourite spot, he wrote to England :—

"*The Hague, Aug. 20th,* 1770.

"MY LADY,—In Italy, however magnificent the objects, and highly elegant the curiosities may be, we in England have the solid, the substantial, and important, which we ought to value above all the rest.

"I have been well gratified with foreign elegances, and shall sit down at home in peace, as the comfortable, useful, and honourable life should be our aim. I am sure I require the most favourable allowance of my friends."[2]

This, and the previous letter to the same lady, written at Stuttgart, enables us to trace Howard's route on his way home, a matter left in obscurity by previous biographers.

---

[1] Brown, p. 98.   [2] Addressed to Lady Whitbread.

CHAPTER V.

ECCLESIASTICAL RELATIONS AT BEDFORD.

1770–1773.

WHEN Howard returned from abroad after his wife's death, he could not at once settle down in his desolate home. Within a short time, he went to Southampton, where he felt so unwell that he requested the prayers of the congregation over which William Kingsbury, an excellent and distinguished pastor of the last century, presided. This circumstance led not only to a pleasant interview, but to a lasting friendship.

Travelling again became his resource; and from Bristol he visited part of Wales and the south of Ireland, accompanied by a servant named Thomasson,[1] who seems to have paid him the most assiduous attention, and who in a MS. journal preserved several particulars respecting his master's life. Upon returning to Cardington, Howard was seized with severe ague, which lasted three-quarters of a year; owing, it would appear, in part at least, to "the low marshy situation of the village," a circumstance which rekindled the sufferer's zeal in promoting sanitary improvement, an object to which more than ever he

---

[1] Much has been said about this man. I reserve any notice of him for the present.

devoted attention after his recovery.   Other subjects occupied his thoughts at this period, for we find him, in the course of four years after his Continental journey, engaged in ecclesiastical, social, and political affairs which require our notice.

It had been his custom, since he went to live at Cardington, to attend divine worship at Bedford. The congregation with which he united had a remarkable history.   A number of godly people in the days of the Civil Wars seceded from the parish churches at Bedford, and chose for their pastor a person named John Gifford.   He was once a zealous Royalist, and being taken prisoner by the Parliamentarians, was sentenced to death; but he escaped through the intervention of his sister and the drunkenness of the guard.   Becoming converted, he joined a few Puritans.   The little band, in the year 1650, elected him to be their spiritual guide ; and the effect of his teaching, followed by an epistle he addressed to them, " upon his departure out of the world," created in the minds of the next generation the most profound reverence for his saintly life and apostolic character. Gifford's epistle has been praised by Southey, who says it exemplifies a wise, tolerant, and truly Christian spirit ; that spirit he infused into the community, as its subsequent history proves.   He was the Evangelist, and the Greatheart of the Bedford pilgrims. His idea of Christian life was, that it springs from spiritual union with the Lord Jesus ; and that the bond of union amongst His followers does not consist in oneness of theological or ecclesiastical opinion, but in religious sympathy and brotherly love.   The Church he founded was neither exclusively Baptist nor Pædobaptist; members of both kinds were admitted on the same terms.

John Bunyan was first a deacon and then the pastor of this unique Society. The humble annals contain several notices of the great allegorist; relating how, when he died, "the whole congregation met to humble themselves before God by fasting and prayer for His heavy and severe stroke upon them, in taking away their honoured brother, Bunyan, by death"; and how it was "agreed by the whole congregation, that care be taken to seek out for one suitably qualified to be chosen an elder among them," and such "care" was committed by all the rest to the brethren living in Bedford. The name of Bunyan continued a household word in that community, and was fresh in the memory and was often on the lips of the people with whom Howard worshipped. Bunyan's "Grace Abounding," and Bunyan's "Holy War," as well as Bunyan's "Pilgrim's Progress," must have been books after Howard's own heart, for the ecstatic expressions contained in his Journals might be taken for echoes of that wonderful man's religious teaching.

. The Church had, in Bunyan's time, several pastors. The Records mention no less than seven. One of them was Nehemiah Cox, "a very excellent, learned, and judicious divine." He appeared in court at the Bedford Assizes, to answer a charge of preaching contrary to the law of the land; and, oddly enough, "he first pleaded in Greek and then in Hebrew"—a piece of pedantry which appeared the more remarkable, as in the indictment he bore the description of "Cordwainer." When the circumstance came to be buzzed about in Bedford, the townsfolk "wound up what they counted a good story, by saying the Judge told the bar, 'Well, this cordwainer has wound you all up, gentlemen.'"

A minister named Joshua Symonds undertook the pastoral office in the Bedford Church the year in which Howard's wife Henrietta died ; and as Howard and he became intimate friends, and he was one to whom he wrote several letters, notice may be taken of him here. Born at Kidderminster, he lived in Birmingham as a young man, when he was encouraged to enter the ministry by the pastor of Carr's Lane congregation, by whose advice he went to the academy of Dr. Conder, at Mile End. There he approved himself to his instructors, and at the completion of his course visited Bedford. His preaching favourably impressed the congregation, and in due time he was ordained their minister.[1] His stated labours were shortened by ill-health, and for some years he was quite laid aside. After his death, John Ryland, a celebrated Dissenting minister, remarked, in a funeral sermon for him, "Few knew where to find a man whose general conversation indicated more godly simplicity and godly sincerity. Having been put in trust with the Gospel, he spoke, not as pleasing man, but God, who trieth our hearts. He used to preach, not himself, but Christ Jesus the

---

[1] I remember the old building, large and cumbrous ; and the departed worthies who worshipped there would have been astonished at the appearance of the present edifice, with its magnificent bronze gates given by the Duke of Bedford. When they were opened, I had the pleasure of delivering an address before the Mayor and Aldermen and a large congregation of townspeople.

Lord; and he meant "—the good man had himself
selected the preacher on this occasion—"that I should
not preach upon the excellences of Joshua Symonds,
but upon the excellences of Jesus Christ." "You
have seen a poor, afflicted, dying man, that has lain,
I may say, at the mouth of the grave for these several
months, under a strong probability, from week to
week, that *that* would be his dying week ; who was
yet supported, comforted, and enabled to wait patiently
for his expected and much-desired change. You
have seen a man who had nine strong ties to earth,"
—this alludes to Mr. Symonds' family,—"drawn by
a far stronger tie toward heaven." He died in 1785.

Mr. Symonds had a daughter whose married name
was Emery, and who lived to a great age. She
knew, when a girl, people who remembered Bunyan ; and to indicate her recollections, it may be
mentioned that she used to tell of her going to
Bridge Street, Blackfriars, by her mother's special
permission, "to stand in a chair at the window, that
she might look at her uncle walking in the street
with an umbrella over his head." She knew three
generations of her ancestors, four of her descendants. Her great grandfather, whom she recollected,
was born in the Revolution year, 1688. She was
acquainted with Newton, Venn, Lady Austen, An-
drew Fuller, the Rylands, and other worthies. She
spoke of her father as "a good Hebrew, Greek, and
Latin scholar," and as a particular friend of the
celebrities just named, especially John Newton, who
addressed to him some of the letters published in
the *Omicron.* What Newton thought of him, appears
from a letter written in 1776 : "If I should outlive

you, and I should have a call to write the life of the Rev. Mr. Symonds, of Bedford, I should perhaps have more to say in your favour than you are aware of; and if you would have the darker side known as well as the brighter, you must write it yourself." [1]

Mrs. Emery talked much about Howard. "Often," says Mrs. Emery's daughter,[2] "have I listened with intense interest to the recital from my mother's own lips, of various little incidents respecting Howard, and beheld with great delight her beaming eyes, while she graphically described his person, dress, and manner, and told of his dignified appearance, of his remarkable punctuality; and how, sometimes, even in the midst of an interesting conversation with her parents, he would look at his watch, instantly rise, and, with a low bow, leave the room."

The Church, as we have seen, was composed of Baptists and Pædobaptist members. Bunyan was a Baptist: Symonds, when chosen, was a Pædobaptist. This did not disturb the harmony of the people, so long as the latter remained what he had been at the beginning; but in 1772 he changed his views, and announced that he could no longer continue to baptize the infants of the flock. This circumstance led to a rupture, and, in the end, to a separation—the Pædobaptists seceding, and forming a second Church on their own distinctive principles. In the secession Howard joined, and it is on this account that these details are introduced, since they

---

[1] Bull's Life of Newton, p. 199.
[2] Reminiscences of a Beloved Mother. Printed for private circulation.

show that, though a man of liberal ecclesiastical views, he attached importance to infant baptism.

As Howard took a decided part in this controversy, I have examined the documents on both sides. The chief grounds alleged by the seceders in a MS. of the period were, that Mr. Symonds, having become an Anti-pædobaptist, was seeking to indoctrinate the whole congregation with his opinions; and that, in this and some other objectionable respects, a large party supported his proceedings. From the Church Book of the Bunyan Meeting, in which Symonds remained after the secession, it appears that the majority who sustained him were prepared to make concessions on condition of the opposite party doing the same. As I am not writing a history of the Church, the reciprocal concessions proposed may as well sink, so far as this narrative is concerned, altogether into oblivion. No doubt much was lying beneath the surface which does not appear ; and those who read between the lines may easily discern the existence of personal feelings such as, alas ! underlie many disputes of greater importance. Painful excitement attended the division ; but it is pleasant to read at the conclusion the following passage in a MS. preserved by the separatists in reference to the brethren from whom they parted :—" Though they cannot but conceive of them as mistaken, yet they hope they are honest in their errors ; and though a difference in judgment and practice, arising from the present imperfections of knowledge and grace, renders it expedient to withdraw from their Society at present, yet they would still conceive of them as brethren, and treat them as such, hoping to unite with them again in the glorious assembly and Church of the first-born, and to spend a happy eternity with them in a world of perfect knowledge, holiness, and joy : where all shall be peace, harmony, and love, and party names and distinctions shall be heard no more." [1] In these charitable views, Howard concurred. Conscientiously compelled to withdraw, he did it with dignity and temper; and, what is rare under such circumstances, he is said to have retained the goodwill of all parties, and to have preserved the forsaken pastor's friendship. [2]

Temporary arrangements followed ; a place was secured for worship until a new Meeting House could be built ; and amongst the ministers who officiated was the son of Howard's old friend, Meredith Townshend of Stoke Newington. " It gratified him highly," says a correspondent of the period, who furnishes these minute but interesting details, " to find that he was appointed to sojourn at Mr. Howard's house during his visit to the people. He found him not

---

[1] The documents on which the statements of the separatists rest were shown to me by my friend, the late Mr. Alliott, at the time minister of the second chapel, called Howard Chapel.

[2] The rules of the new Church are broad and catholic. The first, which is fundamental, runs thus :—" That those whose names are hereunto subscribed, humbly hoping that we have received the grace of God in truth, firmly relying on the mediation and atonement of the Son of God, and sincerely desirous of yielding obedience to all His commandments, having been formed into a Christian Society, do henceforth resolve to walk together as long as circumstances shall permit in the fellowship of the Gospel." The formation of a distinct Church after the rupture, was approved by Dr. Winter, Dr. Gibbons, Samuel Palmer, and other well-known ministers.

disposed to talk much, and supposed that he talked to him less than he would otherwise have done, because he was young in years, and almost boyish in appearance ; besides that, he sat but a short time at table, and was in motion during the whole day. On the Sabbath he ate little or no dinner, and spent the interval between the morning and afternoon service in a private room alone. He had prayer in his family every day, morning and evening, and read the Scriptures himself, but asked his guest to pray. He was very abstemious, lived chiefly upon vegetables, ate little animal food, and drank no wine or spirits. He hated praise ; and when Mr. Townshend once mentioned to him his labours of benevolence, he spoke of them slightingly as a whim of his, and immediately changed the subject."

A new and permanent building for the seceders was speedily raised. Howard gave two hundred pounds, and lent the same amount without interest, on a bond which he afterwards cancelled. He made in this case the present of a pulpit, as he had done before for the Bunyan Meeting House.

The strict observance of the first day of the week, the regular discharge of religious duties at that season, and the avoidance of all business and amusement during its sacred hours, formed a marked characteristic of the Puritans of the seventeenth century, distinguishing them in this respect from most Protestants on the Continent. The same habits were cultivated by Dissenters of the eighteenth century; and though perhaps not so rigid as their forefathers, they carried their punctilious ideas to an excess, and created, in many cases, prejudices against Evangelical religion, with which a more than Jewish abstinence from common habits seemed apparently to be identified. Howard was no doubt a thorough Puritan in his Sunday behaviour; but, whatever might be thought of this, to him it was anything but self-denial. The day in his estimation was "a delight, the holy of the Lord, and honourable;" if he expected it to be so to others, unhappily, he was mistaken. The contrast between English and foreign Sundays struck him forcibly, when travelling abroad, as appears from his correspondence; and amidst the bustle and pleasure-taking of Paris and Brussels he fondly sighed for the quietude of Cardington and the worship at Bedford.

Before the described secession had occurred, Howard purchased or built a house close to the Bunyan Meeting. He had done so that he might have a home in which to spend his Sundays, without being obliged to travel from Cardington to Bedford on the day of rest. According to one tradition, he came over on Saturday and returned on Monday. The building is scarcely, if at all, altered, except that some addition is made on one side. It stands at the corner of Mill Street with a walled-in garden before it. The front is covered with a goodly vine, said to have been planted by Howard himself. It is trailed on lattice-work between the windows, and surmounted by a deep roof exhibiting dormer windows. Two rooms, a sitting-room and a bed-room, occupied by the philanthropist, I lately visited with great interest. They are as plain as possible. The Trustees of the Chapel have lately purchased the premises.

With the pastor of the new Church, the Rev. Thomas Smith, Howard formed a very intimate friendship; and even offered to build him a parsonage house, which was delicately declined.

Howard, I was informed, loved him with a special affection, as one with whom he could sympathize, and in whom he could confide. He, like Mr. Symonds, left behind him a daughter, who used to delight in talking of old times. She spoke of Howard's Sunday morning calls at her father's house. " I remember," she would say, " how anxiously we used to watch his knock, and how pleased we were to walk to meeting by his side." She also told how the two friends would go out on horseback together, ·and Howard would decoy his companion into a ride so long as to preclude his getting home at the usual hour of his mid-day meal, and then would say, as he rejoiced at the success of his manœuvre, "I find, my friend, that you can fast as long as I can; but now you must go to Cardington and spend the day with me, as Mrs. Smith will have dined long before this time." " My father," the lady added, " has often said, those were some of the most delightful hours of his life, for that Mr. Howard would then completely unbend himself, and give the most interesting accounts of his past travels; open to him all his future plans, all his trials and sorrows, in short, every feeling of his heart, in the most free and confidential manner."

Several letters are addressed by the philanthropist to Mr. Smith, indicating the friendship between them, which continued till death. Mr. Smith survived his friend, and removed from Bedford to Foulmire in 1796. He returned to Bedford, and died suddenly in 1801, aged 52.

According to another tradition I heard thirty years

ago, Howard, when he attended at Mr. Smith's place of worship, reserved in the Mill Street house a little parlour for his use on Sundays. There, I learnt, he was wont to tarry in the middle of the day, and take a slight repast between morning and afternoon services. It was his habit, as I was further informed, to walk on these occasions from Cardington and back; and a story was related that some one, whom he had often reproved for his vices, resolved to waylay and murder the philanthropist, when taking this accustomed journey. "Providence," it is said in a funeral sermon preached for him, "remarkably interposed to preserve so valuable a life, by inclining him that morning to go on horseback another road."

Thoroughly identifying himself with the Bedford congregation in Divine worship, he still retained his membership at Stoke Newington; and it is strongly characteristic of his tenacious hold on that early fellowship, of his love to what he regarded as his mother Church, that when his son was to be baptized, instead of requesting the Bedford minister to discharge that service, he sent for his Newington pastor, Mr. Townshend. But practically he maintained communion with Mr. Smith's people and discharged amongst them the duties of benevolence, contributing liberally to the relief of the poor, and assisting them "by every means in his power." He maintained friendly relations with the members; and his urbanity to every one is to this day a subject of praise.

Not within narrow boundaries did he confine his sympathies. He knew no distinction of sect or party. At all times he showed himself willing to do an act of kindness for those of different persuasions from his own. "In every way," says his friend and biographer Dr. Aiken, "in which a man thoroughly disposed to do good with the means Providence has bestowed upon him, can exercise his liberality, Mr. Howard stood amongst the foremost. He was not only a subscriber to various public schemes of benevolence, but his private charities were largely diffused and remarkably well directed."

Howard cultivated friendship amongst the people called Quakers. There was a great deal in their character calculated to attract him. Their purity, simplicity, and unworldliness accorded with his taste. Their vindication of the rights of conscience, and their sufferings on account of it, commanded his respect. Their peaceful disposition and opposition to all kinds of war, were also accordant with his sentiments. Public opinion in reference to the community had undergone a marked change since the time of the Commonwealth. Indiscreet methods of expressing dislike to the Establishment and the predominant sects, had at that period aroused ardent persecution of the Quakers; but the meekness and propriety of their subsequent behaviour, their unblemished morals, and the prosperous circumstances of some of their members, had turned the tide of opinion, and raised Quakerism to more than common respectability. Not only did Howard share in this feeling, but he was drawn towards Friends by affinities of conviction. He had, if I may so say, much of the Quaker in him ; and this was manifested in the singular neatness of his apparel and in the plain furniture of his house.

Another religious body existed, for whom Howard cherished fraternal regards. The Moravians—who

reverently preserve traditions of Bohemian martyrs,
and who in the middle of the last century committed
themselves to noble missionary enterprises beyond
other denominations—had for some time carried on
work at Bedford; and in 1751 consecrated a chapel
for the preaching of the Gospel. Labourers amongst
them sought to promote the spiritual welfare of
neighbouring villages; and their ordinary, Bishop
Johannes de Watteville, visited the Midland District
for the confirmation of converts. All this came
within Howard's knowledge. In gentleness, nonconformity to the world, and morality of life, they were
akin to Quakers; and they had an additional quality
recommending them to his good graces, in their intense Evangelicalism, and the burning fervour of
their hymnology.

There lived at Bedford in Howard's time a large
West Indian proprietor named Barham, who belonged to the Moravian Brethren. His abode was
called "The Great House," and its occupier was like
Gaius of old, for he entertained under his hospitable
roof apostolic men, especially John Newton. He
brings the names of Barham and Howard together
in the following passage :—

" Such a happy family perhaps I never saw, where
the peace and love of God dwell in every heart. I
spoke every morning after breakfast, and attended
the chapel every evening. On Thursday we paid a
morning visit to Mr. Howard of Cardington, when
we had some interesting conversation. May the
Lord bless it. I presented him with an *Omicron*." [1]

<hr>

[1] Bull's Life of Newton, p. 204.

This was in 1773. The clergyman, the Moravian, and the Independent pleasantly met that day, as good men of different denominations ought to do.

CHAPTER VI.

SHRIEVALTY.

1773–1774.

IN the Bedford Corporation Records the name of John Howard appears in 1757 and 1766 as Mayor of the borough. At first sight, it seems as if the subject of our Memoir accepted municipal honours; but a little consideration renders such a circumstance very improbable. The matter is set at rest by discovering that the signature of John Howard the Mayor, is different from that of the John Howard of Cardington; and I am informed that Mr. Howard, the celebrated machinist, father of the present Member for Bedfordshire, when he served the office a few years ago, spoke of an ancestor of his as having preceded him a century before.

A higher honour was conferred upon Howard of Cardington not long afterwards. In 1773 he was selected as High Sheriff for the county, by what means and with what motive, has not been ascertained. The circumstance is peculiar, because Protestant Dissenters had been rendered by the Test Act ineligible for the occupancy of such a position. That Act had entailed pains and penalties of a severe description upon any one who should fill a public office without taking the Sacrament in the Church of

England ; and biographers of Howard have dwelt upon the peril to which he exposed himself by accepting the honour without a legal qualification. But it is forgotten that Acts of Indemnity began to be passed in the reign of George II. for the protection of those who took office without qualification. These Acts were renewed every year, with few exceptions, up to the accession of George III.; after that period the renewal of the indemnity became regular from time to time. Still, Nonconformists were at the mercy of Parliament from year to year, and therefore uneasiness was natural in reference to a statute which, though suspended, was not repealed. Strange stories are told about the Lord Chancellor giving Howard an assurance of indemnification ; but these are reduced to more reasonable dimensions by a communication made to Dr. Brown after he had published the first edition of Howard's Life. He was informed that Howard waited upon the Lord Chancellor and stated his difficulty respecting the Sacrament ; and that the Chancellor told him, though he could not say difficulties were entirely removed, yet if they should arise, his lordship would "do all he could to turn the edge of them." This version was supplied by "a venerable Baptist minister at Bedford," in " the ninety-first year of his age," and more than thirty years after he had received the statement from Howard's lips. There is room for doubting its perfect accuracy, without calling in question the truthfulness of the witness ; but it is possible the elected sheriff consulted the holder of the great seal, and heard that which justified his fulfilment of the office, without any act of occasional conformity.

It was the Test Act, not the Corporation Act, to which Howard is described as laying himself open— the Test Act, passed in 1673, twelve years later than the Corporation Act, was aimed at Roman Catholics, not at Protestant Dissenters. The object was to exclude from office the Duke of York, afterwards James II., then High Admiral of England, Lord Clifford, High Treasurer, and other notabilities, whom it compelled to resign office. The Act declared that all persons holding situations of trust or profit should take the oaths of supremacy and allegiance in public and open court, and also receive the Sacrament according to the usage of the Church of England, in some parish church on some Lord's day, immediately after Divine service and sermon, and deliver a certificate of having done so, under the hands of the minister and churchwardens.[1] The penalties for noncompliance were severe. The delinquent was liable to be disabled from engaging in any lawsuit, from being guardian to a child, from being executor to a will, from receiving a legacy, or bearing any office in England or Wales; and, in addition to these incredible disabilities, he had to forfeit the sum of £500.[2]

A solemn denial of the doctrine of Transubstantiation being included in what was demanded, makes it plain that it was levelled at Papists, not at Dissenters and there was a disposition in the House of Commons at the time to relieve the latter from some of their disabilities. This is no excuse for the injustice

---

[1] Stat. 25 Car. ii., c. 2.
[2] Neal : History of the Puritans, vol. ii., p. 460.

of the law. But the country at the moment was mad about Popery; and Dissenters joined in the policy of excluding Roman Catholics from civil office.

The Test Act and the Corporation Act imposed conformity to the Church of England in receiving the Lord's Supper as a qualification to office. Three different courses had been pursued under these circumstances. Sir John Shorter, in the reign of James II., also Sir Humphrey Edwin and Sir Thomas Abney, in the reign of William III., all three Nonconformists, had, upon accepting the Lord Mayoralty of London, submitted to law, by attending the Church of England and partaking of the Holy Communion. This practice of occasional conformity, as it was called, excited a great deal of violent controversy, many Dissenters resenting it, especially Daniel Defoe, who, in his own trenchant style, with vigorous Saxon idioms employed after a rasping fashion, denounced the practice as utterly inconsistent, saying—that none but Protestants halt between God and Baal, that none but Christians of an amphibious nature could believe one way and worship another.

Proceeding upon Defoe's principle, some Dissenters would on no account whatever accept any office from which they were excluded by the Acts. They objected conscientiously to receive the Lord's Supper according to the rites of the Church, because they deemed those rites unscriptural—sitting at the table, not kneeling at the altar rails, being regarded by them as conformable to the primitive history of this divine ordinance. Other points in the Church service they disapproved, and they could not bring themselves to adopt occasional conformity pursued by some co-religionists.

Another class refused to conform *as a qualification for office*, not because they could not conscientiously receive the Lord's Supper according to Episcopalian usage, but simply because they could not bear to make what the Saviour had ordained as a memorial of Himself, and as a sign of brotherly love, the means of securing entrance upon civil distinctions. They deemed *that* a profanation, calling it the employment of worship as a " pick lock " to place and worldly honour. They could on some occasions, as a token of true Catholic union, join brethren of the Anglican Church in their mode of commemorating Christ's love ; but they could not comply with Acts of Parliament requiring conformity as a qualification for secular acts. This view certainly was taken by the illustrious John Howe, Cromwell's chaplain, William's acquaintance, and a kind of mediator between the strict and the liberal Nonconformists of his day. He proved that a person who, apart from worldly motives, communes with one Church on particular occasions and with another Church on common occasions, does nothing which impeaches his conscientiousness or destroys his consistency. He declared that in 1662, " most of the considerable ejected London ministers met and agreed to hold occasional communion with the now Established Church, not quitting their own ministry or declining the exercise of it as they could have opportunity." [1]

Howard frequently attended the parish church at

---

[1] Howe's Works, vol. v., pp. 265-290.

Cardington ; but whether he ever united with the parishioners in Communion Service I cannot learn. It was his practice to go over to Bedford on Sundays when the Lord's Supper was observed ; but it is not inconceivable that, with his catholic ideas, his love of Christian union, and his habit of worshipping with Episcopalian congregations abroad, he might join with his wife Harriet in receiving bread and wine at the hands of the parish clergyman. I by no means feel sure that he did so; but I think the view taken by John Howe is one in which John Howard shared. At all events, he did not conform when he accepted the office of Sheriff for Bedfordshire, nor were any legal proceedings adopted against him. Such proceedings would have depended upon some officious person informing against him, a circumstance not likely to occur, as the penalties threatened by the Test Act were so serious, that scarcely any one was likely to set the law in motion against a man of Howard's character and reputation. Moreover, the law itself was in such a state of uncertainty, owing to Acts of a contrary character subsequently passed, especially Acts of Indemnity, that a conviction was very improbable. Only six years before Howard's name was pricked for Sheriff, the Corporation of London had failed to enforce the Corporation Act against Dissenters who refused to qualify for the City shrievalty. The judges refused to support the claims of the Corporation, and the Lords affirmed the judgment of the court. Lord Mansfield said, " It is now no crime for a man to say he is a Dissenter, nor is it any crime for him not to take the Sacrament according to the rites of the Church of

England; nay, the crime is, if he does it contrary to the dictates of his conscience." " There is certainly nothing more unreasonable, more inconsistent with the rights of human nature, more contrary to the spirit and precepts of the Christian religion, more iniquitous and unjust, more impolitic, than persecution."[1] Under these circumstances Howard ran no risk by venturing on the shrievalty without the qualification; and a great deal said on the subject is wide of the mark.

There was perhaps some falling off in the outward splendours of the Bedfordshire shrievalty in the year 1773. At that time, and, indeed, within our own recollection, county sheriffs were wont to maintain a very imposing amount of state and ceremony, especially when they went out in their carriages, with an array of attendants, to meet the Justices of Assize. I dare say there was not quite so much that was gorgeous that year in the customary processions, as the Bedfordshire squires and yeomen had witnessed before. The coach was not so smart as usual; the blue livery of the javelin-men was very plain; and I was told at Cardington that, in proof of this, a coat was long preserved by one who wore it, and who carried a javelin on the memorable occasion. No ball would be graced by the Sheriff's presence, nor any play bespoke at the theatre. I can fancy that the bells seemed not to ring so merrily as usual. I am quite sure that, as the Sheriff conducted the Judges into court, and sat beside them with his white wand, he esteemed it anything but a gala day. This eccentric

---

[1] Parl. Hist., vol. xvi., p. 316.

personage, so many thought him, had accepted his responsibilities under a stern sense of moral obligation; and evidently the guilt and misery with which he was brought into contact gave to the discharge of his duties a melancholy colouring. That contact led to important issues. In the opening sentence of his book on prisons he says, "The distress, of which there are few who have not some imperfect idea, came more immediately under my notice when I was Sheriff of the county of Bedford." Further on, he adds, respecting the subject of his great life work, "To the pursuit of it I was prompted by the sorrows of the sufferers, and love to my country. The work grew upon me insensibly. I could not enjoy my ease and leisure in the neglect of an opportunity, offered me by Providence, of attempting the relief of the miserable."

Thus, it appears that Howard's shrievalty gave an impulse to Howard's benevolence as a prison reformer. It was a new path. He had no pioneer. The first man who went up Mont Blanc,—Balmat, hero of Chamounix,—had often walked round the base of the mountain, seeking in vain for a way to the top. Finding his endeavours fruitless, he exclaimed, "This will never do; if there be no path, why I'll make one." Howard had conceived a mountainous enterprise; and with only an energetic will, without any map whereby to pick his steps, without any mortal guide before him, he said, "If there be no path, why I'll make one." And he did. How he did it will appear as we proceed. It was gradually accomplished, and at the commencement he took one step at a time. The circumstance which excited his compassion was seeing persons—who had been declared not guilty, or against whom the grand jury had not found a true bill, or in whose case a prosecutor did not appear on trial—locked up for months, or more, until they paid certain fees to gaolers, clerks of assize, and other officials. Howard's statements are borne out by those of others. "We may trace in the writers of fiction how little the dominion of cruelty, neglect, and extortion had been diminished at the accession of George III. Fielding's Mr. Booth is committed by an ignorant justice to Bridewell, upon a charge of assaulting a watchman, when he had only interfered to prevent an outrage by two men of fortune who bribed the constable to let them escape. When he goes to prison, a number of persons gather round him in the yard and demand *garnish.* The keeper explained that it was customary for every new prisoner to treat the others with something to drink. The young man had no money, and the keeper quietly permitted the scoundrels to strip him of his clothes."[1] "Three street robbers, certain to be hanged, were enjoying themselves over a bottle of wine and a pipe; the man without a shilling in his pocket had the prison allowance of a penny loaf and a jug of water."[2]

Howard immediately began to act, and applied to the Bedfordshire justices to pay a salary to the master of the gaol in lieu of fees. They asked for a precedent to warrant their doing so. Forthwith he rode into several neighbouring counties, and then

[1] Charles Knight's History of England, vol. vii., p. 117.
[2] Fielding's Amelia.

visited most of the prominent gaols in England, to ascertain the general practice regarding this matter.

This first was a winter journey. He set out in the middle of November, 1773, and pursued his researches at intervals during the months of December, January, and February following; but nowhere could he find the precedent of which he was in search. Gaolers in every place were paid out of fees exacted from prisoners, or out of profits upon such articles as were sold to unhappy creatures within prison walls. In some cases he afterwards found, that in small places a public house was used as a Bridewell, and the landlord acted as gaoler, thus turning criminals into customers.

Failure to find an authority of the kind he sought, was important in its consequence. "This I look upon," remarks Dr. Guy, "as a most fortunate circumstance; for had Howard, during some early visit, found that which he sought, he would probably have gone back to Bedford, told the justices of his success, and persuaded them to substitute a fixed salary to the gaoler for these objectionable fees and fines, and with this local reform Howard might have rested satisfied; but travelling, as he was led to do, from place to place, and inspecting prison after prison, he not only found the wrong done at Bedford prevailing everywhere else, but each fresh prison either revealing some new defect of structure or administration, or adding force and piquancy to the lessons which those previously visited had taught him: so that, drawn on and on, and farther and farther, in search of a precedent, he was becoming ever better and better acquainted with the manifold evils, physical and moral, that had made the prisons of England their home."[1]   Still, it must not be forgotten that his experience in the French prison had first taught him the horrible character of gaols, and that the finding of a precedent for paying a salary to gaolers, instead of leaving them to be supported by fees, was not the only object he had in view.   However, the disappointment of his earliest endeavour served afterwards to stimulate his attempt at the extinction of greater evils.   He started another subject of inquiry, "What is the state of Bridewells, and Houses of Correction?"   As soon as he began the examination he discovered "a complication of distress;" but his attention was arrested principally by the prevalence of gaol fever.   He studied the history of that disease, reading Stowe's "Survey" and other books.   A good deal of research was involved in this inquiry.   He found in Baker's *Chronicle* the story of the Black Assizes, when all who were present died within forty hours—"the Lord Chief Baron, the Sheriff, and three hundred more."   The disease was brought into court by prisoners.   Howard felt appalled.   He turned to the "Natural History" by Lord Bacon, and there found that "the most pernicious infection next to the plague is the smell of the gaol."   Further, he learned, that in 1730, at the Lent Assizes in Taunton, prisoners from Ilchester "infected the court," and the Lord Justice, the Sheriff, "and some hundreds besides" died of the distemper.   In 1750, the Lord Mayor and an alderman of London, with many of

---

[1] Paper on "John Howard's True Place in History," read before the Statistical Society, 16th November, 1875.

inferior rank, were carried off in the same way. The opinions of Sir John Pringle and Dr. Lind were cited by Howard in support of the conclusion, that mortality arising from this dreadful affection "was greater than by all other diseases put together." He saw also the effect of vicious example; and remarked, "It is often said, ‘A prison pays no debts,’ I am sure it may be added, ‘A prison mends no morals.’ Sir John Fielding observes that, ‘a criminal, discharged generally by the next sessions after the execution of his comrades, becomes the head of a gang of his own raising, improved, no doubt, in skill by the company he kept in gaol.’ "[1] The three evils of keeping unconvicted people in prison, of allowing the ravages of fever, and of corrupting the morals of a criminal by means of idleness and bad company, rose up as gigantic monsters before the eyes of our philanthropist; and he could give himself no rest till he went forth to slay them. No knightly deed of old could be so noble.

His expedition was difficult. "I found in searching out evidence of fraud and cruelty in various articles, together with other sources of distress, obliged me to repeat my visits, and to travel over the kingdom more than once; and, after all, I suspect that many frauds have been concealed from me, and that sometimes the interests of my informants prevailed over their veracity." It was not, he adds, without some apprehension of dangers that he first visited the prisons, and he guarded against them as much as possible.

---

[1] The State of Prisons, pp. 17–20.

There were three prisons within the limits of Bedford, a county prison, a Town Gaol, and a Bridewell. Unrivalled interest attaches to one of them, as the building where John Bunyan suffered a tedious confinement, and wrote his *Pilgrim's Progress.* The Town Gaol, or Bridge Prison,—long since swept away, but familiar to us from old engravings,—has been commonly identified as the place of his incarceration; no decisive evidence however on this point has yet been found. Our philanthropist could not but inspect all of them, and each certainly appeared "a den,"—as Bunyan called the place where he dreamed his dream. In the County Gaol, Howard states that male and female felons were living together; their night rooms being two dungeons "down steps;" only a single court-yard being provided for debtors and criminals. No apartment was found for the gaoler. The gaol fever had been there twenty years before, and many townspeople had died in consequence. There was a paper put up as follows, "All persons that come to this place, either by warrant, commitment, or verbally, must pay before discharged, fifteen shillings and fourpence to the gaoler and two shillings to the turnkey."[1] This condition of things was terrible; and in connection with the matter of fees, it inspired the indignation of the benevolent Sheriff, and set him to work upon schemes of improvement.

First impressions deepened as he proceeded. "I will show thee greater abominations than these,"

---

[1] State of Prisons, p. 244. He gives a table of fees at Huntingdon. Thirteen and fourpence when discharged from custody. Half-a-crown to the turnkey. Three and sixpence a week for bed. Four and eightpence for two people, if they slept together.

seem to have been words, which, like those addressed of old to the prophet Ezekiel, rung in his ears as he travelled from town to town, searching into the secrets of prison life.

In the February of 1773, the year of Howard's shrievalty, a Bill was introduced into the House of Commons for effecting a reform,[1] like that which he contemplated, before the year expired ; but the connection between these two movements in the same line I am unable to trace. At any rate, the Bill, though read a first time and then committed, came to nothing that session. Next year, however, we find this measure, in an augmented form, re-introduced, and under debate, so as to promise a favourable issue. On the 4th of March, 1774, the House appears resolving itself into Committee, upon a Bill " for the relief of prisoners, charged with felony or other crimes, who shall be acquitted or discharged by proclamation, respecting the payment of fees to gaolers out of the county rates ; and for the more effectually securing the health of prisoners in gaol during their confinement." Prisoners' health, it will be observed here, is an additional object contemplated in the proceedings of this Committee, and Sir Thomas Claver-

---

[1] 1773, 18 Feb. " That leave be given to bring in a Bill for the relief of prisoners charged with felony or any other crime, who shall be acquitted, or discharged by proclamation, respecting the payment of fees, and giving a recompense for such fees out of the county rates ; and that Mr. Popham, the Lord Folkestone, Mr. Cornwall, Mr. Morton, Mr. Fuller, Mr. Feilde, and Sir Thomas Clavering do prepare and bring in the same.

" 19th Feb., Bill read first time and printed.

" 28th April, Committed."—*Commons' Journal.*

ing, the Chairman, reported to the House, that the Committee had examined witnesses, and had gone through the Bill, and made several amendments. These were reported for subsequent consideration.

Another item of the report introduces us to the subject of our biography under circumstances of singular interest, such as have often befallen illustrious soldiers or sailors after fighting victoriously for their country; but such a circumstance rarely has happened to individuals in private life, who have distinguished themselves only by benevolent exertions. Yet, in the esteem of many, these last are more entitled to their country's congratulations and thanks, than warriors whose garments are rolled in blood.

The entry on the Journals is as follows: " Sir Thomas Clavering also reported from the said Committee, that he was directed by the Committee to move the House that John Howard, Esquire, be called to the Bar, and that Mr. Speaker do acquaint him that this House is very sensible of the humanity and zeal which have led him to visit the several gaols of this kingdom, and to communicate to the House the interesting observations he has made on that subject. And Sir Thomas Clavering moved the House accordingly." [1]

It was resolved, *nemine contradicente*, that John Howard, Esquire, should be called to the Bar, to receive from Mr. Speaker's lips the acknowledgments of his country. He was accordingly called in, and Mr. Speaker acquainted him with the said resolution."

Many a subject, far less worthy of the artist's pencil,

---

[1] Commons' Journal, under date.

has called forth an effort of skill, which, handed down to posterity, still commands universal admiration, both of the hero and the picture.

The House of Commons was far different in those days from what it is at present. The portion of St. Stephen's beautiful Chapel, as then fitted up for the use of the Lower House, resembled more a Nonconformist Meeting than anything else. Inartistic benches crowding the floor, lofty and narrow galleries encumbering the side-walls, and projecting over the members' seats ; ugly chandeliers with a few candles, suspended from the middle of a plain ceiling, and from the fronts of a rudely panelled gallery; Mr. Speaker's chair, standing like a pulpit, surmounted by the royal arms, in front of the nation's assembled wisdom. But the unattractive background advantageously throws into relief this noteworthy incident in Howard's life. There sat the Speaker in characteristic dignity, clothed in accustomed robes of office, prolonged curls of an artistic wig falling far down over the front of his shoulders, and a cocked hat crowning his portly figure. The officers of the House, in gowns richer than are worn now, sat at Mr. Speaker's feet ; and the benches, on each side, were filled with gentlemen in the well-known costume of the period, all bewigged, all wearing large cocked hats. Lord North, as Premier, sat on the Speaker's right hand, "a consummate master of debate," with the Attorney General on the one side, and the Solicitor General on the other, "two pillars of the law and state,"—Thurlow of "majestic sense," Wedderburn of "skilful eloquence." And the Opposition benches rejoiced in "the legal acuteness of Dunning," "the profusion and philosophical fancy of Burke," and "the argumentative vehemence of Fox."[1]   To be thanked by such a House was no small honour; and the honour was deserved by Howard. We see him in plain attire, hat in hand, led into the Parliament Chamber with the usual ceremony; bowing to Mr. Speaker, he received from him the unamimously voted form of thanks. "Then he was requested to withdraw."[2]

"As he was then little known, I cannot much wonder," Dr. Aiken remarks, "that so extraordinary an instance of pure and active benevolence was not universally comprehended, even by that patriotic body; for a member thought fit to ask him at whose expense he travelled, "a question which Mr. Howard could scarcely answer without some indignant emotions."[3]   One would like to know whether the Biographer heard this from his friend's own lips. The question of the rude or thoughtless gentleman could not have been asked and answered in the House when he appeared before the Speaker; if really asked at all, it must have been in committee, in the lobby, or somewhere in private. Anywhere, the incident seems odd and improbable; but if Howard told Aiken this story, the authority of course would be indisputable.

It is pleasant to think that amidst party strifes, when violent speeches were listened to with applause in St. Stephen's Chapel, this Apostle of Charity was

---

[1] Gibbon's description of the House of Commons in 1774. He was not returned till the close of the year ; but the ministers he described were in office when Howard received the thanks of the House.

[2] Journals.   [3] Aiken, p. 57.

allowed by the Legislators of his country to tell a Committee the story of his travels, with a view to the amendment of prison laws.   The historian passes over in silence this episode, which deserves to be recorded, as much as any of the debates which elicited cheers from the Government and Opposition benches. "I was examined in the House of Commons in March, 1774, when I had the honour of their thanks," is the modest record of the circumstance.

Three days after this memorable scene, a further report from the Committee on the Prisons Bill was presented, and the next day, March 6th, it was ordered that the Bill be turned into two Bills.   Both Bills were ultimately passed—the first, for the abolition of fees, on the 31st of March; the second, for the cleansing of prisons, and other details relating to prisoners' health, on the 2nd of June.[1]   The making of these laws, we may be pretty sure, gave Howard more satisfaction than the ceremony performed before the assembled House.   No sooner were the Acts passed, than he had copies of them printed to be sent to every prison in the kingdom.

The passing of them was good so far as it went; but they provided no means of efficiently carrying out the contemplated reforms.   No Inspectors were appointed, no machinery whatever was contrived for securing obedience.   Reports from Government officers as to effects of the new legislation will be looked for in vain.   Howard, in his books on prisons, is the only reporter; and if he had not at his own expense largely circulated what he wrote, little or

---

[1] Journals.

nothing would have been known of the prison world,
after Parliamentary Reformers had finished their part
in the enterprise. It is mortifying to discover from
what he describes, so far as it relates to the Kingdom
of Great Britain and Ireland, how little improvement
was accomplished by these new statutes.[1]

[1] Mr. Guy, in his John Howard's Winter Journey,—a book I
did not read till after my Memoir was finished,—makes the
following statement, which corroborates what I have said. " It
was only in fifteen out of one hundred and fifty prisons, that the
law had been strictly obeyed. In the remainder, it had been
imperfectly carried into effect. I am speaking both of the Act
which had for its object the relief of prisoners from illegal extortions, and of that which aimed at the preservation of their health
and the prevention of the gaol distemper."—P. 32.

CHAPTER VII.

BEDFORD ELECTION.

1774.

IT was in the midst of his investigations that Howard narrowly escaped being placed in a position in which, though he might have been a benefactor to his country, probably he would have been in some less degree a benefactor to the world. He was near being seated on one of the benches just described.

A general election occurred in the latter part of 1774. The country was agitated by more than ordinary excitement. The storm created by the famous Middlesex contest, and the echo of the well-known cry, "Wilkes and Liberty," had only just sunk into silence to be followed by the American conflict, then assuming gigantic proportions. The tea-chests had been flung into the waters of Boston harbour, and military movements were proceeding amongst the Colonists. Lord North persisted in taxing the Colony, and his policy involved the kingdom in a struggle with her own children on the other side the water.

"The Americans are our children," said Lord Carmarthen, "and how can they revolt against their parent?" "They *are* our children," replied Burke; "but when children ask for bread, we are not to give

a stone." " When this child of ours wishes to assimi-
late to its parent, and to reflect with a true filial resemblance the beauteous countenance of British liberty
—are we to give them our weakness for their strength,
our opprobrium for their glory, and the slough of
slavery, which we are not able to work off, to serve
them for their freedom ?" The strain of this great
Commoner's eloquence was caught up and repeated
with rival power by the great Peer, Lord Chatham,
who declared, " Had the British colonists been planted
by any other kingdom than our own, the inhabitants
would have carried with them the chains of slavery
and spirit of despotism ; but as they are, they ought
to be remembered as great instances to instruct the
world what great exertions mankind will naturally
make when they are left to the free exercise of their
own powers." The question touched a vital principle,
the principle of self-taxation—the palladium of
English liberty.

Public opinion was divided, but a strong party was
in favour of conciliation and peace. The town of
Bedford shared in the excitement produced by a
struggle tending to such momentous issues. It was
no superficial matter that came before the electors.
Differences of opinion obtained in the Midland
Borough. It entered on a party struggle at the hustings. Some were for the policy of Lord North,
and the subjugation of the American Colony ; and
some supported the Opposition, and condemned the
Ministry with all the party spirit which is common
to Englishmen.

Another element infused itself into the local strife.
The Duke of Bedford had been all but omnipotent in

the town, and had carried in his pocket the key of its elections. But disputes arose in 1769, between his Grace and the Corporation, and the latter determined to shake his yoke from off their necks. Moreover, the Duke was committed to Lord North's policy, and had at an early period in the struggle moved an address to the King, recommending that the leaders of the trans-Atlantic revolt should be brought to condign punishment. He proposed that one of the Secretaries of State should issue a special commission for the trial of the offenders ; and the proposal was carried. No wonder this made the Duke unpopular with the Liberal political party of his day, and exasperated those of the Bedford burgesses who were opposed to the Government. Moreover the Corporation, who had quarrelled with him, were now resolved to take the return of members into their own hands ; and therefore, in prospect of the coming contest, the Municipal body enfranchised five hundred honorary freemen, who could be used for the fulfilment of the Municipal pleasure on this critical occasion.

Municipal corruption, as well as electoral bribery, at that period was sufficiently notorious ; and in this instance the Corporation is said " to have unblushingly offered for sale to the highest bidder," the two seats become vacant through the dissolution of Parliament. This report, however incredible, when one looks at it in connection with the history of the times, seems likely enough to be perfectly true. Sir William Wake and Mr. Sparrow were candidates at this election ; and with them the Corporation made their arrangements.

But a large number of the electors were opposed

both to the Prime Minister and the Bedford magnates. They were averse to the Government; and they resented an invasion on their electoral rights. Hence they looked for candidates of their own.

Their neighbour Mr. Whitbread was selected, chiefly perhaps on personal grounds. He was well known to the inhabitants, and had won their favour by social virtues. Mr. Howard, on similar grounds, and also perhaps from his previous shrievalty, was put forward at the same time. His philanthropy and general character made him popular with the Liberal party, and he strenuously opposed a war with America.

The latter selection is said to have taken the object of it by surprise; and we are further informed it was only twelve days before opening the poll, that he came to a decision. " He was actually forced to the hustings, without time to deliberate upon the propriety of the step his friends were about to take." Another element entered into the strife. Howard was a Nonconformist; and Nonconformists, though admissible to Parliament, laboured under disadvantages, and were objects of dislike to the High Church party; and that party was prepared to employ all possible methods to prevent the return of a Dissenting candidate. In consequence of such circumstances, the Bedford election of 1774 was fiercely fought. Howard's opponents looked on him as the representative of " Presbyterians, Moravians, and other sectaries," with whom, they said, the borough swarmed. But it appears that Howard, as well as Whitbread, had supporters among Churchmen ; and the report goes that a parish clergyman took sides with the popular candidates and inexcusably selected for his text—" Are not two sparrows sold for a farthing? Fear ye not therefore, ye are of more value than many sparrows." When speeches had been made, and the poll books were closed, the declaration showed—for Wake, 527 votes; for Sparrow, 517 votes; for Whitbread, 429 votes, and for Howard, 402 votes.

The defeated candidates knew enough to justify their presenting a petition against the return. Howard was already so absorbed in his prison work, that, immediately after the bustle of the contest, he travelled as far as Yorkshire, and visited several gaols and Bridewells; but in December we find him and his colleague lodging their petition to the House of Commons; and in March 1775 they were engaged before a Committee for trying its merits. The injustice of such trials before the Grenville Act of 1770, is notorious; but though that measure produced some amendment, its success was imperfect. Parties fought for majorities in Committee; and the ablest men, "most feared by their opponents, were almost invariably struck off,—a process familiarly known as knocking the brains out of the Committee,—and then the Committee became at once partial and incompetent." "A Whig candidate had scant justice from a Tory Committee; a Tory candidate pleaded in vain before a Whig Committee." Most likely the Committee on the Bedford election to some extent resembled others; but the issue shows there must have been a measure of impartiality. One main question was, as to the legality of honorary freemen's votes; another, as to the admissibility of voters who were recipients of the famous Harpur Charity. The legality of the first and the admissibility of the second were conceded by the Committee.   The first concession told in favour of Wake and Sparrow ; the second, in favour of Whitbread and Howard.   Howard lamented the one while he was glad of the other ; and said he would rather lose his seat than allow an abuse of power by the Corporation.

He communicated the decision of the Committee in the following note to Mr. Symonds.

"DEAR SIR,—I would beg to acquaint you that the great question relative to honorary freemen was determined in favour of them.   The certificate voters are allowed, and this day at three o'clock the recipients of Harpur's Bounty were declared not disqualified, which determination, most probably, will give us our seats ; yet, as our opponents declare they shall object against other votes, the contest still continues. I would have the deepest sense of that Hand which ruleth the hearts of men, and turneth them which way soever He pleaseth.   We are in the hope that the Committee will report to the House that great abuse of power in the Corporation, by which influx your liberties are destroyed.   Could I have gained the first question at the expense of the seat, with pleasure I would have embraced it.

"I   desire   my   sincere   compliments   to   Mrs. Symonds, with my best thanks for your assistance, care, and concern ; a grateful sense I hope I shall ever retain, being with much esteem, Sir, your affectionate friend and obliged, humble servant,

"JOHN HOWARD."

The scrutiny went on and the balance wavered. The numbers at one time stood thus :—Whitbread

574, Howard 542, Wake 541, Sparrow 530. Then, by a decision of the Committee, that all persons who had received parochial relief within six months before the election, should be struck off the poll, Whitbread's supporters amounted to 568, Wake's to 541, Howard's to 537, and Sparrow's to 529. Whitbread and Wake were accordingly declared to be the sitting members.

Howard's feelings in reference to the contest are expressed in a letter which he wrote to his friend Mr. Symonds; and from this it appears how much the question of Nonconformity had to do with the election.

"Accept my best thanks for your kind assistance and zealous attachment, in an affair in which it has pleased God to rebuke us; I may say *us*, Dissenters; for having the honour of being supported by them, and being a Dissenter, I was the victim of the Ministry. Most surely I should not have fallen in with all their severe measures relative to the Americans; and my constant declaration, that not one emolument of five shillings, were I in Parliament, would I ever accept of, marked me out as an object of their aversion. Two or three of the members told me of it on Monday, but I insisted, as the Committee were on oath, that they must be consistent in their resolution as to the charities, and as ancient usage was the line they went on; the free men they never would disqualify in the town, as we knew many non-residents who were paupers, but we never objected to them. Yet alas, when one would not do, both must be brought; even resolutions were tortured, sooner than one independent person should have a seat.

"I sensibly feel for an injured people; their affection and esteem I shall ever reflect on with pleasure and gratitude. As to myself I calmly retire. It may be promotive of my best interests. My large and extensive acquaintance, and the very kind part the Protestant Dissenters of all denominations took in the affair hurt me not a little, yet in the firm belief of an overruling Providence, I would say, It is the Lord, let Him do what seemeth right. He maketh light to arise out of darkness."

Attempts were made afterwards by the townspeople of Bedford to induce Howard to come forward as candidate a second time; but he was proof against their solicitations.

Mr. Whitbread, associated with Howard in the Bedford election, was related to him. In his will he calls this gentleman his cousin. Samuel Whitbread was grandson of William Whitbread, who married Letitia Leeds of Croxton.[1]   It must have been

[1] The following inscription on a monument in Cardington Church gives an interesting account of the family :—

"Ive Whitbread, Esq., of this parish, and of the City of London, merchant, erected this monument to the memory of his ancestors, who, coming into England with the Normans, settled at Ion, in the parish of Upper Gravenhurst, in this county of Bedford, upon an estate given them by the Conqueror, and continued there until the year 1650, when William Whitbread, Esq., purchased lands and settled in this town of Cardington, where the family have ever since continued, and many of them upon their decease have been interred in this church. His eldest son, Henry Whitbread, Esq., succeeded, and after him his eldest son, William Whitbread, Esq., who espoused the cause of his country in the reign of King Charles I., and accepting of a commission in the army, behaved with the greatest courage and gallantry, and was many years Receiver-General and Justice of the Peace for this county. He married

through Howard's second wife, Henrietta Leeds, that he traced a kind of cousinship to the Whitbreads, and the cousinship became pleasant in consequence of the friendship existing between him and the Bedford Member. They co-operated in plans for the improvement of Cardington. Mr. Whitbread had large property there, and was Lord of the Manor.

Lettice, daughter of Edward Leeds, of Croxton in the county of Cambridge, Esquire, by whom he had two sons and six daughters. She died 4th June, 1698, aged 69 years. He died 4th August, 1701, aged 74 years. His eldest son, Henry Whitbread, Esq., succeeded to his estates and the office of Receiver-General, and first married Sarah, daughter and co-heiress of John Ive, of London, merchant, and had by her three sons and three daughters. She died 27th December, 1710, aged 36 years. He died 13th October, 1727, aged 62 years.

Sarah		10th March, 1699		11 months.
William	died	16th July, 1721	aged	28 years.
Lettice		21st Dec., 1721		25 years.

John, Ive, and Rachael are living. He married his second wife, Elizabeth, daughter of Phillip Read, of New Sarum, in Wilts., M.D., and had by her two sons and one daughter. She died 9th January, 1746, aged 59 years. Henry, the eldest son, died 22nd April, 1742, aged 22 years. Samuel and Elizabeth are living. MDCCL."

A later addition goes on to say—

"The above mentioned John Whitbread, Esq., died a bachelor, 12th February, 1762, aged 67 years. Rachael married Oliver Edwards, Esq., of the City of London, who died 29th August, 1757, aged 66 years. Ive Whitbread, Esq., the above and first mentioned, married Elizabeth, daughter of Peter Hinde, of Theobalds, in the county of Hertford, Esq. He died 7th May, 1765, aged 65 years. She survived him only to 7th July, 1766, aged 46 years. Their remains are interred underneath. They had one daughter, Catherine, who died an infant, 13th June, 1748, and one son, Jacob, now living. MDCCCXVI."

In an immense map of the estate,—kindly shown me by the present Member for Bedford, great-grandson of old Mr. Whitbread,—there are marked out a number of holdings, long thin strips of ground, reminding one of the open field system in Saxon times, illustrated by Mr. Seebohm in his "English Village Community."

Whilst Howard was looking after his small tenantry, Whitbread was doing the same with his very much larger one. Noble trees still adorning the road-side were planted by them together; and the delightful appearance of things all round the church is ascribed to their benevolent co-operation.

Mr. Whitbread was a remarkable man. He was born at Cardington in 1720, and married Lady Mary Cornwallis in 1769. She died in 1770. He was the seventh child of a country gentleman, and was educated at Northampton. In the fourteenth year of his age he entered a London brewery, and from that time to the end of life distinguished himself by extraordinary industry and business aptitude. Morning, noon, and night, he was busy in his secular vocation, but never neglected other duties of life. He would sit up whole nights to attend to operations going on; but, in the small hours, he was accustomed to devote two of them to reading, meditation, and prayer. He read the writings of Doddridge, Watts, Thomas à Kempis, and other works of various communions. His ancestors included Nonconformists; and it was interesting to me to find, in the early records of the Church under Mr. Symonds' care, the name of Whitbread next to that of John Bunyan, amongst members admitted when Gifford was pastor. Mr. Whitbread himself contributed to the funds of the Bunyan Meeting House, and left it an endowment of £500, though he was a decided member of the Church of England. A conscientious observance of the Sabbath marked his weekly life, but far from restricting religion to particular seasons, he spread its influence over all his time; and in a MS. book, kept for the purpose, he recorded the progress of his Christian experience. Not slothful in business, he was fervent in spirit, serving the Lord. He could concentrate his mind upon what interested him at the passing moment. Those who saw him with his children would suppose he had nothing to do but to attend to them. The same wholeness of purpose appeared in his daily employment.

He occupied Bedwell Park in Hertfordshire—with its pointed roof, old staircase, and antique windows—for some time, and invited Clarkson there for several months, when he was preparing for the anti-slavery crusade. Small meetings at an early period were held in the drawing-room of his town residence, where friends of the cause simply *inquired* into the evils of the slave-trade, with a view to its abolition. He was the first man who called Mr. Pitt's attention to the subject in the House of Commons. He, and his illustrious son, Samuel, to be noticed hereafter, always voted together on anti-slavery questions, though differing politically on some questions. He founded the Cancer Ward in Middlesex Hospital, and contributed £8,000 to the General Infirmary at Bedford.

He had in his possession Bunyan's pulpit Bible, and a bowl which he used when in Bedford gaol;

and in the Howard House at Cardington there are two portraits of him, one in a brown wig and the dress he wore at business, another in evening costume, with an elegantly curled wig of silvery whiteness. The face in each case is full of intelligence, decision, and suavity.

Amongst his private memoranda occurs the following characteristic passage :—

"I most humbly acknowledge with a grateful heart the goodness of God shown to me an unworthy servant, in blessing my labours abundantly through a long course of years, even near fifty years, with great increase year by year, almost beyond example ; and it was not acquired by the public funds, or contracts with Government, or speculations, or legacies, but by fair trade only.

"Lord, what shall I render ? Thou art my God, and I will thank Thee. Thou art my God, and I will praise Thee. Oh, give thanks unto the Lord, my soul ; and indeed I may truly say with David, 'What am I, O Lord God ; and what is my house, that Thou hast brought me hitherto ?' And I pray God to establish and continue to bless my house and the house of my fathers, and that Thy Name may be magnified among them for ever.   Amen.

"And I further pray God, that my posterity may with comfort and peace enjoy the fruits of my labours for many generations ; and in order to their doing so, I beseech them to follow and practise the advice of St. Paul, when he charges those that are rich in this world, that they be not high-minded, nor trust in uncertain riches, but in the living God, who giveth us richly all things to enjoy ; that they do good, that

they be rich in good works, ready to distribute, willing to communicate, laying up in store a good foundation against the time to come.

"S. W."

"*August,* 1790."[1]

[1] I am indebted for all the information and extracts here
given, to Lady Isabella Whitbread, who permitted me to inspect
the papers.

CHAPTER VIII.

1773–1780.

BEFORE I enter further into this subject, it may be well to observe that such miseries as Howard discovered had not been unnoticed and unlamented in former years. In 1701 the Society for Promoting Christian Knowledge, which then undertook benevolent work beyond what the title would at first suggest, turned attention to English prisons. A committee was appointed to visit Newgate; and having done this, they extended their inquiries to the Marshalsea and other places. Dr. Bray, chairman of that committee, drew up a paper, entitled "An Essay towards the Reformation of Newgate and other Prisons in and about London." The document remained unnoticed amongst the Society's archives until it was discovered by the Secretary, the Rev. J. B. Murray, who mentioned its existence to Mr. Hepworth Dixon. By him it was published for the first time.[1]

The Essay produced no practical effect. But, in 1729, General Oglethorpe was chairman of a Parlia-

---

[1] It is printed in Hepworth Dixon's "John Howard and the Prison World of Europe, 1849." See what Mr. Field says in the preface to his "Life of Howard," and his "Howard Correspondence." It appears that Dixon was indebted to Field for his knowledge of the "original and authentic document" incorporated in his memoir.

mentary Committee, then appointed to make investigations into the state of prisons. The subject once more fell into abeyance till 1773, when Mr. Popham, as we have seen, brought his Bill into the House of Commons to accomplish what Howard so earnestly desired.

It was just at this time that Howard began his prison explorations. We have witnessed their commencement. From the 15th to the 27th of November in 1773, he was engaged in visiting the counties of Northampton, Leicester, Nottingham, Derby, Stafford, Warwick, Worcester, Gloucester, Oxford, and Buckingham.

He found that dungeons were deep and damp and dark, and that prisoners slept upon wretched mats of the thinnest description. At Nottingham twenty-five steps had to be descended to reach three cells of a less miserable kind, which prisoners had to pay for; twelve more to lower dungeons, cut out of the well-known sandy rock, contained poor creatures without money or friends. They were stowed away, it might be, for years. Twenty-six underground steps he counted at Worcester; and at Gloucester, prisoners had died, as he thought, partly in consequence of stench from a dunghill close to the stairway.

In December of the same year he set off again to visit Hertford, Berks, Wilts, Dorset, Hants, and Sussex. At Salisbury he saw outside the prison gate a chain passed through a staple in the wall, at each end of which stood a debtor, padlocked by the leg, offering for sale nets, laces, and purses.

A surgeon at Winchester told him that twenty prisoners had died of gaol fever in one year; and in his Rutland and Yorkshire journey he found that there were cells of such narrow dimensions, that they did not measure more than seven feet six and a half, by six feet and a half. They let in light and air through small perforations in the door ; yet within this horrid confinement three people were locked up together, night after night, from fourteen to sixteen hours.

In the summer of 1774, he undertook a new tour to the West of England, winding round into South Wales. Stopping at Cardiff, where a new prison had been erected, he heard of a poor man who for an exchequer debt of seven pounds had spent ten years in a dungeon, and then died of despair. This touched to the quick the sensibilities of the prison explorer, as he entered the empty cell.

Hermits of old tormented themselves by constructing wretched abodes in which they could not stand upright ; and thus they strove to expiate their sins. The prison authorities of Plymouth, whither Howard went after leaving Cardiff, contrived a place for felons of the same order, and for a similar purpose, only they emulated the Anchorites, not as a penalty for their own offences, but as a punishment for other criminals committed to their charge. When he struck down into the beautiful county of Devon, and visited what is now the queenly seaport of the South, he found there a gaol, which in its horrors vied with the famous Nitrian caves, inhabited by Eastern monks in the fifth century. " No yard, no water, no sewer. The gaolers live distant," are ominous words recorded in Howard's note-book.[1]

[1] State of Prisons, p. 380.

This horrid establishment had in it a place called the Clink, seventeen feet long, eight feet wide, and five and a half feet high. No light could struggle inside, no air could penetrate the den except through an opening five inches by seven. Three people had once been shut up within this receptacle for two months, preparatory to transportation. By turns they took their stand at the opening to catch what light and air could by this method be obtained. The door had not been unfastened for five weeks before Howard paid his visit. He insisted upon entering, and there found, amidst intolerable filth and stench, a human being who had been confined in it for no less than seventy days. The unhappy creature confessed he would rather have been hung at once, than endure a lingering death in this fearful grave.

Howard was at Exeter twice in 1774, once in February and once in September. The gaol belonged to the Walter family, who had the grant of it from the Duchy of Cornwall ; and the gaoler paid for it a rent of twenty-two pounds a year. It seems incredible, but we are assured that the surgeon said he was by contract excused from attending in the dungeons prisoners with gaol fever. The gaoler permitted his captives to seek charity in the city, but the box containing the collection was broken open by the man who conducted them on their begging excursions. He stole the money and ran away.[1]

At the end of 1774 we meet with Howard in East

[1] State of Prisons, p. 372. Howard suggests :—

" If any gentleman would undertake the disposal of the contributions, this would not only prevent such a fraud, but the money laid out for meat, firing, etc., would be far more bene-

Anglia. Norwich Castle,—an old Norman fortress on the top of a hill overlooking a city of gardens, long since turned into a prison, and now refaced with stone, which destroys its venerable appearance,—attracted the traveller's especial attention. He found within the great square keep—comprising two gaols, upper and lower, with a small area in the middle,—a dungeon down a ladder of eight steps for men, a small room for women, and two airy apartments for the sick. The gaoler was humane and respected by the prisoners, who sold at the gates laces, purses, and nets. Here, as elsewhere, the careful inspector observed the most minute particulars; and it is amusing to notice how frequently he was counting steps and measuring walls. His allusions to mitigating circumstances shows that he was not getting up a case in favour of his own views, but was conscientiously endeavouring to ascertain the truth.

And it may also be remarked that Howard brought his scientific habits to bear on his benevolent enterprise. He noticed the effects of the poisonous effluvia in prison upon cloth, which became so offensive that without changes of raiment he could not bear the inside of a post-chaise, and therefore felt obliged to travel on horseback. He also found the leaves of his memorandum book so tainted that he could not use it till he had spread it an.hour or two before the fire. He notices that Dr. Hales, Sir John Pringle, and others had observed how " air, corrupted and putrified, is of such a subtle nature, as to rot and dissolve heart

ficial than their spending most of it in liquor." The suggestion indicates the good man's simplicity and benevolence.

of oak ;" and how walls had been impregnated with pernicious matter for years together. The sanitary laws of the Hebrews recognised the fact, and in our time it is acted upon, when certain fevers have entered a dwelling.

Swaffham, Wymondham, Thetford, and Yarmouth underwent his scrutiny, with results differing a little in detail, but agreeing in proofs of mismanagement and misery.

Suffolk was visited the same year. Howard had been there in the month of February, and again he visited the town in December. At those periods he examined the County and Town Gaol of Ipswich, and all the particulars are minutely recorded in his "State of Prisons." One entry shows a ray of light falling on the darkness :—

"A neat chapel lately built. Mr. Brome, the chaplain, does not content himself with the regular and punctual performance of his stated duty, he is a friend to the prisoners on all occasions."

Another prisoners' friend, unknown to fame, at that time resided in Ipswich ; and with him, most likely, Howard would now come in contact. His name was David Edwards, and, in the very year of Howard's first visit, he published "Sermons for the use of condemned criminals." At the end of the book he gives an account of two prisoners executed at Ipswich, whose treatment casts an extraordinary light upon prison affairs in those days.

The men were visited by Mr. Edwards, who was a Nonconformist minister, and he made a deep impression on their minds. They wished to hear him preach ; and though in gaol under sentence of death, such was

the incredible laxity of rules, that they obtained permission to attend a week evening service in the Independent Meeting House.   Stranger still, they went,
as it were, haphazard, for on their arrival they found
the Church privately assembled for the transaction of
business.   Rumours in the town brought many of the
inhabitants together that night, to see and hear what
went on; and it was determined by the pastor that ecclesiastical affairs should be put aside.   He forthwith
ascended the pulpit and preached to the condemned.
"The prisoners came in with their fetters and shackles
on."   "They shed abundance of tears" as they listened
to a discourse from the words, "This is a faithful saying, and worthy of all acceptation, that Christ Jesus
came into the world to save sinners."   "The house was
thronged," the preacher informs us; "and I suppose,
not a dry eye in the whole place, nothing but weeping and sorrow; and the floods of tears which gushed
from the eyes of the two prisoners were very melting.
When we had concluded, I went and spoke to them
some encouraging words, by way of supporting them
under their sorrow.   They then desired to see me in
the evening,"—the same evening, it would seem,—
"which I did, and called upon Mr. Brindle by the
way.   The old gentleman went along with me to the
prison, and was one who prayed with them, with much
fervour and enlargement of heart.   We spent nearly
two hours with them, and *a crowd of people was present.*
At parting, they earnestly entreated me to attend
them to the place of execution the next day.   I told
them I could not bear it.   Mr. Brindle likewise
observed that it was an unprecedented thing; that a
Dissenting minister was never known to do it in this

county. To which they calmly replied, 'I hope, sir, it will be no disgrace.' I told them, as the minister of the parish"—probably not Mr. Brome, who acted as chaplain in 1774—" was to give them the Sacrament next morning, it was his province to attend them to the place of execution, or some clergy of the town. I left them after I had explained to them the nature of the Lord's Supper, pointing out the qualifications of a sincere communicant.

"About ten o'clock the next morning a messenger came from the prisoners, saying they desired I would meet them at the place of execution; I did not at first feel willing to comply, but begged they would get some clergyman to go. By-and-by another messenger came, to tell me *that not one clergyman in the town would go;* that the practice had for some time been laid aside." Mr. Edwards went. "I conversed with them," he says, "and then prayed most of the way; but my place was so uneasy, that after I had gone about a mile, I ordered the cart to stop, and stepped into the chaise again. Soon after, we came to the fatal tree. I then got out, and, inquiring for the sheriff, was told that his deputy was there; to whom I applied to know how long the prisoners had to live? He courteously replied, *'there was no time particularly fixed.'* 'Sir,' said I, 'the prisoners are both of them young, and there are abundance of young people present; will you suffer me to give them a word of exhortation on this melancholy occasion?' He answered 'With all my heart.' I asked what time he would allow me? to which he replied, *'Take your own time; your time shall be mine.'"* The minister ascended the cart "and gave out part of a hymn at the end of Sternhold and Hopkins' Psalms, entitled *The Lamentation of a Sinner*, which was sung to Windsor tune." He addressed the multitude. They were deeply affected. " There was the utmost decency observed in every part. There was no tumult or talking, but a solemnity in every countenance, highly becoming the occasion. I then kneeled down and prayed, then gave my last advice, told them to take time, and concluded with the benediction."[1]

According to this singular narrative, which I give as I find it, the good minister seems throughout to have acted with the utmost sympathy, and with a deep concern for the welfare of the culprits ; but the purpose for which I introduce the account is to throw light upon the want of order, rule, and discipline in the conduct of prison authorities and officers. The manacled criminals walk through the streets to a place of worship! The officers have not ascertained what preparations had been made for receiving them! They invite a preacher to the prison, and he takes whom he likes, whilst there is a crowd to hear what he says! The clergy are indifferent! No particular time is fixed for the execution! The deputy sheriff is polite, and gives full liberty to the preacher to do as he pleases. I wonder whether Howard became acquainted with this strange incident ? Most likely he did.

In January, 1775, and again in the same month of the following year, he is in the picturesque city of

---

[1] Mr. Edwards' narrative is printed in *The Evangelical Magazine*, 1802, p. 257.

Durham, where the Prince Palatine Bishop, who sat enthroned in the rock-built Norman Cathedral, held as his property the High Gaol, which he granted by patent to a county baronet, as perpetual sheriff. There were two sorts of debtors in the place ; the common-side debtors, who had no courtyard, and the master-side debtors, who had miserable privileges, for which of course they paid. There was a debtors' hall, used for a chapel, from which some were excluded on the Sunday Howard was there. He saw six prisoners chained to the ground, and he adds : "Their straw on the stone floor was almost worn to dust." He saw the common-side debtors eating boiled bread ; and they told him this was the only nourishment they had for nearly a twelvemonth. For an entire bedchamber, *without* a bedfellow, three and sixpence a week was paid ; *with* a bedfellow, two shillings, and one and threepence. A man who found his own bed and bedding, and allowed a bedfellow, got off for fourpence a week. Oddly enough, in the table of fees, occur sums to be paid by knights, ten shillings a week for diet and ten shillings on quitting the prison. For squires and gentlemen, seven shillings and sixpence a week, and three and ninepence when discharged. A yeoman was put down at six shillings for board, and eight and eightpence at the end of his imprisonment. These charges are puzzling. Keepers were allowed fourpence every time they accompanied prisoners who went abroad.[1] At Morpeth three dirty rooms were used as a County Bridewell, and over the way was a warehouse, where the gaoler

---

[1] State of Prisons, pp. 417–419.

carried on a clothier business, and employed the prisoners as his workpeople.[1]

Overleaping foreign travel, which I reserve for separate consideration, I notice that from November, 1775, to May, 1776, he spent his time on long journeys of home inspection.

In the autumn of the latter year, he visited Knaresborough—with its lofty cliff, its ruined castle, its winding river, its romantic bridge—and there he was told of an officer confined some years before for a few days, who took with him a dog as a defence against vermin infesting his cell. The dog was soon destroyed, and the unprotected captive suffered in consequence by the attack of rats.[2] Terrific tales perhaps were told which the good man too readily believed ; but when due allowance is made for exaggeration, enough of horror remains.

We cannot follow him through the counties of York, Derby, Leicester, Warwick, and Oxford. At the close of this journey he stopped at Berkhampstead, and saw in the Bridewell a dungeon underground with a damp earth floor, and walls without a window. No courtyard, no straw, no water, and fortunately no prisoners.[3]

No sooner home, than he was off again down into Norfolk ; then through Suffolk, Essex, and Hertford, finding at the County Gaol, in the last place, that fever had carried off seven or eight prisoners and two turnkeys, and that four were still sick, with no infirmary to put them in. A week afterwards, he is in

---

[1] State of Prisons, p. 428.   [2] Ibid., p. 410.
[3] Ibid., p. 214.

Essex and Suffolk again; then he darts away down to Gloucester, Somerset, and Wilts. In 1774–6, he inspected a prison at Manchester, the town then advancing beyond what it had been in the reign of Charles II., when it is described as a mean market town of 6,000 people, lagging far, indeed, behind the Lancashire metropolis of the nineteenth century. The new prison was finished in 1774, and had separate court-yards, and apartments for men and women, also workrooms as well as dungeons, and an iron-grated door into each court, with "fastenings of a contrivance singularly curious."[1] This house of correction is represented by an odd old woodcut, as it appeared in 1776. The description given in words is more intelligible than the engraving. The prison frontage has five windows, three being cross-barred. "From two of these are suspended five long ropes, bags being tied to the ends to receive contributions; while prisoners stand at the windows to solicit alms, in money, tobacco, or food, from the passers by. At the door the beadle is pushing in an unwilling captive." "On the Salford side, are trees repeating themselves in the translucent Irwell. Upon the green margin at Hunt's Bank, sits a disciple of Izaak Walton, angling with due patience for eels."[2]

Not to weary the reader with a repetition of particulars abounding in sameness, I hasten on to the year 1779, when Howard appears driving through Hertfordshire again; in the county gaol he was "well informed" that a prisoner had been brought

---

[1] State of Prisons, p. 440.
[2] Memorials of Manchester Streets, by Proctor, p. 15.

out as dead from one of the dungeons, and " on being *washed under the pump*, showed signs of life and soon after recovered."   Our author adds, " Since this, I have known other instances of the same kind."[1]   At St. Albans, the gaoler paid rent to the corporation for premises used as a prison ; where two soldiers and a girl were locked up all day together.[2]   He passed through Essex, and noticed the new county gaol at Chelmsford, where a prohibition of spirituous liquors was painted on a board.   At Colchester Castle, there was no water.   At Halstead, prisoners were employed in spinning, but not allowed to participate in what they earned.   At Harwich the room had no chimney.   At Canterbury the prison was unhealthy because of offensive sewers ; there was no bedding but mats, and prisoners slept in their own clothes.   Rochester he visited in 1779, and again in 1782, when he tells us the city Bridewell is in a house with an inscription over the door : " Richard Watts, Esq., by his Will dated 22nd of August, 1579, founded this charity for six poor travellers, who, not being rogues or proctors, may receive gratis for one night, lodging, entertainment, and fourpence each."

Watts' charity has been immortalized by Charles Dickens in his " Seven poor Travellers " ; but he says nothing of the Bridewell that Howard describes. The philanthropist would scarcely have recognised the place in the novelist's description.   " I found it to be a clean white house of a staid and venerable air, with the quaint old door, choice, little, long, low, lattice windows, and a roof of three gables. The

---

[1] Appendix, p. 181.   [2] Ibid., p. 182.

silent High Street of Rochester is full of gables with old beams, and timbers carved into strange faces. It is oddly garnished with a queer old clock that projects over the pavement, out of a grave red building, as if Time carried on business there, and hung out his sign."

In the Sussex county gaol at Horsham Howard saw two spacious courts with water in each, and a wall enclosing the whole prison. "The felons," he says, "on their entrance are washed with warm water, and each man is clothed in a green striped uniform of coat, waistcoat, and breeches ; and has two shirts, two pairs of stockings, a pair of shoes, a hat, and woollen cap." This entry he made with immense joy. Sussex "set a noble example of abolishing all fees, and also the tap ; " in consequence of this, "the gaol was as quiet as a private house."[1] At Kingston-upon-Thames "one woman was in a bed on the men's side, and two women in the room for faulty apprentices, but they pay for this privilege. There is a door from the men's court into that of the women ; and one of the men keeps the key, and can let any of the prisoners into the women's apartments."[2] At Newport Pagnell the prisoners were almost suffocated in hot weather. The prison at West Wycombe consisted of two garrets in the keeper's dwelling house. Buckingham town gaol was new, built at the expense of Lord Cobham—a fact inscribed over the portal. On October 14th there were "no prisoners but a raving lunatic."[3] Howard learned that the Cambridge town Bridewell had recently been a

[1] Appendix, p. 189.   [2] Ibid., p. 192.   [3] Ibid., p. 195.

thorough fever-den ; seventeen women had been confined in a work-room without fire-place or drainage.
This made it so exceedingly offensive that it generated
gaol fever, which so alarmed the vice-Chancellor that
he emptied the Bridewell ; and two or three inmates
died in a few days.[1]   Beccles Bridewell had no separate
apartment for women, though there was plenty of
room for one in the keeper's garden ; and in a room
called the Ward, was a window opening into the
street, where numbers of idle people gathered round,
to look in, and, perhaps, gossip with the prisoners.
At Lavenham the keeper had a number of thumb-
screws.   At Clare three men wore a heavy chain, and
two had logs fastened to them as well.   Our investi-
gator reports at a later date, that a Coventry felon
received a royal pardon ; and on the letter to the
clerk of assize conveying it, there was written : " The
Secretary of State's fee is £1 7s. 0d., and my fee
£1 1s. 0d., which you will take care to receive on the
back of the pardon, from the officer who receives
him."   The man could not pay the fees ; hence, says
Howard, " I found the poor wretch in May 1782,
languishing in prison, on his pound of bread a day."[2]
In Oxford Castle the rooms were the same as they
had been at the time of the Black Assize ; and the
benevolent inspector thought it probable there would
soon be another similar visitation.[3]   In Worcester
county gaol, prisoners were all night chained by
means of linked fetters, and iron rings fastened to
the floor.[2]   From Gloucester county gaol he writes :
   No proper separation of the sexes, or of the Bride-

---

[1] Appendix, p. 199.   [2] Ibid., p. 209.   [3] Ibid., p. 222.

well prisoners from the rest." The magistrates' in-attention to this important point occasioned most licentious intercourse; and all endeavours by the Chaplain to promote reformation was necessarily defeated. "Many children have been born in this gaol."[1] In Liverpool Bridewell he met with an odd contrivance; in the court was a bath, "at one end of it was a standard for a long pole, at the extremity of which was fastened a chair. In this all the females, not the males, at their entrance, after a few questions, were placed with a flannel shift on, and underwent a thorough ducking, thrice repeated, a use of the bath which I dare say the Legislature never thought of, when, in their late Act, they ordered baths with a view to cleanliness and preserving the health of prisoners : not for the exercise of a wanton and dangerous kind of severity."[2] These are but a few of the many items which cover page after page in the book on prisons; but they are more than sufficient to cast a fearfully lurid light on the prison world of the last century.

Howard speaks of evils being perpetuated after his former visits, in spite of his exposures and suggestions. Magistrates were too careless to trouble themselves about improvements, and gaolers who farmed the prison estates considered it to their interest to allow things to go on as they were. There was reform, however, in many instances. A second visit found things better than the first, and a third better than the second. Walls were white-washed; water was supplied; debtors were separated

---

[1] Appendix, p. 231. [2] Ibid., p. 258.

from felons ; the sexes were kept apart ; drink was forbidden ; fees were abolished. Our philanthropist had not laboured in vain.

When we read Howard's books and memoirs, we are often puzzled in attempts to follow the chronological lines of his life. It is frequently difficult to determine at what period a particular incident took place. Dr. Brown again and again gives the months and days without any clue to the year of occurrence. We are also surprised at the zigzag course of the traveller's tours. He rushed east, west, north, south. He raced over a few neighbouring counties, and then returned home, to race again over distant parts of the kingdom,—when one thinks it would have saved expense, labour, and time to have taken journeys in consecutive order. But it serves to explain what looks at first like a vagrant career, that Howard by degrees, and not by a large plan prepared at first, pursued his inquiries. The future opened as he went on and on, far beyond what he dreamed of at the outset. If the map of his life had been spread out before his shrievalty year, he would have started back in astonishment, and pronounced its filling up to be impossible. But light fell, thoughts arose, purposes were formed, deficiencies were supplied, and faulty designs improved as journeys were repeated, as years rolled on, as experience widened.

When he started, he only thought of finding instances authorizing an abolition of gaol fees. When in search of that object, he stumbled on monstrous evils, which were as new as they were terrible, and as startling as they were new ; a sort of benevolent fascination led him forward. He began with gaols ;

then he encountered Bridewells. "Seeing in two or three of the county gaols some poor creatures whose aspect was singularly deplorable, and asking the cause of it, I was answered, 'They were lately brought from the Bridewells.' *This started a fresh subject of inquiry.* I resolved to inspect the Bridewells, and *for that purpose travelled again* into the counties where I had been, and indeed into all the rest, examining houses of correction and city and town gaols." Here we have one instance out of several. A casual answer given to a question started a fresh subject of inquiry. These subjects of inquiry rose before his mind in swift succession. Inquiring after gaols and Bridewells, he soon inquired after hospitals and other institutions. What he saw in one place he wished to compare with what could be seen in another. He read, thought, studied ; and, wishing to be quite accurate, he laid down his pen, packed up his luggage, called his servant, and started off on an expedition of many miles, to verify a fact or to rectify a suspected mistake. He went abroad, and that suggested comparison with things at home, about which he was anxious to be quite sure. Thus journeys grew out of journeys, and on the way divergencies in his route arose ; and probably by the time he returned home he had wandered into quarters he did not dream of when he first set out. Here is a clue to the maze in which at times we are lost in our study of his life.

Before I dismiss this part of my subject, a word or two ought to be said respecting his mode of travelling. It is scarcely needful to remark that no such conveniences existed as are familiar enough now. Sometimes in a stage coach, in such parts of the country as could boast of the provision ; sometimes on horse-back, and sometimes in a post-chaise, he made his excursions. One day a postilion annoyed him greatly. He would move slow or fast, just as he pleased, in spite of commands from one accustomed to be obeyed. When they stopped to change horses, Howard told the landlord of the inn to send for any poor widow he might know and could recommend for honest industry. Placing her before him, he gave her double the amount of the gratuity expected by the postilion; and then turning to the latter, said that he had for-feited all claim to the customary reward, and it was therefore withheld, not on the score of meanness, but on the score of justice. He did not grudge money, but he disapproved of incivility ; and so sent the man about his business.[1]

This may be thought eccentric. Still more eccen-tric is the following fact. Reaching an hotel, he would order a dinner like any other gentleman, only stipulating that his own servant should wait at table. When the repast was ready and brought in, and when the waiter had retired, the travelling attendant would obey his master's order by shifting the dishes on the sideboard, and preparing a basin of bread and milk. Howard not only paid the bill for the dinner he did not eat, but gave liberal fees to the waiters whose services he declined ; for it was a maxim with him, never to destroy the pleasure of a journey for the sake of saving a few shillings or a few pounds. He soon became pretty well known on the road; and it is unnecessary to remark, that a traveller of so ex-

----

[1] Aiken, p. 218.

traordinary a description found a welcome wherever he went.

Moving about England in those days was neither comfortable nor secure. The public stage was inconvenient; so, in some respects, was the post-chaise ; whilst highway robbers, all over the kingdom, were the order of the day as well as the night. Flying highwaymen, riding on "grey," "sorrel," and "black" steeds, were subjects of common talk. Ruffians attacked coaches laden with passengers, and rode up to carriage windows pistol in hand. Not only were there desperate characters who obtained a sort of professional income on the road ; but I have been assured by one who knew him, that a tradesman at eventide, after shutting up shop, would mount a swift horse, and do a little business amongst travellers in the neighbourhood. At noon day, gentlemen on charitable errands were stopped just outside a town, and under threat of "Your money or your life," had to surrender their purses and their watches.[1] Amidst a state of things like this—hard to be realized now-a-days—Howard performed his journeys ; and it ought to be distinctly remembered, as illustrative of his courage, together with his philanthropy, that though scarcely a gentleman in England travelled more than he did, he was never robbed by a highwayman but once. Of this I was informed by his coachman's son.

Howard's exploration of prison life in London, which I now take up by itself, began in March, 1774. He called at the Marshalsea in Southwark, where

---

[1] These incidents I became acquainted with many years ago, on the testimony of persons concerned.

buildings were out of repair; charges were exorbitant; debtors and felons, young and old, men and women, were mingled together; lodgings were let to people not prisoners, who lived there with a family, and also kept a shop; the sick had no infirmary, the healthy no regular food. In dark, narrow rooms, four men slept on two beds; the tap was let out to a prisoner, and there inmates lay upon the floor. To show the habits of drinking, Howard states, that one Sunday, six hundred pots of beer were brought in from a neighbouring public house, because the beverage supplied by the regular tapster did not meet the customers' taste.

In April, Howard visited Clerkenwell. It had not been whitewashed for years. Those who could not pay for beds, slept on a little straw spread over the floor. One room was so crowded, that some climbed into hammocks slung from the ceiling. A penny loaf a day was the whole allowance. He went there again in 1777, and found thirty convicts committed for a term of years, some of whom were ill, and their feet turned black through long confinement. In 1783, one was dying, with little covering on the body, another was dead. In the women's sick-ward were twelve persons in their clothes on barrack bedsteads, or on the floor without bedding of any kind.

Of course he examined the state of things at Newgate. He describes the condemned cells. Fifteen of these existed before the prison was rebuilt in 1778 and 1780. In twelve years, four hundred and sixty-seven executions took place, and the processions to Tyburn were amongst the London sights—thousands on thousands lining the road and looking down from roofs and windows on the grim spectacle. The cells in which criminals spent their last night were lined with planks studded with broad-headed nails, and altogether so forbidding in appearance, that wretched inmates were struck with horror; and some of the most hardened are said, at the sight, to have burst into tears.

Parodies of judicial forms were the amusement of felons and juvenile offenders; if the latter resisted an initiation into deep mysteries of villany, they underwent a mock trial by an impudent patriarch, who tied on his head a knotted towel, in imitation of a wig. Prisoners of course had to pay garnish for riotous entertainments.

Howard describes what he witnessed in the Fleet. "They play in the courtyard at skittles—and not only the prisoners; for I saw amongst them several butchers, and others from the market, who are admitted here as at any other public house. The same may be seen in many other prisons, where the gaoler keeps or lets the tap. Besides the inconveniences of this to prisoners, the frequenting a prison lessens the dread of being confined in one. On Monday night, there was a wine club, on Thursday night, a beer club, each lasting usually till one or two in the morning. I need not say how much riot they occasion, and how the sober prisoners are annoyed by them."[1]

"Passing under Ludgate the other day," Howard states, "I heard a voice bawling for charity, which I thought I had heard somewhere before. Coming

---

[1] State of Prisons, p. 158.

near to the gate, the prisoner called me by name, and desired I would throw something into the box." I heard myself, half a century ago, from people living in Windsor, that a prison in the royal town had iron bars, through which the people could look into the street; and that when George III. passed by, they had been known to say to him, "Please, your majesty, let us out." The exposure of prisoners to the common gaze, and faces peering out of cells and court yards, may still be seen in Spain, in Egypt, and in Syria.

We are furnished with a glimpse of New Ludgate, in Bishopgate Street, a prison for debtors free of the City, and for clergymen, proctors, and attorneys. The common-side debtors were placed in two large garrets—called the Forest, and the Dock—without fireplaces. The walls were black; and a bath, as well as an infirmary, was a thing unknown.

At the Wood Street Compter, Howard saw a room thirty-five feet by eighteen, with twenty-three beds ranged round the walls, on three tiers of shelves; and in one of his visits, he found thirty-nine debtors, seven with wives and children. The place swarmed with vermin; but there could be seen in the court, a chapel—and a tap-room.

Westminster Gate House was empty; but the King's Bench, Southwark, overflowed in the summer of 1776; for debtors, with their families, made up a population of over a thousand.

An incident connected with London, and illustrative of Howard's force of character, may be here introduced. It occurred in 1782. A riot broke out in the Savoy, then used as a place of military confinement. Two hundred ruffians gained the ascendant over their keepers, and ruled as masters in that old historic building. Everybody was afraid to go near the spot. The philanthropist heard of what went on, and determined to subdue the gang. It was in vain that friends tried to dissuade him from the enterprise. His heart melted like wax under the hot touch of human sorrow; but his will was like iron, which no opposition could break or bend. In he went, and stood face-to-face with the outlaws, who had already murdered two officers. The effect is said to have been amazing. What Howard did, and how he did it, is not described, only the effect. The lions were as lambs before the marvellous peacemaker. They stated their grievances; he pledged himself that they should be inquired into; and on the faith of his word they ended the struggle, and were led without further resistance back to their cells.[1]

Of the Lock Hospital he makes particular mention; and his forcible remarks are worthy of consideration by persons apt to look askance upon objects of charity such as he describes. "Many a worthy woman has here to lament the diabolical profligacy of an abandoned husband. Many a poor and helpless infant to deplore its being the offspring of a distempered parent. Many a young creature of tender years, yea, even in infancy itself, has to bewail the inhuman violence of a diseased, filthy, and loathsome ravisher. Others who have been led away by the arts and wiles of seducers, by promises made only to be broken, and fair words meant only to deceive.

---

[1] Anecdote related by Howard's friend, Dr. Brown, who must not be confounded with the biographer of that name.

L

And lastly, many who inadvertently have sought their own ruin, have also been cured in this hospital. Some of these, whose lives have happily been preserved, have kissed the rod of affliction, by the blessing of God have turned from their iniquity, and have been happily restored to their family, the country, and themselves. Therefore, their having brought on themselves disease by their own sin and folly, is no reason why they should be left to perish. A life lost to the public, from whatever cause, is still a loss. If we speak of the matter in a Christian view, how dare any, who profess to know the grace of our Lord Jesus Christ, make this an objection ? Suppose the Redeemer had urged such a plea against becoming poor for our sakes ; suppose He had said of us, ' Leave those sinners to the consequences of their sins and folly ; they are miserable, guilty, lost, and undone, but it was their own fault; let them perish eternally ; let the law take its vengeance on them. I'll not become poor for their sakes, to save them from its curse, for they do not deserve that I should.' Had this been the language of our Lord, where had we now been ? " [1]

He did not visit the prisons in Wales till the summer of 1774. At Flint he saw offenders in two dark closets, called the *Black Holes*—each measuring five feet by four. They were too small to allow of anyone lying down ; yet women sometimes were doomed to dwell in these chambers of horror. At Ruthin, he met with cells only three feet wide. At Caernarvon and Dolgelly, receptacles of the same kind, dirty,

---

[1] Lazarettos.

offensive, and insecure. In 1779, he revisited the
northern parts of the Principality; and though his
efforts to better their condition had not been very
effective, " he saw improvements enough to forbid
despondency."

Scotland he visited repeatedly. He was there in
1775. In Glasgow, where his fame had gone before
him, he was welcomed and entertained with distinguished hospitality, and had presented to him the
freedom of that city. There he noticed what afforded
him much satisfaction, namely, a regulation to the
effect, that the gaoler, every morning and evening, at the opening and shutting up of the prison,
should personally visit every part of it. Four years
afterwards, 1779, he recorded in notes of a Scotch
tour : " The prisons which I saw in Edinburgh, Glasgow, Perth, Stirling, Jedburgh, Ayr, etc., were old
buildings, dirty and offensive, without courts, and
also generally without water. They are not visited
by the magistrates, and the gaolers are allowed the
sale of most pernicious liquors."

He mentions the Tolbooth at Edinburgh. No
particular interest attached to it when he wrote down
the name in his crowded journal ; but now that Scott's
" Heart of Midlothian " has given to it a wide and
lasting fame, one does not glance with indifference at
the brief and dry entry. " In the Tolbooth at Edinburgh, July 6, 1779, there were thirteen debtors and
nine felons ; and in the Canongate Tolbooth, there
were five debtors and one felon." " March 28, 1782,
there were in the Tolbooth four debtors and twenty-
three criminals ; in the Canongate, two debtors."[1]

[1] Appendix, p. 149.

"There are in Scotland," he says in his "State of Prisons," "but few prisoners ; this is partly owing to the shame and disgrace annexed to imprisonment, partly to the solemn manner in which oaths are administered and trials and executions conducted, and partly to the general sobriety of manners, produced by the care which parents and ministers take to instruct the rising generation." "In the southern parts of Scotland it is very rare that you meet with any person that cannot both read and write. It is scandalous for any person not to be possessed of a Bible, which is always read in the parochial schools."[1]

In 1782 he again appears on the other side of the Tweed, welcomed at Edinburgh, as he had been at Glasgow, and receiving the freedom of the city from the Corporation of Modern Athens. The prisoners of war confined there were, according to his account, well treated ; but he pitied *poor* creatures in the Tolbooth, shut up in a horrid cage, and chained to an iron bar. "I say poor," he adds, "because such as have money have too much liberty. For, in the same prison, I lately saw some who were confined for a riot, drinking whisky in the tap-room, in company with many profligate townsmen, who were readily admitted as they promoted the sale of the gaoler's liquor."[2]

Howard met with various adventures in travelling ; and I heard many years ago, from the son of his favourite servant, John Prole, the following anecdote : —Once, in Scotland, his master and he came to a little public-house, where the only fare consisted of

---

[1] Appendix, p. 148.　　　[2] Ibid., p. 151.

black bread, eggs, and oatmeal. They placed this humble refreshment, in a large awkward dish, upon a three-legged stool, and proceeded to cut slices with a garden knife, the house furnishing neither table-knives nor forks. Howard, however, was pleased with the humble hostess, for on being asked, how she could live in such a lonely place "without privileges," —a current phrase for religious ordinances,—she readily replied, "Moses, sir, had greater privileges while keeping his father Jethro's flock in the wilder-ness than when in the court of Pharaoh."

I may add that the same faithful attendant, in a pamphlet already noticed,[1] relates the following in-cident:—"How kindly did that Great Preserver protect me and my good master in that hazardous journey into Scotland in the deep snow, when we went through drifts in many places far deeper than our horses and ourselves. And in a remarkable manner was I preserved in our journey from New-castle; for, about five o'clock in the morning, as I was riding on before my master, getting out of the road, both the horse and myself fell into a pit, which I could not see, it being made level by the snow, and in which we were covered; but having a strong horse, he worked himself out with me on him, without any hurt; among many other dangers we were in our journey preserved from; while many as we heard of lost their lives in that severe season. And all our escapes from death were owing to that kind hand which, in the moment of danger, is often remarkably seen."

---

[1] Legacy to his Children.

Howard visited Ireland in 1779, and found prisons there in as bad a state as they were in Scotland. The country had no houses of correction, and people acquitted were kept in confinement till they paid their fees. Boys, almost naked, might be seen detained for the payment of some forty shillings; and of course their intercourse with old and hardened criminals produced most mischievous effects.

Once more he arrived in Dublin about the beginning of the summer, 1782. A Committee of the Irish Parliament had been appointed to inquire into the state of Irish gaols, and he afforded them some valuable evidence. He visited prisons in Dublin and Tuam, and reports that they were dirty and crowded; that men and women were huddled together; that there was no religious service; that pigs in the latter place were more cared for than prisoners, inasmuch as what had been intended for a bath had been turned into a sty. A good deal of discomfort was endured by him in his journeys through the sister Isle. Along bad roads he had to make his way, and often met with no other provision than what could be obtained in the huts of peasants. A basin of milk, or a little water with which to make a cup of tea, were all he asked for; and this, with biscuits, which he had provided at starting, satisfied his wants. In connection with this mode of living, it may be mentioned that once an Irish nobleman invited Howard to dinner, and after some hesitation he consented, on condition he should have nothing provided but potatoes. When he sat down to table he was surprised to see seventeen covered dishes. He thought the pledge had been broken; and what

was his surprise when he found each dish contained
potatoes cooked in different ways. The abstemious
guest reproached himself for having caused more
thought and trouble in the kitchen, than if no condition had been imposed. [1]

In Dublin he was highly honoured. University
degrees had been conferred on him before, now a
diploma of LL.D. was added by the University of
the Irish capital.

An incident is related in *The Gentleman's Magazine*
(Dec., 1790) which may here find a place. "In the
summer of 1783, Mr. Howard was returning from a
tour through the Irish prisons, and I sailed with him
from Dublin to Holyhead. His son was with him,
and while we were on the deck of the packet spoke
with great roughness to a child that was playing with
his coat, and drove it from him; this appearance
of inhumanity his father instantly took notice of,
and reprimanded him for not behaving with greater
tenderness. But at night Mr. Howard had an opportunity of showing his disposition more plainly. On
coming to take possession of his berth, he found that
a maid-servant, belonging to some of the passengers,
was not provided with a bed, and, immediately giving
up to her his own, he spent the night upon the cabin-
floor, choosing rather to inconvenience himself than
to disturb that son on whose account he is now
calumniated. In these little incidents we see a man
alive to every feeling of humanity; uneasy at a word
spoken with harshness to a child; submitting to an

---

[1] Related by Dr. Brown in his Memoirs (p. 523) on the authority of the Rev. Mr. Bealey.

inconvenience to relieve from a trifling distress a stranger whose rank gave no claim to attention ; and leaving his son in possession of an accommodation which his own age rendered almost necessary. These were not the effects of a mind heated by enthusiasm, but the effusions of a truly benevolent heart to which that noble sentiment, '*Humani nihil a me alienum puto*,' might deservedly be applied. I knew not Mr. Howard's name during these transactions, and learned it only by accident a short time before we landed."

When at Dublin in 1787, he was introduced to John Wesley. "I had the pleasure," says the founder of Methodism, "of a conversation with Mr. Howard, I think one of the greatest men in Europe. Nothing but the mighty power of God can enable him to go through his difficult and dangerous employments." Wesley was pleased with Howard. Howard was pleased with Wesley. " I was encouraged," Howard told Alexander Knox, " to go on vigorously with my designs. I saw in him how much a single man might achieve by zeal and perseverance, and I thought, Why may not I do as much in my way as Mr. Wesley has done in his, if I am only as assiduous and persevering ? and I determined I would pursue my work with more alacrity than ever."[1] Again, in 1789, an interview occurred between these two extraordinary men. "Mr. Howard," writes Wesley, "is really an extraordinary man ; God has raised him up to be a blessing to many nations. I do not doubt but there

---

[1] Life of Henry Moore, p. 271, quoted by Tyerman in The Life and Times of John Wesley, vol. iii., p. 495.

has been something more than natural in his preservation hitherto, and should not wonder if the
providence of God should hereafter be still more
conspicuous in his favour." [1]

The American orator already noticed has drawn
a parallel between the two. They resembled each
other in person, both were of short stature; in habits,
both were ascetic and self-denying ; in working
power, both sacrificed sleep, food, society, to the fulfilment of their mission ; in courage, both overcame
prejudice, passions, and perils; in executive ability,
both had clear-cut purposes, and carried them into
practical effect ; in self-reliance, they resolved not on
other peoples' opinions, but on their own judgment ;
in entire consecration, both were above the temptations of riches and honours ; and in their manner of
travelling, both lived on horseback, travelling by
night and by day, careering through the three kingdoms, making themselves equally at home in the
city and hamlet, among the rich and the poor. [2] The
parallel is clever, but it does not give prominence to
what brought the two most closely together—they
were united in a faith substantially the same, in spite
of their Calvinistic and Arminian difference. Both
trusted simply and entirely to the same Saviour.
Both constantly felt that salvation is all of grace,
and on their knees could join in the same prayers,
and in adoring worship join in the same psalmody.
In each case religious principle was the root of enterprise, heroism, perseverance, and success.

At the same time we see he met Knox, private

---

[1] Tyerman, vol. iii., p. 581.   [2] Bellows' Howard, p. 57.

Secretary to Lord Castlereagh, known as the friend and correspondent of Bishop Jebb. He wrote Essays on the political circumstances of Ireland ; and his " Remains," eulogized by his episcopal friend, have not in them "a page which has not some energetic truth or some happy illustration, and these illustrations always powerful arguments."

On the whole, the journeys in Great Britain and Ireland we have described were not in vain. The last of them found things better than they were at first. Some gross abuses had been stopped, gaols and Bridewells had been cleansed, and were more and more systematically arranged. His recommendations had borne some fruit. He was becoming more and more a power in the country; his presence everywhere commanded respect, and his counsels in numerous cases carried weight.

Between 1776 and 1782 he paid repeated visits to the hulks on the river Thames—hulks being a new mode of dealing with criminals, whose number greatly perplexed the Government. In nineteen years eight thousand convicts, save one, were divided between an old ship named the *Justicia,* moored at Woolwich, and two others in Langton and Portsmouth harbours. Out of six hundred and thirty prisoners in the *Justicia,* one hundred and seventy-six died within nineteen months. This led to a Parliamentary inquiry, which had a beneficial effect on the health of the convicts, which Howard gratefully acknowledges. In 1787 the system of transportation to New South Wales commenced; and two years afterwards our benevolent voluntary Inspector found the *Justicia* converted into an hospital, a frigate named the

Censor being employed for receiving prisoners. Both showed signs of improvement—the second less than the first, which set him to search out causes, which he soon ascertained, and then suggested fitting remedies. In 1783 he reports :—" The men in the *Justicia* looked well, which I doubt not was in a great measure owing to their being employed, and also restrained from spirituous and other strong liquors. Of late but few of them have died ; this shows that their situation is better with respect to health, but the association of so many criminals is utterly destructive to morals." [1]

The hulk system worked badly. Howard was examined by a Parliamentary Committee, and related what he knew. Some other method of home punishment was desirable.

In 1779 an Act was passed for the erection of two English penitentiaries, under three competent superintendents. Howard was one, Dr. Fothergill was another. Fothergill was of Quaker extraction, and studied medicine at Edinburgh, where he took a degree, and afterwards distinguished himself in his profession. To scientific attainments he added extraordinary beneficence. He paid much attention to the restoration of persons after being drowned, and decidedly opposed intramural interments. A common philanthropy drew these two men closely together, and disposed them to unite in the Penitentiary scheme, however reluctant they might be on other grounds to undertake the difficult task. Howard's scruples were overcome by the persuasion of Sir William Blackstone, who is to be remembered amongst

---

[1] State of Prisons, 4th edit. enlarged, pp. 466, 467.

his acquaintances. The third superintendent was Mr. Whatley, treasurer of the Foundling Hospital.

The arrangement failed. The superintendents could not agree on a site. Howard and Fothergill preferred Islington, Whatley chose Limehouse. Time was lost in this way, and the philanthrophist's patience was nearly exhausted. Blackstone died, saying in his last hours to Fothergill, "Be firm in your opinion."

"That advice," Howard remarked to his friend, "seems to me to be the most important direction in our conduct. We are fixed upon as the proper persons to determine on a plan and situation for a penitentiary. Why then transfer the office to other persons, whose station in life and other engagements must render them very unfit for entering into such a matter? Let us, when we meet, absolutely fix on one situation as the best on the whole, according to our ideas ; and, specifying our reasons, let us submit the approbation or rejection of this one plan to those in whom the law has invested such a power ; but not give them the unnecessary trouble, nor us the improper degradation, of determining in our stead the respective advantages of such different plans." Whatley was obstinate, and Fothergill died. Howard now stood alone, and did not choose to fight a single-handed battle with his colleague. Accordingly he resigned. "My Lord," he wrote to Earl Bathurst in January, 1781, "when Sir William Blackstone prevailed upon me to act as a supervisor of the buildings intended for the confinement of certain criminals, I was persuaded to think that my observations upon similar institutions in foreign countries would, in some degree, qualify me to assist in the execution of the statute of the nineteenth year of his present Majesty. With this hope, and the prospect of being associated with my late worthy friend, Dr. Fothergill, whose wishes and ideas upon the subject I knew corresponded entirely with my own, I cheerfully accepted His Majesty's appointment, and have since earnestly endeavoured to answer the purpose of it ; but, at the end of two years, I have the mortification to see that not even a preliminary has been settled. The situation of the intended buildings has been a matter of obstinate contention, and is at this moment undecided. Judging therefore from what is past, that the further sacrifice of my time is not likely to contribute to the success of the plan, and being now deprived, by the death of Dr. Fothergill, of the assistance of an able colleague, I beg leave to signify to your lordship my determination to decline all further concern in the business, and to desire that your lordship will be so good as to lay before the King my humble request that His Majesty will be graciously pleased to accept my resignation, and to appoint some other gentleman to the office of a supervisor in my place." [1]

When Howard retired the scheme collapsed. Botany Bay took the place of penitentiaries for many a year. Convicts were shipped off to the other side of the globe, to demoralize one of the most beautiful regions in the world ; and only at a comparatively late period have our countrymen worked out the true idea of penitentiaries by founding establishments at Pentonville, Portland, and Dartmoor.

---

[1] Dated January, 1781. Printed in Brown's Memoirs, p. 309.

Another unfortunate class of persons inspired Howard's compassion. England, in the eighteenth century, had been involved in one war after another. The dispute with America led to hostilities in 1773; our country in 1777 became embroiled with France, which allied itself to the revolted colony; in 1778 Spain joined France, and thus we had to deal with a third foe. In 1780 a rupture with Holland came to be added to other calamities. The consequence was, that a number of war prisoners were confined, both on the Continent and in England, when the last of these quarrels had continued for awhile; and people at the present day have little idea of the misery which, in consequence of being taken captive in a time of war, existed at the close of the last hundred years. Not only were foreign soldiers and sailors liable to be captured, but peaceable people crossing the sea were in peril. A vessel belonging to a country with which we were at war, might by one of our ships be attacked, be run down and seized, and persons of the upper as well as lower class on board be arrested and brought over to England. I remember hearing, when I was a boy, of romantic adventures on both sides. I had a schoolmaster who in one of these turns of fortune was seized in a vessel, and conveyed to a French prison, where for the space of some years he remained in confinement. One odd occurrence I heard related. A gentleman eloped with a lady, and the fugitive pair set out for the Continent. As they were crossing the Channel a French crew took them prisoners; and they were separated and detained abroad for several years.

Howard discovered the privations to which prisoners on both sides the Channel were exposed, and he gives details of what he saw both in French and English prisons. It is needless to repeat them or to indicate his suggestions for improvement; but it is worth while to record a remarkable incident which happened in connection with his work amongst foreign prisoners. Above three hundred Dutchmen, kept in confinement on the banks of the River Severn, had been so neglected that they were left almost naked. Some benevolent people heard of it and made a collection for the sufferers' relief. A worthless official interfered to prevent the benevolent design; he wished, it appears, to force them into acts of enlistment, that, under a British flag, they might fight against their own country. Such manœuvres were not uncommon in those days. Howard no sooner heard of this than, with characteristic promptitude, he came to the rescue. Not sending to make inquiries, not trusting to official reports, he repaired to the spot, saw the poor Netherlanders, examined their statements, ascertained the particulars, commenced a subscription, put down his name for ten guineas, and ordered articles for the prisoners' relief to be sent the next day. He went himself to see how things proceeded, no doubt greatly to the chagrin of officials. He had the captives brought before him, and having distributed the clothing, urged them, as men and patriots, never to fight under the flag of a country not their own.

CHAPTER IX.

PRISON RESEARCHES ABROAD.

1775–1781.

HOWARD'S home and foreign journeys succeeded each other so rapidly, that readers of his life become confused. I have therefore thought it best to keep his researches on the Continent distinct from those in Great Britain and Ireland, that a clear impression may be left respecting the lines of his philanthropy.

In April, 1775, he started for France. Louis XVI. was on the throne. Marie Antoinette in the pride of her beauty presided over her luxurious court. The finances of the country were in a state of wretched disorder. Turgot, Maurepas, and Necker were busy with theories for filling an empty exchequer. The country was discontented, and cries for reform came from the lips of all classes, premonitory of a crash which soon startled the world. Still, fashion and folly were rampant in the metropolis and the provinces. Splendid equipages rolled along the streets, balls and masquerades dazzled the aristocracy in the halls of Versailles and the hotels of Paris, whilst peasants groaned under the salt tax and cursed the rich, who generally were unmindful of their sufferings. Amidst these lights and shadows Howard made his appearance.

Reaching the city on the banks of the Seine by some lumbering diligence, or some scarcely more convenient chaise, he began immediately to thread narrow, winding, dirty streets, amidst din and bustle, searching for the *Conciergerie*, the *Grand* and *Petit Châtelet*, the *Fort L'Evêque*, and the *Bicêtre* prisons. His first question everywhere was—"Whether the gaoler or keeper resided in the house?" An answer always came in the affirmative. In most cases he found four or five gates ; the inner one called a turn-stile. Five or six turnkeys were seen on patrol, watching for plots and surprises. No prisoners were in irons, a fact which astonished one familiar with chains in England. Courts were clean, air was fresh, and he seldom perceived offensive smells. Mass was daily said, from which the attendance of Protestants was excused. He measured the cells, tested the supplies, copied the regulations, interrogated the gaolers, and picked up information respecting men and women in confinement. He found few debtors, owing to a law which made persons who committed them to prison, responsible for the payment of nine shillings a month towards board and lodging. In default of payment, prisoners recovered their liberty.

The *Bicêtre*, an hospital built on an eminence two miles from Paris, included paupers and lunatics. About five hundred rooms had an occupant in each. *La Cour Royale*, in this edifice, had eight dungeons, with chains fastened to the wall, and a stone funnel in each cell to let in air. Prisoners made straw boxes, toothpicks, and other articles, which they were allowed to sell to visitors. [1]

[1] State of Prisons, p. 92.

M

The Bastille—so huge, so strong, so walled and moated, so full of mystery, that Carlyle exclaims, "Could one but, after infinite reading, get to understand so much as the plan of the building." The Bastille, so covered in everybody's thoughts with stories of injustice and cruelty, of innocent lives sacrificed, or, what was worse, lengthened out in misery, —that inaccessible fortress, of course, inspired the curiosity of the traveller. Of his attempt to explore its secrets, which might be wrought up into a sensational story, or, painted by a skilful artist, would make a capital picture—he gives the following account—a perfect specimen of sententious simplicity. "The Bastille may occur to some of my readers as an object concerning which some information would be acceptable. All that I can give them is—that I knocked hard at the outer gate, and immediately went forward through the guard to the drawbridge before the entrance of the castle. I was some time viewing this building, which is round, and surrounded by a large moat. None of the windows look outwards, but only towards a small area; and if the State prisoners are ever permitted to take the fresh air, it must be on the leads, which have high parapets. But whilst I was contemplating this gloomy mansion, an officer came out of the castle, much surprised; and I was forced to retreat through the mute guard, and thus regained that freedom which, for one locked up within those walls, it is next to impossible to obtain."

This incident, recorded with conscientious accuracy, I find to have been also entrusted to tradition as well as to paper ; and instead of being worn away by long handling, it has recently developed into the following romantic dimensions. "He boldly drove up to the gates in a handsome carriage and four, with several servants in livery, dressed himself like a gentleman of the court. Stepping out of the carriage, with an air of authority, he desired to be shown over the building. The officials, taken by surprise, and never doubting from his deportment his right to be obeyed, permitted him to examine everything he chose."[1]

This comparison of an original and authentic statement in writing, with a story told by one person to another over and over again, well illustrates the marvellous effect of tradition. How the traveller gained admittance to other prisons, he explains by reference to a law, which allowed of charitable individuals visiting the inmates, to bestow alms, either by their own hands or through the medium of a gaoler. The latter method alone was allowed in the case of dungeon-prisoners.

In the provincial gaols of France, Howard saw little worth noticing; and in May we follow him to Belgium. Near Brussels is the town of Vilvorde, where William Tyndale, the English translator of the Scriptures, was imprisoned, strangled, and burnt. Whether or not the prison explorer thought of that tragedy I do not know, but he stopped to see the House of Correction, and took down the dimensions of rooms and the number of steps.

At Mechlin, under the shadow of its grand cathedral, he sought out the prison, and was glad to find no debtors in it. The criminals lodged "up stairs," not in filthy dungeons; each was provided for with

---

[1] Memories of Seventy Years, edited by H. Martin, p. 59.

" straw and two blankets," and " clean linen every week from a charity."

At Bruges, he heard the far-famed Carillon ring out its mysterious music from—

> The belfry old and brown :
> Thrice consumed, and thrice rebuilded, still it watches o'er the
> town.

There too were pictures quaint and beautiful, having charms for most travellers ; but in a book on " The State of Prisons," he only tells us how debtors and criminals were treated ; the former receiving an allowance from their creditors, the latter not shut up in underground cells. He records the care taken of the sick, and states that a list of charities hung up in the council chamber.

In Ghent, the Hôtel de Ville told of Charles V., and the streets, of the Brewer, Jacob Van Arteveld. The name of the city further suggested to an Englishman, recollections of " time-honoured Lancaster ; " but Howard had one thing to do. In *La Maison de Force* he tells us that prisoners had bedsteads, mattresses, pillows, sheets, and blankets, also good and sufficient food. Men and women were separated, the former weaving, the latter washing, spinning, and mending. Spirituous liquors were prohibited ; and altogether he pronounced the establishment " a noble institution." But the prison belonging to the Benedictine Monastery presented a contrast, with its dreary subterranean dungeons. Howard's habit of counting steps and measuring doors and windows greatly displeased the governor, who soon cut short his stay, and thus put an end to his inquiries.

He visited a nunnery,—the famous Béguinage, I apprehend,—where the women in black gowns and the ancient Flemish *faille*, kneeling on the floor at Vespers in a dim light, present a picture which no tourist who has seen it can forget. The Sisterhood attend the sick; and Howard speaks of the place as "the Hospitable Mansion," not inhabited solely by nuns, but destined for the reception of men who were insane, and aged women who were sick. "The tenderness," he adds, with which both were treated, "gave me no little pleasure."[1]

He went to Delft, or Delfshaven,—that interesting Dutch town so intimately connected with the story of the Pilgrim Fathers. There they engaged in wearisome correspondence with the English Court, and were much troubled by hard terms exacted by merchant adventurers, till a few brave-hearted brethren resolved to start for America at all hazards. There John Robinson preached to this advanced guard, from the pertinent text—"Then I proclaimed a fast there, at the river of Ahava, that we might afflict ourselves before our God, to seek of Him a right way for us, and for our little ones, and for all our substance."[2] And there "sundry of the Dutch strangers that stood on the quay as spectators could not refrain from tears," and "the scene was remembered there a quarter of a century afterwards."[3] What Howard saw and chiefly thought of at Delft, however, was the prison.

---

[1] State of Prisons, p. 140.   [2] Ezra viii. 21.

[3] "History of Plymouth Plantation, and Hypocrisy Unmasked," quoted in Dr. Dexter's "Congregationalism of the last three hundred Years."

"At Delft there were nearly ninety in the House of Correction, men and women quite separate ; all neat and clean, and looked healthy. They told me their allowance was five stivers a day.[1] All were employed in a woollen manufacture ; women spinning, carding, etc., men were weaving from coarse to very fine cloth ; their task was to earn thirty-five stivers a week. Some earned a small surplus, but they had only half of it." If a prisoner behaved well for a few years, and gave proofs of amendment, the magistrates abridged the time for which he was sentenced.[2]

All this delighted our friend, and suggested to him what might be done in English prisons. Opposite to Rotterdam, on the other side of the river, he noticed a House of Correction as "airy, and built round a court, in which is a basin of water communicating with the Maes." An outbreak of patriotism occurs here. " I mention this edifice, on account of the sentiments of veneration it inspired, when I trod on the ground under which such piles of my brave countrymen lie buried, it having been used as a military hospital after the siege of Bergen-op-Zoom." The brave countrymen to whom Howard alludes fell in the year 1747. The son-in-law of George II., Prince William of Nassau, Stadtholder of Holland, being then engaged in defending his country against the invasion of a French army sent by Louis XV., British soldiers, under a son of George II., were despatched to help the Dutch. " Our two young heroes agree but little," said Mr. Pelham, " our own is open, frank, resolute, and perhaps hasty ; the other, assuming, pedantic,

---

[1] A stiver is about a penny.   [2] State of Prisons, p. 132.

ratiocinating, and tenacious." The Duke of Cumberland fought with desperation; but the British were sacrificed by the Dutch, whom they went to help, and who got out of the fight as quickly as possible.[1] At Bergen-op-Zoom there followed terrible work; and it was over the buried bones of the English soldiers that Howard expressed veneration for English courage. He hated war, but he appreciated valour.

An Institution at Amsterdam, similar to that at Delft, arrested his attention. Men were winding silk as well as rasping wood; and as Howard looked with a keen eye on what went on, he seems to have made the authorities suspicious. "I wished," he says, "to know more particulars of this famous prison, but could scarce ever get from the *cautious old keeper* a direct answer to any one question, though I paid him five visits with that intent." In the Spin House he saw thirty-two females, some abandoned characters, yet now sitting, in the presence of the mistress, quiet and orderly. He watched them as they went to dinner. The keeper, whom they called Father, presided at table. "First they sang a psalm, then they went in order down to a neat dining-room, where they seated themselves at two tables, and several dishes of boiled barley, agreeably sweetened, were set before them. The Father struck with a hammer; then, in profound silence, all stood up, and one of them read, with propriety, a prayer about four or five minutes. Then they sat down cheerful, and each filled her bowl from a large dish, which contained enough for four of

---

[1] Pelham's Letter to Mann, quoted by C. Knight, History of England, vol vi., p. 180.

them. Then one brought on a waiter slices of bread and butter, and served each prisoner." [1]

In Holland he was greatly interested in the *Rasp Houses* for men, and in the *Spin Houses* for women. Men rasped wood, women spun worsted. Work was Howard's delight; and he rejoiced in the maxim on which these Dutch systems were founded; "*Make them diligent, and they will be honest.*" He relates the following story in illustration: "I have heard in England that a countryman of ours, who was a prisoner in the Rasp House at Amsterdam several years, was permitted to work at his own trade, shoemaking; and by being constantly employed, was quite cured of the vices which brought him to confinement. My informant added, that the prisoner received at his release a surplus of his earnings, which enabled him to set up in London, where he lived in credit, and at dinner commonly drank " Health to his worthy masters at the Rasp House." [2]

Of all foreign countries, Howard liked Holland best; and he learnt there more than he did anywhere else. "There is one short paragraph in his Journal in Holland," says Mr. Bellows, "that contains undeveloped every sound and reformatory idea that has since entered into prison science.

It is this: "The principal cause that debtors as well as capital offenders are few, is the great care that is taken to train up the children of the poor, and indeed of all others, to industry. The States do not transport convicts; but men are put to labour in the Rasp Houses, and women to proper work in the Spin

---

[1] State of Prisons, pp. 126, 127.   [2] Ibid., p. 122.

Houses upon this professed maxim : 'Make them diligent, and they will be honest.' Great care is taken to give them moral and religious instruction, and reform their manners, for their own and the public good; and I am well informed, that many come out sober and honest. Some have even chosen to continue and work in the house after their discharge. Offenders are sentenced to these houses, according to their crimes, for seven, ten, fifteen, twenty, and even ninety-nine years; but, to prevent despair, seldom for life. As an encouragement to sobriety and industry, those who distinguish themselves by such behaviour, are discharged before the expiration of their term." [1]

These are now primary principles in prison reform, and they were adopted by Howard when most Englishmen were ignorant or unconvinced of their efficacy. The Dutch were far before us in those days.

Howard from Amsterdam made his way to Utrecht, carrying letters of introduction to Dr. Brown, English chaplain, to Groningen, to Lewarden, where prisoners were at work, and to Bremen, where a workhouse had done much to relieve the streets of beggars. At Hamburg, however, he was horrified. "Among the various engines of torture," he says, "which I have seen in France and other places, the most excruciating is kept and used in the deep cellar of this prison. It ought to be buried ten thousand fathoms deeper. It is said the inventor was the first to suffer by it, the last was a woman not two years ago."

[1] John Howard, his Life, Character, and Services, by H. H. Bellows, p. 35.

In the kingdom of Hanover, then under the English crown, he found, at Luneburg, criminals employed in digging chalk, preparing it for the kiln, grinding, sifting, and packing it in barrels. At Hanau, the chief town of a small principality, he tells us the galley slaves were divided into *honnêtes* and *déshon-nêtes;* the former had their term of imprisonment shortened on account of good behaviour. They worked on the public roads, and told Howard they preferred it to being idle. The *déshonnêtes* were never let out of the town, and had to perform "disagreeable services." The following entry furnishes a curious instance of grim humour.

"At Mannheim, Monsieur Babo, Counsellor to the Regency, very politely gave orders to show me every room of *La Maison de Force.* Prisoners committed to this house are commonly received in form with what is called the *bien venu,* or *welcome.* A machine is brought out, in which are fastened their necks, hands, and feet. Then they are stripped, and have, according as the Magistrate orders, the *grand venu,* of twenty to thirty stripes; the *demi venu,* of eighteen to twenty; or the *petit venu,* of twelve to fifteen. After this, they kiss the threshold and go in. Some are treated with the same compliment at discharge. The like ceremony is observed at some other towns in Germany."[1]

In June, 1775, we find him in the fair city of Bonn on the banks of the Rhine, whence he wrote to Mr. Symonds.

---

[1] State of Prisons, p. 112.

"*Bonn, June* 20*th*, 1775.

"DEAR SIR,—I flatter myself a line will not be unacceptable. As one's spirits are tired with the same subject, it is a relaxation and pleasure to write to a friend; which indeed is my case at present, being just come from the prisons in this place. I had visited many in France, Flanders, and Holland; but I thought I might gain some knowledge by looking into the German police. I have carefully visited some Prussian, Austrian, Hessian, and many other gaols. With the utmost difficulty did I get access to many dismal abodes; and through the good hand of God I have been preserved in health and safety. I hope I have gained some knowledge that may be improved to some valuable purpose. Though conscious of the utmost weakness, imperfection, and folly, I would hope my heart deceives me not, when I say to my friend, I trust that I intend well. The great Example—the glorious and Divine Saviour;—the first thought humbles, abases, yet, blessed be God, it exalts and rejoices in that infinite and boundless source of love and mercy.

"The state of the weather makes travelling not a little fatiguing. I have the pleasure of now coming homeward. There are many travellers at the first, or great houses; but these three or four weeks I have not met one Englishman. We are here surrounded with vineyards, so I must not say it is hot; yet I cannot help wishing for my refreshing bath.

"I have spent some Sundays with the French Protestants. I love and esteem them. Though separated, yet truly united. I trust and hope we shall make one great and glorious body.   In which wish, I truly remain, etc.,

"JOHN HOWARD."

"P.S.—Mr. Castleman, Mr. Freelove, etc., with gratitude.   I think of their late instance of affection, and with pleasure in some sacred moments.   Adieu ! I pray God bless you ; and may many be your crowns of rejoicing in that great and glorious day.—J. H."

Howard returned to England in July, 1775 ; but in May, 1776, he again crossed Dover Straits on his way to Switzerland.   After tarrying two or three weeks in Paris, he proceeded to Lyons, where he examined the prison of St. Joseph—formerly a convent—containing twenty-nine criminals, who, on account of the heat, wore no other covering than shirts.   The Swiss cantons deeply interested him ; Geneva and Lausanne confirmed his conviction of the good effects resulting from industry.   At Bern, most of the prisoners he saw were employed in cleaning the streets.   Four or five dragged a wagon, and the rest loaded it.   They wore a collar with a hook projecting above their heads, a contrivance which must have been a great torment, seeing that it weighed five pounds.   He asked, " whether they chose to work thus, or be confined indoors." " Much rather work thus," they replied.

The effect of this visit is noticed by Archdeacon Coxe, who, writing in 1801, informs us that the House of Correction, in such a deplorable state at the time Howard visited the city, had undergone a great change through the efforts of M. Manual, a member of the Council.   Prisoners were classified and distinguished by the colours of their dress.   The men and women were lodged in different parts of the building and were constantly employed. They were also taught to read and write, and instructed in various trades, so as to render the establishment nearly self-supporting.[1] Switzerland reaped benefit from the philanthropist's visit.

At Basle, he heard a strange story, "When I was in the room [of a felon] and took notice of the uncommon strength of it, the gaoler told me a prisoner had lately made his escape. I could not devise what method he took, but heard it was this : He had a spoon for soup, which he sharpened to cut out a piece from the timber of his room ; then by practice he acquired the art of striking his door, just when the great clock struck, to drown the noise, and in fifteen days he forced all the bolts. But attempting to let himself down from the vast height by a rope, which he found, the rope failed him ; and by falling he broke so many of his bones, that the surgeon pronounced his recovery impossible. But his bones were set, and with proper care he did recover, *and was pardoned.*"

From Basle Howard revisited Germany; and at Metz his eye caught a significant symbol, over the door of the House of Correction. It was a carving, which represented a wagon drawn by two stags, two lions, and two wild boars, with an inscription explaining the device, *i.e.*, "If wild beasts can be

---

[1] Coxe's Travels in Switzerland, vol. ii , p. 232. The author was a friend of the Whitbread family, and accompanied Samuel Whitbread, the statesman, on his grand tour. To him he dedicated his travels. He most likely knew Howard. Howard commends a tract which Coxe published on foreign prisons.

tamed to the yoke, we should not despair of reclaim-
ing unruly men."

Howard was far removed from a mere theorist.   He
had, of course, ideas of prison reform, but they were
not with him a substitute for facts.   No *imagination*
of what prisons were or ought to be filled his mind.
His philanthropy arose from what he saw, and operated along lines established accordingly.   Not more
consistently had Bacon dwelt in.thought on the principle of induction, than did Howard in practice act
upon it.

In the month of August, 1776, he completed his
journey by a re-inspection of the Ghent prisons; but
he scarcely touched his native shores, before he was
travelling through England to compare things at
home with things abroad.   The spring of 1778 saw
him commencing another Continental tour, by crossing over to Helvoetsluis on the way to Amsterdam.
There he met with a serious accident.   A runaway
horse caught him by the coat, and threw him on a
heap of stones.   The pain he suffered brought on an
attack of fever, which confined him for six weeks;
and during this period he kept a diary, in which he
recorded his spiritual experience.

" In patience may I possess my soul, and say, It is
the Lord, let Him do what seemeth Him good."
" Righteous art Thou in all Thy ways and holy in all
Thy works."   " May this great affliction be to try me,
to prove me, and to do me good in my latter end, to
wean my affections from this world and fix them on
the rest that remaineth for the people of God."
When he was better he proceeded to Hague and
then to Rotterdam.

Holland was a favourite land of John Howard's, and this time he wrote the following passage in his Journal. "I leave this country with regret, as it affords a large field for information in the important subject I have in view. I know not which to admire most, the neatness and cleanliness appearing in the prisons, the industry and regular conduct of the prisoners, or the humanity and attention of the magistrates and governors."

At Osnaburgh, then under the government of the Duke of York, Prince Bishop of the Dominions, he saw much to disapprove. At Brunswick things were not better; but at Magdeburg he noticed prisoners employed on the fortifications, while in the House of Correction large chambers were occupied by women tending silkworms.

He wrote from Berlin, on the 28th of June, 1778, a letter in which he said, "We are here on the eve of an important event—the king of Prussia in Silesia and the enemy encamped within a few miles of him; 40,000 men ready to destroy one another as the prejudice or passions of an arbitrary monarch may direct. This would be matter of great concern to a thinking mind, had it not the firm belief of a wise and overruling Providence. I hope in about a fortnight to be clear of the armies, and to be at or near Vienna." Curiously enough, about two years before this, an ex-Prussian officer, one Major Kaltenborn, wrote,—as Carlyle tells us in his Life of Frederick the Great,—the following words respecting a review: "What a sight, and awakening what thoughts, that of a body of 18,000 to 20,000 soldiers, in solemn silence and in deepest reverence, awaiting their fate from one man."[1]   The two passages were written by different men with different sentiments.   They point to stirring times, and to encampments, and to the great Bavarian succession quarrel.   War was threatening in the year 1778.   "Who," it was asked, "shall succeed to the throne at Munich—Karl Theodore, Elector Palatine, or one of the Imperial Austrians?"   Frederick said, "Not an Austrian."   So Prussia and Austria prepared for war.   This historical reference explains Howard's letter.   Negotiations were going on at the moment.   What the King offered, the Emperor rejected ; what the Emperor offered, the King rejected.   An ultimatum was sent on June 13th, offering to Austria a small piece of Bavarian territory.   Austria returned, on the 24th, a note of non-acceptance.   Frederick, enraged, issued his declaration of war on the 3rd of July.   This outburst of passion, this kindling of the war-blaze, lights up a picture of our philanthropist in his hotel chamber at Berlin, writing home to his friend, Mr. Smith, reflecting upon the formidable belligerents.

Presently Howard forgets the armies, on his way to Spandau, looking after criminals who were rasping log-wood, carding wool, or tending silkworms.   At Dresden, on the Elbe, rich in pictures, curiosities, and historical associations, he finds, to his sorrow, slaves and prisoners heavily ironed, even some who were sick, women as well as men, fastened by a chain to a staple in the wall.

At this very time we find, as Carlyle tells us, the

---

[1] Carlyle's Frederick the Great, vol. x., p. 81.

"Elbe, and his branches, and the intricate shoulders of the giant mountains," thick with armed men. "From Königsgrätz, northward by Königshof, by Arnau up to Hohenelbe, all heights are crowned, all passes bristling with cannon. Rivers Aupa, Elbe beset with redoubts, with dams in favourable places, and are become inundations, difficult to tap. There are ditches eight feet deep by sixteen broad. Behind, or on the right bank of the Elbe, it is mere entrenchments for five-and-twenty miles."[1]

Frederick, on his war-horse, reconnoitered his army on the 8th of July, just at the moment when Howard, in a modest travelling carriage, drove past, perhaps on the opposite side of the river, full of humane projects. The contrast between the two men is notable. So do mortals in this troubled world meet and pass one another little heeding, as they are bent on different enterprises all under the eye of Heaven.

Somehow or other, Howard reached the grand city of Prague, where the people were frightened by martial noise and fury, which signified nothing or next to nothing ; for, after all, the two armies did not close with each other. Everybody who has visited the quaint old place, with its never-to-be-forgotten bridge striding the Moldau, and searched after mementos of Jerome of Prague, has been sure to visit the Hradschin and the Dom, and to have noticed beyond them, if they have not reached it, the Monastery of Strahow, whose famous Library is the admiration of bibliographers. Perhaps that may be the building to which Dr. Brown, Howard's biographer,

---

[1] Life of Frederick the Great, vol. x., p. 116.

alludes, when speaking of a *Capuchin Convent*, though it is in fact an establishment of Premonstratensian monks.   He tells an amusing story about it on the authority of Howard's servant.[1]   It was dinner time, on a day when rigorous abstinence was prescribed ; but instead of scanty and simple fare, delicious viands loaded the brotherhood's table.   Invited to sit down, and enjoy the hospitality of the house, Howard administered a sharp rebuke, saying he had heard they lived a life of seclusion for self-denial and prayer, whereas he found in the convent revelry and drunkenness.   He informed them that he was going to Rome, and it would be his duty to make a report to the Pope of what he had seen ; whereupon the brethren were troubled, and a deputation afterwards went to his hotel, to beg he would spare them the threatened exposure.   He intimated that reformation would be their best safeguard.

From Prague he travelled to Vienna, crossing the bastions, and plunging into that strange network of streets, well compared to a spider's web, the cathedral of St. Stephen's being a centre, the suburbs a circumference.   There, as everywhere, he looked after prisons, and was shocked at the dungeons of La Maison du Bourreau, where he thought he had found an unhappy victim of gaol fever, but it turned out otherwise.   He was pleased with the hospitals of Vienna, and a little amused with a contrivance for punishing bakers who sold bread of defective weight. The culprit was put into his own basket, fastened to the end of a long pole, and in this way underwent a

---

[1] Brown, p. 249.

good ducking in the Danube waters. As an exception to his general rule, Howard visited the Court, and dined with the Queen of Hungary, when he met some of the nobility and the foreign ambassadors. He also accepted an invitation from the English minister, Sir Robert Murray Keith, when the following conversation took place :—

" 'The glory of abolishing torture in his own dominions,' remarked a German gentleman, 'belongs to his Imperial Majesty.'

" ' Pardon me,' said Howard ; 'his Imperial Majesty has only abolished one species of torture to establish in its place another more cruel ; for the torture which he abolished lasted at the most a few hours, but that which he has appointed lasts many weeks, nay, sometimes years. The poor wretches are plunged into a noisome dungeon, as bad as the Black Hole at Calcutta, from which they are taken only if they confess what is laid to their charge.'

" ' Hush,' said the ambassador ; 'your words will be reported to his Majesty.'

" ' What,' replied Howard, ' shall my tongue be tied from speaking truth, by any king or emperor in the world ? I repeat what I asserted, and maintain its veracity.' " [1]

This uncourtly but honest conversation does not seem to have given offence, for the character of the man could not be separated from his speech.

True to his mission, he hastened from Vienna to Gratz, from Gratz to Lambach, from Lambach to Trieste. At Gratz,—a town surrounded by fortified

---

[1] Brown, p. 252.

ramparts which command an extensive view,—he observed in the House of Correction that the prisoners were more healthy than were those at Vienna, and that they had beds and coverlets. Of Lambach—an ancient village on the borders of the Salzkammergut, near the Traunfalls, with a Benedictine monastery— he omits particulars respecting the prison, because he could not say a word in its favour.

Trieste was then rising in commercial and maritime importance in proportion as Venice in this respect decayed. The Altstadt, with its narrow streets, scarcely passable by carriages, formed a fourth of the whole town ; and the Duomo, or cathedral, of San Giusto, a Byzantine edifice founded in the fifth century, telling of old Lombard times, crowned the hill near the castle. Its tower is said to stand on the site of a temple of Jupiter, the foundation of which still exists. Like the queen of the Adriatic, the new town rises on ground reclaimed from the sea or salt marshes close on its borders ; and a broad canal, named after the Empress Theresa, carries on its bosom vessels whose cargoes can be unshipped close to the doors of the merchants' warehouses. A motley crowd throng the streets. Greeks, Armenians, Dalmatians, Slavs, Germans, and Jews presented, a hundred years ago, odd varieties of costume, and languages as confused and as confounding as those spoken round the Tower of Babel.

Such was the place now reached by Howard. He found offensive rooms in the prison. Pale countenances told of misery. In the castle eighty-five slaves (*condannati*) seemed healthy and well. They worked on the roads round the harbour, and some were in a lighter, raising mud close to the windows of Howard's hotel. To prevent escape, these men were guarded by six soldiers. They had two pounds and a half of bread and four farthings a day. Howard heard them called over, and saw them receive their pay as they entered the castle. They had two shirts each, and good beds with coverlets in airy rooms. "They were distinguished from other labourers by a light chain on their legs, and a chain supported by a girdle of leather at their waists."[1] So particular was the observation of this remarkable inspector, and so minute are the details which he jotted in his pocket-book. What he did thus at Trieste is a specimen of what he did everywhere.

From Trieste, in a small shallop, he crossed the Gulf of Venice and entered the Lagoons, landing on the marble pavement of the Piazzetta.

"At Venice," he remarks, "the great prison is near the Doge's palace, and it is one of the strongest I ever saw." Much has been written on this subject. The *piombi*, prisons under the leads, have been dramatically described by Casanova, who was confined there in 1755. Rogers, in lines familiar to everybody, paints them in fearful colours :—

> "But let us to the roof,
> And when thou hast surveyed the sea, the land,
> Visit the narrow cells that cluster there
> As in a place of tombs. There burning suns
> Day after day beat unrelentingly,
> Turning all things to dust ; and scorching up
> The brain till reason fled, and the wild yell
> And wilder laugh burst out on every side,
> Answering each other as in mockery."

[1] Appendix to State of Prisons, p. 65.

A French author, Jules Lecomte,[1] has attempted to remove the impression generally entertained ; and he condemns as extravagant what several have written. Mr. Ruskin, too, regards much that is said about the *piombi* as unfounded.   But Howard certainly was struck with the terrific condition of any one confined in those strange chambers, for he says : " The rooms for the State prisoners are over part of the palace in the leads, which renders confinement in the heat of summer almost intolerable." My own recollections of them, as they were twenty-five years ago, are in accordance with Howard's statement ; though, except as to the heat, I cannot agree with the description of them given by some writers.

The *pozzi*, or dungeons, are worse than the *piombi*. They are connected in one's thoughts with the *Ponte dei Sospiri*, or Bridge of Sighs, across which prisoners were led to receive sentence.[2] Between three and four hundred prisoners were confined in these loathsome and dark cells for life, when Howard saw them, in 1778. Some of them I can testify have only a loophole in the wall ; and to enter is to be smitten with imaginations of unutterable horror.   Howard inquired of those he saw whether they would not prefer the galleys, to which they answered "Yes."   Mercifully there were no irons ; happily there was no fever.   He however noticed a corpse lying on the sands of a lagoon, which he concluded to be that of a galley slave who had committed suicide ; for no one could hope to escape by swimming with seven-and-twenty

---

[1] Venise, ou Coup-d'œil Littéraire, Artistique, etc. p. 217.

[2] I visited them three years ago ; they are frightful enough, but are now disused.

pounds of iron fastened to his limbs. " If the galley slave," he said, "had light and air, which the cell captive had not, his fetters counterbalanced the advantage."

Next to Venice he visited Padua, and could hardly fail to see Giotto's paintings in the Arena Chapel, though anti-pre-Raphaelite prejudices were then in the ascendant. For the *Palazzo della Ragione* in the old market-place, with its allegorical devices, Howard would not care, nor much for its Duomo and Baptistery ; but the prison he explored, without giving us any account of its condition. Ferrara he passes over with a bare mention ; but at Bologna, besides its three prisons, he mentions the hospital *S. Maria de Vita*, which I am at a loss to identify amongst several *ospedali* boasted of by the citizens. It afforded him great pleasure. "All was clean ; and the wards were lofty and not in the least offensive. The wards of the men and women were of the same size, each containing thirty-eight beds, nineteen on each side. The bedsteads were of iron, and the coverlets were white and clean. Each ward had fourteen windows, seven on a side, and all had curtains. They had folding wooden casements, and on the outside wire lattices." These minute specifications, with others in a foot-note, are characteristic ; [1] and it is a relief to find so pleasant an exception to his catalogues of miseries.

He proceeded to Florence. Upon his arriving there he was presented by the famous English ambassador,

---

[1] Appendix, p. 67. "Over each curtain was a slip of black marble with the number of the bed."

Sir Horace Mann, to the Grand Duke of Tuscany, who promised special facilities for obtaining information ; and to his prison inquiries Howard devoted himself.

In his Appendix he speaks of two prisons. In the great prison *Palazzo degl' Otto*,—I suppose the *Palazzo del Potesta*, or *Bargello*, is meant,—there were twenty criminals, six of them confined in strong secret chambers. They were left unchained. But in the torture room he saw a sort of guillotine, " a machine for decollation, which prevents that repetition of the stroke which too often happens when the axe is used." He mentions another prison, which he calls *Delle Stinche*, the approach to which was through five doors, which he carefully counted ; the first surmounted by the words, *Oportet misereri*, "We ought to be compassionate." There was a new infirmary. In the place were forty-two men and fourteen women. Debtors were not divided from other inmates.[1] To the prisoners he gave some money for the purchase of beef and mutton, of tea and sugar ; and this so delighted them, that they saluted him with hymns and choruses, " and would have sainted him had he not prevented it."[2] It was like the reception of Paul and Barnabas at Lystra.

Howard's description of Florentine prisons in 1778 is very different from that by Charles Dickens in 1846 : " In the midst of the city, in the piazza of the Grand Duke, adorned with beautiful statues and the fountain of Neptune, rises the Palazzo Vecchio with its enormous overhanging battlements, and the great tower

[1] Appendix, p. 67.   [2] Brown, p. 254.

that watches over the whole town. In its court-yard, worthy of the castle of Otranto in its ponderous gloom, is a massive staircase that the heaviest wagon and the stoutest team of horses might be drawn up. Within it is a great saloon, faded and tarnished in its stately decorations, and mouldering by grains, but recording yet in pictures on its walls the triumphs of the Medici and the wars of the Old Florentine people. The prison is hard by in an adjacent court-yard of the building " (he means the Bargello, a distinct building altogether, and at some little distance), " a foul and dismal place, where some men are shut up close in small cells like ovens, and where others look through bars and beg; where some are playing draughts, and some are talking to their friends, who smoke the while to purify the air; and some are buying wine and spirits of women vendors; and all are squalid, dirty, and vile to look at. 'They are merry enough, signore,' says the jailer. 'They are all blood-stained here,' he adds—indicating with his hand three-fourths of the building. Before the hour is out, an old man eighty years of age, quarrelling over a bargain with a young girl of seventeen, stabs her dead in the market place full of bright flowers, and is brought in prisoner to swell the number." [1]

If these two accounts be true, prison life at Florence did not improve in the space of sixty-eight years.

On this journey Howard paid a second visit to Rome. It was then under the rule of Pius VI., a handsome dignified person, reputed for his patronage of litera-

---

[1] Pictures from Italy, p. 265.

ture and art, and making himself agreeable by his
gracious manners.   His administration is reported
to have been mild and liberal, and all this accords
with an anecdote related respecting the Papal sovereign and Mr. Howard.   The latter was honoured
with an interview in one of the Pontifical palaces,
when the usual ceremonies were dispensed with, and,
after conversation with the English visitor, his Holiness, taking him by the hand, said, "I know you
Englishmen do not value these things; but the blessing of an old man can do you no harm."[1]

A parallel instance of Papal courtesy occurred
many years afterwards, when Stephen Grellet, a well-
known member of the Society of Friends, and in
some respects resembling John Howard, visited the
palace of the Quirinal.   It is interesting to place the
incidents side by side.   "We went upstairs," Mr.
Grellet says in his diary, "through several apartments in which were the military body-guard."   "In
a large parlour were several priests; one dressed like
a Cardinal, but who is the Pope's valet de chambre,
opened the door of his cabinet and said in Italian,
'The Quaker has come,' when the Pope said, 'Let him
come in.'   He was sitting before a table; his dress was
a long robe of fine white worsted, and a small cap of
the same.   He had read my reports to the Cardinal
respecting many of the visits I had made to Rome,
to prisons, etc.   He entered feelingly on some of these
subjects, and intends to see that the treatment of
prisoners and of the poor boys in the House of Cor-

---

[1] I do not feel sure whether this occurred in the first or second
visit.

rection, and various other subjects that I have mentioned, should be attended to, so that Christian tenderness and care be exercised. On the subject of the
Inquisition, he said he was pleased I had seen for
myself what great changes had been brought about
in Rome in this respect; that it was a long time
before he could have it effected; that he has made
many efforts to have similar alterations introduced
into Spain and Portugal, had succeeded in part to
have the Inquisition in those nations conducted with
less rigour, but was far from having yet obtained
his wishes. 'Men,' he said, 'think that a Pope has
plenitude of power in his hands, but they are much
mistaken; my hands are greatly tied in many things.'
He, however, expressed his hope that the time was
not far distant when Inquisitions everywhere will be
totally done away." Friend Grellet addressed him
with great solemnity, and adds, "The Pope, while I
thus addressed him, kept his head inclined and
appeared tender; then, rising from his seat in a
kind and respectful manner, he expressed a desire
'that the Lord would bless and protect me wherever
I go,' on which I left him."[1]

Of the Inquisition Howard laments, the chambers
were silent, melancholy, and inaccessible. "In this
city," he remarks, "and in many others in Italy, is a
confraternità della misericordia, called *S. Giovanni di
Fiorentini*." Members of such a fraternity are still
to be seen; and their strange costume, enveloping the
whole person from top to toe, leaving only two openings for the eyes, makes a ludicrous impression;

---

[1] Abridged from Memoirs of Stephen Grellet, vol. ii., p. 69.

I shall never forget witnessing it for the first time. The Society consists of about seventy, chiefly nobles of the best families. After a prisoner is condemned, one or two of them come the midnight before his execution, to inform him ˙of his sentence, and continue with him till his death. They, with the confessor, exhort and administer comfort, and give him the choice of most delicate food. "All the fraternity attend the execution, dressed in white. When the prisoner is dead, they leave him hanging till the evening; then one of the fraternity, generally a noble, cuts him down and orders him to be conveyed to the burial-place which they have appropriated to malefactors." The men "are interred in the same dress in which they were hanged, for in Italy coffins are not in general use." [1]

The hospital of St. Michele, with its manufactories and shops, met with his warm approval—so far as its industrial arrangements were concerned. "The hospital of St. Michele," he says, "is a large and noble edifice. It consists of several courts, with buildings round them. In the apartments of one of these, boys who are orphans and destitute, are educated; all learning different trades. When I was there the number was about two hundred. At twenty years of age they are completely clothed, and a sum of money is given to set them up in the business they have learned. In another court are apartments for the aged, in which were nearly five hundred. Here they find a comfortable retreat, having clean rooms and a refectory. They appeared happy and thankful.

---

[1] Appendix, p. 75.

Another part is a prison for boys or young men. Over the door is this inscription: 'Clemens XI., Pont. Max. Perditis Adolescentibus corrigendis instituendisque ut qui inertes oberant instructi reipublicæ serviant, MDCCIV.' In the room is inscribed the following admirable sentence, in which the grand purpose of all civil policy relative to criminals is expressed: *Parum est coercere improbos pœnâ, nisi probos efficias disciplinâ.*[1] The regulations of this prison, and the Latin maxim just quoted, delighted the visitor amazingly; and Dr. Aiken remarks, "He would, I believe, almost have thought it worth while to have travelled to Rome for that alone."[2]

Travelling to Naples a second time, he visited prisons and galleys; also certain hospitals for the cure of wounds inflicted by stilettos—a mode of violence, as he reckoned, causing more deaths in a year than all the murders in our three kingdoms put together.

At Civita Vecchia he noticed, in a spacious hospital for galley-slaves, a particular room for such as had cutaneous disorders, and another for consumptive patients; for in that country "physicians are persuaded that consumption is a contagious disorder."[3] From Civita Vecchia he went on board a vessel bound for Leghorn. The captain landed the second night and pitched a tent, when the sky and shore were full of Italian beauty, to find in the morning all changed. For there arose a fearful tempest of thunder and lightning, and the bark was driven on an island, where the

---

[1] "It is of little advantage to restrain the bad by punishment, unless you render them good by discipline."

[2] Aiken, p. 97.   [3] Appendix, p. 78.

people would not permit them to land, because they were supposed to come from a plague-stricken port. Next day they were swept as far as the African coast, where they could not step on shore without submitting to quarantine. As they declined this detention, they had to put out to sea again ; and at last, after another rough night, they reached the island of Gorgona, where the Governor courteously welcomed the philanthropist, and entertained him for five or six days. On his travels again, he may be traced from Leghorn to Lucca, and from Lucca to Lerici, along shores adorned by charming scenery and ennobled by allusions in Virgil and Homer. But prisons, prisons, were all this benevolent man seemed to think of—strong, invincible, victorious everywhere, was his one fixed idea. As at home he would deny himself the pleasure of accepting hospitable invitations, and sometimes even decline to look at a newspaper, lest his attention should be diverted from the great business of his life, so abroad scenery and recreation were often avoided. Once he was persuaded in Italy to attend a concert, " but finding his thoughts too much occupied by the melody, he could never be persuaded to repeat the indulgence." " No other man," says John Foster, "will ever visit Rome under such a despotic consciousness of duty as to refuse himself time for surveying the magnificence of its ruins. Such a sin against taste is far beyond the reach of common saintship to commit."

" His attention was so strongly and tenaciously fixed on his object, that even at the greatest distance, as the Egyptian pyramids to travellers, it appeared to him with a luminous distinctness as if it had been nigh, and beguiled the toilsome length of labour and enterprise by which he was to reach it. So conspicuous was it before him, that not a step deviated from the direction, and every movement and every day was an approximation. As his method referred everything he did and thought to the end, and as his exertion did not relax for a moment, he made the trial, so seldom made, what is the utmost effect which may be granted to the last possible efforts of a human agent ; and, therefore, what he did not accomplish, he might conclude to be placed beyond the sphere of mortal activity, and calmly leave to the immediate disposal of Providence." [1]

From the unity of his purpose there arises a great deal of sameness in the record of his journeys ; but now and then some striking incident is brought to light, tinged, however, with the character and spirit of the traveller. For example, on reaching Milan, he met with a young man imprisoned for bigamy. He worked in the manufacture of fine gold brocade ; and on conversation with him Howard discovered he could converse in four or five languages. His imprisonment had produced a good effect ; and the visitor, finding his liberation could be accomplished by the payment of a fine, not only advanced the money, but made a present to pay his expenses to another country. The rescued youth manifested his gratitude by respectful attention to his benefactor during his stay in the Lombardic capital.

Leaving Milan for Turin, Howard crossed Mont Cenis, and overtook a lady on horseback, to whom

---

[1] Essay on Decision of Character, Letter iii.

he gallantly offered a seat in his carriage, which she politely declined. At Chambery, he renewed his prison inspections, and then, on the same errand employed himself at Geneva. Winding his way up to Berne, he heard of an odd occurrence in prison life. Twelve convicts managed to escape; five were re-taken, and, strange to say, " the magistrates ordered they should not be punished, as every one must be desirous of gaining his liberty, and they had not been guilty of any violence in obtaining theirs." " The punishment, therefore, fell where it ought to fall—upon the keeper "[1]; that was Howard's judgment.

On his way home he found instruments of torture in the old city of Augsburg, and dungeons for people convicted of witchcraft—so long did that superstitious idea linger in Europe. At old Munich (the new part of the city was not then erected) was a room contain-ing a table and six chairs for the magistrates and their secretaries, all covered with black cloth and fringe, and elevated above the floor by two steps of the same sable hue. Various engines of torture, some stained with blood, hung on the walls. When these were applied, candles were lighted, as the windows were closed to prevent the sufferers' cries from being heard abroad. At the venerable Ratisbon and the picturesque Nuremberg torture chambers—still re-maining though happily not used—were visited by the explorer: at one place he saw prisoners grinding glasses and polishing steel buttons, and at another, male convicts working up the marble of the neigh-bouring mountains. Passing through Wurtzburg,

[1] Brown, p. 267.

Frankfort, and Cologne, he noticed prisoners employed in useful ways; and at Aix-la-Chapelle on Sunday evening, November 8th, 1778, he writes, " Hallelujah, blessing, honour, glory, and power be unto the Lamb for ever." Refreshed with spiritual joy, he wended his way homewards through Liége, where he had prison sights that filled him with horror, though the city was under episcopal dominion. But he could not resist the temptation to cross into Holland, where he made copious notes of all his observations, and then, after his characteristic zig-zag fashion, he darted southward, and having stopped at Lille, prolonged his pilgrimage as far as Paris. Two mornings were spent at the Bicêtre; and the hospitals of St. Louis and l'Hôtel Dieu were examined. On reaching Calais, he paid attention to the prisoners of war, and relieved the crews of English vessels wrecked on the coasts. There he ended a journey of 4,636 miles. After his return he reflected on what he had seen, and compared the whole with the state of prison life in England. The balance was much in favour of what he had seen in the Netherlands.

" When I formerly made the tour of Europe for the benefit of my health, which I did some years ago, I seldom had occasion to envy foreigners anything, either as it respected their situation, religion, manners, or government. In my late journeys to view their prisons, I was sometimes put to the blush for my native country. The reader will scarcely feel, from my narrative, the same emotions of shame and regret as the comparisons excited in me on beholding the difference with my own eyes; but from the account I have given him of foreign prisons he may judge whether a desire of reforming our own be visionary ; whether idleness, debauchery, disease, and famine be the necessary, unavoidable attendants of a prison, or only connected with it in our ideas, for want of a more perfect knowledge and more enlarged views. I hope, too, he will do me the justice to think that neither an indiscriminate admiration of everything foreign, nor a fondness of censuring everything at home has influenced me to adopt the language of a panegyrist in this part of my work, or that of a complainant in the rest. Where I have commended, I have mentioned my reasons for so doing; and I have dwelt, perhaps, more minutely upon the management of foreign prisons because it was more agreeable to me to praise than to condemn. Another motive that induced me to be very particular in my account of foreign houses of correction, was to counteract a prevailing opinion among us, that compelling prisoners to work, especially in public, is inconsistent with the principles of English liberty ; while, with a strange absurdity, taking away the lives of numbers of our countrymen, either by the hands of the executioner or by diseases which are almost inevitably the result of long confinement in our close and damp prisons, seems to be little regarded. Of such force is custom and prejudice in silencing the voice of good sense and humanity! I have only to add that, fully sensible of the imperfections which must attend the cursory survey of a traveller, it was my study to remedy that defect by a constant attention to the one object of my pursuit alone, during the whole of my two last journeys abroad." [1]

[1] State of Prisons, last edition, p. 45.

He compared modes of execution at home and abroad, and he remarks, " An execution day is too much with us a day of riot and idleness ; and it is found by experience that the minds of the populace are rather hardened by the spectacle than affected in any salutary manner." This conclusion, of late, I am thankful to remember, has been adopted by our legislators, and the horrid scenes witnessed once in front of Newgate executions are abolished. Howard seems to have preferred a private mode of putting criminals to death, and notices that at Aix-la-Chapelle decollation is concealed from the view of the public by a scaffolding round the spot where it is performed.[1] Mr. Field, after quoting the sentence, adds this paragraph of his own :—

" The writer,"—who, as a gaol chaplain, may be cited as an authority on the subject,—"cannot forbear expressing an earnest hope that the day is not far distant when in his own country a somewhat similar plan shall be adopted, when the officers of justice alone shall witness the execution of the criminal ; and, for the satisfaction of the community, a certain number of persons—perhaps two or three hundred— shall be allowed to see and sufficiently examine the corpse of the offender to identify his person and remove all doubt as to his death."[2] This sentence was written in 1850. It has carried with it public opinion ; and now the chaplain's hope is fulfilled.

[1] Life of Howard, p. 173.   [2] Ibid., p. 174.

CHAPTER X.

LATER RESEARCHES.

1781–1783.

HOWARD was exceedingly careful in the record of facts, but he seems to have had little power of generalization ; hence, in reading his voluminous reports, it is difficult to summarize the result of his inquiries.   Here and there he makes a comprehensive remark, but, in most cases, he is content to note down measurements, rules, occupations, the state of health, and a number of sanitary facts.   Therefore it is no easy task to give a compact yet complete view of his journeys ; and now that I take up later expeditions, I am under the necessity of making a selection from a large mass of material.

The tour which began in May, 1781, and ended in December of the same year, was to the countries of Denmark, Sweden, and Russia, which he had not visited before.   Passing through Holland and a part of Germany, he reached the city of Rendsburg, in the Duchy of Holstein, on the bank of the Eider.   There he found seventy-seven slaves receiving their daily dole of bread whilst employed on fortifications that had stood many a siege.   He calls attention to a post at the entrance of the town, exhibiting the figure of a man with a sword by his side and a whip in his hand, premonitory of consequences attendant on crime; and to the strange sight of people, under the charge of an officer, walking through the streets encased in tubs, which covered their bodies, their heads projecting through a hole on the top, their legs moving through the open bottom; the contrivance being termed "a Spanish mantle." Gibbets and wheels used for executions were placed on eminences; but the common mode of putting criminals to death was beheading. Capital punishment, however, was rare in Denmark. Condemnation to the spinning houses seems to have been regarded as worse than death. Rooms in the citadel of Copenhagen were clean and whitewashed, and had chains fixed to the walls; but in the Blue Tower, set apart for State prisoners, the dirtiness of the male wards contrasted with the cleanliness of the female ones. There were dungeons, however, which drew forth the exclamation, "The distress and despair in the pale and sickly countenances of these slaves were shocking to humanity." In walking to their work, prisoners, branded for their crimes, were chained hand to hand.

Crossing the Sound at Elsinore, which reminds one of Shakespere and Hamlet, Howard entered Sweden, and made some stay in Stockholm, with its picturesque streets alive with people, its waters alive with boats, and its bridges alive with traffic. Executions there were performed with an axe by a headsman; and women,' after being beheaded, were burnt together with the scaffold, which was set on fire at the four corners. Torture had been abolished, but prisons were dirty and offensive. Our philanthropist, with his own hand, distributed bread among starving prisoners, remarking that their punishment seemed severe, to which the gaoler replied, " It was good for their health." Coffins were kept ready for those who died ; but the place of confinement reserved for the condemned seems to have been comparatively comfortable.

Howard found the Swedish houses generally neater than Danish ones ; whence he inferred that he should find Swedish prisons also in better condition. This was not the case ; and altogether Swedish travels gave him no satisfaction, personal inconvenience being added to his disappointments. He therefore gladly proceeded to Russia.

Russia was then the talk of Europe. It had not long emerged from barbarism, under the discipline of Peter the Great, yet it aspired to artistic refinement, under the profligate Empress Catherine, who had just purchased the Walpole collection of pictures to adorn her palace walls. Howard naturally felt some curiosity about an empire which made such a start in civilization ; but especially, he wished to see what was the operation of its criminal laws, and the state of its criminal population. To escape observation—for he was now a famous man all over Europe—as he approached St. Petersburg, he stepped from his carriage, and walked into the city alone, wishing to remain unrecognised, and to examine prisons in their usual state, not as they might be specially prepared for inspection. The Empress heard of his arrival, and, whatever might be her motive, immediately invited him to Court. He replied that he had come to visit prisons, not palaces. The Empress's character might have something to do with this curt reply; but probably, had she been as virtuous as she was base, he might have shrunk from a visit.

In his notes on Russia he is more concise and comprehensive than usual; therefore I cannot do better than use his own words.

"In Russia the peasants and servants are bondsmen or slaves, and their lords or masters may inflict on them any corporal punishment, or banish them to Siberia, on giving notice of their offences to the police. But they are not permitted to put them to death. Should they however die by the severity of their punishment, the penalty of the law is easily evaded.

"Debtors in this country are often employed as slaves by Government, and allowed twelve roubles yearly wages, which goes towards discharging the debt. In some cases of private debts, if any person will give sufficient security to pay twelve roubles a year as long as the slave lives, or till the debt is paid off—as also to produce the slave when he is demanded—such person may take him out of confinement; but if he fails to produce him when demanded, he is liable to pay the whole debt immediately.

"There are no regular gaolers appointed in Russia, but all the prisons are guarded by the military. Little or no attention is paid to the reformation of prisoners. There is no capital punishment for any crime but treason; but the common punishment of the knout is often dreaded more than death, and sometimes a criminal has endeavoured to bribe the executioner to kill him. This punishment seldom

causes immediate death ; but death is often the consequence of it." [1]

Howard saw the different instruments of death and
torture—the axe and block, a machine for breaking
arms and legs, a knife for slitting noses, a contrivance
for branding by puncture and black powder, and the
cat—a whip of from two to ten strings.

The knout, a whip with a wooden handle, consisted of thongs two feet in length, twisted together
and ending in a thick one, measuring a foot and a
half. Howard, wishing to know all about this instrument, took a coach and drove to the house of
the executioner. The man was astonished at such a
visitor. But his manner overawed the official, who,
very unwillingly, made his confessions. Can you inflict the knout in such a manner as to occasion death
in a short time ? " " Yes, I can." " In how short a
time ? " " In a day or two." " Have you ever so inflicted it ? " " I have." " Have you lately ? " " Yes,
the last man died of the punishment." " How do you
render it mortal ? " " By one or more strokes on the
sides, which carry off large pieces of flesh." " Do you
receive orders thus to inflict the punishment ? " " I
do."

He afterwards witnessed what he thus describes.

" August 10, 1781. I saw two criminals, a man
and a woman, suffer the punishment of the *knout.*
They were conducted from prison by about fifteen
huzzars and ten soldiers. When they arrived at the
place of punishment, the huzzars formed themselves
into a ring round the whipping post, the drum beat

---

[1] Appendix to the State of Prisons, ed. 1784, p. 40.

a minute or two, and then some prayers were read, the populace taking off their hats. The woman was taken first, and after being roughly stripped to the waist, her hands and feet were bound with cords to a post made for the purpose, a man standing before the post and holding the cords to keep them tight. A servant attended the executioner, and both were stout men. The servant first marked his ground and struck the woman five times on the back. Every stroke seemed to penetrate deep into her flesh. But his master, thinking him too gentle, pushed him aside, took his place, and gave all the remaining strokes himself, which were evidently more severe. The woman received twenty-five and the man sixty. I pressed through the huzzars and counted the number as they were chalked on a board ; and both seemed but just alive, especially the man, who yet had strength enough to receive a small donation with some signs of gratitude. They were conducted back to prison in a little waggon. I saw the woman in a very weak condition some days after, but could not find the man any more." [1]

In the fortress were vaulted rooms, insufferably hot, where deserters lodged, and whose doom was to work on the fortifications and to drag wood out of the river Neva. Slaves were seen with logs fastened to both legs. He found debtors, as well as criminals, in close confinement, the former subsisting upon alms collected in boxes hung out of the window. Yet there were lights amidst the shadows. New and better prisons were being erected, the hospitals of St.

---

[1] Appendix, p. 41.

Petersburg were well managed. The Empress had
established a school for the education of the nobility,
and a limited number of common people; on Howard's
visiting this institution, the pupils made him a present of some ivory work, which he took home and
placed in the root house at Cardington.

From St. Petersburg he passed on to Cronstadt,
where he found culprits and debtors taking ballast
out of ships; the men had healthy faces and were
robust, and though scantily fed were warmly clothed.
He paid repeated visits to prisons and hospitals, and
then started for Moscow, by which means, to use his
own words, he *travelled his ague off.* He declined a
military escort, and proceeded in his simple fashion,
accomplishing five hundred miles in less than five
days, *without ever taking off his clothes.* He astonished
the drivers by his liberality; and on offering each
about the value of half a crown, instead of the accustomed fee of twopence or threepence, they were afraid
to accept so large a gratuity till he told them, as he
had committed his life to their charge, he must insist
upon paying them for their care.

He tells some frightful stories of what he saw in
different Russian prisons. But he also says, "I
found no traces of any such prisons or dungeons as
were common formerly in the castles of England,[1]
and in several foreign countries. That cruel mode of
confinement in many of our prisons has been a principal cause of the gaol fever. I saw no symptoms of
the gaol fever in Moscow or in any part of Russia."[2]

[1] See Burns' Justice, edit. 1780, vol. ii., p. 345.
[2] Appendix, p. 51.

On his reaching Moscow, he sat down to write the
following letter to Mr. Smith at Bedford, dated September 7th, 1781 :—

"I am persuaded a line will not be unacceptable
even from such a vagrant. I have unremittedly pursued the object of my journey, and have looked into
no palaces, or seen any curiosities, so my letters can
afford little entertainment to my friends. I stayed
about three weeks at Petersburg. I declined every
honour that was offered me, and when pressed to
have a soldier to accompany me, I declined that also.
Yet I fought my way pretty well, five hundred miles,
and bad roads, in less than five days. I have a
strong yet light and easy carriage, which I happily
bought for fifty roubles (about ten guineas). This
city is situated in a fine plain, totally different from
all others, as each house has a garden, which extends
the city eight or ten miles, so that four and six horses
are common in the streets. I content myself with a
pair, though I think I have drove to-day near twenty
miles to see one prison and one hospital. I am told
sad stories of what I am to suffer by the cold ; yet I
will not leave this city till I have made repeated visits
to the prisons and hospitals, as the first man in the
kingdom assured me my publication would be translated into Russian. My next step is for Warsaw,
about seven or eight hundred miles. Every step
being homeward, I have spirit to encounter it, though
through the worst country in Europe. I bless God I
am well, with calm easy spirits. I had a fit of the
ague a day or two before I set out for Petersburg, but
I travelled it off, the nights last week being warm. I
thought I could live where any men did live ; but this

northern journey, especially in Sweden, I have been pinched ; no fruit, no garden-stuff, sour bread, sour milk; but in this city every luxury, even pineapples and potatoes."[1]

Howard's medical knowledge was turned to good account wherever he went, and an instance of its successful application occurred during his Russian travels. An English lady was seized with typhoid fever during the absence of her husband, and was supposed to have expired, the usual signs of life having disappeared. The servants were laying her out as a corpse when Howard, who happened to be in the neighbourhood, was informed of the circumstance. On examining the body he saw that animation was not. extinct, and by the employment of restoratives saved the patient from a premature grave. Some time afterwards she brought a daughter to England ; and one of the first objects of interest in London to which her mother conducted the young lady, was the statue of her deliverer in St. Paul's Cathedral.

Leaving Russia, he passed through Poland, and had sights of misery at Warsaw ; but on entering Silesia thankfully discovered humane methods of treating criminals. .

He returned to Germany, and in the Prussian dominions had an adventure which brought out one of his peculiarities. His firmness offered resistance like granite rock, when any one, no matter who, strove to crush it. On this occasion he met a royal courier, who had neglected the prescribed precaution of blowing a horn as he came to a narrow piece of road

---

[1] Brown, p. 331.

which admitted of only one carriage at a time. The messenger insisted upon proceeding, asserted the authority of his master, Frederick the Great, and told the Englishman to turn back. The Englishman refused, on the ground that he had observed the law, but the courier had broken it.[1] There they sat, looking each other in the face, till the officer had to give way to an opponent whose strength consisted in a sense of right.

After stopping at Brunswick he repaired to Holland. Whether it was on his way thither I do not know, but he certainly stopped at Osnaburg during this journey, and whilst there had an interview with the Duke of York, Prince-Bishop of that small dominion. He informed him of the continued infliction of torture in the Principality. The young prince desired to learn the particulars. Howard declined to enter into the subject, thinking the recital would be too much for his Highness ; but he begged him to institute an official inquiry. After this interview he forwarded a copy of the new edition of "The State of Prisons," with a ribbon fixed at the page which described the visit of 1778, where he had expressed a hope, "that it might engage the notice of an amiable Prince who is the present Bishop, and so be the means of alleviating the sufferings of the miserable prisoners."

One more visit to Antwerp, one more inspection of Vilvorde, Ghent, and Bruges, and the traveller reached his native shores. At the last of these towns a Sister of Charity asked him, "Are you a Catholic ?" "I love people of all religions," was his catholic

---

[1] Aiken, p. 219.

reply.   " Then," said the lady, " we hope you will die a Catholic."[1]

It was in the year 1781, when the fourth prison journey was performed, that Burke pronounced his memorable eulogium. " I cannot name this gentleman without remarking that his labours and writings have done much to open the eyes and hearts of mankind. He has visited all Europe—not to survey the sumptuousness of palaces or the stateliness of temples ; not to make accurate measurements of the remains of ancient grandeur, nor to form a scale of the curiosity of modern art ; nor to collect medals, or collect manuscripts—but to dive into the depths of dungeons, to plunge into the infection of hospitals, to survey the mansions of sorrow and pain, to take the gage and dimensions of misery, depression, and contempt, to remember the forgotten, to attend to the neglected, to visit the forsaken, and compare and collate the distresses of all men in all countries. His plan is original ; it is as full of genius as it is of humanity. It was a voyage of discovery, a circumnavigation of charity. Already the benefit of his labour is felt more or less in every country ; I hope he will anticipate his final reward by seeing all its efforts fully realised in his own."[2]

Howard's next tour abroad was to the South, and for this he left Falmouth in January, 1783, bent on visiting Portugal and Spain, which he had not seen before.

In the month of November, 1755, as noticed al-

---

[1] Appendix to State of Prisons, p. 104.
[2] Speech delivered at Bristol.

ready, Lisbon had been shattered by an earthquake, and soon afterwards Howard made an attempt to reach the spot, not that he might behold a sensational spectacle in the ruins, but that he might administer relief to suffering citizens. The attempt, as we have seen, was frustrated. Many years had elapsed and the city was now restored, including one building in particular, towards which the traveller was drawn by a fascination which influenced him as a Protestant and a philanthropist. He would fain see one of those famous establishments which the Romish Church had employed for crushing the Reformation; and would also fain endeavour to mitigate the sufferings of those immured within its mysterious walls. A Portuguese gentleman, the Chevalier de Oliocyra, had in vain sought the abolition of this institution; it still remained, doing its accustomed work. It is curious to notice that the Jesuits, who are credited with the introduction of the tribunal into the country, were, three years after the earthquake, expelled from Portugal; the engine, however, which they are said to have raised, went on with its machinery down to Howard's visit, and long afterwards. He would be sure to hear of the *autos da fé*, which had been recently held, with all the ceremonies attending the occasion, and of the *quemadero*, where victims of all sorts had been burnt to ashes. He tried to get into the prisons of the Holy Office on the banks of the Tagus, but in vain; he heard, however, of its nineteen vaulted rooms, some of them called *secret*, totally dark, and separated from each other by walls sixteen feet thick.

From Lisbon he entered Spain, and visited Badajoz, which had existed in Roman times, and passed through varied fortunes under the Moors, till Alonso IX. recovered it for the Christians. There our traveller found things in a better state than in Portugal. The prisons were clean and had fountains in the courtyard, which gratified him much ; but he mourned to find that torture was still used to obtain confession. He entered Toledo with its Alcazar crowning the height, reminding most Englishmen who see it, of Durham and its grand Norman cathedral ; but he was chiefly interested in the prison where people were loaded with irons. A short journey brought him to Madrid, when Fernando VI. was on the throne, just at the end of a war for the recovery of Spanish dominions which at different times England had conquered and annexed. Peace was agreed by treaty in September, 1783.

There is much in the metropolis of Spain to interest a traveller, in spite of the cutting winds which come from the Sierra and sweep through the *Puerta del Sol* in early spring—the season when Howard entered it. But there, as everywhere, prisons and hospitals were his chosen haunts. The largest of the former, the *Carcel de Corte*, he describes as having stone beds with hooks to which the prisoners were chained ; but there happened at the time to be a gaoler who, exercising a discretionary power, treated people under his charge with compassion and forbearance. In the prison intended for the city it was otherwise ; dungeons were filthy, and walls of the torture chamber showed bloody stains. In another place where convicted criminals were confined, a mischievous practice obtained of revising sentences already passed ; but in a building provided for petty offences judicious regulations existed—adults were employed, and young criminals were under instruction.

The Inquisition is a characteristic Spanish institute, and in Madrid it exercised a terrible sway. The memory of old horrors is perpetuated in works of art, as if they were objects for admiration ; and to this day may be seen in one of the smaller rooms of the immense Museum an enormous picture, displaying with minute accuracy all the details of an *auto da fé*, happily now amongst things of the past. Such scenes secured sympathy a hundred years ago; and though the Inquisition then was beginning to totter before its final fall, Spaniards whom Howard saw tolerated the tyranny of the Holy Office. When I was in Madrid, last spring, I had the pleasure of meeting with the British Episcopalian chaplain and the Scotch Presbyterian missionary, who hold Protestant worship respectively in two large apartments of an extensive building known as No. 1 in the Leganitos, a much-frequented street in Madrid. I was informed, by those acquainted with the facts, that this edifice was formerly devoted to Inquisitionary business, and I was shown over it from top to bottom. Underground there are long passages with openings here and there, now bricked up, which led, I was informed, into dungeons, where victims were shut up in darkness and misery. Howard in vain sought to penetrate into these recesses; but he managed to secure an interview with the Grand Inquisitor, who received him at seven o'clock one morning and led him into the room where the accused were examined. The judge's seat was hung with scarlet, and over it rose a crucifix. A table stood in the middle, with two

chairs for secretaries ; and at the further end a stool
supported the miserable being brought before the
tribunal.   What Howard saw and described is represented in old engravings.

The hospitals at Madrid were magnificent, the
Royal Hospital in particular.   There nine hundred
patients were accommodated ; but the critical eye of
the uncommon visitor detected things he disapproved :
numerous people allowed to come in, disturbed the
sufferers, and rooms for convalescents were so close
as to retard recovery.

He mentions particularly the Hospital of *San
Antonio*, and informs us that "in a room in this
hospital, a charitable society, called the *Hermandad
del Refugio*, met every evening, and then went about
the streets, giving notice of their presence by striking
the pavement with sticks shod with iron.   Whatever
poor and distressed people they met with in their
perambulations, they conducted to this hospital, and
supplied them with a supper of bread and eggs, one
night's lodging, and a breakfast of bread and raisins.
The sick they sent to the general hospital, where one
of eighteen physicians always attended to examine
and admit patients.   In that part of the hospital
next the street, was a place into which the sick put
notices of distress, in consequence of which they were
immediately visited and relieved.[1]

It is a mistake to suppose that, in this and other
journeys, Howard's attention was confined to prisons.
He took cognisance of hospitals, schools, and every
kind of benevolent institution existing in the cities
and towns he visited.

[1] Appendix, p. 117.

He proceeded to Valladolid, the main centre, after Seville, of Protestant excitement in Spain at the period of the Reformation. There, in the Plaza Mayor, Philip II. had looked on ladies and gentlemen of high rank condemned to the flames for reading the Bible and holding religious meetings. Outside the city lay the Quemadero, where executions took place after the ceremony of the *Auto da Fé.* Something of that wonderful history of Protestant faith and fortitude Howard would remember ; and, as in Madrid, so here he sought access to the Inquisition, and with more success than he did in Lisbon.

In one room he saw a picture of the *Auto da Fé* of 1667, when ninety-seven people were burnt. The room of the tribunal resembled that at Madrid ; but he further mentions an altar, and a door into the Secretary's cabinet, surmounted by an inscription denouncing the greater excommunication against any one who should dare to enter within it. Prohibited books, some in English, multitudes of crosses, beads, and small pictures, together with a painted cap and a *sanbenito* for condemned heretics, were freely shown. Then he approached a passage with several doors, when his guide told him "none but prisoners could be admitted." Our eager and inquisitive friend actually said, "I would be confined for a month, to satisfy my curiosity." "None come out under three years," rejoined the attendant. Howard learned that the cells had double doors and were separated by double walls, and that over the intervening space rose a chimney, or funnel, with perforations to let in gleams of light. At the back of the prison sat a great mastiff.

On his way towards France, Howard stopped at the romantic city of Burgos, with its picturesque bridge and gateway, and its glorious cathedral. In the prison he witnessed more humane treatment than in some other places—a circumstance which gave him greater pleasure than any architecture, however wonderful. Pausing again when he reached Pamplona, he discovered an odd abuse of power. The governor twice a year released as many prisoners as he pleased, without assigning any reason for it.

From Pamplona he wrote to his friend, Mr. Smith :—

"I am still in Spain. The manner of travelling by mules is very slow. I was fourteen days in coming from Lisbon to Madrid, a distance of only four hundred miles. In this country you must carry all your provisions. The luxury of milk for my tea I can very seldom get ;[1] but I one morning robbed a kid of two cups of its mother's milk. I bless God I am well, and enjoy calm spirits. . . . I have been in this city three days, and must stop a few days longer before I cross the mountains. The Spaniards are very sober and honest; and if a traveller can live sparingly and lie on the floor, he may pass tolerably well through this country. I have come into many an inn and paid only fivepence for the noise (as I may term it) I made in the house. No bread, eggs, milk, or wine do they sell. Peace has not been declared ; many will hardly believe it. The Spaniards speak of General Elliott with a spirit

---

[1] My experience in the north-east of Spain last spring resembled Howard's.

of enthusiasm. Never were two nations so often at war who had such esteem and complacency one towards another. I travelled some time with an English gentleman; but finding my stoppages to visit the prisons inconvenient to him, he went forward with his Spanish servant. I go through Bayonne, where I shall only stop one day. I shall proceed to Bordeaux, where I shall find many horrid dungeons. I hope to be in Ireland in July. In England I have little more to do before I go again to press, after which I hope to be in comfort at my own fireside."

From Bordeaux, where Howard found what he expected—deep dungeons and plenty of irons, he travelled to Paris, where matters had somewhat improved; the worst dungeons were unused, air and light were admitted into cells, and some sort of classification was adopted. A newly-erected prison presented a gratifying contrast to the old ones. In Lille, things were as bad as ever; but the General Hospital and the workhouse received commendation. At the *Tour de St. Pierre* he caught a fever, to the cure of which he thus alludes: "I have abundant reason for thankfulness to Divine Providence for recovering me from a fever. . . . I gratefully record and remember the mercy and goodness of God. For many days I have been in pain and sorrow; the sentence of death was, as it were, upon me; but I cried unto the Lord and He delivered me, blessed for ever be His name. O God, do my soul good by this affliction; make me more sensible of my entire dependence upon Thee, more serious, more humble, more watchful, more abstracted from the world, better prepared to leave it. May I live a life of faith in the Great Redeemer, whom having not seen, yet I hope I love, and desire to serve to the end of my days." [1]

Amsterdam, Utrecht, and Ghent again saw the philanthropist within prison walls. Applying for permission to enter the *Maison de Force*, in the last of these cities, he was told by the burgomaster, " The Emperor has prohibited access to visitors ; but you, sir, are an exception to all rules." There he found the manufactory given up, because it was thought injurious to the trade of the country. The building was neglected for want of funds, and dirt accumulated as a necessary consequence.

The traveller reached England in the summer of the same year, 1783, having completed a distance of three thousand three hundred and four miles.

[1] Brown, p. 380.

CHAPTER XI.

LAZARETTOS.

1785–1788.

TWO impulses moved Howard to undertake the researches described in this chapter. The primary one was a desire to diminish the sufferings of mankind, and this motive shaped before him a practical result which he contemplates in the following passage from his work on Lazarettos :—

"Although the subjects of the Turkish Empire be little enlightened by the modern improvements in arts and sciences, I conceived that from their intimate acquaintance with the disease in question [the plague], and from the great difference between their customs and manners and ours, some practices might be found among them, and some information gained, not unworthy the notice of more polished nations. I was also pleased with the idea, not only of learning, but of being able to communicate somewhat to the inhabitants of these distant regions, if they should have curiosity enough to inquire, and liberality to adopt the methods of treating, and of preventing contagious diseases which had been found most successful among ourselves."

With the motive here expressed, another blended itself. In early years he had shown a taste for studying medicine. Without attaining to any large acquaintance with healing *science*, he acquired some skill in the healing *art*. He prescribed remedies, he administered drugs; and the means by which infection spread and the methods by which it might be stamped out excited in him a beneficent curiosity, like that which induces our physicians to study the secrets of Asiatic cholera.

He had heard of plague-stricken cities; he had seen the perils of contagion; he had felt troubles attendant on quarantine laws; and he conceived the purpose of a new tour in order to study the whole of this perplexing subject. "I had been led," he remarks, "by the view of several lazarettos in my travels, to consider how much all trading nations are exposed to that dreadful scourge of mankind, which those structures are intended to prevent; and to reflect how very rude and imperfect our own police was in respect to this object. It likewise struck me that establishments effectual for the prevention of the most infectious of all diseases, must afford many useful hints for guarding against the propagation of contagious distempers in general." He was a man devoid of fear, dauntless respecting danger; therefore, trusting himself to the Almighty's protection, once more he took leave of his native shores. But he was not rash. He took precautions. "I answer, once for all," he said, "that next to the free goodness and mercy of the Author of my being, temperance and cleanliness are my preservatives. Trusting in Almighty Providence, and believing myself in the way of my duty, I visit the most noxious cells, and, while thus employed, I fear no evil. I never enter an hospital or prison before breakfast ; and in an offensive room I seldom draw my breath deeply."[1]

Lazarettos, it may be observed in passing, were established to check the ravages of the plague, and are said to have originated at Venice in the twelfth century; but Jewish laws respecting leprosy seem to have been an anticipation of the quarantine which obtained in the Middle Ages. In Mediterranean ports quarantine is still enforced, and it usually lasts from six to fifteen days, for which period travellers are detained. Lepers were called Lazari ; and a leper house, or church for them, outside the walls of Jerusalem, is mentioned in a monastic chronicle, as dedicated to Saint Lazarus. Several such buildings are noticed in Mediæval literature.[2] The St. Lazarus of " Legendary Art" is identified as "the brother of Mary and Martha, and is often represented as a bishop; but the Lazarus, whose name is connected with the buildings called Lazarettos, must have been him in the parable who is mentioned as lying at the gate of the rich man, 'full of sores.'"[3] I do not find the name of Lazarus in Butler's " Lives of the Saints."

At the close of autumn in 1785, Howard set sail once more for Holland. There he wished to prepare for his business by collecting opinions respecting the plague. Moreover, he desired to examine the Lazaretto at Marseilles, and for this purpose had requested the English Foreign Secretary of State, Lord Carmarthen, to seek for him permission from the French Government to visit that institution. He

---

[1] Brown, p. 251.   [2] See Du Cange's Glossary.
[3] Mrs. Jameson's Legendary Art.

waited at the Hague for the arrival of an answer; when it came, he learned that the application had not been successful, and that if he showed himself in France, he was likely to be thrown into the Bastille. Determined to overcome resistance, he planned a scheme which had in it a touch of romance. He went to Brussels, took a place in the diligence to Paris with another passenger, who wore a "black wig," and reached the French capital at night, where, as secrecy was essential, he sought an obscure hotel near the office of the Lyons diligence by which he meant to travel southwards. He went to bed about ten o'clock, and at midnight was aroused by loud knocking at his chamber door. Presently the *femme de chambre* entered with a man behind her, dressed in black, wearing a sword, and keeping his hands warm in an enormous muff. "Is not your name Howard?" "Yes; what of that?" "Did you come in the Brussels diligence in company with a man in a black wig?" Our irritated traveller answered, that he had paid no attention to any such trifling circumstance, whereupon his interrogator vanished. This strange interruption between twelve and one o'clock in the morning excited suspicion; and knowing enough of France to be aware not only of the extensive practice of espionage, but of the facility with which arrests were made, he thought it wise to leave the place as soon as possible. So, having discharged his bill the night before, he early shouldered his small portmanteau, and marched away to the office, whence he set off at the appointed hour for the city of Lyons. In the course of this journey, a lady was taken ill, for whom he was able to prescribe medicine which gave relief; acting the part of a physician made a favourable impression upon his fellow travellers, and this enabled him to proceed on his critical journey with all the more confidence. Critical indeed it was; more so than at the moment he imagined, even after the warning at the Parisian hostelry. The fact was, that the French ambassador at the Hague had been informed of the Englishman's movements in consequence of his application to visit Marseilles. The man in the black wig was a spy employed to watch him; but it so happened that an official, who might otherwise have ordered his arrest, had gone over to Versailles, and was absent from the metropolis on the night of his arrival. Evidently Howard had a narrow escape; yet, though privacy would have been the best policy—and he did keep himself out of public company—he ventured to visit the prisons and hospitals at Lyons before he started for Avignon, where again he stopped to fulfil his charitable mission. At Lyons he found the Hôtel Dieu worse than it had been on his former visit. Rooms were offensive, windows were unopened, two patients were lying in one bed, and fringed furniture retained infection.[1] At the pontifical Avignon he saw no prisoners in irons, for the thick walls, the Argus eye of the gaoler, and the presence of fierce watch-dogs, made escape impossible; but he heard that implements of torture were employed, so that blood issued from the pores of racked victims. Arrived at Marseilles, he learned the true story of the black-wigged man, and was informed how he himself had escaped snares cunningly laid for him.

[1] Lazarettos, p. 53.

Monsieur Durand, a Protestant pastor on whom he called, addressed him in alarming terms. " Mr. Howard," said he, " I have always been happy to see you till now. Leave France as soon as you can ; I know they are searching for you in all directions." But Howard would not leave France without seeing the Marseilles Lazaretto, the very thing he came for. He did see it, in spite of spies and police. He tells us that he visited *Le Bureau de Santé* at the end of the port ; that there was an iron lattice with a door opened only by servants of the directors, dressed in a blue livery ; that letters from captains performing quarantine were received with a pair of tongs and dipped in vinegar ; and that the Lazaretto stood on an elevated rock commanding the entrance to the harbour, where he found numerous rooms, guards, passengers with wire contrivances to prevent contact between them and other people. The building had a governor's house, and a chapel where religious service was daily performed. He does not omit to inform us there was also a tavern.[1]

He made further inquiries, through which he heard a report that in the Toulon Arsenal a Protestant was confined simply on account of his religion ; where- upon he determined to proceed to that place, and assuming the disguise of a fashionable Parisian, and speaking French with facility, he succeeded in obtain- ing access to the building. There he was assured the report was false ; and that the last prisoner for not being a Roman Catholic had left eight years before. This did not satisfy him. He found out the man

---

[1] Lazarettos, p. 4.

of whose imprisonment he had heard, and from him ascertained that he had been a slave in the galleys forty-two years,—the charge against him being, that at the age of fourteen he had joined other boys in a quarrel with somebody who lost a gold-headed cane. After being doomed to a life-long imprisonment for so small an offence, the man had become a Protestant, and been steady in his attachment to the reformed faith : now past work, he lived in a galley set apart for the aged and infirm, who received a small daily allowance from the king. Relieving this sufferer, and purchasing of him some musical pipes which he had ingeniously cut and tuned, the philanthropist took the opportunity of seeing the galleys moored near the Toulon Arsenal. The galleys were moored near each other, with names painted on the stern—the *Firm*, the *Brave*, the *Intrepid*. They contained about six hundred prisoners, all wearing caps differently coloured. The grey denoted deserters ; the green, smugglers ; the red, thieves ; the last were branded on the left shoulder. The galleys had one deck, swept twice every day ; and windows on the roof were open. Some slaves had been on board forty, fifty, and even sixty years ; but they had good clothes and good bread, and a small allowance in money. Those who worked had three sous a day for wine. Some were making shoes, others baskets ; and some on shore outside the Arsenal were employed in digging and sawing.

Howard gives a touching story which he heard at Toulon. The brother of a lady related to his informant, was apprehended by dragoons as he came out of a Protestant conventicle. His son saw soldiers seize him, and immediately went to the governor, offering to take his father's place. Accepted as a substitute, he was sent to the galleys for life. At the end of ten years he obtained his liberty through the intercession of a friend. The parent lived long enough to see his noble son at liberty, and then expired.[1]

Howard's next destination was Nice. At Nice—not the French fashionable watering-place it is now—there were two hundred and fifty galley slaves living in dirty rooms near the water. They were employed in pontoons for clearing the harbour. Sundays and Thursdays were idle days; and as the expiration of imprisonment approached, the prisoners had a measure of liberty allowed.

From Nice, on the 30th of January, 1786, he wrote to Mr. Smith :—"I had a nice part to act," he says. "I travelled as an English doctor; and, perhaps, among the number of empirics I did as little mischief as most of them. I never dined or supped in public. My secret was only trusted to the French Protestant ministers. I was five days at Marseilles, and four at Toulon. It was thought I could not get out of France by land, so I forced out a Genoese ship, and have been many days striving against wind and tide—three days in an almost desolate island overgrown with myrtle, rosemary, and thyme."

"Last Sunday fortnight, at the meeting at Toulon, though the door was locked and the curtains were drawn, one coming late put the assembly in fear, even so as to make inquiry before the door was opened. I was twice over the Arsenal, though strictly

---

[1] Lazarettos, p. 55.

prohibited to our countrymen. There is a singular slave who has publicly professed himself a Protestant these thirty-six years—a sensible, good man, with an unexceptionable and even amiable character."

"I am bound this week for Genoa, and then to Leghorn, where a Lazaretto has been built within these few years. I know, sir, you will not treat any new attempt as wild and chimerical, yet I must say, it requires a steadiness of resolution not to be shaken in order to pursue it.

"I write this with my windows open, in full view of an orange grove, though the mountains at a great distance are, I see, covered with snow."

He then coasted the beautiful shore and reached Savona, where, in an hospital, he discovered a delicate provision which greatly delighted him—an alcove recess concealed by linen curtains between beds in the women's ward.

He proceeded to Genoa, which he had visited before, and where he noticed an arrangement similar to that in Savona. He tells an odd story about benefactors to the charity. They were rewarded by having statues placed in the wards and on the staircase, the attitudes assumed according with the amount of their contributions. Many were standing, others occupied a chair,—this latter distinction being secured by giving a hundred thousand crowns. One statue had its foot under the chair,—a diminution of dignity, consequent upon a subscription of only ninety thousand crowns.

At Genoa he found a Lazaretto, spacious and convenient, "plentifully supplied with a stream of water descending from the mountains." At Varignano, by the Gulf of Spezia, on a rising ground near the port, he copied the plan of some new buildings; and at Leghorn he was grieved to see plague-ships admitted, "instead of being chased away and burnt." There, the Grand Duke of Tuscany invited him to dinner, an honour he declined, though he admitted " The repeated visits which I have paid to his prisons and hospitals have given me the fullest conviction that he is the true father and friend of his country." [1] At Pisa he felt delighted with the alterations which had taken place. The Hospital had a ward on the ground floor, with iron grated doors opening into "an elegant botanic garden, which through the iron gates affords a pleasant view." [2] At Florence he experienced a similar enjoyment, for things had improved there since his visit seven years earlier.

On the 19th of March, he landed at Malta. Sir William Hamilton, friend of Lord Nelson, had given him a letter to the Grand Master of the Knights of St. John. Climbing up steep streets like staircases, lined with shops full of curiosities, and crowded with people of all nations, he reached the Hospital of the Order, and on presenting his introduction, obtained permission to see whatever he wished. What he saw distressed him exceedingly. For he witnessed the utmost inhumanity on the part of servitors, who, as he thought, should have been gentle nurses; instead of which, he says, "I once found eight or nine of them highly entertained with a delirious dying patient." There were twenty-two persons employed in attending above five hundred patients; whereas the Grand Master's fifty horses had forty grooms.

<hr>

[1] Lazarettos, p. 7.　　　　　[2] Ibid., p. 57.

"The slaves," as he calls prisoners he saw, "have many rooms, and each sect, their chapel or mosque, and sick rooms apart. A woollen manufactory is carried on by some of them, but the majority are blacks, and unhappy objects ; for the Religious,—the Knights so called,—being sworn to make perpetual war with the Turks, carry off by piracy many of the peasants, fishermen, or sailors from the Barbary coasts. How dreadful, that those who glory in bearing on their breasts the sign of the Prince of peace, should harbour such malignant dispositions against their fellow-creatures, and by their own example encourage piracy in the States of Barbary. Do not these Knights by such conduct make themselves the worst enemies to the cross of Christ, under pretence of friendship ?[1]

At a later interview with the Grand Master, His Highness asked what he thought of the place. "I told him my sentiments," he says, "and made some of the remarks that I now publish, adding, if he himself would sometimes walk over the hospitals, many abuses would be corrected. But my animadversions were reckoned too free; yet, being encouraged by the satisfaction which the patients seemed to receive from my frequent visits, I continued them ; and I have reason to believe they produced an alteration for the better in the state of these hospitals, with respect to cleanliness and attention to the patients."[2]

Howard often met with coldness on the part of officials, and saw plainly enough they were displeased at the freedom of his remarks; but the grateful smiles

[1] Lazarettos, p. 58. [2] Ibid., p. 60.

of relieved patients and prisoners were a recompense
for what he had to put up with, and encouraged him
to proceed with his mission of mercy.

A convent called *Casa della Maurisa*, founded for
the accommodation of travellers at a small expense,
was a pleasant religious retreat in which Howard
spent two afternoons, and found "all still, quiet,
agreeable." The passages, the rooms, and the church
were neat and clean ; and over each door hung a picture representing "some one celebrated for virtue and
piety." Windows looked into a garden. The refectory was decorated with Scripture subjects.

A peculiar interest attaches to this visit at Malta,
from the circumstance that the Order of St. John was
then on the point of being extinguished.

Emmanuel de Rohan was a French Knight, raised
to the supreme dignity, the last but one; and he held
the office when Howard delivered his letter of introduction. The affairs of the Order then looked promising. The fraternity were at peace with one
another. "If their galleys," it is remarked by their
last historian, "cruised in the Mediterranean rather
as a pleasure-trip, than a warlike demonstration, the
tranquillity of the times brought with it many substantial benefits to the island." [1]

This statement does not accord with what Howard
wrote to his friend, Mr. Whitbread, on reaching Zante.
"I took my final *congé* of the Religious, as they are
called, who are detested by the Maltese for their
pride and profligacy. In short, they are a nest of
pirates, running on the Barbary coast, and catching

[1] Knights of Malta, by Porter, pp. 641, 642.

all the little boats of fishermen and traffickers in the creeks, bringing them with their wives and children into perpetual slavery. They wear the cross, the ensign of the Prince of peace, and yet declare eternal war and destruction to their fellow-creatures."[1]

The French Revolution brought destruction on the brethren. " The institution of the Hospital, remarks the author just quoted, was far too aristocratic in constitution to escape the antagonism of the *sans culottes*, whose cry of *à bas les aristocrats* was ringing through France. Everything marked the Order as one of the fitting victims to revolutionary fury and popular clamour." This is true, but far from the whole truth. The scandalous repute into which the Knights had fallen must be taken into account, before any one can decide on the merits of the question. It was enacted in 1792 that the Order should cease within the limits of the French Government. De Rohan died in 1797, and in 1798 his successor, D'Hompesch, surrendered Malta to the French nation.

During Howard's stay in the island he wrote the following letters :—

" *Malta, March* 31*st*, '86.

" JOHN PROLE—I am well,—with intrepid, firm spirits and resolution, in pursuing my determined object ; but have had a sad winter to combat with. Some days on a desolate island on the south of France, and last Sunday morning, a sad storm from twelve to four o'clock—we expected a watery grave.

---

[1] Zante, May 1st, 1786. Letter to S. Whitbread, Esq., printed in " Howard's Correspondence," by Field.

Though our sailors all cried to St. Anthony to save them, it was God that had mercy on us.

"I have had my audience of the Grand Master, and he granted my request, so that every place is flung open to me. We are here as warm as June, yet the first salutation is, 'It is cold, sir,' which they find, as they are wrapped up in great coats. I see peas and beans in plenty in the streets, but I take my tea in the morning, and a little weak chocolate in the evening.

"I sail for Turkey in ten days, if everything succeeds as I have laid my plan, I have hopes to be at Vienna in Germany, on my return home, the latter end of July or the beginning of August. My object is great, and liable to a fatal miscarriage. My zeal I hope will not abate, nor will I look back. My best compliments to my Cardington friends, Mr. Smith, Mr. Gadsby, Mr. Cosin, Mr. King, Mr. Leach, etc., etc.

"The old smith's shop you and Joseph may take down. Mr. Smith may directly have all the materials for the hen house that he desired. He is to set it up with his workmen ; and tell him I will allow and pay him the expense thereof. You will then make foot-path—the side of some hurdles—that you will put up all neat.

"I remain, yours to serve you,

"JOHN HOWARD."

We find another letter written from Malta, addressed probably to a maternal relative, Mr. Tatnall.

"*Malta, April 9th*, 1786.

"DEAR SIR,—As the French Minister thought proper to deny Lord Carmarthen's request for me, I travelled *incog.*, as on a physician's tour, and did my business both at Marseilles and Toulon. In the latter place, in one of the galleys in the arsenal, there is one Protestant who openly makes the profession thereof; and his exemplary character for thirty years does us credit. I was informed that no strangers are to enter, but particularly no Englishman on any account. However I passed several hours there on two days, but was advised to get off by shipping as soon as possible. My advisers were the Protestant ministers, who alone were trusted with the secret, and who perhaps were the only persons to be trusted. At Genoa and Leghorn I was received in the most generous manner, was allowed to visit the Lazarettos; the plans sent to my lodgings to copy, etc.

" I visited Florence, Rome, and Naples, about a fortnight in each place, to review the places in my line. I then took shipping for this island. We lay by contrary winds several days close to Messina, Catania, Syracuse, etc., and saw the dreadful effects of the earthquake about two years ago in Sicily. Soon after we met a sad storm ; but happy for us, it lasted only four hours, and we arrived here about ten days ago. I have paid two visits to the Grand Master. Every place is flung open to me. He has sent me, what is thought a great present, a pound of nice butter, as we are here all burnt up ; yet peas, beans in plenty, melons ripe, roses and flowers in abundance ; but at night tormented with millions of fleas, gnats, etc.

" I am bound for Zante, Smyrna, and Constantinople. We have here many Turks, the accounts from them are not favourable. A ship to-day arrived from Tripoli, the plague now ravages that city.   The crew, etc., went into strict quarantine.

" One effect I find during my visits to the Lazaretto, viz., a heavy headache, a pain across my forehead ; but has always quite left me in one hour after I have come from these places.   As I am quite alone, I have need to summon all my courage and resolution.   You will say it is a great design, and so liable to a fatal miscarriage.   I must adopt the motto of a Maltese baron—Non nisi per ardua.   I will not think my friend is amongst the many who treat every new attempt as wild and chimerical, and as was first said of my former attempt, that it would produce no real or lasting advantage.   But I persevere 'through good report and evil report.'   I know I run the greatest risk of my life.   Permit me to declare the sense of my mind in the expressive words of Dr. Doddridge, 'I have no hope in what I have been or done.'   Yet there is a hope set before me.   In Him, the Lord Jesus Christ, I trust.   In Him I have strong consolation.

" These days (Sundays) I go little out.   I have the notes of several sermons, and my Bible with me.   It is a pain to see in almost all the churches in large gold letters—

'Indulgentia Plenaria.'

And before the crucifixes of canvas or stone in the street with—*Qui elucidant me vitam eternam habebunt,* and poor creatures starved and almost naked, putting into the box grains, five of which make one half-penny.

" I am, I bless God, pretty well ; calm steady spirits.   All see at the inns, etc., that I have the mode of travelling, and try to oblige me; but I inflexibly keep to my mode of living, with regimen or low diet. The physicians in Turkey, I hear, are very attentive too in the time that the plague is there.

"In many instances God has disappointed my fears and exceeded my hopes.

"Remember me to any of our friends. A share in your serious moments. Thanks for kindnesses shown to mind and body. With great esteem, I am,

"Dear Sir,

"Your affectionate Friend,

"JOHN HOWARD."

Leaving Malta, Howard for the first time visited Asia. He entered a new world. Two civilizations rose in contrast, and must have produced startling effects on so keen and careful an observer. Now he saw a mosque and a minaret, so different from European cathedrals and churches; and came in contact with the green-turbaned Mohammedan, descended from the Prophet's family, and the vagrant Arab child of Ishmael, Abraham's son. Such a transition opens a new world of ideas; the traveller seems as if translated back to the patriarchal era.

Landing at Smyrna, there stretched before him a long line of flat coast, backed by a range of hills, calling to mind the primitive age, when Polycarp under their shadow died at the stake. European-looking edifices,—an extended group of shops, warehouses, and dwellings, first caught his eyes, as he stepped on the quay; and these objects were seen melting into a mass of unmistakable Oriental architecture. The first sight of a bazaar is never to be forgotten—the

open stall—the counter on which the salesman, pipe
in hand, sits motionless and sleepy, as if the disposal
of his goods were the last thing he thought of ; the
stock closely packed within the smallest possible
compass ; the neighbourhood of various trades, each
working in its own way—a row of goldsmiths here
and of saddle-makers there ; the narrow street or
alley, shaded from the sun by an awning of extended
mats ; the donkey creeping along under a burden of
wood ; a camel stalking through the crowd with a
load of building materials ; and a white ass richly
caparisoned trotting amidst the crowd, bearing on his
back a turbaned military officer. All these objects
produce on a European unaccustomed to them a sort
of theatrical effect, as if he were mingling in a crowded
fancy ball or wandering amidst the stalls of a fancy
fair.

Beyond other contrasts, perhaps, is that between
religious buildings in these two divisions of the world.
A mosque is utterly unlike a church ; a minaret is
utterly unlike a steeple or a spire. Then, thinking of
an Eastern mausoleum and an English graveyard,
what surprise overtakes the stranger from the West
when he enters the tomb of a Turk, fitted up with
carpets and cloths of silk as though it were the home
of a living man ; or when he wanders amidst rows of
cypresses, which overshadow graves with turbaned
headstones. Of these contrasts Howard was sensible.

Oriental prisons, however, he chiefly thought of,
and they certainly are equally curious and distressing.
Small attempts are made to confine either the accused
or the condemned. They are seen herding together
in open walled areas, or in stable-like cells, like

neglected cattle ; no discipline, no classification, no employment. The laxity of restraint has the terrible accompaniments of nakedness and want. Ghastly forms huddled in corners, peering through grates,— these are pictures which meet one's eye in Eastern prisons. Howard came up to a gate of this kind, and found three Turks squatted on the ground idly smoking ; and he procured admission to the interior, because he was taken for a professor of the healing art—a sacred personage in Eastern lands, one holding a pass key into all manner of secret places. A poor creature in one of the dens had been bastinadoed from hand to foot ; his relief and restoration by plasters of salt and vinegar,—not a pleasant remedy,—and the administration of a dose or two of medicine, procured for this reputed physician the highest respect.

Smyrna came within the limits of the Levant Company, which appointed chaplains to their stations, or Factories, as they used to be called. The neglect of religion by English merchants and travellers at that period greatly distressed our devout friend. " Here," he said, " I had an opportunity which in this tour I did not enjoy at any of the hotels of the ambassadors, of attending public worship on Sunday, performed by the worthy chaplain of the Factory. I take this occasion of mentioning a secret source of contagious irreligion, that most of our ambassadors have no chaplains, nor any religious service in their houses. With pain I have observed on Sundays, many of our young nobility and gentry, who are to fill eminent stations in life, instructed in their houses, by example at least, especially in Roman Catholic countries, to make the Lord's day a season of diversion and amusement. How have I been mortified by the comparison, when, after calling at their hotels, I have seen upon my return from thence, the chapels of the Spanish and French ambassadors crowded."

Amongst other adventures at Smyrna, our traveller threaded the narrow streets and the crowded bazaars in company with the Cadi, as he went his rounds, to test the weights and measures used by tradespeople. Faultiness incurred imprisonment, or the strokes of a bastinado. The poor Turks expressed in their countenances the terror felt at the appearance of the officer; and well they might, for justice was not the invariable rule of his proceedings; various motives, often selfish, would lead to the punishment of innocent people.

The hospital, as well as the prison and the market, came under Howard's inspection; and he found in one an aged superintendent, called a prior, who, having suffered from the plague, was devoting himself to the nursing of others under the same calamity. This beautiful instance of charity was in fulfilment of a vow; but his success was unequal to his wishes, for he told his visitor that half the patients were swept off by death.

From Smyrna he proceeded to Constantinople. On his way he saw the plains of Troy and Mount Ida, caught a distant view of Mount Athos, and perhaps touched at Gallipoli. The Dardanelles were beautiful; and passing on to the Sea of Marmora, the charms of the scenery increased.

The first sight of Constantinople, which is as it were a strip of Asia, bound on the edge of Europe,—the Golden Horn full of shipping, with caraques gliding

on the still waters of the harbour,—Scutari on the
Bosphorus, with its palaces and minarets climbing
up the rocky bank, a vision of rare beauty,—all this
makes an arrival at the City of Constantine a
memorable moment. Howard must have felt the
charm. Pera and Stamboul, the long walls of the
latter, the line of cypresses, as tower after tower, gate
after gate are passed ; the gloomy cemeteries with
Turkish graves ; the Palace of Sweet Waters, the
gardens and kiosks answering to the name; the
Sultan's Seraglio, *the Sublime Porte ;* the Arsenal,
once a church, echoing with the music of Chrysostom's
eloquence; the Mosque of St. Sophia, with an ex-
quisitely contrived group of domes ; the old Hippodrome, commenced by Septimus Severus, and the
obelisk of Theodosius ; these and other objects of
fascinating aspect rise in remembrance, as forming
the background of Howard's pilgrimage of charity in
the wonderful city, which has seen such marvellous
revolutions in succession.

"At Galata," he says, "I found the sick lying on
the floors. All were neglected, for none of the faculty
would attend them. I requested a young physician
who accompanied me to this hospital to set the charitable example. In another, I saw many sick and
dying objects lying on dirty mats on the floors. In
the midst, however, of this neglect of human beings, I
saw an *asylum for cats*, an instance of attention which
astonished me." He would find no asylum for dogs.
In the prison at Galata were eighteen debtors, and
they depended for their subsistence partly upon
charity. A bag, he observed, fastened in the middle of
the street leading to the prison, as a receptacle for

any kind of charity people were disposed to bestow. Meat, as well as money, was deposited. Greeks, Jews, Armenians, and Turks, being members of different religious bodies, had separate apartments allotted to them in prison ; and, he says, " It may be worth mentioning as a general observation, that I always found fewer prisoners of the Mahometan than of other religions." [1]

Whilst at Constantinople he heard of a recent occurrence illustrative of the methods of detecting and punishing distinguished officials at that period. The Grand Vizier sent for the Grand Chamberlain, who supplied the city with bread and the garrison with biscuits.

" Why is the bread so bad ? " asked the superior.

" Because the last harvest was so bad," replied the Chamberlain.

" Why is the weight so short ? " came as the next question.

On which followed this answer—

" It might have happened by accident to two or three amongst such an immense number of biscuits ; but the greatest care shall be taken for the future."

The Chamberlain left the Vizier's presence, but before he got home an executioner overtook him and cut off his head in the street, putting it under the arm of the corpse, which remained there three days, and placing the light biscuit by his side.

" It being very hot weather, I said,"—Howard wrote this to his friend, Dr. Hermott,—" it was impossible it could remain three days in the street."

---

[1] The chief information respecting his Eastern tour is supplied by the book on Lazarettos.

"'Yes, it did,' replied the informant ; 'for our three days may be only five or six and twenty hours. If one half-hour before sunset, we call it a day ; and so, if half an hour after sunrise, we call it another day.' My mind reverted to the glorious event of the Resurrection that is our joy and rejoicing."

Howard's medical fame went before him ; and if it gave him influence it caused him trouble. A daughter of one in high position at the Porte suffered from a disease which baffled Turkish physicians. The English visitor was called in ; he prescribed for the young lady with success. The overjoyed father sent him a purse of two thousand sequins, worth about £900, which he, of course, declined, saying, " He never took money, but a plate of grapes would be acceptable." So long as he remained in the city, grapes were never wanting on his table.

No doubt Howard met with much courtesy. The polite Turk would pour out coffee, and pile up sweets, and offer other luxuries abounding on the banks of the Bosphorus ; but the English visitor cared for none of these things ; he preferred to thread the dirty alleys of Stamboul, in quest of prison cells and pining captives.

He saw day by day sad scenes. " I am sorry to say," he told Dr. Aiken, " some die of the plague about us ; one is just carried before my window ; yet I visit where none of my conductors will accompany me. In some hospitals, as in the Lazarettos, and yesterday among the sick slaves, I have a constant headache ; but in about an hour after it always leaves me." [1]

[1] Aiken, p. 133.

After all, though he had heard so much of Lazarettos, he had not entered one. This thought struck him, hence he resolved nobody should in future have reason to make the deprecatory remark. With characteristic promptitude he returned to Smyrna, and on his way came in contact with the plague. A passenger on board the same boat with him fell ill. Fetid breath, and a black spot behind the ear, plainly showed what ailed the sufferer. Howard, to whom the case had been referred, ordered that the patient should be placed in a cabin by himself. The day after his arrival at Salonica the man died.

Howard wrote the following letter[1] on his arrival at Salonica :—

" Salonica, July 22nd (1786).

"With pleasure I will converse an hour with my worthy friend, who, I doubt not, has been informed of my intention to visit and collect all the plans, regulations, etc., of the principal lazarettos in Europe. I have been at Marseilles, Genoa, Leghorn, Naples, Malta, etc. Several questions (with consulting fees) have been put to the first physicians of those places, relative to their treatment of persons in the plague ; but thinking I should gain more knowledge in the Greek hospitals for that disorder, I have been at Zante, Smyrna, and Constantinople, and I came hither about a week ago. I visit boldly, but am forced to keep it secret. I always have in those places a painful headache ; but it has ever left me in an hour after my removal.

" I came hither on Saturday in a Greek boat, full of passengers, one of whom being taken ill, he was

---

[1] Brown, p. 439.

brought to me, as I always pass for a physician. I felt his pulse, looked at the swelling, and ordered him to keep warm in a little cabin, as he had caught cold; in two hours after I sent for a French captain, desiring him to give no alarm, but said that I was persuaded that man had the plague; and, on Tuesday after, I saw the grave in which he was buried. I visit all the prisons to inform myself, but my interpreters are very cross with me. I am bound for Scio, as in that island is the most famous hospital in the Levant. My quarantine of forty days' imprisonment is to be, I hope, at Venice. I could easily have made my route by land to Vienna, without being stopped, as no quarantine is performed on the confines of the Emperor's dominions; but should such an establishment for our shipping be ever introduced into England, things which now may appear trivial, may be of future importance in case of such a new foundation; I have therefore procured from the Venetian ambassador the strongest recommendation to assist me in the minutest observations I may make during my quarantine. I bless God I am quite well, calm, and in steady spirits; indeed, I have at times need of determined resolution, as, since I left Helvoetsluys, I have never met with any English ship, or travelled one mile with any of my countrymen.

"I am persuaded I am engaged in a good cause, and confirmed of having a good God and Master; His approbation will be an abundant recompense for all the little pleasures I may have given up. At Smyrna, the Franks', or foreigners', houses are shut up; everything they receive is fumigated, and their provisions pass through water; but in Constantinople, where many of the natives drop down dead, houses of the Franks are still kept open. I there conversed with an Italian merchant on Thursday, and had observed to a gentleman how sprightly he was ; he replied, he had a fine trade, and was in the prime of life ; but alas ! on Saturday he died, and was buried, having every sign of the plague.

"A line through our ambassador's, at Vienna, will be a cordial to the drooping spirits of—

"Your affectionate Friend,

"JOHN HOWARD."[1]

Salonica is the ancient Thessalonica, "where was a synagogue of the Jews: and Paul, as his custom was, went in unto them, and for three Sabbath days reasoned with them from the Scriptures, opening and alleging, that it behoved the Christ to suffer, and to rise again from the dead ; and that this Jesus, whom, said he, I proclaim unto you, is the Christ."[2] Howard could not fail to think of this as he walked within the lofty stone walls, five miles in circuit, rising from the sea—a vast triangle surmounted by a fortress of seven towers. The Grand Mosque resembles that of Constantinople, and there are in the city Greek churches and Jewish synagogues, successors to that in which the Apostle preached. The place rejoices in the marble propylæum of the Hippodrome—one of the finest specimens of ancient art remaining in the world.

Howard visited a Jewish hospital, it was "a sort of

---

[1] The address of this letter, inserted in Brown's Memoirs of Howard, is not given.

[2] Acts xvii. 1–3, Revised Version.

spacious shed, lightsome and airy;" and being quite open, without any surrounding walls, it would have greatly pleased his esteemed friend, Dr. Jebb, who says in his work on prisons, "lofty walls and iron doors and grated windows enclose disease as well as misery of other kinds."[1]

Landing at "Scio's rocky Isle," where he does not appear to have troubled himself about Homer, he sought a leper house, where he found what pleased him—lepers lodged in separate apartments, with little almond, fig, and grape gardens, two streams of mountain water flowing amidst the trees. He recommended, in addition, baths separately for men and women.

Meeting with a vessel bound for Venice, whose foul bill of health was passport to a Lazaretto, he, with courage,—some would call it hardihood,—embarked at once, and whilst making the trip met with an adventure painted in highly sensational colours by one of his biographers.[2] After leaving the Morea, where the captain touched and took in fresh water, a ship hove in sight, wearing no friendly aspect, and presently commenced an attack. We are told there was only one gun of large calibre on board, and that Howard took charge of it, and rammed it almost to the muzzle with nails and spikes, and then, waiting his opportunity, sent the contents with murderous effect on the enemy's deck. Aiken's Memoirs and Brown's MSS. are cited in support of the narrative, but they do not bear out this version.

On turning to Howard's own description of what

---

[1] Lazarettos, p. 65. [2] Dixon's John Howard, p. 343.

took place, a very different impression is received. "A few days after leaving Modon, we had a smart skirmish with a Tunisian privateer. In this skirmish *one* of our cannon, charged with spike nails, etc., having *accidentally* done great execution, the privateer immediately, to our great joy, hoisted its sails and made off. The interposition of Providence saved us from a dreadful fate, for I understood afterwards that our captain, expecting that either our immediate death or perpetual slavery at Tunis would be the consequence of being taken, had determined to blow up the ship rather than surrender." Howard's habitual modesty might have prevented him from mentioning any share he had in this naval engagement ; but at all events the mention of "*one* of our cannon having *accidentally* done great execution," diminishes the blaze of colour in the imaginative sketches of his biographer.[1]

The vessel now went on its way over the Mediterranean, touching at Corfu and Castel Novo ; but the treacherous weather of that latitude so baffled them, that the captain and his illustrious passenger did not reach Venice until the end of two months. Many a discomfort fell to his lot ; and after mentioning the action with the Barbary pirate in a few simple words, he adds : "I remember I had a good night when, one

---

[1] Aiken (p. 134) remarks that there was a smart skirmish, and the corsair was beaten off by "a cannon loaded with spike nails and bits of iron, and pointed by Mr. Howard himself." If true, the author must have learned it from Howard's lips. He adds, "It afterwards appeared to have been the intention of the captain to blow up his vessel, rather than submit to be taken into perpetual slavery."

evening my cabin baskets were floated with water, and I thinking I should be some hours in drying it up, I went to bed and forgot it." Working their way up the gulf, they at length reached the beautiful city, which seems to float on the waters, so that one who visited it has said: "Buildings with their strange Eastern architecture seemed, like fairy ships, to totter, to steady themselves, and come to anchor one by one; and where the shadow was, and where the palace was, you scarce could tell."[1] Such thick-coming fancies, as we write or think of this and other enchanting spots on the shores of Italy, serve to bring out, in all the more bold and sublime relief, those moral qualities which shine forth calmly in Howard's life, making us feel that, after all, in such self-denial as his there is a true spiritual beauty, surpassing that of blue seas and marble palaces and all the pictures painted by Titian and Tintoretto.

On reaching Venice, where he had been before, Howard had to submit to quarantine laws, and was confined first in one Lazaretto, then in another; the second, perhaps, rather the best of the two. He tells us: "A messenger came in a gondola to conduct me to the new Lazaretto. I was placed with my baggage in a boat, fastened by a cord ten feet long to another boat in which were six rowers. When I came near the landing-place the cord was loosed, and my boat was pushed with a pole to the shore, where a person met me who said he had been ordered by the magistrates to be my guard. Soon after unloading the boat, the sub-prior came and showed me my lodging,

[1] Faher's Foreign Churches and Peoples, p. 282.

which was a very dirty room, full of vermin, and without chair, table, or bed." [1]

The old Lazaretto of Venice originated in 1448 by decree of the Senate, when rules and tariffs were devised by the heads of the far-seeing Republic ; and similar arrangements were afterwards adopted in other European Lazarettos. Over the gateways of two large warehouses were carved in stone the images of three saints, San Sebastian, San Marco, and San Rocco, who were esteemed patrons of the Venetian Lazaretto. Formerly, when persons who had the plague were brought out of the city, they were put into one Lazaretto room for forty days, and then into another for a like period. It must have been a tormenting circumstance, to be kept in durance outside the City of St. Mark, amidst broad, muddy, and,— in bad weather,—most dreary lagoons. Yet he says : " I had a pleasant view, but the rooms were without furniture, very dirty, and no less offensive than the sick wards of the worst hospital. The walls of my chamber, not having been cleaned probably for half a century, were saturated with infection. I got them washed repeatedly with boiling water, to remove the offensive smell, but without any effect. My appetite failed, and I concluded I was in danger of the slow hospital fever. I proposed white-washing my room with lime slaked in boiling water, but was opposed by strong prejudices. I got, however, this done one morning through the assistance of the British Consul, who was so good as to supply me with a quarter of a bushel of fresh lime for the purpose ; and the consequence was, that my room was immediately ren-

---

[1] Lazarettos, p. 12.

dered so sweet and fresh that I was able to drink tea in it in the afternoon, and to lie in it the following night."[1]

Howard escaped the plague; but the experience of the Lazaretto and his observations upon it were valuable in relation to the object he had in view; and when he was liberated he rejoiced in his freedom, though the blessing was accompanied by great debility. He heard many a story in such Venetian circles as he chose to enter. I insert two:—

"A German merchant happening to be in Venice on business, supped every night at a small inn, in company with a few other persons. An officer of the State Inquisition came to him one evening, and ordered him to follow whither he led, and to deliver to him his trunk, after having put his seal upon it. The merchant asked why he must do this, but received no answer to his inquiry, except by the officer's putting his hand to his lips as a signal for silence. He then muffled his head in a cloak, and guided him through different streets to a low gate, which he was ordered to enter; and, stooping down, he was led through various passages underground to a small, dark apartment, where he continued all that night. The next day he was conducted into a larger room hung with black, with a single wax light and a crucifix on its mantelpiece. Having remained here in perfect solitude for a couple of days, he suddenly saw a curtain drawn, and heard a voice questioning him concerning his name, his business, the company he kept; and particularly whether he had not been, on a certain day, in the society of persons who were

[1] Lazarettos, p. 11.

mentioned, and heard an abbé, who was also named, make use of expressions now accurately repeated. At last he was asked if he should know the abbé if he saw him, and, on his answering that he should, a long curtain was drawn aside, and he saw this very person hanging on a gibbet. He was then dismissed.

A senator of this Republic was "called up from his bed one night by an officer of this same Inquisition, and commanded to follow him ; he obeyed the summons, and found a gondola waiting near his door, in which he was rowed out of the harbour to a spot where another gondola was fastened to a post. Into this he was ordered to step, and the cabin door being opened, he was conducted into it, and, as a dead body with a rope about its neck was shown him, he was asked if he knew it. He answered that he did, and shook through every limb as he spoke ; but he was then conveyed back to his house, and nothing more was ever said to him upon the subject. The body he had seen was that of the tutor to his children, who had been carried out of his house that very night and strangled. The senator, delighted with this young man's conversation, used to treat him with great familiarity, and in those unguarded moments communicated to him some political matters of no great importance, but which he thoughtlessly mentioned again to others—an imprudence for which he paid dearly with his life, whilst his generous patron was thus admonished of his indiscretion by the sight of his strangled body." [1]

---

[1] These occurrences Howard described to his friend Dr.

Howard left the Lazaretto and spent three days in crossing the Gulf of Venice to Trieste. The hospital fever was creeping over his system as the result of confinement; and he heard of the death of the last ambassador from Constantinople through the same fearful complaint. He was now bound for Vienna, if his health would permit ; and fortunately an Austrian sub-governor lent him an easy carriage, in which he rode for five days, stopping only a single night by the way. The fatigue reduced him in body and mind, but he blessed God for "steadiness of resolution," and on he went, mile after mile. What followed on his arrival at Vienna requires a few words to be said respecting the Emperor of Germany.

Joseph II., eldest son of the illustrious Maria Theresa, occupied the throne. Frederic the Great, of Prussia, who had kept in check the Emperor's ambition, died in 1786, the year of Howard's visit ; and the former was now beginning, in alliance with Catherine of Russia, a war against the Turks. He had distinguished his reign by abolishing the separate jurisdictions of Austria, and subdividing the monarchy into thirteen uniform civil and judicial circles. Besides, he had abolished feudal servitude, and substituted a fixed tax in the room of feudal dues. He had taken away the censorship of the press, established universities, schools, and libraries, and, above all, granted toleration to Romanists, Protestants, and Greeks. Other innovations were of a still more startling character. He forbade pilgrimages and processions, treated marriages as a civil contract,

Brown, from whose MS. memoranda they were copied by the biographer.—Brown's Memoirs, p. 456.

would allow no Papal bulls to be published in his dominions without consent, and prohibited pomp in conducting funerals. The character of the man may be inferred from these proceedings.

As soon as Howard arrived at the great city on the Danube, he devoted himself at once to prison in-inquiries and the inspection of hospitals. The Emperor Joseph had reared an enormous building in the Alser Vorstadt—called Allgemeine Krankenhaus—containing ten quadrangles, one hundred and eleven chambers, and altogether accommodation for 3,477 patients. Connected with it was a lying-in hospital, to which persons were admitted with the utmost secrecy and in the easiest manner. Vienna also boasted of asylums for the insane, for the deaf and dumb, and for the blind, so that there was plenty of work for the philanthropist to do in the Austrian capital. Upon the whole, he was delighted. He said that these institutions were "objects of the Emperor's particular attention ; and having been either founded or improved by him, they manifested a public spirit which did him great honour, and gave a striking example to other potentates."

Howard was now a man of renown, and he might well attract the notice of a person like Joseph II. Shortly the English ambassador informed him of the Emperor's desire for a private interview. "Can I do any good by going?" he asked. He could have no such reluctance to comply as he might feel when invited by Catherine. Assured that the conference would prove useful, he consented. Still there was a difficulty, as, having finished his business of inspection, he felt anxious to leave early next day. A second message informed him his Imperial Majesty would receive him next morning.

It was Christmas day when the interview took place. Reaching the Imperial palace in the old city, encompassed by the wonderful glacis now covered with gardens which lie embosomed within vast circles of public and other buildings, he was conducted into a kind of "counting-house room," where he found his Imperial Majesty attended by a secretary, and was then taken into another apartment, "so plainly furnished that it had neither looking-glass nor chair."

The first inquiry made by the august personage related to the Military Hospital. The Englishman was frank, saying, "It is ill constructed; one defect particularly struck me, the care of the sick is committed to men who are very unfit for that office, especially when it is imposed on them as a punishment, which I understand to be the case here." Turning to the workhouses, Howard said, "There are many defects; the people are obliged to lie in their clothes; little or no attention is paid to cleanliness, and the allowance of bread is too small. "Where," he was asked, "did you see any better institutions of this kind?" He replied, "There was one better at Ghent, but not so now, not so now," alluding to alterations recently made there. He wrote the following in his diary:—

"*Christmas Day*, 1786, *Vienna.*—I this day had the honour of near two hours' conversation in private with the Emperor; his very condescending and affable manner gave me that freedom of speech which enabled me plainly and freely to tell him my mind.

His Majesty began on his Military Hospital, then the
Great Hospital, also the Lunatic Hospital, the defects
of which I told him.   On prisons I fully opened my
mind.   It pleased God to give me full recollections
and freedom of speech.   His Majesty stopped me
and said, '*You hang in your country.*'   I said, ' Yes ';
but death was more desirable than the misery such
wretches endure in total darkness, chained to the
wall, no visitor, no priest, even for two years together ;
it was a punishment too great for human nature to
bear, many lost their rational faculties by it.   His
Majesty asked me the condition our prisons were in
at London.   I said they were bad, but in a way of
improvement ; but that all Europe had their eyes on
His Majesty, who had made such alterations in his
hospitals and prisons.   I said, the object was, to make
them *better* men and *useful* subjects.   The Emperor
shaked me by the hand, and said I had given him
much pleasure.   He freely and openly conversed with
me.   I admire his condescension and affability, his
thirst and desire to do good, and to strike out great
objects.   He was not a month on the throne before
he saw every prison and hospital ; now he continually
and unexpectedly looks into all his establishments.
I have seen him go out in his chariot with only one
footman, no guards, no attendance ; sometimes drives
himself, with only his coachman behind ; looks into
everything, knows everything, I think means well.
The Emperor told his minister he was greatly pleased
with my visit ; I had not pleaded for the prisoners
with soft and flattering speech that meant nothing ;
some things I advised he *should* do, others he should
not do."

The conversation bore fruit, for he afterwards ascertained that orders were issued to rectify evils which he had pointed out.

In the great prison he found few dungeons empty, and all inmates were kept in darkness. They were chained to the wall, and no priest or clergyman had been near them for eight or nine months—a punishment so great that he says, " they complained to me with tears in the presence of their keepers." But a new prison had been erected when Howard visited the capital, and he found it so constructed that the dungeons were less horrid than in the old one. Criminals sent off to Hungary were first brought to the House of Correction and clothed in uniform. They were divided into companies of five, chained together, with iron round their necks and feet. Their doom was to draw boats up the Danube, which wore them out so fast that they rarely survived beyond four years.

He next met with a German Countess who treated him differently from what the Emperor had done. She haughtily asked about some prisons in her husband's province. " The worst in all Germany," Howard curtly answered, " particularly as it regards the female prisoners ; and I recommend you, Countess, to visit them personally, as the best means of rectifying abuses." " I go to prisons !" she indignantly exclaimed as she left the room ; then she heard him calling after her, " Madam, remember that you are a woman yourself, and must soon, like the most miserable female prisoner in a dungeon, inhabit but a small space of that earth from which you originally originated." This bore no resemblance to the accents of a German courtier ; it had the tone of John Knox or of an old Hebrew prophet.

With this incident all that is interesting in the Lazaretto journey comes to an end. He returned home through Frankfort, Aix-la-Chapelle, Bois-le-Duc, and Amsterdam, and reached London in February, 1787.

Two things greatly agitated Howard at this time.

One was the conduct of his son. Repeated allusions occur to it in his letters. "It is with great concern I hear the account of my son's behaviour. I fear he gives you, as well as others, a great deal of trouble. A great loss to children is their mother, for they check and form their minds, curbing the corrupt passions of pride and self-will, seen very early in children. I must leave it to Him with whom are all hearts, and sigh in secret, trusting that the blessing of such an excellent mother is laid up for him."[1] Again, "I have a melancholy letter from John Prole relative to my unhappy young man ; it's indeed a bitter affliction—a son, an only son."[2] It is apparent how deeply amidst his later travels this domestic trial penetrated his heart, how exquisite was the pain inflicted by it. The whole melancholy story can better be related in a subsequent chapter.

The other trouble was of a different kind. The fame of this friend of humanity travelled far and wide, and supplied matter for newspaper reports, public speeches, and private conversation : in his

---

[1] Letter to Prole, Oct. 31, 1786.
[2] Letter to Mr. Smith, Jan. 18, 1787.

life-time there were zealous admirers, who wished to see a monument for the perpetuation of his memory. A correspondent of *The Gentleman's Magazine* for May, 1786, stated that he had met Mr. Howard in Rome, and described him "as the most truly glorious of mortal beings," whom "he all but worshipped." He therefore proposed the collection of a fund for the erection of a statue, which should hand down his name and acts to posterity. Most persons, except those who were so intimate as to be aware how discordant with his taste was such an idea, took it up with warmth and eagerness; and even Dr. Lettsom, who knew him well, seconded the proposal, in a letter written to the same magazine in the following month. "Virtue," he said, "whether shining in the public walks of life or emitting the soft rays of human benevolence in the dungeons of misery, will ever obtain its own internal reward beyond all the powers of sculpture; but to exhibit that evidence to the public, to excite emulation in virtuous pursuits, and to induce specta-tors to go and do likewise, nothing seems more conducive than a monument to Howard."

About the same time the following prospectus was issued :—

"Many sincere admirers of Mr. Howard,
'*The friend to every clime, a patriot of the world,*'
anxious that his transcendent philanthropy may not wait for the tardy, and, as it should seem, almost un-willing gratitude, of posthumous acknowledgment from the public, entertain a hope, from the hint thrown out in *The Gentleman's Magazine* for May, and so nobly improved upon in that for June, that a statue may be

erected to him, to perpetuate the memory of it before
it be taken from mortal eyes, and during his absence
upon a God-like errand which carries him to Turkey,
to try to restrain the ravages of the plague. And
who knows not with how truly Christian a spirit and
undaunted courage he before went about doing good ;
how gloriously he has devoted a great part of his life
and property to repeated visits to most of those
mansions of misery and infection, the gaols of
Europe ; and how many a weary prisoner whom he
came unto has been bound to bless him, for the
removal of at least some horror, for the alleviation of
at least some anguish, which, with the iron entered
into his soul, when it was cast down and disquieted
within him ! Those persons, therefore, who, feeling
like men, Christians, and Englishmen, the exalted
merit which does so much honour to their nature, their
religion, and their country, wish to avail themselves
of the humble possessor's absence, for the pleasure of
expressing that feeling, in doing something towards
erecting such a monument of public gratitude to
him, and of encouragement to equal virtue, if it be
possible, in others, are hereby invited to send their
contributions to Messrs. Goslings, Bankers, Fleet
Street ; Dr. Lettsom, Basinghall Street ; or to J.
Nichols, Printer, Red Lion Passage, Fleet Street."[1]

It was in May, 1786, that the erection of the
monument was proposed, and the idea excited interest amongst all ranks—peers, ministers, and other
people of distinction placing their names on the
list. All sorts of projects were discussed—columns,

---

[1] Nichols' Literary History, vol. ii., p. 682.

statues, chapels, almshouses, being suggested by different persons. The public prints contained references to minute details, such as the site of the monument, whether St. Paul's Cathedral, or Westminster Abbey, or St. George's Fields, or Shooter's Hill. Zealous supporters went so far as to contend with each other as to the most appropriate kind of inscription, whether it should be Latin or English, in prose or in poetry. As soon as Howard heard of all this, he protested against it with his whole might. "It distresses my mind; whoever set it afoot I know not, but sure I am they were totally unacquainted with my temper and disposition. I once before, on an application to sit for my picture to be placed in public, hesitated not a moment in showing my aversion to it, as I knew I was going on a dangerous expedition. Thomas will remember almost the last word I said to him, ' If I die abroad, do not let me be moved, let there be only a plain slip of marble placed under that of my wife Henrietta with this inscription, "John, died —, aged —. My hope is in Christ.'" These were private expostulations. He added public ones. He wrote a letter to the subscribers, afterwards printed in *The Gentleman's Magazine*.[1] " Gentlemen, I shall ever think it an honour to have my weak endeavours approved by so many respectable persons, who devote their time and have so generously subscribed towards a fund for relieving prisoners and reforming prisons. But to the erecting a monument, permit me, in the most fixed and unequivocal manner, to declare my repugnancy to it, and that the

[1] Vol. lvii., Pt. I., p. 101.

execution of it will be a punishment to me. It is therefore, gentlemen, my particular and earnest request that it may for ever be laid aside." The letter is dated Vienna, Dec. 15, 1786.

Soon afterwards he wrote to England, saying, " I hope the statue will be entirely destroyed by my letter, which Mr. Willoughby will deliver on Wednesday sennight, as the popular frenzy seems abated. Our ingenious friend, Aiken, endeavoured by a letter to throw a damp on the scheme at first, but to little purpose. Is it known who wrote the first letter in the magazine? However intentionally good, yet most assuredly a stranger to my temper."

Amsterdam, Jan. 18, 1787.

The letter privately addressed did not stop the enterprise. Another public appeal appeared in *The Gentleman's Magazine,* urging the continuance of endeavours to erect a statue, as reflection would "correct the wrong suggestions of sensibility, and Mr. Howard would at last respect that decision which he was unable to control." This led to the following address on the part of the man whom so many delighted to honour :—

" *To the Subscribers for erecting a Statue, etc., to Mr. Howard.*

"MY LORDS AND GENTLEMEN,—

"You are entitled to all the gratitude I can express for the testimony of approbation you have intended me, and I am truly sensible of the honour done me ; but at the same time you must permit me to inform you that I cannot, without violating all my feelings, consent to it, and that the execution of your design will be a cruel punishment to me.   It is, therefore, my earnest request that those friends who wish my happiness and future comfort in life would withdraw their names from the subscription, and that the execution of your design may be laid aside for ever.

"I shall always think the reform now going on in several of the gaols of this kingdom, and which I hope will become general, the greatest honour and the most ample reward I can possibly receive.

"I must further inform you that I cannot permit the fund which in my absence and without my consent has been called the Howardian Fund to go in future by that name; and that I will have no concern in the disposal of the money subscribed; my situation and various pursuits rendering it impossible for me to pay any attention to such a general plan, which can only be carried into due effect in particular districts by a constant attention and a constant residence.

"I am, my Lords and Gentlemen,
"Your obedient and faithful
"humble servant,
"JOHN HOWARD.
"*London, Feb.* 16*th,* 1787."

No argument could move Howard's decision.   He was firm as a rock, and felt pleasure when some one said to him, "Mr. Howard, you may be sure you would have seen my name in the subscription set on foot during your absence, if I had thought the measure would be acceptable to you."   "My dear friend," he replied, "I am sure you know me too well. I thank you, and all my best friends, for judging so correctly of my sentiments, and not assisting to wound my feelings." To Mr. Smith he declared, " Conscious as I am of many sins and imperfections, I must always view with pain and abhorrence every attempt of my friends to bring me forward to public view and public approbation. If, therefore, you love me, if you value my peace of mind, you will use your utmost endeavours to prevent any similar attempt." On another occasion he waived all claim to merit,—"Oh, dear sir, as for the merit, I'll say it is my hobby-horse." With a touch of humour he said to Prince Kaunitz, who told him, that though no statue might be erected to him in his own country, one would be raised in the prisons of Vienna. " I have no objection to its being erected where it is invisible." Ultimately, about £500 of the fund was returned to the donors, and the remaining £1,035 13s. 6d. was invested. Part of this was given to prisoners, part for striking a medal in honour of Howard, and the rest was appropriated to the erection of the monument in St. Paul's Cathedral.

The curious dislike Howard felt even to his portrait being taken, is illustrated in the following anecdote:—

" I have detected a fellow at work upon this face of mine (ugly as it is) even as I have been walking in the streets of London ; and, if a hackney coach has been within call, I have popped into it, drawn up the blinds, and sat snug till I got to my own door, as if I was apprehensive a bailiff was at my heels. Nay, I have often had my door itself infested by a lurking artist, who was literally in wait to take me off." Looking into a shop window once, he found some one trying to take his likeness; but he frustrated the design by throwing his face into such contortions that, as he said, "the resemblance between my actual self and the copy would have been just as striking as I could wish it to be."[1]

It should be added before I close this chapter, that after Howard's return from his tour for examining Lazarettos, he applied himself afresh to the investigation of prison life in England.

He found little improvement, in 1787, amongst London gaols. The City authorities were lukewarm in the matter; fees were still extorted, filth was abundant, disease prevailed, moral contamination deepened and spread. New buildings perpetuated old defects. "The Borough," he said, "is a new gaol on a bad plan. The wards of the men and women join, so that the prisoners associate together. The whole prison very dirty. Garnish not abolished."

Soon after he revisited Ireland. New gaols had been erected, but not on a plan which he approved. The interest of the revenue prevailed over the interests of the nation; and the Commissioners of Excise granted licences to village tippling houses, in opposition to gentlemen living on the spot, who saw plainly enough that these places were fountains of mischief. Drinking in prison was a great curse. "At the Newgate one lay dead from this cause in the infirmary, and another was killed in a drunken affray a few days after." Irish County Hospitals were maintained in part by County rates, and King's letters for

---

[1] Gleanings, vol. i., p. 226. Quoted by Field in his Howard Correspondence, p. 138.

collections and contributions—an old practice which was still carried on. All this was insufficient. It left selfish and short-sighted county people to do as they liked, and to think more of their own purse than of the public welfare. Still, he thought things were on the mend, and hoped that his comments would accelerate progress.

He had much to say about charter schools in the Sister Island. He laid the conclusions he reached on the subject before a Committee of fifteen gentlemen who had the management of these institutions. He also placed a report before the House of Commons. He extended his visits to all the establishments, thirty-eight in number; and ventured, as was his wont, upon unsparing criticisms.

Though a zealous Protestant, he disapproved of the manner in which zeal for a cause he valued, sometimes betrayed itself. "I hope I shall not be thought, as a Protestant Dissenter, indifferent to the Protestant cause when I express my wish that these distinctions (between Catholic and Protestant) were less regarded in bestowing the advantages of education; and that the increase of Protestantism were chiefly trusted to the dissemination of knowledge and sound morals." He adds an exemplary instance of good management in Chester Blue Coat Hospital; and copies the rules of a Quaker school at Acworth, as excellently adapted to promote "decent and regular deportment in youth."

He gives a bad account of Ireland in letters written to his friend Mr. Whitbread.—

"*June 8th*, 1787.—There is a spirit of improvement, but it has to struggle with the vice of persons, from the highest to the lowest, who make a job of every public institution."

"*Dublin, July 6th*, 1787.—In this country every public institution is a private emolument; all are corrupt, or totally inattentive, from the highest to the lowest. It never can be a rich, united, or independent State. Many parts are as savage as the inland parts of Russia."

"*Dublin, April* 28*th*, 1788.—I am sorry to say I know no country that is so profligate, so wild, so cruel. On the road I myself passed, the most cruel murder was committed on the day before; yet people talk as calmly of it as we do of a pick-pocket; and as to perjury, it is a general evil."

During his journeys in Ireland "several of the principal towns presented him with their freedom; and the University of Dublin conferred on him the honorary degree of Doctor of Laws"; Howard, however, would never use the title. Whilst there, in 1788, he gave authority to a bookseller to sell a large case of his first work on prisons, and his account of the Bastille, at the original publication price, and to pay over the amount realized to the Mercers' Hospital; but the vessel conveying the present was wrecked, and therefore his generous design was frustrated.

It was during this tour that he wrote a letter to Dr. Price, from which the following is an extract:—

"*Dublin, March* 23*rd.*

"My journey into this country was to make a report of the state of the charter schools, which charity has been long neglected and abused, as indeed most public institutions are made private emoluments, one sheltering himself under the name of a bishop, another under that of a lord, and for· electioneering interest breaking down all barriers of honour and honesty. However, Parliament now seems determined to know how its grants have been employed. I have, since my visits to these schools in 1782, been endeavouring to excite the attention of Parliament ; and some circumstances being in my favour,—a good Lord Lieutenant, a worthy Secretary (an old acquaintance), and the first Secretary of State, the Provost, a steady friend, I must still pursue it ; so I next week set out for Connaught and other remote parts of this kingdom, which indeed are more barbarous than Russia. By my frequent journeys my strength is somewhat abated, but not my courage or zeal in the cause I am engaged in." [1]

Whether it was during this Irish tour, I am not certain, but the following story appears to relate to it : " Towards persons confined for trifling debts, or unjustly detained in custody for their fees, he frequently exercised a liberality which, considering the comparatively narrow limits of his means, should make our rich ones blush. I have often seen him come to his lodgings," says the Journal of his attendant on most of his tours, " in such spirits and joy, when he would say to me, ' I have made a poor woman happy ; I have sent her husband home to her and her children.' He would often tell me, too, of such and such a man being kept in prison for his fees, which he had paid, and sent the poor man to his family and home."

He went over once more to Scotland, and relates

<hr>

[1] Aiken, p. 148.

this circumstance respecting the House of Correction at Edinburgh. " In the three close rooms were forty-seven women, some of them lying sick. No magistrate ever looked in upon them, and no clergyman ever attended them, or used any endeavours to reclaim them. The Lord Provost said, they were so hardened it could have no effect. I differed in my opinion from his Lordship, and told him that on seriously conversing a few minutes with several of them, I saw tears in their eyes."[1]

I conclude this chapter with two testimonies to the effect of Howard's visits and influence.

On the foundation-stone of a new prison at Manchester, this inscription was engraved :—

" That there may remain to posterity a monument of the affection and gratitude of this county to that most excellent person, who hath so fully proved the wisdom and humanity of the separate and solitary confinement of offenders, this prison is inscribed with the name of JOHN HOWARD."

At a later period, Sir G. O. Paul proposed the erection of a penitentiary at Gloucester, and began his proposal with the remark, " It is impossible to enter on this subject without paying a tribute of respect to the indefatigable Mr. Howard, the presiding genius of reform of these melancholy mansions of oppression and distress—to him whose disinterested and diffusive philanthropy is scarcely unknown to any, although not attended to as it ought to be by those for whose information his researches and observations are intended ; for to him all future reformers

---

[1] Brown, p. 527.

are indebted for seeing what they see and feeling what 'they feel. They only reflect the rays of his benevolence on mankind." [1]

[1] Sir G. O. Paul on Prison Discipline, vol. i., p. 12.

CHAPTER XII.

AUTHORSHIP.

1777–1789.

HOWARD, in all his travels, had an eye to the publication of results; and in 1777 his first book appeared, entitled " The State of Prisons in England and Wales." An Appendix followed in 1780, containing a " Further Account of Foreign Prisons and Hospitals." An enlarged edition was issued in 1784. Also in 1780 he published "An Account of the Principal Lazarettos in Europe, with various Papers relative to the Plague; together with Further Observations on some Foreign Prisons and Hospitals, and Additional Remarks on the Present State of those in Great Britain and Ireland." Howard's " Translation from a French Account of the Bastille," is dated the same year; and, to 1789 belongs his English version of the Duke of Tuscany's " New Code of Civil Law." The fourth edition of " The State of Prisons," in 1792, contains much more matter than the first.

Respecting the design of his publications, he says distinctly, " The whole conduct of this matter must be ascribed to Providence alone; and God by me intimates to the world, however weak and unworthy I am, that He espouses the cause; and to Him and

Him alone be all the glory." Throughout, the man was consciously fulfilling a Divine vocation. He did not propose to establish a new theory of prison discipline, pitting one scheme of treatment against others, tenacious, as many reformers are, of certain ideas which they are proud of calling their own. Much less did he think of entering the domain of criminal jurisprudence. Philosophers were at work upon that subject, whilst he was practically studying details. A remarkable impetus to speculations upon the treatment of criminals was given about that time. Nugent published his English translation of Montesquieu's "Spirit of Laws" in 1766; and questions were then raised as to the power of punishment, and the proportions between penalty and crime. The Italian Beccaria gave to the world his Treatise on Crimes and Punishments in 1764, which had an amazing run amongst the reading public, and was translated into several languages; an English translation of it appeared in 1766. Its popularity showed that public interest was beginning to be felt on this long-neglected point. Paley scantily noticed it in his "Moral and Political Philosophy," dated 1785; devoting a chapter to " The Administration of Justice." Evidently, the philosophy of crime and its treatment had come to be a spirit in the air, making its presence felt throughout all Europe. Howard did not soar into lofty regions, but kept his footing firm upon the ground, going about, knocking at prison doors, and talking to gaolers, turnkeys, and prisoners, to find out the real condition of things and the best methods of mending them. He not only saw, but *looked;* not only heard, but *listened.* His object was thoroughly practical. Maxims of reforms he suggested and enforced. The situation, construction, and furnishing of buildings ; the separation of criminals according to their offences ; the provision of baths and ventilators for the promotion of health, and of infirmaries for recovery from sickness; the classification of debtors and felons apart from one another; the employment of criminals in various kinds of useful labour ; the appointment of honest, active, and humane gaolers ; the suppression of taps and liquor bars within prison precincts ; care in the selection of chaplains, and in the orderly conduct of Divine Service ;—these were expedients for improvement at that time most urgently needed, and these he commended with all the force derived from extensive observation and eminent personal authority. He would not have criminals tormented, he said ; nor would he have them indulged. Starvation and extravagance he alike opposed, and misrepresentations as to these points sometimes involved him in controversial argument. He was not qualified to enter into the philosophy of the subject; he had no genius akin to that of Romilly or Bentham ; but as a plain practical man, he opened the way for reforms which have now become established, more or less, throughout the civilized world.

The modesty of the author is touching. "A person of more ability, with my knowledge of facts, would have written better; but my ambition was not the fame of an author. Hearing the cries of the miserable, I devoted my time to their relief. In order to procure it, I made it my business to collect materials, the authenticity of which could not be disputed.

For the warmth of some expressions where my
subject obliges me to complain, and for my eagerness
to remove the several grievances, my only apology
must be drawn from the deep distress of the sufferers,
and the impressions the view of it excited in me—
impressions too strong to be effaced by any length of
time." [1]

The book on the State of Prisons gives a bare
account of what he had seen, coupled with statistics
in the driest tabular form ; but at the close of the
volume the Author attains to real eloquence. [2]

"What I have proposed throughout my work, is
liable, I am sensible, to some objections ; and these
will doubtless be heightened by the cavils of those
whose interest it is to prevent the reformation of
abuses on which their ease or emolument may
depend. Yet I hope not to be entirely deserted in
the conflict; and if this publication shall have any
effect in alleviating the distresses of poor debtors and
other prisoners—in procuring for them cleanly and
wholesome abodes, and thereby exterminating the
gaol fever, which has so often spread abroad its
dreadful contagion—in abolishing, or at least reduc-
ing, the oppressive fees of clerks of assize and of the
peace, and checking the impositions of gaolers and
the extortions of bailiffs—in introducing a habit of
industry in our Bridewells, and restraining the shocking debauchery and immorality which prevail in our
gaols and other prisons—if any of these beneficial
consequences shall accrue, the writer will be ready
to indulge himself with the pleasing thought of not

---

[1] State of Prisons, p. 488.   [2] Ibid., p. 489.

having lived without doing some good to his fellow-creatures, and will think himself abundantly repaid for all the pains he has taken, the time he has spent, and the hazards he has undergone."

Then he adds a passage somewhat prophetic of what is now being done in the way of Parliamentary inquiries, and the publication of Blue Books. In that long and dreary but useful procession, his own modest collection of facts may be considered to take the lead. "Nothing effectual will however, I am persuaded, be done in reforming the state of our prisons, till *a thorough Parliamentary inquiry concerning them be set on foot, on which may be grounded one comprehensive statute for their general regulation.* Should this be undertaken, I would cheerfully (relying still on the protection of that kind Hand which has hitherto preserved me, and to which I desire to offer my most thankful acknowledgments) devote my time to one more extensive journey, in which the Prussian and Austrian territories, and the most considerable free cities of Germany would probably afford some new and useful lights on this important national concern."

Howard's method and style of treatment improved as the volumes succeeded each other. The first edition of the Appendix, in point of interest exceeds the earlier work. The second edition of the Appendix is fuller than the first, containing as it does some remarkable and even romantic narratives. The book on Lazarettos is best of all. When he wrote that, he had gained a better method of arranging material, and a superior dexterity in the use of his pen.

In the allusion he makes to a Parliamentary inquiry, he recommends what is now a basis of statistical science. Blue Books form a staple on which Statists employ their industry for practical purposes ; but in the case before us, quite independent of the aid of Parliament, going up and down England and the Continent at his own expense as a noncommissioned inquirer,—except as Divine Providence employed him in that capacity,—our philanthropist may be said to have laid the foundation, or at least one of the corner-stones, of that kind of literary and scientific enterprise which is now promoted by the Statistical Society. Dr. Guy indicates this as Howard's true place in history. " His highest place in the annals of the world is that of a philanthropist ; yet he is worthy of a place in the annals of civilization as an *original Statist.* Undoubtedly he was the discoverer or inventor of that modern method of dealing with social wrongs, which is gradually building up for us a civilization worthy of the name." [1]

In preparing his MSS. and carrying them through the press, he stood in need of assistance. And he found what he wanted in two friends who claim a distinct place in this biography.

The first to be mentioned, is Richard Densham, who, after being a fellow-pupil with Howard under the tuition of Mr. Eames, became assistant master in his Academy. Eames filled the Divinity chair, and gave lectures on Oriental languages, Densham attended to mathematics and philosophy. Between him and Howard a friendship arose which was terminated only by death. He is expressly represented

---

[1] Dr. Guy's Paper, read before the Statistical Society, Nov. 16, 1875.

as helping his friend in preparing his work on prisons. He received materials which he carefully arranged, no doubt correcting inaccuracies as to spelling and grammar. Densham was poor, and Howard never lost sight of his early companion ; when disabled, the former received an unlimited draft on his friend's banker. This, however, the needy man, who had only twelve or thirteen pounds a year, respectfully declined to employ. Mr. Whitbread's son also befriended the scholar, and settled on him an annuity for life. Densham, in return, left a legacy of eighty pounds to that gentleman, which he, as might be expected, delicately refused ; so that in these incidents we have refreshing examples of kindness, independence, and gratitude.

Another assistant is well known. Dr. Richard Price, it will be remembered, was pupil at the Newington Academy. His name is conspicuous in English Literature as a politician, a philosopher, and a divine. He sympathized in the American War of Independence, and preached a sermon in 1789, entitled " The Love of Country," which made no small stir. In it he dilated upon truth, virtue, and freedom, as blessings on which the country depends, and for the attainment of which patriotism should be the guide of our endeavours. At the close he bursts into an impassioned eulogium on the French Revolution, before the Reign of Terror had come, and whilst its indescribable atrocities were lying in the bosom of an unknown future. As metaphysician and financier, he made a broad mark ; and it is said that William Pitt was much indebted to Price's work on " Reversionary Payments and Annuities." As a divine, he exhibited freedom of thought, and deviated from orthodox lines, though not to the extent often supposed.   He held no particular theory about the Divine existence and the relations between Father, Son, and Holy Spirit, but sought to follow a middle course between Calvinistic and Socinian Schools, rejecting the doctrine of our Lord's simple Humanity, and holding an Arian theory as to His exaltation and glory.   He refused to say anything of Substitution or Satisfaction ; but he believed in some kind of Atonement, and, though denying Predestination, he interwove the doctrine of philosophical Free-will into the web of his speculations.

" Although Dr. Price's middle scheme seems to have been better received by the Trinitarians than the Socinians, it had but little effect in satisfying either of them." [1]

Whilst an intimate friend of Lord Shelburne, Price was shunned by Dr. Johnson ; and at Oxford the latter left a room as soon as Price entered it.   Praised by friends, he was denounced by enemies.   Priestley, at Dr. Price's funeral, eulogized him as a patriot and philosopher, a paragon of virtue and religion.   Burke described him as connected with "intriguing philosophers and political theologians," and painted scenes of desolation and misery as the practical outcome of speculations such as his. [2]

Howard could have no sympathy in Price's distinctive views.   Yet it seems that with aberrations from orthodoxy the latter combined singular fervour

---

[1] Memoirs of Dr. Price, by William Morgan, p. 110.
[2] Reflections on the Revolution in France.

in devotion,[1] and this might the more endear him to the intensely Evangelical philanthropist. A friendship undoubtedly existed between them, arising out of early association in Mr. Eames's Academy, and fostered by intercourse, when the two were living as neighbours at Stoke Newington. Such a friendship is remarkable, and perhaps was not approved by zealots in opposite camps; but it shows the breadth of Howard's social affections, and how he could embrace in fraternal love persons whose intellectual apprehensions and whose religious peculiarities differed from his own. Dr. Stennett remarks: "His candour, as might naturally be expected in a man of his exemplary piety, was great. As he steadily adhered to his religious principles, so he abhorred bigotry. Having met with difficulties in his inquiries after truth, he knew how to make allowance for those who met with the same."[2]

Howard was largely assisted by Dr. Price. "I am ashamed," he says, "how much I have accumulated your labours; yet I glory in that assistance, to which I owe so much credit in the world, and, under Providence, success in my endeavours. It is from your kind aid and assistance, my dear friend, that I derive so much of my character and influence." Our author received further assistance. He chose for his printer a Mr. Eyres, of Warrington, in Lancashire, "induced by various elegant specimens which had issued from his press,"[3] and because there the printing could be

---

[1] Priestley's Funeral Sermon for Price, p. 19.
[2] Funeral Sermon by Dr. Stennett, preached at Little Wild Street.
[3] Aiken, p. 62.

executed under his own inspection. But an additional attraction appears in the family of the Aikens, who then resided there.

The Aikens, on the mother's side, descended from Sir Francis Wingate, who lived in the neighbourhood of Bedford, and owes his notice in history to the discreditable fact of his committing John Bunyan to Bedford Gaol. A daughter of this knightly Justice was married by a Nonconformist minister, named Jennings, tutor to Dr. Doddridge, who succeeded him as superintendent of his Academy. Doddridge fell in love with Jennings' daughter Jane, when she was only fifteen ; but the young lady gave her heart and hand, not to him, but to John Aiken, who became Doctor of Divinity, and was placed at the head of a distant Academical Institution at Warrington. Jane had a brother, Francis Jennings, a brewer at Bedford, who communed with the Church where Howard attended Divine worship, and who offended some precise fellow members by wearing red slippers—his wife aggravating the offence by the profusion of ringlets which adorned her neck. Howard probably became first acquainted with the Aikens through the Jennings' connection at Bedford,[1] and it has been lately stated,[2] that after the death of his Henrietta, he made an offer to Ann Letitia, the daughter of Dr. Aiken, afterwards the well-known Mrs. Barbauld. This lady, in after life, was very fascinating, but her girlhood must have been peculiar; for when a young gentleman

---

[1] This circumstance was suggested to me by my friend the Rev. John Brown, of Bedford, and the suggestion is confirmed in " Memories of Seventy Years," recently published.

[2] In the publication just referred to.

went into her father's garden to woo the damsel, she climbed up a tree and disappeared on the other side of the garden wall.[1] If Howard really did make her an offer, it is to be hoped she treated him in a different way. Certainly he knew, and I have no doubt admired, that remarkable woman. She married Mr. Barbauld, a Frenchman, and lived at a distance from Warrington when Howard was carrying his book through the press. But in the Aiken circle he would be often present, feeling himself quite at home there.

The Warrington Academy—"first located in a respectable terrace, which stood in a pleasant garden, overlooking the Mersey, a little westward of the Bridge,"[2] and afterwards removed to a square in the eastern part of the town—had in 1777 seen its best days ; but it continued under the care of Dr. Aiken ; and he and his family formed a centre of social attraction in the neighbourhood. The Doctor had a son John, who became a physician, and distinguished himself as an author. He it is who, then living at Warrington, assisted Howard in preparing his work for the press. The former, in his memoirs of the latter, makes the following statement : " On his return from his tours, he took all his memorandum-books to an old retired friend of his, who assisted him in methodizing them, and copied out the whole matter in correct language. They were then put into the hands of Dr. Price, from whom they underwent a revision, and received occasionally considerable alterations."[3] " With his papers thus corrected, Mr. Howard came to the

---

[1] Memories of Seventy Years, p. 109.
[2] Lancashire Puritanism and Nonconformity, vol. ii., p. 402.
[3] Aiken, p. 64.

press at Warrington ; and first he read them all over carefully to me, which perusal was repeated sheet by sheet as they were printed. As new facts and observations were continually suggesting themselves to his mind, he put the matter of them upon paper as they occurred, and then requested me to clothe them in such expressions as I thought proper. On these occasions, such was his diffidence that I found it difficult to make him acquiesce in his own language, when, as frequently happened, it was unexceptionable. Of this additional matter, some was interwoven with the text ; but the greater part was necessarily thrown into notes, which, in some of his volumes, are numerous." Aiken informs us further that Howard resided in Warrington during the whole time of printing, and his attention to business was most indefatigable. During a very severe winter, he made it his practice to rise at three or four in the morning for the purpose of collating every word and figure of his daily proof-sheet with the original.

He took lodgings near the printer's shop, and sometimes rose even as early as two in the morning, because the stillness of the hour favoured him in his work. At seven he dressed. At eight he finished breakfast, and proceeded to the printing office, where he continued several hours, and then took a stroll out of the town, with bread and dried fruit in his pocket. His evenings he spent with friends, then returning to his lodgings, he took tea or coffee, after which he retired to rest ; but not until he had engaged with his manservant in family prayer. Such minute particulars give a lively picture of the good man at this period of his life ; and we can ·imagine him passing the pleasant garden on the banks of the Mersey, or entering the Academy House in the Square at the eastern part of the town.

A stray anecdote is worth picking up in connection with days at Warrington. Once, when leaving the printing office, he heard some oaths and curses; whereupon, buttoning up his pockets, he said to the workmen, "I always do this whenever I hear men swear; as I think that any one who can take God's name in vain, can steal, or do anything that is bad."

The particular account of Howard's employment relates to the printing of his first book on "The State of Prisons;" but as subsequent works were also executed at Warrington, it may be inferred that the author paid repeated visits to the place. His labours as an author were very considerable. From about 1780, they "had been greater than in any former equal period; yet it could not be expected that the matter absolutely new which he had collected should be proportionably great. It was, however, enough to employ him very closely during several months of the year 1784, in printing an Appendix and a new edition of the main work, in which all the additions were comprised." The last book Howard sent into the world, was his account of the Lazarettos. As Aiken says: "It composes a quarto volume, beautifully printed, and decorated with a number of fine plates, which, as usual, are presented to the public; and so eager are the purchasers of books to partake of the donation, that all the copies were almost immediately bought up."[1]

---

[1] Aiken, p. 151.

As so many references have been made to Dr. Aiken, it may be proper to state, that after his father's death, in 1784, the time when Howard was busy with the Appendix, he went to the University at Leyden, and then removed to London in 1792, after Howard's death. He seems to have been of a restless disposition ; for, after commencing practice as a physician in the metropolis, he settled for a while at Yarmouth, where he cultivated acquaintance with the clergy. But friendly relations between him and them ceased in consequence of a pamphlet which he published relative to the Test and Corporation Acts. The effect of this pamphlet was heightened by sympathy, which he felt and expressed, in the earliest stages of the French Revolution.

Aiken, in his "View of the Character of Howard," has much to say of his social, or, as some thought them, unsocial habits. His acquaintance with the subject of his biography was probably confined chiefly, but not entirely, to what they saw of each other at Warrington. The distance of their abodes at other times, and the philanthropist's Continental journeys, must have limited their intercourse to occasional opportunities. The biographer speaks of his hero as not very "companionable;" yet while "he assiduously shunned all engagements which would have involved him in the forms and dissipation of society, he was by no means disinclined to enter into conversations on his particular topics ; on the contrary, he was extremely communicative, and would enliven a small circle with the most entertaining relations of his travels and adventures."[1]   And

[1] Aiken, p. 231.

again, "He was fond of nothing so much as the conversation of women of education and cultivated manners, and studied to attach them by little elegant presents and other marks of attention. Indeed, his soft tones of voice and gentleness of demeanour might be thought to approach somewhat to the effeminate, and would surprise those who had known him only by the energy of his exertions."

It seems to me, that the writer was here thinking of what he had witnessed at Warrington during Howard's visits, particularly when Mrs. Barbauld was present.

CHAPTER XIII.

LATER PRIVATE LIFE.

1770–1789.

CARDINGTON, not Warrington, was Howard's home. We can watch his private habits in that favourite retirement. His memory, wherever he went, constantly carried a number of matters connected with his household and estate; and he exercised his judgment upon them at a distance, undisturbed by the main scheme of his life. Cutting timber, sorting tiles, preparing lime, underpinning barns, trimming hedges, nailing up matting—all manner of minor things he used to think of when far away. Notices of them occur in his letters, and they indicate how much he looked after affairs at home.

Though Henrietta was gone, he persevered in doing what he knew she liked. When abroad, he continued to devise liberal things for poor neighbours and tenants, such as she would have approved; and, considering how much his heart and time were engaged in greater enterprises, "it was surprising with what minuteness he would send home his directions about his private donations. His schools were continued to the last."[1] The memory of the departed had for him special charms, and threw a halo round

[1] Aiken, p. 37.

associated objects. He said to his nephew, as he offered the Cardington residence rent free, "You will find the house and grounds just as they were in your Aunt's time, and I have no doubt you will keep them so." It has been indicated already that he would have nothing touched which bore the impress of her gracious hand.

Some thought that the widower might one day seek an occupant for the vacant chair beside his solitary hearth. I have repeated a story current in the Aiken circle. There is another to this effect,—that once in Holland he sat near an elderly gentleman, who had with him a young lady somewhat resembling Henrietta. So struck was Howard with the likeness, that he set his servant to ascertain who she was. It turned out that she was the elder gentleman's *wife.*[1] Another anecdote is given. He derived so much pleasure from the works of an unnamed authoress, that he made an expedition to the neighbourhood where she lived, that he might seek an interview, if private inquiries confirmed his favourable impression. On reaching his hotel he fell into conversation with some one he had travelled with, from whom he ascertained that the lady had another and a favoured admirer. "His chagrin," it is added, "however, was somewhat lessened by sympathy, when he discovered that his companion, having travelled upon the same errand, was as much disappointed as himself."[2] I mention these stories for what they are worth. Reticence with regard to his own plans, provoked curiosity. Incidents which

[1] Aiken, p. 234.   [2] Field, p. 351.

really occurred were magnified, and mere imagination at times stood in the place of facts. Had he known all that was said about him, he would have been greatly diverted.

But whatever questionable things might be rumoured, this is certain, that he steadily continued dispensing such charities as he had commenced in earlier days. A pleasant instance of thoughtful kindness has been related. A journeyman wheelwright succeeded his master in business, and married a respectable woman in the parish. Howard was absent at the time, but on his return told the new couple it was not too late to make them a present. Forthwith he ordered his bailiff to look out the best cow in the farmyard, and drive it to the wheelwright's cottage. "On second thoughts," he added, "the poor fellow has nothing to keep her on this winter; we will keep the cow for him till she has calved."

It is worth while to add, that Howard never returned from distant journeys without bringing presents for his tenantry and servants; and on visiting the North of England he would buy for them articles of cutlery and other hardware.

Cardington was no place for sumptuous hospitality. His habits were abstemious; for he lived upon vegetables, and "never tasted animal food, not so much as an oyster." Yet "his meals were always served up, whether he had company or was alone, in a style suited to his rank in life; and those who saw him the most frequently, and under circumstances of strict reserve, declare that they never were in a house where domestic arrangements exhibited more regularity and comfort."

A stray anecdote may fitly fall in here. One day an elderly gentleman on horseback, attended by his servant, stopped at an inn in Cardington, and began to catechise the landlord about the merits of this much-talked-of man. "Characters," he said, "often appear very well at a distance, which would not bear close inspection"; and he had therefore come to Howard's home to ascertain his real character. He went into the garden, saw the dwelling, questioned the household, examined the tenantry, noticed everything he could on the premises, and narrowly examined the interior of the cottages which were built for the tenantry. The stranger departed, satisfied that Howard at home was the same as Howard abroad. This careful inquisitor turned out to be the eccentric Lord Monboddo.

Howard's sister died in 1777, and left him a house in Great Ormond Street, where he resided when afterwards in London. In the first half of the last century it was a street of fine buildings, that side of it *next the fields*, being "beyond question one of the most charming situations about town." It runs out of Queen Square, and the immediate neighbourhood is little altered from what it was a hundred years ago; but it is amusing to read of its side " next the fields," seeing that now it requires a walk of some miles to get into a region such as was then contiguous. The old houses, of which a large majority remain, are tenements of a rather ordinary description; and in one of the most moderate the philanthropist lived, in a style such as is hardly conceivable when we remember who were his neighbours. They included several celebrities. Dr. Hickes, and Dr. Mead, and Dr. Stukely, and the Duke of Powis. There, too, resided the grim Lord Chancellor Thurlow, Cowper's friend ; and from his house, one night in 1784, the great seal of England was stolen by burglars, who got in at the window. Probably it was when the Chancellor and the philanthropist were neighbours, that his Lordship, in a debate upon the Bill for releasing insolvent debtors, remarked, "He had lately had the honour of a conversation upon the subject with a gentleman who was, of all others, the best qualified to treat of it ; he meant Mr. Howard, whose humanity, great as it was, was at least equalled by his wisdom, for a more judicious, or a more sensible reasoner upon the topic he never conversed with." During Howard's residence in Ormond Street, a woman of rather forbidding appearance made repeated ineffectual attempts to gain an interview ; at last she succeeded. He thought from her looks that one of the other sex had come with a mischievous intent. He therefore rang the bell, and told his servant not to leave the room. The stranger turned out to be a woman rather crazed, but an infatuated hero-worshipper, who poured out a flood of compliments, and then took her leave, declaring that, as she had seen the object of her admiration, she should go home and die in peace.

During his occasional residence at the West End he regularly attended Divine worship in Little Wild Street. We can follow him in his Sunday haunts through Bloomsbury Square,—which had scarcely ceased to be one of the wonders of the metropolis,— to a turning out of Drury Lane, where few vestiges even then remained of the pride and fashion which marked the neighbourhood before the Revolution. In Wild Street stood a meeting-house with a curious history. It had been a Roman Catholic chapel, first for the Portuguese, and next for the Spanish ambassadors ; and, as a Protestant place of worship, it had an endowment for an annual sermon in commemoration of the destructive storm in 1703.

In the rebellion of '45 members of this Church formed themselves into a volunteer corps, and turned their place of worship into a parade ground ; and it may be further noticed as a fact in connection with Howard's shrievalty at Bedford, that a member of the Wild Street Church was one of the gentlemen who, in 1754, refused either to serve as sheriff or to pay a fine of five hundred pounds for not serving.[1]

These traditions were rife in Howard's time, and were often on the lips of old-fashioned folks who frequented the spot.

Holloway, the famous engraver, and Joseph Hughes, afterwards one of the founders and secretaries of the British and Foreign Bible Society, were Howard's co-worshippers.

Dr. Stennett was minister, and between him and Howard a warm friendship sprang up, and that is a

---

[1] Amongst other remarkable members was one Thomas Laugher, born in 1700, and lived till 1812. He remembered having seen Queen Anne go to the House of Peers seated on a pillion behind the Lord Chancellor, and could recollect bread being sold at twopence farthing the quartern loaf, and butcher's meat at a penny a pound. He had a son who died before his father, at the age of eighty. " If," said he, " the young fool had taken so much care of his life as I have, he might now have been alive and hearty."

reason for noticing the place and the man. He was born at Exeter, and educated by tutors of competent learning. He maintained Nonconformist opinions in an age marked by looseness of principle and eccentricity of opinion ; and though separated from the Established Church, he was free from sectarian bigotry.

Partaking of the piety which distinguished early Nonconformists, he lamented irregular attendance on worship, and inveighed against conformity to the world. Monkish austerity and criminal indifference were alike the objects of his aversion.[1] Such a man suited Howard's taste, and, though the latter remained an Independent, he identified himself with the Wild Street congregation, contributed to the support of its institutions, and aided in the erection of a new chapel in 1788.

Howard wrote from Smyrna to his friend, saying : " The principal reason of my writing is most sincerely to thank you for the many pleasant hours I have had in reviewing the notes I have taken of the sermons I have had the happiness to hear under your ministry. These, sir, with many of your petitions in prayer, have been and are my songs in the house of my pilgrimage. With unabated pleasure I have attended your ministry ; no man ever entered more into my religious sentiments, or more happily expressed them. It was some little disappointment when any one else entered your pulpit. How many Sabbaths have

---

[1] I here follow the description, and use language employed in a Funeral Sermon for Dr. Stennett, Dr. Kippis, and Dr. Harris, by John Evans. I have also before me "A Brief History of the Baptist Church in Little Wild Street."

I ardently longed to spend in Wild Street ; on those days I generally rest, or, if at sea, keep retired in my little cabin. It is you that preach, and, I bless God, I attend with renewed pleasure. God in Christ is the rock and portion of my soul. I have little more to add. I pray God reward you a thousand-fold." [1]

"You know, my friends," said Dr. Stennett in his funeral sermon for Howard, "with what seriousness and devotion he attended for a long course of years on the worship of God among us. It would be scarce decent for me to repeat the affectionate things he says in a letter sent to me from a remote part of the world, respecting the satisfaction and pleasure he had felt in the religious exercises of this place. I shall, however, be excused if I just observe that his hours of religious retirement, whether on land or at sea, were employed in reviewing the notes he had taken of sermons delivered here. 'And these,' adds he, 'are the songs in the house of my pilgrimage. Oh, sir, how many Sabbaths have I ardently longed to spend in Wild Street. God in Christ is my rock, the portion of my soul.'"

Dr. Stennett had a remarkable ancestry. His father, Joseph Stennett, occupied the same pulpit before him ; and his grandfather, another Joseph, was a distinguished seventh-day Baptist in the reign of William IV., celebrated in John Dunton's doggerel as—

> " Stennett the patron and the rule of wit,
>   The pulpit's honour and the saints' delight."

Dr. Stennett, the grandson, was more than fifty

---

[1] This letter is printed in the " Brief History."

years member of the Wild Street Church, and forty-seven of them its minister ; having assisted his father some time before he himself became sole pastor. He published several volumes, amongst them one, once rather popular, on " The Parable of the Sower" ; and historians of Dissent have said, that "in a soft, tender, and insinuating persuasion and influence he was a master." [1]

The decay of the neighbourhood whither Howard wended his way on Sundays has increased since then. Sunday traffic is carried on there now, vegetables are exposed for sale, and plenty of fowls may be seen feeding on scattered garbage. Amidst it all a Mission Chapel has been built of late on the site of the old meeting-house, where good work is being done. The beneficent spirit of Howard lives in that neighbourhood still.[2]

Having glanced at Howard's private life in Cardington and London, we turn to look at his appearance and general habits.

He is described as of middle height, with " a speaking" benevolence in his face, and when young decidedly handsome. A rude engraving represents him with a wig, cocked hat in hand, ruffles at the wrists, buckles on his shoes, and in attitude resembling a polite Frenchman. He is thus portrayed by one who knew him. " Personally, John Howard was about the middle size, stout and well-made, dark complexion, with dark quick eyes and aquiline nose.

---

[1] Bogue and Bennett, Hist. of Dissenters, vol. ii., p. 650.

[2] Lord Justice Lush, as a young man, worshipped in Wild Street ; and it is to his family that the work here noted is chiefly owing.

He used to wear a bag wig, and had much the air of a foreigner."[1]

William Brodie Gurney, the short-hand writer, and one of the founders of the Sunday School Union, delighted to tell how, when a boy, he had seen Howard "in his pepper-and-salt coat, scarlet waistcoat, and cocked hat."

His voice, which was musical, his countenance combining humour and gravity, his manner of conversation, at once courteous and courageous, attracted the timid and over-awed the bold. Above all, he had an imperial decision which none could resist. Of his personal influence we have seen a proof in his Savoy prison exploit. Another of a different kind has been recorded. When Ryland, the engraver, was under sentence of death for having committed forgery, a gentleman told Howard of the mysterious concealment of a servant girl who had lived in the prisoner's family. What became of her no one could say. The condemned man would give no information. The philanthropist undertook to bring her to her friends in twenty-four hours, and he succeeded. Somehow or other he managed to elicit the secret, and to recover the lost.

An individual who professed to know him well, tells us, that when Howard travelled it was usually in the public stage or diligence, and that on the road he would sometimes change name and character with the servant who attended him.

" Persons of all descriptions," he adds, " have obtruded themselves into his presence to catch one glance

---

[1] Cooper MSS. in Bedford Library.

U

of his features ; and indeed so very troublesome and alarming to him did these frequent visits become, that he at last suspected his life to be endangered by the promiscuous admission of strangers. Some particular publications of the Bastille—which he had procured under the disguise of an old fruit-woman, and at the immediate hazard of his life, and which he had printed—gave rise to his fears."

It is also said, by the same authority, "He was invited by Mr. B. Pryce, of Wilton, to dine at his house ; and, as an inducement, that gentleman spoke of the painting and sculpture at Wilton House as worthy of attention. Howard politely assured him 'that he never stopped to see any famous houses or the curiosities they contained.'"[1]

I feel hesitation in repeating these stories. They contain possibly some grains of truth ; at all events they show the interest taken by contemporaries in the private habits of this extraordinary man. But I am satisfied we are on sure ground in what now follows. "No time was lost with him," says his faithful servant, John Prole, "but improved for the most valuable purposes."[2] He calculated how long it would take to walk or ride to fulfil an engagement with such nicety that he seldom was a second behind. The brisk step which tradition ascribes was significant of his active mind ; the neatness of his person and the order of his apparel also corresponded with the

[1] "Anecdotes of the Life and Character of John Howard, Esq., F.R.S., written by a gentleman whose acquaintance with that celebrated philanthropist gave him an opportunity of learning particulars not generally known."

[2] A Father's Legacy to his Children.

method of his plans and the regularity of his life. And with all his self-sacrificing devotion, he did not lack a wise measure of prudence and precaution. When visiting prisons, he used to smell vinegar and change his apparel ; and he was careful, as he states, never to enter an hospital before breakfast, and in offensive rooms never to draw his breath deeply. Moreover he had a great distaste for luxuries. "No parade of equipage, or outward appearance," to quote again the words of his attendant, "no superfluities nor indulgences in eating or drinking ; but the strictest abstinence from everything that could in the least be a let or hindrance to him in performing what he well knew was his incumbent duty as a rational and immortal being, who would be called to a strict and impartial account of the talents with which a good and gracious Creator had endowed him."[1] I may add, that he was entitled to be called a teetotaller and vegetarian. "Animal foods and fermented and spirituous drinks he utterly discarded from his diet. Water and the plainest vegetables sufficed him. Milk, tea, butter, and fruit were his luxuries; and he was equally sparing in the quantity of food and indifferent as to the stated times of taking it. Thus he found his wants supplied in almost every place where man existed, and was as well provided in the posadas of Spain and caravanseras of Turkey as in the inns and hotels of England and France. Water was one of his principal necessaries, for he was a very Mussulman in his ablutions; and if nicety or delicacy had place with him in any respect, it was in the perfect cleanliness of his whole person."[2]

[1] A Father's Legacy to his Children.   [2] Aiken, p. 222.

He could endure what would have been insupportable to most men. In some of his journeys he was subject to distressing privations, to protracted fatigue, to painful illness. We have seen how he travelled off a fit of the ague when travelling in Russia, and how in the Venetian lazaretto, lying amidst water, he employed his time in translating and abridging the rules of the establishment. When from home, he sent letters full of minute directions to his servant, respecting his property. Of this habit I give an example :—

"JOHN PROLE,—I suppose the posts and rails are down ; the quick and hollies all planted ; and that the carpenters at Fenlake are off. Desire Sharp to cut the hedge in Allen Brown's close, as also that at the upper end of Smith's close ; the same as he has done all along the road side.

"Let Mr. Easton go on with the finishing Calleman's house, by putting up the doors, shelves, closets, dressers, etc. ; and to put down the new posts and gates at your pickle ; before which, tell John Joice and Thomas James to range the posts and rails between Gulliver's and the new gates, by putting them more back in the close, as I ordered and their own view will direct, as this post wants coming about a foot out. Tell Mr. Calleman to put down the stones and slabs you brought ; and then, from the front of one of the houses, the width of the stone before the door, dig two spit of mould out of the intended palisade doorway. Carry the mould to the new hedge and then gravel it as a footpath to the house. Let it be done by a line. The four or five load of gravel may be dug from the pit in the close. · Let it be done to either house that I may see it when I come down, which cannot possibly be next week ; but it will be the week after, when I can stay to see very little done, as many affairs take up my time and thoughts. The well, the side of Calleman's house dig out and finish by putting the pump (Mrs. Thody's) down, as it suits to have the labourers. Give yourselves room and do it at once (getting it as deep as possible) by Joe and two or three more hands at work ; the kerb bricks, etc., being all ready for it. Write on Tuesday or Wednesday. Let me know how much wheat and barley we have. Let Joe thresh all the oats out. When will he probably finish ? It is time, the first dry weather, to get the rood of potatoes planted. Be particular as to the quantity. The yard is not now so littery, if Conquest has been a couple of days since.

"I enclosed £10, so you have £20 5s. 8d. in hand. Never hardly was known such a time, nobody will part with any money; the American War, unjust and cruel, has brought the nation into contempt, and many individuals to poverty and misery. You will get Mr. Green's and Mr. Coombs' bills. I will pay and settle everything before I go on my arduous task. Did I not stay myself on a better strength, wisdom, and righteousness than my own, I should faint. I do see my danger by the commotions in Europe, but I bless God my spirits do not fail me.

"Yours,

"J. HOWARD."[1]

---

[1] I copied this from an autograph in the possession of my friend the late Sir Charles Reed. *Pickle* means, enclosure.

Several things are remarkable in this letter. The distinct view which our practical farmer has of his estate, so that it lies like a map before him and he can point to each part without any hesitation; the clear directions, in spite of confused grammar, which he gives to Prole respecting what ought to be done on the farm; the trust in Providence, which cannot be concealed even in a letter consisting of orders to a servant; and an under-current touching the great enterprise of his life. Prison journeys, surrounded by perils, were ever within his view.

He was singularly modest, forming a low estimate of his own character. "I am not at all angry," he once wrote, "with the reflections that some persons make, as they think, to my disparagement; because all they say of this kind gives God the greater honour—in whose Almighty hand no instrument is weak, in whose presence no flesh must glory. The whole conduct of this matter must be ascribed to Providence alone; and God by me intimates to the world, however weak and unworthy I am, that He espouses the cause, and to Him, to Him alone, be the praise."

He shrunk from publicity, and uniformly combated arguments against his scrupulous dislike of it. That dislike, his friend Mr. Smith felt sure, "did not arise from false modesty, or even from any reserve of disposition, but from truly Christian principles, as he would come forward with great readiness and energy whenever he thought he could render a service to his fellow-creatures."

He never wished to be known beyond a circle of chosen friends. These were but few. It is remarkable, that one who occupied so prominent a position on the Continent as well as in England, and could not but have an immense number of casual acquaintances, should have so small a number of intimate associates. The Whitbread family, his pastors Symonds and Smith, with Dr. Stennett and Dr. Price, the Aikens, and perhaps two or three more, exhaust the list. In harmony with the habit which made him shrink from observation during his lifetime, he did all he could to prevent notice being taken of him after his death. Some of his last days were spent in destroying letters and papers which would have been most valuable in the preparation of his Memoirs.

As we have seen, he knew John Wesley; and we meet with him in 1789, calling at City Road Chapel House, to present a copy of the book on Lazarettos. The busy preacher and ecclesiastic was not at home. The author left this message, " Present my respects and love to Mr. Wesley, tell him I had hoped to see him once more—perhaps we may meet again in this world, but if not, we shall meet, I trust, in a better." [1] Wesley was then eighty-six. Howard but sixty-one. There is no account of their meeting afterwards. The next year, in January, the latter was in his Russian grave: the former expired in 1791, aged eighty-eight.

Dr. Lettsom was a distinguished physician, born on a small island of the Atlantic, and sent to England for his education. Here he was received into a family in which a celebrated Quaker minister happened to be residing; and in process of time the young visitor

---

[1] Quoted in Tyerman's Life of Wesley, vol. iii., p. 495.

adopted the tenets of this zealous and persuasive person. An old engraving represents him as a rather prim-looking gentleman in a neatly curled wig, a plain cravat, and a collarless coat. Nichols, the historian of eighteenth century worthies in literature, boasts of his undeviating friendship, which had afforded " most grateful and rational enjoyment," and pronounces him "an ornament to society, the liberal friend to merit, and an example of beneficence to every avenue of human distress." " He was equally distinguished for public and private benevolence, and for every species of useful exertion, both in the medical profession and as a member of society at large."[1]   In illustration of his character there is related an "extraordinary and well-founded fact, of his having been attacked on Finchley Common by a highwayman, with whom his remonstrances and pecuniary assistance operated so powerfully, that in the result a public robber, impelled to transgression by extremity of want, was converted into a useful member of society." This incident was such as to delight Howard. Dr. Lettsom had a villa at Grove Hill, Camberwell,—then a charming rural suburb, eulogized in " an elegant poem " of the period, which describes the interesting scenery and the beautiful landscapes with which it abounded. A museum of natural history, a botanical garden, and a rich library attracted to his residence the virtuosi of the day. Perhaps Howard, who does not seem to have cared much for such objects, never visited " this terrestrial Elysium," but he was one of Lettsom's acquaintances and correspondents.

[1] Nichols' Literary History, vol. ii., p. 657.

It was Lettsom who, in co-operation with the literary printer John Nichols, and a Dr. Warren, not mentioned by Fame, started the idea of a monument. Lettsom, in writing to the typographer when sending a subscription, observes :—

"Persuaded as I am, that his character and writings will survive the most durable monument of friendship; yet such an example of approbation appears to me calculated to promote many beneficial purposes, though it cannot augment the zeal of this amiable man in the pursuit of lessening human misery. Public approbation of private and public virtues, whilst it acknowledges a debt due to intrinsic merit, reflects the highest honour on the community; for to reward virtue is a pleasing proof of its prevalence, and that it does prevail, the monument of Howard will testify. Virtue, whether shining in the public walks of life, or emitting the soft rays of human benevolence in the dungeons of misery, will ever obtain its own reward beyond all the powers of sculpture; but to exhibit that evidence to the public, to excite emulation in virtuous pursuits, and to induce spectators to go and do likewise, nothing seems more conducive than a monument to Howard. The present moment, during his absence in Turkey, is the most proper to accomplish such a design. With goodness of heart, he unites exemplary humility, and a perfection of mind rarely equalled is veiled by a modesty that shuns praise and adulation; but the public applause, which is due to great and virtuous actions, cannot be ungrateful to the God-like breast of Howard." [1]

[1] Nichols' Literary History, vol. ii., p. 682.

Lettsom called on Howard, to overcome his obstinate scruples to accept this public testimonial ; but all in vain. Two or three hours' attempted persuasion produced not the slightest effect.

Capel Loft, who patronized rising merit and cheered the heart of Kirke White by his sympathy and praise, when stung by the attacks of heartless reviewers, is also numbered in the circle of Howard's acquaintances. Another is found in the famous Dr. Warton, historian and critic of English poetry ; and of this fact I find a memento in a copy of the " State of Prisons,"—now on the shelf of the Athenæum Club Library,—containing an inscription of his name as a " friend," written by the author. Another literary man Hayley, author of the " Life of Cowper," belonged to the class of Howard's admirers ; and this is demonstrated in an anonymous book entitled : " The Eulogies of Howard : a Vision "—a singularly strange production. " I am," says Hayley, writing in 1791, " particularly desirous that the author of the little work I have mentioned may for the present remain unknown. That it may not appear even at the press in my hand, I must still detain the manuscript about a week, till I can get it copied under my own roof. I flatter myself, however, you will receive pleasure when I tell you that the chief aim of this performance is to honour the memory of our departed friend, the excellent Howard, with a view to quicken and extend the generosity of the nation in subscribing to his monument." The work is in prose, and entitled " The Eulogies of Howard: a Vision." " To show how much all ranks of men are interested in his glory, I have represented, in this visionary form, persons of different professions pronouncing different panegyrics on his incomparable character. The work altogether does not amount to a hundred pages." [1]

This curious letter is addressed to Mr. Nichols; and in an earlier one, dated 1789, Hayley mentions a printer's proof of "The Young Widow," a novel he had written, saying, "If it be ready, be so good as to despatch it by Tuesday's coach, with a line to tell me if you received my letter to Mr. Howard, and if it has found him in England." The absurd vision represents Heaven, where eulogies are pronounced on the philanthropist, and a funeral sermon is delivered.

Here, before I proceed any further, I may fittingly introduce the sequel of Howard's sad domestic story; and it is a painful task. His son when about nine years old, just as his father had determined to travel abroad, was placed in an Academy at Pinner, no long drive from the residence of his aunt, then living in Ormond Street. With his aunt the boy spent his holidays during his parent's absence. About the time of her death he was removed to an Academy at Daventry, which had been under the care of Dr. Doddridge, at Northampton. To this circumstance, it may be, we are to attribute the once current report that Howard purposed making his son an Independent minister. As John Howard's father had sent him as a lay pupil to an academy for the education of ministers, so John Howard himself sent his boy to an institution of the same kind. Neither of them, in doing this, thought of the holy office. When the boy went to Daventry he was too young for his father

[1] Nichols' Literary History, vol. iv., p. 741.

to have a purpose in that direction. But this should
be noticed : the tutor, Mr. Robins—eulogized by
Robert Hall, for "delicacy of taste and elegance of
diction," and as having imparted to that great pulpit
orator his first perception of those qualities, as he
heard him preach—must have been a teacher of no
mean order, and the lad, therefore, enjoyed distinguished advantages. During his parent's absence
he had the additional benefit of Mr. Smith's care ;
that gentleman "considering him a charge over which
he was bound to watch with as unceasing a solicitude
as he felt for his own children. He, therefore, at his
father's request, often wrote to him at school, giving
him the same excellent advice as was contained in
the very affectionate letters which that father himself
frequently addressed to him during the course of his
various tours." [1]

At this early period there is no reason to doubt
the boy's filial affection. Though he had been taught
to submit implicitly to parental commands, he had
loved as well as feared his father, and was accustomed, at a later period, to speak of him with reverence. But an evil power, so it is said, worked in a
contrary direction. A servant named Thomasson,
standing high in Howard's estimation, gained an as-
cendency over the stripling, and turned it to the
worst of purposes. When the latter was rising out
of boyhood, the former led him into temptation. In
London, at Ormond Street, he had opportunities of
doing so ; and he employed them, we are assured,
in a manner truly diabolical. Nor were there wanting

[1] Brown, p. 406.

people who, looking with a jealous eye on the far-famed parent, insinuated that he was spending money upon amiable eccentricities, which ought to be saved for his son and heir. To the credit of the misguided youth, however, it is recorded that he said himself when such insinuations reached his ear, "What good can I do with money, which will bear any comparison with the good he has done?" Howard became too late aware of what went on; and when his son was eighteen or nineteen, he took him to Edinburgh, and placed him under the care of Dr. Blacklock. But habits of dissipation had taken too strong a hold to be destroyed, or even checked, by judicious discipline. He is described as having been, at that time, "a fine, tall, pleasing, and promising young man." Soon afterwards signs of mental aberration made their appearance. These were betrayed in his intercourse with fellow-students; "but whatever was the prevailing disposition of the moment, if the name of his father was mentioned he never failed to manifest the strongest degree of filial affection, and spoke of him with that exultation which manifested the pride he took in his descent." Removed from Edinburgh, he came to reside at Cardington, where he lived in greater style than ever his father did.

Now came a change of disposition. He could not bear his father's expostulations, he had independent property, and therefore did not rely upon resources beyond his own; yet no open breach occurred, for when, in 1784, he entered St. John's College, Cambridge, as a gentleman commoner, his father introduced him to particular friends, including the Baptist minister, Robert Robinson, predecessor of Robert

Hall, in the University town. In spite of all that could be done, young Howard became worse and worse; insanity took a decided form. He vexed the authorities, frightened the gownsmen, played mad tricks in the neighbourhood, turned against his friends, became the enemy of his tempter—and altogether behaved in such a way, that the maternal uncles engaged two keepers from an asylum to remove the young man to Cardington, where he was kept under restraint.

Of course, Howard has been reproached for what happened. Many think that personal superintendence of his son's education might have prevented the mischief—that home interests were neglected, and that *therefore* the child of his beloved wife fell into evil hands. The fact is, Howard, feeling himself called to fulfil a mission which took him far from home, it was a matter of necessity, if he obeyed the call, that he should devolve the education of his son on other people. Whether, for the sake of one's own child, a work for the welfare of multitudes in all coming time should be set aside, is a case on which different persons would give different opinions. But no one reflecting on the habits of Howard's mind and the peculiar genius of his character leading him to sacrifice the individual to the universal, will wonder at the conviction which *he* formed of his own duty. At the same time, it is plain he did not think his son's proper education need be neglected. Nor can he be charged with omitting such attention to his son as philanthropic toils allowed. His letters and memoranda, when abroad, contain proofs how near his heart lay the welfare of the child; for a man who used terms of endearment as real coin, not as mere counters, could scarcely be wanting in parental attachment. That the son, whilst sane, felt convinced of his affectionate solicitude, is evident from the fact that, when once asked whether his father would not be angry, he answered, "*Not angry, but unhappy.*"

Yet, after all, whilst admitting what may be urged in Howard's excuse, I am constrained to say that he thought too much of parental authority as being *absolute kingship*, to which implicit submission was due ; and further, I confess that his idea of the end of education, as being to teach obedience rather than to inspire love, is not the true idea. Therefore I must think that in this respect he erred, yet that he was cruel appears entirely false.

A distinction is to be made between the man and his method. He is to be judged by the times in which he lived, his method is to be judged by unchangeable principles. In his day, ideas of parental and school discipline were different from what they happily are now. They were based more on the inspiration of fear than on the inspiration of love. They were stern, rather than amiable. A father was a ruler, the child a subject; a schoolmaster wielded the rod, a pupil expected stripes. There was no mutual confidence. Busby, not Arnold, was a type of past pedagogues. This must be remembered. In prison management Howard was above his age, in educational rule he was on a level with it. Much may be said in excuse of the man, nothing in excuse of the system.

A letter published not long ago for the first time, brings to light the condition of Howard's private affairs in 1785.   Not from a profuse expenditure in housekeeping, or on works of art, but from his "reforming schemes," as he called them, he anticipated pecuniary difficulties.

In a letter from Cardington, written on June the 21st, of the year just mentioned, he entrusted Mr. Whitbread with "a secret," namely—that about Christmas he would probably take a final leave of Cardington.   He adds, "You might guess, that prior to my sister's death, I was somewhat involved by my reforming schemes.   Her death, and her great kindness to me,[1] enlarged my ideas, and I persevered ; though I foresaw the prosecution thereof would prevent my living in the easy manner I had done. Viewing the great expense thereof, and knowing that with my very moderate parts, nothing but a long and continued application to the subject would carry me through it, I did not allow myself my natural rest, and for some years hardly the necessaries of life.   I quitted my town house (where I know not that there were a dozen joints of meat in the seven years) and came to Cardington.   Some money I have laid out in necessary repairs, and every bill was paid to Lady day ; but I do see that with strictest economy here, my expenses will exceed my actual certain income, so I propose living in some airy lodgings in town, and perhaps, with my attendance on the hospitals of which I am Governor, I may wear out my life usefully."

Mr. Whitbread replied that the news "struck him

---

[1] She bequeathed him about £20,000, as well as the house in Ormond Street.

like an alarum bell," adding, "it requires revising again and again." Howard did not finally leave Cardington, probably influenced by his friend's wise expostulations.

A letter at a later period addressed by him to the same gentleman, indicates the strong determination Howard felt to accomplish his last great journey :—

"Affliction you know I have, but I am not cast down, and I shall face every danger with calmness and resolution; and should it please God to give me the health and strength I now enjoy, I shall endeavour to take a far more extensive journey than I have yet taken. As to a return to my own country, there is little probability of it. I have a firm and fixed determination, and that tried at the bar of a calm judgment, that a retirement to ease would be cowardly, sinful, and base. The season of zeal and activity is passing away, and fain would I give some check to greater ravages than any occasioned by the destructive weapons of war. Harriet[1] and my younger friends will rank me with enthusiasts; but probably that they have long done; yet have patience with me, for *finis coronat opus.*"[2]

Shortly before Howard left Cardington for the last time, an incident occurred in the Whitbread family calculated to give him pleasure. His young friend, Samuel Whitbread, had been educated at Eton, and then removed to St. John's College, Cambridge. He came of age in 1778; and probably it was somewhere about that time that he made the grand tour

---

[1] Mr. Whitbread's daughter.

[2] This letter is dated, Cork, May 12th, 1788.

X

of Europe under the companionship of a gentleman afterwards known as Archdeacon Coxe. Coxe was a great Whig, and in politics agreed with John Howard ; and beforehand, as well as when they were on their travels, Howard would be sure to feel an interest in the plans and adventures of the tourists, being himself so well acquainted with their route. But the event to which I more particularly refer, is the marriage in 1789 of Mr. Whitbread. He then was united to Lady Elizabeth, eldest daughter of the first Earl Grey ; and six years later the lady's brother, Sir Charles, married the bridegroom's sister. In 1790 Mr. Whitbread, the son, entered Parliament as member for the borough of Steyning, and distinguished himself as a strenuous supporter of the Whig party. Such an event would probably be anticipated by Howard ; and when his eyes were for ever closed, the rising statesman did not fail to mark the philanthropist's memory with expressions of love and honour.

This chapter may be fitly closed with an extract from a letter written by Lucy Aiken, daughter of John Aiken, M.D., and niece of Mrs. Barbauld :—

"Several months ago you asked me whether I had not seen Howard, the patriarch of English philanthropists. I answered that I had ; and that, eight years' child as I was, I retained the most distinct recollection of his person, his manners, and his interesting conversation with us children, to whom he was ever full of kindness.

"It was in the summer of 1789 that John Howard, previous to setting out on his last mission, passed ten days at Yarmouth in consultation with my father.

Child as I was, the impression he made on me was indelible: a small man, brisk in his movements, with a lively eye and expressive countenance, extremely fond of children, and entertaining them with narrations fitted to them. His image is still before my eyes." [1]

[1] Memories of Seventy Years.

CHAPTER XIV.

HIS LAST JOURNEY.

1789, 1790.

HOWARD determined on another expedition to foreign fields. His object—not definitely indicated by himself, but guessed at by intimate friends—seems to have been to explore regions entirely new to him, such as Asiatic Turkey, the land of Egypt, and the coasts of Barbary; and also, by retraversing old ground, to detect aspects of things he had before overlooked, and to gather fresh material for enforcing lessons of improvement. "If to these motives be added the long-formed habitude of pursuing a certain track of inquiry, and an inquietude of mind proceeding from domestic misfortune, no cause will be left to wonder at so speedy a renewal of his toils and dangers."[1]

It is sometimes given to the children of mortality to detect in the distance a gathering of the death cloud. The dark shadow is discerned moving across the landscape. Howard was one in whom this presentiment was strong. Even in his second book on prisons, when announcing his intention to revisit Russia and other countries, he remarked he was not

---

[1] Aiken, p. 184.

insensible of the dangers attending the journey, yet he could calmly resign himself to the disposal of unerring Wisdom. " Should it please God," he went on to say, "to cut off my life in the prosecution of this design, let not my conduct be uncandidly imputed to rashness or enthusiasm, but to a serious, deliberate conviction that I am pursuing the path of duty, and to a sincere desire of being made an instrument of more extensive usefulness to my fellow-creatures than could be expected in the narrower circle of a retired life."

The apprehension which he publicly avowed was privately expressed in more touching tones. To one he said, " If we never meet each other more below, I trust we shall meet in heaven ";—to another, " You will probably never see me again, but be that as it may, it is a matter of no concern to me whether I lay down my life in Turkey, in Egypt, in Asia Minor, or elsewhere ";—to a third, " We shall soon meet in heaven, and the way to heaven from Grand Cairo is as near as from London ";—to a fourth, " I am going a very arduous journey. Probably, my friend, we shall never meet any more in this world ; but it is the path of duty ; and with respect to myself, I am quite resigned to the will of God." It is remarkable that amongst the countries where he anticipated danger, it does not appear that he mentioned Russia.

Before his departure, he made a will specifying certain characteristic bequests. A considerable part of his property, after providing for his son, he left to the poor. It included a donation of five pounds each to ten Cardington cottagers who had not been in an alehouse for twelve months preceding his death ; a

like donation to ten poor families who had been
most constant in attending Divine worship during
the same period ; and fifty pounds to the poor of
the parish " where he married his last invaluable
wife." His servants were all remembered. His body
was to be buried wherever he died, and the cost of
the funeral was not to exceed ten or fifteen guineas.
By a codicil he directed five hundred pounds to be
applied for alleviating the miseries of public prisons.[1]

He gave directions to his friend and pastor, Mr.
Smith, as to the text from which he was to preach a
funeral sermon, in case of the journey proving fatal.
The text is the last verse of the seventeenth psalm.
" That text," said he, " is the most appropriate to my
feelings of any I know, for I can indeed join with the
Psalmist in saying, ' As for me, I will behold Thy
face in righteousness : I shall be satisfied, when I
awake, with Thy likeness.' At the same time he laid
a strong embargo on any attempt to hold him up to
the admiration of survivors."

There were many leave-takings on the eve of this
last journey. Among the letters of Ridley, the mar-
tyr, is one written on the eve of his fiery trial, in which
he reviews scenes and companions much endeared,

---

[1] " When Mr. Howard was making his will, and had named
all his relations, his legal adviser said to him, ' Whose name
shall we add as your heir, in case all these should die ?' Mr.
Howard replied, turning to Mr. Whitbread, who had entered
the room, ' My friend here ; I will leave it to his second son.'
Mr. Howard's relations died, and my father, Samuel Charles
Whitbread, the second surviving son, inherited Mr. Howard's
property at Cardington." I give this interesting anecdote as
communicated to me by Miss Whitbread, who resides in the
Cardington House.

and by name bids farewell to each. It is unutterably solemn—this shaking hands with old friends, and especially with Time itself, the oldest of all, under the shadow of the eternal doorway. Howard seems to have gone about in a very tender, subdued spirit, bidding *good-bye* to one after another, especially the members of the Whitbread family. He had a loving interview with Mr. Smith, in which he commended to him the oversight of the Cardington schools. The last night he walked round the dear old garden, with Joshua Crockford, and took a parting look at the firs planted by Henrietta, thinking that now at last everything had been arranged as she would have liked. He called at John Prole's cottage and gave the good wife two relics—her lady's miniature, and a little tea-caddy. Such treasures were carefully preserved, and more than sixty years afterwards were publicly exhibited at Bedford in Howard's Chapel, as the meeting-house where he worshipped came to be called. Mention was made of an ivory thimble which Howard had carved in early days and given to Henrietta before her marriage, being found in a work-box after her death. It was bestowed on her lady's-maid as an heirloom. It remained in the possession of the Prole family.

Howard set out on horseback for London accompanied by the faithful old servant, to whose dame, already enriched with presents, the master gave a guinea in compensation, as he said, for her husband's loss of time. So he rode away—for ever. Arrived in London, he sent back his trusty domestic, saying, "John, these two horses are yours when you get home"; and to this gift he added a large parcel of

tea and sugar for his wife, who was a favourite with
Howard as she had been with his wife.

It is a great mystery,—after reading the accounts
by Howard's biographers of Thomasson having been
the ruin of the son,—to find in the will, made when
all the mischief had been done, and within a year of
Howard's death, this same Thomasson named as
an annuitant of ten pounds for life. It is even still
more strange, to find this man accompanying his
master in the last journey abroad, and attending him
in his dying moments, apparently without having
forfeited his confidence. It would seem, from these
circumstances, that the father could not have believed
reports about him circulated by fellow-servants and
other persons ; but the puzzle involved in the affair
no one has explained, and we must leave it as it is,
amongst the hidden things of this world.

It is, however, to be remembered, that the evidence
against Thomasson rested on incidents of misbe-
haviour and treachery of which his master had no
personal cognisance, that Thomasson, before his
misconduct, had been a favourite servant, possessed
of his master's confidence, that, afterwards, when suspected by people about him, he would cunningly
do all he could to retain his master's good-will, that
the testimony of other servants against him might
be put down to the account of either prejudice or
jealousy, and finally, that there was this peculiarity in
Howard—he had a high opinion of his own judgment,
paid little attention to what other people said, if he
did not like it, and made up his mind upon what
he saw, or could ascertain by personal investigations.

Early in July, 1789, he embarked for Holland, and on reaching the capital, wrote to Mr. Whitbread.

"Amsterdam, July 10*th,* 1789.

" As to my affairs, I am perfectly easy about them. Having food and raiment, I trust I shall be content. I have lately seen how unfit I am to bustle in the world. My affairs are pretty clear."

From Amsterdam he travelled to Utrecht; and the subject at that time uppermost in his mind, appears in his note-book. " It is very probable that the plague flies about from one country to another, as accident or negligence gives it opportunity ; so that disease rises spontaneously, that is, without our being able to trace its imported infection, though it must have originally taken its rise in some particular place, as perhaps in Egypt or the coast of Barbary. Important is the inquiry whether it is ever found thus to arise spontaneously. But as to the nature or cause of this malady, I don't entertain much hope of seeing that investigated and ascertained with precision, any more than the essence or cause of the small-pox or measles. I would look to the moral source, from whence all evil and suffering have been derived, and would at least endeavour to diminish their bitterness."

Whilst at Utrecht, he departed from his usual practice of declining invitations to dinner. His friend Dr. Brown, under whose roof he sojourned, relates the following incident :

" There resided at this time in Utrecht a very worthy and humane gentleman of the name of Loten, who had been for many years the Dutch Governor of

Ceylon. I had the honour of his particular acquaintance; and he expressed to me the strong desire he felt to be introduced to Mr. Howard, though, as he was confined to his house by asthma, he could not go out to wait on him. I mentioned this circumstance to Mr. Howard, and described to him Mr. Loten's character in that amiable point of view in which it so fully deserved to be placed. The philanthropist immediately requested me to introduce him to my friend, and added, ' For such a man as you have described this gentleman to me, I will depart from my rule; and if he does me the honour of asking me to dinner, I will certainly accept the invitation.' This reply I reported to Mr. Loten, and he sent an immediate invitation to Mr. Howard, who dined with him accordingly, though without violating his constant regimen, in abstaining from animal food and wine." [1]

Leaving Utrecht, he went to Osnaburgh in Germany, to find prisoners in noxious cells, ironed hand and foot; and to Hanover, to find torture perpetuated —a circumstance which so depressed him that he exclaimed, "Have I not reason with a sigh to say, I labour in vain and spend my strength for nought? But I have resolved by the help of God to give myself wholly to this work."

At Brunswick, he learned that eighteen years had elapsed since torture was practised, and the chamber had not since been opened.

He called on a public executioner—an official holding a different position from his pitiable compeers

---

[1] Brown, p. 564.

in this country[1]—and saw horrid instruments, then unused. The man seems to have been very communicative on points connected with his dreadful calling, and informed his visitor that he had "been several years in that occupation at Hanover, though here," in Brunswick, "he had only beheaded four or five." On his being asked if nothing was put into a tortured person's mouth, he replied, "No; the Osnaburgh executioner thinks they suffer less,"—and on his describing some. modes "which the art of devils and men had invented," he said, "Sir, the Osnaburgh torture is still ruder."

Places next mentioned are Berlin,—where men and women were seen marching about in "the Spanish mantle;"—and Spandau, where he met with an Englishman as gaoler;—and Könisberg, where people were sent "to perish from nastiness and neglect." He begged that irons might be taken off some who were dying; and says the very magistrates who accompanied him "were covered with vermin." At Riga, he entered within the Russian confines. Here, in the military hospital, he found "three hundred sick, crammed into two dirty and offensive wards;" and he learned, without surprise, that five hundred recruits had lately died there. Men with slit nostrils and scarred cheeks appeared in a prison ten miles from Riga; and he was told how the head knout-master at St. Petersburg had quarrelled with two of his colleagues, and had struck off the heads of both, in a

---

[1] I remember lighting some time ago upon a funeral sermon preached by a German divine on the death of an executioner, in which he is described as an important functionary, and as having been a most exemplary character.

fit of passion. For this, he was sentenced to two hundred and seventy strokes of the knout, and imprisonment for the rest of life.

Together with the nature of the plague, the subject of vegetable diet occupied much of his attention; and at Riga he wrote in his pocket-book on the 23rd of August,[1] "I am firmly persuaded, as to the health of our bodies, herbs and fruits will sustain nature in every respect far beyond the best flesh meat. Is there any comparison to be made between a herb market and a flesh market? The Lord planted a garden for mankind in the beginning, and replenished it with all manner of fruits and herbs;—this was the place ordained for man: if these had still been the food of man, he would not have contracted so many diseases in his body, nor cruel vices in his soul. The taste of most sorts of flesh is disagreeable to those who for any time abstain from it; and none can be competent judges of what I say, but those who have made trial of it.

"I hope I have sources of enjoyment that depend not on the particular place I inhabit; a rightly cultivated mind under the power of religion, and the exertion of beneficent dispositions are a ground of satisfaction little affected by *heres* and *theres.*

"I hope my soul thirsts for the ordinances of God's house, which I am this day deprived of, but I will make it a day of rest. Through mercy brought here in safety, I have this morning read over some solemn transactions of my soul many years past,

---

[1] This and other extracts from the pocket-book are given by Brown, and repeated by Field.

and in the most solemn and devout manner renew those vows, which, alas, have been too often broken, and acknowledge Thee the Almighty Jehovah for my Lord and my God. O God, hear my prayer, and let my cry come before Thee."

Here, simply for his own use, he refers to a Covenant made at home with God long before : and he now devoutly renews it in a land of strangers.

At St. Petersburg he found things much in the same state as they had been eight years before, except that a new House of Correction was almost finished. In hospitals judicious improvements had taken place. He inspected the Foundling and another Institute for the practice of inoculation; and with regard to opinions of what he saw, the travelling critic was as outspoken as usual. The Marine Hospital at Cronstadt appeared to him worse than ever. He wrote home to Mr. Whitbread, " Let us, my dear friend, think of the mercies of so long a life, and offer up songs of praise. Our souls break 'the mist of human things' and know their emptiness. Ere long we shall be gathered to our fathers, not scattered and lost in the abyss of annihilation, for we know that our Redeemer liveth ; we are going to a land peopled with our fathers and our kindred and the friends of our youth. This makes us, even amidst our doubts and fears, cry out, 'I would not live always.'"

" *St. Petersburg. Sunday, Sept. 6th,* 1789."

He proceeded to Moscow, with which Englishmen are now much better acquainted than they were then. In a prison he noticed the want of bedding for the sick, though in one room were eighty-eight men, several of them in a state of high fever; prisoners subsisted on charitable contributions, and did not seem to be in lack of necessaries. " Hence," he says, "I conclude that the nation is humane; and in travelling through a great tract of the country, the peasants appear to me of a kind and hospitable disposition." One prison he saw, he pronounced "a disgrace to any civilized country."

From Moscow he wrote to Dr. Price. The letter contained a notice of his plans, and a forewarning of his fate—"I arrived a few days ago in this city, and have begun my rounds. The hospitals are in a sad state; upwards of seventy thousand sailors and recruits died in them last year. I labour to convey the torch of philanthropy into these distant regions, as in God's hands no instrument is weak, in whose presence no flesh must glory. I go through Poland into Hungary. I hope to have a few nights of this moon in my journey to Warsaw, which is about a thousand miles. I am quite well, the weather clear, the mornings fresh, thermometer 48°, but have not yet begun fires. I wish for a mild winter, and shall then make some progress in my European expedition. My medical acquaintance give me but little hope of escaping the plague in Turkey; but my spirits do not at all fail me; and indeed I do not look back, but would readily endure any hardships and encounter any dangers to be an honour to my Christian profession."

In this journey, as in others, he diverged from his intended route, and hastened through the deserts of Tartary to the Euxine Sea.

Vast plans rose on his mind : one country after

another, one city after another opened before him,
but he would first see more of Russian hospitals. So
he accomplished a long, dreary journey to Crements-
chuok, on the banks of the river Dnieper, proceeding
thence to Cherson.

Cherson, or Kherson, is a town near the mouth
of the Dnieper on the shores of the Black Sea. It
was built by Prince Potemkin so late as 1778; and
in Howard's time, though young, was of importance,
but it declined as Odessa rose. It consists of four
divisions—the Citadel, the Admiralty, the Greek
suburb, and the military suburb. The population,
thirty years ago, amounted to thirty thousand. It
has a Cathedral, Courts of Justice, and Government
offices, with extensive docks and barracks. In the
eyes of Englishmen it possesses a claim to particular
notice from its connection with Howard in his last
days; and what we know of it forms the background
of our final story.

He wrote from this place to Mr. Whitbread,—

"Cherson in Tartary, Nov. 14th, 1789.

"I was somewhat sensible of the dangers I had to
encounter and the hardships I had to endure in a
journey thirteen or fourteen hundred miles with only
my servant. I went on pretty well till on the
borders of Tartary, when, as I depended on my
patent chain, my great trunk and hat-box were cut
off from behind my chaise. It was midnight, and
both of us having travelled for four nights, were fast
asleep. However we soon discovered it, and having
soon recovered the shock, I went back directly to
the suspected house and ran in among ten or twelve

of the banditti. At break of day I had some secured, and search made; my hat-box was found, but my great trunk I almost despaired of, though I stayed before the door in my chaise two days. Providentially the fourth day it was found by a peasant. The brass nails glistened in a part where the oilskin was worn. His oxen would not go on, he beat them, but they would not go on, he then saw something, but durst not approach till another peasant came up; when, after signing themselves with the cross, they went up to it and carried it directly to the magistrate of the village. He sent after me to a town about eighty miles off, where I was to stay two or three days, and I returned. I found by my inventory that not a single handkerchief was lost; and they missed about a hundred guineas in a paper, in the middle of the trunk. My return stunned them, all would have been moved off before light. I have broken up the band; four will go into—— I am well.

"The wild Cossacks who live underground in the Crimea, must look sharp if they rob me, as I will not go to sleep any night on the road, and I am well armed. I am persuaded no hurry or fear will be on my mind. My journey, I still think, will engage me for three years; and as I have a year's work in England, I think little of Cardington.

"The land for several hundred miles is the finest garden mould, not a stone mixed with it, not a single tree, nor any inhabitants. A person may have any quantity for ten years, and after that, by paying the Empress fifteen roubles (about 1¾ guineas) a year. Fine haystacks a person showed me; two-thirds he took, and one-third he gave the Empress, but no rent."

A fragment from a letter written at Cherson, dated November 17th, has been preserved, in which he says, "Many here are shivering with the ague, and a morass of twenty miles is before my window. I give the ounce of bark and drachm of snakeroot and wormwood, which has not failed me once." He goes on to say, seventy thousand recruits had died in Russia the preceding year.

In Cherson he received a newspaper in which he read with joy an account of the fall of the Bastille ; presently we find him plunging again into prison work, and off through a treeless country to a place he calls Witowka, where he saw "many brave fellows who had fought well for their country before Otschakov, suffered to perish with filth, neglect, and vermin." Others were lying dead by the road side. He laboriously sought, first to measure, and next to remedy the distressing evils before him ; and, though he had to deal with people who, as he suspected, were ready to impose on him, he succeeded to some extent in his benevolent designs. At this time, in a more than usually pathetic vein, he expressed his feelings, dwelling upon the condition of exiles, forced from their homes and dearest connexions, and comparing them with others, cheerful and happy at a wedding or village festival. "Let them," he says, "be viewed quitting their birth-place, with all their little wardrobe, and their pockets stored with roubles, the gifts of their relations, who never expect to see them more ; now joining their corps in a long march of two or three thousand versts ; their money gone to the officer, who conducts them and defrauds them of the allowance ; arriving fatigued and half-naked in a distant dreary country, and exposed immediately to military hardships with harassed bodies and dejected spirits; who can wonder that so many droop and die in a short time without any apparent illness? The devastations I have seen made by war among so many innocent people, and this in a country where there are such immense tracts of land unoccupied, are shocking to human nature."

At Cherson, great preparation had been made in expectation of the renowned visitor: the shifting of patients, the coverlids on beds, and the presence of surgeons waiting to receive him, showed an anxiety to make a favourable impression, but he had not faith in his own influence over them. He told the officers, "that in none of the countries he had ever visited had he found so little attention paid to the military as in Russia. He knew, however, what he said would have no other effect on them, but to make them despise him; he should, however, assuredly relate, what he had beheld with so much concern and indignation."

About that time he wrote the following sentences in his journal :—

"May I not look on present difficulties, or think of future ones in this world as I am but a pilgrim or wayfaring man, that tarries but a night; this is not my home, but may I think what God has done for me, and rely on His power and His grace, for His promise is, His mercy endureth for ever: but I am faint and low, yet I trust in the right way pursuing, though too apt to forget my Almighty Friend and my God. Oh! my soul, remember and record how often God has sent an answer of peace. Mercies in the most seasonable times, how often, better than thy fears, exceeded thy expectations. Why should I distrust this good and faithful God? In His word, He has said, 'In all thy ways acknowledge Him, and He will direct thy path.' Lord, leave me not to my own wisdom which is folly, not to my own strength which is weakness. Help me to glorify *Thee* on earth, and finish the work *Thou* givest me to do; and to *Thy* name *alone* be all the praise."

The last entry in his memorandum book indicates his opinions on the Temperance question.

"How many patients do I see," he exclaims, "in many disorders, which, I am persuaded proceed from the use of spirituous liquors! What strict care should be taken that the attendants do not bring any to sell in the hospital! Have I not seen unmixed spirits served round to sick and dying patients by persons intoxicated themselves, when to my great surprise I was told that the physician had ordered it as a *treat* to the patients! If my visits had any share in promoting this, I fear I killed half a dozen of them; or, at least, put them some days sooner out of their misery!"

Russia now was at war with Turkey. The fortress of Bender—higher up the Dnieper, near which Charles XII. of Sweden found a retreat after the battle of Pultawa in 1709—fell before the victorious arms of the great Northern Power, just after Howard's arrival at Cherson. Pausing in a career of conquest on account of the season, the general allowed his officers to visit the Russian port. Accordingly they flocked into the new city, and were welcomed with rejoicings. Balls, masquerades, and other scenes of gaiety made winter evenings bright as day, and filled many a young heart with gladness, soon to be dashed with terrible sorrow. For, as, in Brussels, a midnight dance was followed by death at Waterloo, so, in Cherson, festivities were succeeded by an outbreak of fever, which the soldiers had brought from Bender. A lady of sixteen was attacked, and her friends, hearing of Howard's skill, sent for him. At first, from various unselfish reasons, he hesitated to comply, but afterwards he paid her more than one visit, requesting he might be informed of the effect of the medicine he prescribed. A letter to him was delayed for eight days, and when he received it he resolved at once, on a rainy night intensely cold, to ride to his patient on a dray horse, for he could procure no better animal. He sat down by the bedside and watched her till morning. That day she died ; and at the same time the visitor felt he had caught the fever.

Returning to Cherson, he remained in his lodging a day or two, after which he was able to visit Admiral Mordvinof. He stayed later than usual, and on reaching home, took *sal volatile* in a little tea. He appeared better, but soon had a violent attack, accompanied by fits, which made his face black and his breathing difficult.

Prince Potemkin sent a physician; and his friend, Admiral Priestman, paid him assiduous attentions. One day he found him sitting by the stove in his bedroom, exceedingly ill. After a vain attempt by the visitor to rally the patient's spirits, the latter solemnly replied, "Priestman, you style this a dull conversation, and endeavour to divert my mind from dwelling upon death; but I entertain very different sentiments.

Death has no terrors for me ; it is an event I always look forward to with cheerfulness, if not with pleasure, and be assured the subject is more grateful to me than any other. I am well aware that I have but a short time to live, and my mode of life has rendered it impossible that I should get rid of this fever. If I had lived as you do, eating heartily of animal food and drinking wine, I might, perhaps, by altering my diet, be able to subdue it. But how can such a man as I am lower his diet, who has been accustomed for years to live upon vegetables and water, a little bread and a little tea ? I have no method of lowering my nourishment, and therefore I must die. It is such jolly fellows as you, Priestman, who get over these fevers."

He then gave directions respecting his funeral. "There is a spot near the village of Dauphiné, this would suit me nicely ; you know it well, for I have often said I should like to be buried there. And let me beg of you, as you value your old friend, not to suffer any pomp to be used at my funeral, nor any monument, nor monumental inscription whatsoever to mark where I am laid ; but lay me quietly in the earth, place a sun-dial over my grave, and let me be forgotten."

He further requested that the burial service of the Church of England should be read over his remains. A letter came from England just at the last, containing a hopeful account of his poor son.

"Is not this comfort for a dying father ? " he exclaimed.[1]

It was the 20th of January. The snow was lying

---

[1] Brown, pp. 587–589.

on Russian fields ; cold winds blew round the house ; a few strangers were beside his bed. Admiral Mordvinof came in to see him. A change had taken place. A messenger rushed for the physician. Ere he came, the object of solicitude had passed into a region of which the Lord of it has said, " There shall be no more death, neither sorrow nor crying ; neither shall there be any more pain."

The people honoured Howard with general mourning ; but the best tribute to his memory was rendered by peasants and slaves, who wept over him, wondering much how a gentleman should have left the comforts of his home to look after the prisoner and the captive. "On the day appointed for his interment thousands assembled to witness it. The coffin was placed on a bier drawn by six horses. The carriages of the Prince of Moldavia, Admiral Priestman, Admiral Mordvinof, the General and staff officers of the garrison, and the Cherson magistrates and merchants followed the remains. A large body of cavalry attended, with other persons on horseback, and two or three thousand on foot." [1]

Howard's son survived him about nine years. His father's estate descended to the unhappy man, who remained totally incapable of managing his affairs. His uncle, brother of Henrietta Leeds, looked after them ; and account books and letters relating to him and to his property are in the possession of Mr. Whitbread, at Southill. Amongst the papers is an account of money received and paid by the agent at Cardington, showing great care, and that a steady

---

[1] Clarke's Travels, vol. ii., p. 339. See also pp. 175–179.

watch was preserved, all the way through, by the uncle over his subordinate. Letters contain reports of the patient's state of mind and body. Now he appears in a frantic condition, and then in a state of sullen obstinacy, refusing every kind of food. Nourishment had to be administered by force. Health wavered, —now better, then worse,—until death put a period to miseries which had covered the greater portion of his life. Particulars were carefully given by Mr. Leeds to the person employed to conduct the funeral; and the uncle appeared anxious to carry out what he judged would have been the wish of the parent had he survived his son. He was buried at Cardington, near his mother. Their names are united with that of the philanthropist on a tablet in the Parish Church :—

"John Howard, only son and heir of J. and Henrietta Howard, died the 24th of April, 1799, aged 34 years. In hope of a resurrection to eternal life through the mercy of God, through Jesus Christ, rests the mortal part of Henrietta Howard, wife of John Howard, daughter of J. Edward Leeds, Esq., of Croxton, in Cambridgeshire, who died the 31st of March, 1765, aged 39. ' She opened her mouth with wisdom, and in her tongue was the law of kindness.'—Proverbs xxxi. 26.

" John Howard died at Cherson, in Russian Tartary, January 21st, 1790, aged 64. Christ is my hope."

Howard's friend, Mr. Whitbread the elder, died in 1796, and was interred in his family vault. Not far from it, in Cardington Church, is an elaborate monument, designed by Bacon, representing the deceased in the attitude of prayer. The dying man's left hand extends to an open Bible, which is on the floor, and his finger is on the passage, " I am the resurrection and the life : he that believeth in Me, though he were dead, yet shall he live."   Underneath is the following inscription :—

" Sacred to the memory of Samuel Whitbread, Esq., who was born in this parish, August 20th, 1720 ; and died at Bedwell Park, in Hertfordshire, June 11th, 1796. By the indefatigable exertions of honest industry he acquired an ample fortune, which his large but discriminating generosity rendered service-able to the encouragement of virtue, the diffusion of knowledge, and the relief of the afflicted. He was humane without weak-ness, liberal without prodigality, and religious without bigotry or ostentation. He endeavoured to live as all men when they are about to die would wish they had done, and died in the earnest hope and firm belief of a resurrection to eternal life."

In the same aisle is also a monument to the memory of the popular statesman who, like his father, was one of Howard's friends. The monu-ment is surmounted by figures of a man and woman kneeling, the latter leaning on the former. The fol-lowing inscription is on the slab :—

" To the memory of Samuel Whitbread, of Southill, in this County, only son of Samuel Whitbread, of Bedwell Park, Hert-fordshire, born 18th January, 1764 ; married 27th January, 1788 ; died 6th July, 1815. Elected Member of Parliament for the Borough of Bedford, 1790, which Borough he represented to the time of his death. A statesman of unblemished integrity, a man of truth, constancy, and virtue ; he loved freedom and peace, and applied in their behalf talents, eloquence, energy, and perseverance ; sincere in his attachment to the Christian faith, he abhorred all persecution as unwise, unjust, and un-righteous ; he never relaxed in his endeavours to promote the extension of religious and political liberty. Those who looked to him followed him as a faithful guide, those who differed from him, respected him as an honest man. Also to the memory of Elizabeth, his wife, daughter of Charles, 1st Earl Grey, born 7th

April, 1765, died 28th November, 1846. She was pious, virtuous, and charitable. Her duties were pleasures. She drew from her religion her sweetest counsel in prosperity and her chief consolation in affliction."

Howard's death was announced in the *Gazette*—a distinction, it is said, never conferred before on a private person. Unnumbered tributes were paid to his memory, and many laudations sent to periodicals never appeared for want of room. Many funeral sermons were preached, and those by Dr. Stennett, Mr. Smith, and Mr. Palmer were published. The last of these preachers remarked, " That others upon his decease would be excited to prosecute some of his schemes for the public good, he himself had a firm persuasion. This made him the less anxious about his own life, which his friends thought of so much importance. In the last conversation I had with him, when I expressed my fears for his safety, and my wishes that he could have been prevailed upon to continue at home, in order to carry into execution the generous plans he had formed for the good of his country, his answer was, ' When I am dead, somebody else will take up the matter and carry it through.' "

Death having removed the only obstacle to the erection of a monument in his honour, the design was renewed and prosecuted with ardour. Instead of being what so many wished, a statue of the living man, it was a funereal memento in the metropolitan cathedral.

" The first statue admitted to St. Paul's," observes Dean Milman, " was not that of statesman, warrior, or even of Sovereign; it was that of John Howard, the pilgrim, not to gorgeous shrines of saints and martyrs, not even to holy lands, but to the loathsome depths and darkness of the prisons throughout what called itself the civilized world. Howard first exposed to the shuddering sight of mankind the horrible barbarities, the foul and abominable secrets of those dens of unmitigated suffering. By the exposure, he at least let some light and air into those earthly hells. Perhaps no man has assuaged so much human misery as John Howard; and John Howard rightly took his place at one corner of the dome of St. Paul's, the genuine apostle of Him, among whose titles to our veneration and love, not the least befitting, not the least glorious, was that He went about doing good."

The following inscription, written by Mr. Whitbread, the statesman, is engraven on the south side of the pedestal :—

This extraordinary man had the Fortune to be honoured whilst living,
In the manner which his Virtues deserved ;
He received the thanks
Of both Houses of the British and Irish Parliaments,
For his eminent Services rendered to his Country and to Mankind.
Our National Prisons and Hospitals
Improved upon the Suggestions of his Wisdom,
Bear testimony to the solidity of his Judgment,
And to the Estimation in which he was held.
In every Part of the Civilized World,
Which he traversed to reduce the sum of Human Misery ;
From the Throne to the Dungeon his Name was mentioned
With Respect, Gratitude, and Admiration.
His Modesty alone
Defeated various efforts that were made during his Life,
To erect this Statue,
Which the Publick has now consecrated to his Memory.

He was born at Hackney, in the County of Middlesex,
Sept. ii[d], MDCCXXVI.
The early Part of his Life he spent in Retirement,
Residing principally upon his paternal Estate,
At Cardington, in Bedfordshire ;
For which County he served the Office of Sheriff in the
Year MDCCLXXIII.
He expired at Cherson, in Russian Tartary, on the xx[th] of Jan.
MDCCXC.
A Victim to the perilous and benevolent Attempt
To ascertain the Cause of, and find an efficacious Remedy
For the Plague.
He trod an open but unfrequented path to Immortality
In the ardent and unintermitted Exercise of Christian Charity :
May this Tribute to his Fame
Excite an Emulation of his truly glorious Achievements.[1]

---

[1] Another inscription has been preserved ; and it is interesting
from the circumstance that it was composed by the poet Cowper.
But it could not have been intended for St. Paul's Cathedral.
It relates to a monument intended for his grave, or for one
proposed to be erected at Cherson. The following letter and
its appendage are printed in " Howard's Correspondence," edited
by the Rev. J. Field. It appears as if Bacon, the sculptor, was
at work on another monument besides the one intended for the
great metropolitan church, and also that the artist had consulted the poet respecting the inscription it should bear.

"Weston Underwood, Sept. 7th, 1790.

" DEAR SIR,—

" I have found no need to make a new inscription, your own
being, in respect of the matter of it, unimprovable. The
alterations that I have made in the expression, I have made
merely on this principle, that the merit of all monumental
writing consists in a strict adherence to classical neatness of
phrase and connection, that the members of which the whole
consists may slide harmoniously into each other, and that there
may not be one syllable redundant.

"You will find my labours on the other side, for which I can say nothing, but that I have done my best, which best is always most readily at your service. I am, with Mrs. Unwin's respects, yours, dear Sir, very affectionately,

"WM. COWPER."

"JOHN BACON, ESQ."

Sacred to the Memory of
John Howard,
who
devoted life and fortune to the service of his fellow creatures.
Author of many merciful regulations
In the Gaols of his own native England,
He compassed Europe
That he might communicate them
To other Countries also.
Prompted forth a second time
By the desire and hope
Of alleviating that dreadful calamity the plague,
He terminated his course of benevolence
at this place,
Jan. 9, 1790.   Aged 64.
With many virtues,
Each worthy of a memorial,
All springing from the faith and animated by the charity
of a Christian,
He refused a statue at home,
But has here a monument
That posterity may share with us the benefit of his example.

Whether the letter and inscription relate to a monument placed over his grave, or to one proposed at Cherson, Mr. Field could not ascertain.

CHAPTER XV.

HOWARD'S CHARACTER.

FROM the sketch I have given of Howard's private life, taken in connection with the story of his journeys, we see what manner of man he was. The elements of his character, all which can be attributed to his original constitution of mind and body, to the influence of early circumstances, and to his natural predilections and habits—all these are manifest from what has been described in former chapters.

Such a person could never have been an artist, a poet, or a philosopher. He had not the rich ideality, or the passionate imagination, or the subtlety and comprehensiveness of such gifted children of "the Father of lights." But he might have been a successful lawyer, an eminent merchant, an ingenious discoverer, a useful statesman, or a distinguished admiral or general. Indeed, looking steadily into the man, one finds that his common sense, his observant mind, his methodical habits, his punctuality and prudence, his activity, enterprise, courage, endurance, and firmness, bear more than a slight resemblance to the qualities of a Wellington. The warrior and the philanthropist were a good deal alike. Out of similar primitive materials were formed the Waterloo soldier and the prison philanthropist. Into such diversified shapes

can two rough pieces out of the same quarry be hewn
and carved. But what was natural in Howard took
a different turn from being wrought into what was
higher than itself.

The religious aspect of his character we shall notice
presently.

In the meanwhile he is to be viewed as a *Traveller*,
a *Sanitary Reformer*, a *Statist*, a *Prison Revolutionist*,
and a *General Philanthropist.* He made no geographi-
cal discoveries, threw no light on the habits, the language, and the physical peculiarities of barbarous
races ; did not make observations on the government
and laws of civilized Europe ; collected no political
information of any kind, and had no power of picturesque narrative ; was perhaps incapable of criticizing
architecture, statuary, and pictures. But he had a
courage like that of wonderful explorers. His journeys in Russia with a single servant over thousands
of dreary miles and amidst untold privations, are a
proof of this. There was in him remarkable curiosity,
associated with disregard of peril and persistency in
carrying out a purpose on which his will was bent.
Witness his visit to the Bastille—the only man who
ever left it reluctantly—his adventures on the way to
Marseilles, and his conduct on reaching that port.
This especially is to be remembered, that if the published result of his travels be not an eminently read-
able book, if it do not supply philosophical details
and principles, or reveal political secrets, it does what
far more materially concerns the well-being of mankind ; for it assists society to reform its greatest enemies, and stimulates people of all descriptions to cultivate a spirit of humanity and benevolence.

Sanitary matters were shamefully neglected during the last century. Such neglect, perpetuated for ages, then reached a frightful culmination. In a total disregard of cleanliness we recognise the main causes of pestilential outbreaks such as ever and anon come under our notice as we turn over the chronicles of age after age; and what renders that disregard the more remarkable is, that at the same time the minutest attention was paid to the habits of the people in a variety of ways—sumptuary laws, interferences with trade, regulations enacted by guilds and companies, and the adoption of merchants' marks with other devices to protect vested interests—these were the order of the day. Indulgence in dirt was chief amongst English liberties; and out of abundant dirt sprung abundant disease. The accumulated evils which it produced defy accurate description. House drainage, the state of streets and roads, dens of filth in great cities, tumble-down thatched cottages in the rural districts, were a disgrace to England; and though in one sense insufferable, they were tolerated without an effort for their removal. Even in my own time I have witnessed in the northern counties what would seem incredible to the present generation.

All the more credit then is due to Howard for his sanitary crusade. The cleanliness of prisons was one of the objects he promoted in his prison tours; but it is a great mistake to suppose that those criminal abodes were the exclusive or the principal spheres of that purifying process he sought to promote. Indeed, he began with the cottage and ended with the gaol. With no precedents to guide, with no extensive sympathy to encourage, Howard, aided by Whitbread, set to work at Cardington to remove long-continued nuisances, to provide clean and decent dwellings, and to transform the whole into a model village. Afterwards, in every visit he paid to prisons, the sanitary condition of cells and court-yards became an object of careful inquiry, and improvement in these particulars was the subject of his earnest suggestions. A wonderful endeavour after the proper lodgment of the poor is at this moment exciting sympathy and assistance. Outcast London is now filling our newspapers with descriptions and appeals. All this will, we trust, form a volume of sanitary improvement, to which Howard may be said to have produced a modest but original preface more than a hundred years ago.

Of Howard as a *Statist* I leave another to speak :—

"We who are now living know that Howard was the founder of an epoch, because we are the witnesses from day to day of the adoption by the State of the very method of procedure which Howard used on the many occasions on which he found work to do.

"Howard found his first opportunity of rendering a great public service in the year 1756, when he was thirty years old, and soon after his election as a Fellow of the Royal Society. He was captured on the high seas and imprisoned in France, where he shared the sufferings of large numbers of his fellow-countrymen ; but having been liberated on parole, he remained in France till he had made himself master of all the painful facts and figures relating to their captivity. He then came to England, and submitted these facts to the 'Commissioners of Sick and Wounded Seamen,' who thanked him for his services, and, remonstrating with the French Government, brought about an exchange of prisoners, and, as I infer, a redress of the grievances that Howard had pointed out. In this instance ⌈Howard's self-imposed duty began with a most laborious investigation of the facts of the case, and ended when he had placed the matter in the hands of the Commissioners, who proved to be both willing and able to obtain redress."⌉

" Some person among those lookers-on who proverbially see more of games than the players themselves, happens to become cognisant of some cruel injustice, the inheritance perhaps of remote times, the product, may be, of some brisk and thriving industry, and he exposes it. ⌈If there is real ground of complaint, the public is brought to sympathize with the sufferers, the press gives the needful publicity, and possibly some benevolent association lends its support. The subject is brought under the notice of Parliament, or laid before some executive department of the Government. A Parliamentary Committee or a Royal Commission is appointed, witnesses are examined, evidence taken. The results are embodied in a Report. At length an Act of Parliament is passed, and inspectors are appointed, with power in some cases to bring about the punishment of those who neglect its provisions or set them at defiance; in others, to give, by means of periodical reports, that publicity which either checks malpractices or, pointing out legislative shortcomings or defects, paves the way for improved legislation. It is by such successive processes as these that our great social evils and wrongs are first exposed, then prohibited, then watched, checked, and destroyed.⌋

" Now every word of this description applies in

its full force to the method of procedure of John Howard."

As a *Prison Revolutionist* he has scarcely been *discriminately* appreciated. Vague eulogiums are pronounced on his career, without trouble being taken to understand wherein lay the strength and value of his life-work. He was far from believing that men and women are mere creatures of circumstance, that their misdoings are mainly the fruits of social wrongs committed from age to age by such as are chiefly rulers of the world. He felt strongly the individual responsibility of human beings, that everybody has a personal will, that every one is a free agent. He also was convinced that sin and misery, that crime and penalty, are linked together by laws of God as well as by laws of man. He did not adopt modern theories of punishment for capital offences; and he approved, though reluctantly, of the infliction of death on murderers and other extreme felons. He had no notion of petting the condemned, and treating them as if they were heroes. But he felt indignant when he witnessed brutal conduct under the guise of justice. He could not admit that imprisonment, transportation, and death should be executed as if they were acts of vengeful retaliation. He advocated the blending of humanity with justice, and looked upon the sufferings of a culprit as chastisement to be administered in mercy. The reformation of the offender he constantly sought. He aimed at making a prison a school for amendment. It was his cherished maxim, that idleness is the mother of crime. "Make them diligent, and they will be honest," he had seen written over the Spin and Rasp Houses of Holland; and the words never departed from his memory.

The efficacy of his labours has been thus described by an American at the National Prison Congress :—

"It is wonderful how little of his indignation or wounded sensibility he wasted in the first report of his early experiences,—the most disheartening because of their newness,—upon words and sentimental reproaches. His moral fury all went into work. He did not make a moment's parade of his fine feelings, nor call in the neighbours to witness his transports of indignation. He quietly records, for his own use, his distressing observations, and reflects with practical good sense, and without speculative profundity, upon their causes. Strange to say, his personal unsupported inspections, without warrant or authority, were not without some immediate effect, for Howard carried in his small and homely stature, a certain grave and potent personality, made up of unaffected earnestness, simplicity of purpose, and religious courage, which awed and commanded from the first, alike prisoners and prison keepers."

"What other man has made his personality for so many years so directly felt by the very persons for whose improvement and reform he was labouring? Associated beneficence, deputed and vicarious sacrifices for the vicious, organized corporations for charity and for reform ; we all know their necessity, their advantages, and their power. But do we not also know their limitations, their dangers, their exposures to superficiality and perfunctory work, their tendency to become at last only costly machines, run largely or mainly for the sake of officers who administer them ? John Howard was a sublime exception to the rule which trusts more to the machinery than the power that drives it, to the wheels than the spirit in the wheels. His personal labours were as abundant as his public reports were few and far between ; his inquiries as minute, special, and particular, as they were numerous, broad, and universal. He swept the whole field, but it was carefully as if he had only a single threshing-floor." [1]

Of his character as *universal philanthropist,* numerous illustrations have been afforded in the chapter on his private life. Broad in spirit, minute in detail, he sought out the troubles and inconveniences of the poor, with a hand ever open to the bestowment of substantial help as far as resources allowed. His quiet beneficence at Cardington has been eclipsed by brilliant achievements in the great theatre of Europe. Many who have heard of what he did in France, Italy, Spain, and Russia, know nothing of what he accomplished in Bedfordshire. Yet the Cottage Reformer deserves to be remembered as well as the Reformer of Prisons.

His *Evangelical piety* has sometimes been represented as if it were enthusiastic and fanatical, a drawback on his character, a blot on his escutcheon. Whereas this really is to be regarded as the mainspring of his vast philanthropy. It was not simply an addition to character otherwise noble. It was the source of that nobility. Religion was everything to him, in his work, his endurance, and his intercourse with mankind.

Religion was his guide, his stay, his solace, his

[1] John Howard : his Life, Character, and Services. An address delivered before the International Prison Congress, July, 1872. By Henry W. Bellows, of New York, pp. 27, 31.

delight. It was not confined to Sundays and places of worship, but breathed itself over journals and letters, and hallowed the whole breadth of a wonderful activity. His devotion, his trust in God, his obedience to Divine precepts, his loving covenants with the supreme Friend of Souls, his steady confidence amidst perturbations of circumstance, his insight into the spiritual world, his glimpses of celestial scenes flooded with eternal love, meet us ever and anon, as we turn over the modest records of his private spiritual life. Faith in Christianity properly so called, in the glorious Gospel of the blessed God—this is conspicuous in his papers. A man must be the best exponent of his own motives and impulses; and Howard ever expresses Evangelical convictions as lying at the basis of his efforts.

The Bible, in the sum of its revelations, was the guide of his faith, the charter of his joys, the guide of his life; but he looked on the New Testament as the consummation and finished glory of the Old. He has been described as realizing the ideal of a Hebrew patriarch, devout and dignified. The fact is, he was vastly more of a Christian than a Hebrew. Like Abraham, in his moment of evangelical rapture, he saw "the day of Christ," yet not far off, but near; "he saw it and was glad." His models were not patriarchs, prophets, and kings, so much as apostles, and their Divine Lord. His precepts were the words of Jesus, rather than the institutes of Moses; the Spirit which filled his soul was not that which emanated from Sinai, but that which descended at Jerusalem on the day of Pentecost.

In the letters and notes from which most of the

information in this volume is drawn, are found passages such as the following :—

"God considers what weak creatures we are, therefore gives us every motive to do good.

"Jacob speaks of the angel who had been his guide in all his journeys, and had delivered him out of all his dangers; and Jacob's God, I trust, is *my* God, and my guide, and my portion for ever.

"An approving conscience adds pleasure to every act of piety, benevolence, and self-denial. It inspires serenity and brightens every gloomy hour ; disarming adversity, disease, and death. Is it my ambition to put on the Lord Jesus ? 'to have the same mind in me which was also in Him'?

"The peculiar doctrines of Christianity,—the degradation of human nature, our inability to restore ourselves, our need of a Mediator, and of Divine aid,— are doctrines which strike at the root of vain glory. We are justified by faith, by the grace of God, through the redemption that is in Jesus Christ. Where then is boasting ? It is excluded (Rom. iii. 27). Aim at what is praiseworthy, and then at the approbation of God, who alone is an impartial, infallible Judge. Let it be my earnest inquiry how I shall best serve God in the station which He has assigned me.

"Our superfluities should be given up for the convenience of others. Our conveniences should give place to the necessities of others. And even our necessities give way to the extremities of the poor.

"O God! may the angel which conducted the Israelites through the desert, accompany and bless me!

"In all my dangers and difficulties may I have full confidence in that unseen Power, to believe in hope, as the Lord orders all things ; therefore I leave every-thing to Him, trusting He will always give His angels charge concerning me, and then I am equally safe in every place; therefore I will fear no evil, for Thou art my God."

In other memorandum-books the following passages are inserted :—

" O God ! succour me in time of trial, and help me to maintain my integrity. My eyes are up to Thee, O God ! to help me to encounter the danger ; leave me not to my own strength, but may I rely on Him in whom is everlasting strength. I come to the throne of God for mercy and help in time of need, and that I might finish my course in peace. Diffident of myself, I look up to God.

" Where there is most holiness there is most humility. Never does our understanding shine more than when it is employed in religion. In certain circumstances retirement is criminal ; with a holy fire I would proceed. What is our profession of religion, if it does not affect our heart ? Shall I desert His cause ? O God ! may I through Divine grace persevere to the end ! *My* end too is approach-ing." " My desire is to be washed, cleansed, and justified in the blood of Christ, and to dedicate myself to that Saviour who has bought us with a price."

Howard felt he was saved by Divine grace, and for the glory of that grace he lived and died. It is re-markable that of the great enterprise of his life, as far as the matter related to himself, he felt disin-clined to talk. He would not dwell on his own achievements. He did not derive satisfaction from that source. His eye was fixed, not on his own philanthropy, but on Divine love, which he fervently adored. Visiting the prisoner was only a specific form into which his benevolence was shaped. The benevolence itself cannot be accounted for except by attributing it to the influence of religion. Till a man shall be found *without that*, doing what he did, or anything like it, Christianity must retain the glory of making him what he became. His philanthropy is the reflection of that which only one book in the world reveals.

It is exceedingly unfair to speak of what he did as platform philanthropy, as an anticipation and pattern of Exeter Hall compassion. Yet some have indulged in this strain, who ought to have known better. He did not make appeals to the public to execute what he proposed, nor even to help him in his efforts. He worked alone, draining his own purse for needed supplies. No contrast, as to modes of operation, can be greater than between the course he pursued and that adopted in later times. Societies have their place, and some of them are due to his inspiration ; but he himself preferred to stand on his own foundation, and to fulfil a mission in his own way. Nor is compassion for the prisoner, pity for the criminal, to be sneered at, as weak sentimentalism ; for whilst it appeals to our purest natural sympathies, it reflects the spirit of that Divine One who devoted His life to the diminution of individual suffering, to the seeking and saving of them that are lost.

The resemblance of Howard to his Divine Master is striking. Well has it been said, "We cannot contemplate the example of Christ without asking,

If He were now living on earth, where should we be obliged to go if we wanted to see Him ?   We should have to go to the back streets, and alleys, and courts of our large cities,—to the bedside of the untended, uncared-for sick,—to the squalid home of poverty and ignorance,— to the garret or cellar where father and mother and child are pining and dying for want of bread.   This is where Christ would certainly be found."   And it was amidst the poor and imprisoned that Howard was to be found.   Of those who shall be at the right hand at the last day, to whom will Christ's word be more applicable than to Howard? " I was an hungered, and ye gave Me meat : I was thirsty, and ye gave Me drink : I was a stranger, and ye took Me in : naked, and ye clothed Me : I was sick, and ye visited Me : I was in prison, and ye came unto Me.   Inasmuch as ye have done it unto one of the least of these My brethren, ye have done it unto Me."

In connection with his religious character, it cannot be too distinctly remembered, that it had not in it an atom of bigotry.   He had his own theological and ecclesiastical convictions.   He acted upon them with consistency ; but he never refused to those who differed from him catholic rights of love and fellowship, which the Divine Head of the universal Church has conferred upon all His spiritual followers.   His catholicity is conspicuous in an age when sectarian lines were strongly marked, when the opposite of what some now condemn as Latitudinarianism was in the ascendant.   An age of intense religious beliefs *has not in the past* been an age of tolerance and unity, though no religious belief ought to be stronger than this—that we are all one in Christ Jesus. Such belief, carried to a pitch of intensity, would revolutionize Christendom. Howard had much more of it than most Christians a hundred years ago. His fraternizing with other Churches than his own, and his social friendliness with those from whom he differed on momentous points, are facts which ought to be pondered in the present day.

It is said of a hero amongst the Hebrews, " We shall not find any occasion against this Daniel, except we find it against him concerning the law of his God." [1] The same may be said respecting the subject of our memoir. His conscientiousness, sometimes thought to be punctiliously scrupulous ; his unworldliness, by some accused of ascetic excess ; his humility, on certain occasions carried to the length of an unreasonable self-abnegation ; his devotional fervour, appearing to unsympathetic minds as enthusiastic and fanatical—these qualities sprung from intense religious convictions, from unaffected conscientiousness. Not a speck of sin or weakness can be detected on his moral purity, his uprightness, his veracity, and his brotherly love for all mankind.

The drawbacks of his character are to be attributed wholly to natural eccentricity [2] and to mental misjudgments. That he was, like other excellent per-

---

[1] Daniel vi. 5.

[2] A curious instance of his eccentricity occurred at Venice. The Venetians were "astonished at his going about the streets during a hard winter without boots or gaiters, with no great coat, and sometimes even no cravat on ; though at this time the poorest citizen dared not to venture out of doors unless he was almost buried in furs or in broadcloth."—Brown, p. 458.

sons, especially men of independent mind, very odd in certain ways, no one can dispute after reading what has been recorded relative to his habits. The only thing I can find in his character seriously objectionable, is the method of domestic education which he felt constrained to adopt. I say *felt constrained*, for it does not appear to have proceeded at all from the absence of affection and sensibility. Proofs that he loved his unfortunate son are abundant. The child of his Henrietta he regarded with the utmost attachment. But he had a theory of family discipline which, however conscientiously formed, will be approved by only a few in the present day. His idea of obedience was, not the submission of love, but a subjugation of will through the influence of fear, or through the force of authority. But we see in his case, not parental unkindness, not insensibility, not a hard, severe, ungenerous mind—only a *misjudgment*, an *unwise* opinion. All he did, he really meant to be for his son's good ; and he felt surprised when the result turned out otherwise. As I have intimated already, it can be pleaded in excuse of the mistake, that he carried out persistently, and to an advanced degree, the notion of juvenile discipline then fashionable in public schools, and in the homes of all classes, especially the uppermost.

To those whom Divine Providence has placed in circumstances of affluence or of competency, so as to raise them above the need of a trade or profession, he presents a specially appropriate example. It shows how such persons may nobly consecrate their leisure and resources ; and it ought to stimulate them to industry in what Dr. Barrow significantly calls, their " particular calling as gentlemen." [1]   Yet wealth is far from being a *sine quâ non* for beneficence. Sarah Martin as well as Elizabeth Fry was a heroine in the same list as that graced by Howard's name.

Further, in an age when *association* for benevolent purposes is so widely developed and is so liable to abuse —when people lean so much on one another, looking for precedents, waiting for examples, tarrying on the borders of beneficence till more daring spirits beckon them on, the story of Howard's individuality and independence, shrinking from praise, comes as a corrective.   Not that it ought to interfere with united action wisely conceived ; but it ought to supersede feeble developments in the way of servile reliance, by inspiring a manly resolution, guided, not by the doings of others, but by a consciousness of individual power and obligation.   In these times, when Christians are fond of having their good deeds reported and emblazoned, and when so many are extravagantly disposed to raise memorials of persons whom they admire, and not a few are equally glad to receive them, the tale of Howard's self-forgetfulness supplies a correction, checking base-born pride and bidding every worker look for his reward in the approval of conscience and " the praise of God."

" Lay me quietly in the earth," said Howard ; " place a sundial on my grave, and let me be forgotten."   That he cannot be ; but we are constrained to recognise his resemblance to One who " made Himself of no reputation."

[1] See Barrow's Sermons.

CHAPTER XVI

A GOOD man's influence does not die with him. In Howard's case the fact is conspicuous. Could we collect all instances in which his memory has consciously touched ministers of mercy in this world of sorrow,—still more, if we could trace all streams of moral power which, flowing from him, have unconsciously reached multitudes of workers,—the record of these manifold and mysterious impulses would make a marvellous history.

A few examples may justly close the present volume.

As early as 1772, a clergyman at Bedford Chapel set on foot subscriptions for the relief of small debtors who were confined in prisons with the vilest criminals. A Society was instituted for its permanent promotion, "James Neild, a jeweller in St. James Street who amassed a large fortune and became High Sheriff of Buckinghamshire, was a zealous supporter, and filled for some years with great success the office of Treasurer. He won the title of a second Howard, and distinguished himself amongst those who were anxious to raise a monument in honour of Howard the first."

Mr. Neild in 1800 published, "An Account of Persons Confined for Debt in the various Prisons of England and Wales, together with their Provisionary Allowance during Confinement." He states himself that during a period of twenty-eight years he visited most of the prisons in England, endeavouring everywhere to separate the debtor and vagrant from the abandoned felon. He tells sad stories illustrating the wretched effect of "the laws betwixt debtor and creditor," which he with other wise men anxiously desired to reform. The law of bankruptcy was then on the carpet, as it has been so recently in our time. Ten shillings in the pound would be offered to a creditor and not accepted, and then the money would be spent on the fees, the lodging, and the maintenance of the debtor, during perhaps a long incarceration. If, after arresting and putting a man in gaol for what he owed, a creditor forgave the debt, liberation did by no means take place as a matter of consequence. "No," says the gaoler, "my demand for prison fees and lodgings amounts to so-and-so, and I will detain him till these are paid." Thus a gaoler acted as judge, jury, and executioner; and this abominable system Mr. Neild strove to overturn. Window duty was imposed on prisons, and therefore, for economy's sake, light and air were excluded from the captive's cell. Hence disease was engendered, gaol fevers raged, and this painstaking person, in his beneficent labours, caught the pestilence, from which he did not recover for twelve months. As he contemplated the Association with which his journeys were connected, he exclaimed with pardonable excitement, "This little rivulet shall one day swell into a wide and copious stream that shall diffuse plenty and prosperity on every side of it; it shall abound like Euphrates and like Jordan in the time of harvest!" He volunteered, in connection with Sir John Mild-

may, in 1802, to examine and report on the management of convicts in Portsmouth harbour. His per-
sistent endeavours after reform put gaolers on the
alert, inspiring a salutary fear of being visited; and
so he helped to keep these dismal domains in a state
of preparation for the eyes of gaol critics like himself;
and at the same time magistrates were stirred up to
make themselves better acquainted than they had
been with the inside of a county prison. Mr. Neild's
name, coupled with that of Howard, received honourable mention from judges on the bench; and better
still, gaols at Aylesbury, at Gloucester, at Dorchester,
at Chelmsford, and even at Edinburgh, were improved, as the result of his influence.

He seems to have been somewhat eccentric. One
day he wrote stating that he had been surprised by
receiving a bank note for £1,000 in a blank note
addressed to James Neild, Esq., Cheyne Walk,
Chelsea. He presented it to the Committee of his
pet Society, saying it must have been intended for
them, he being their Treasurer. Lord Romney was
of a different opinion; but the Treasurer insisted upon
the money being thrown into the Society's exchequer.
The bank note could not be traced, being of three
years' earlier date; and Mr. Nichols informs us,
"Happening at that time to be an acting commis-
sioner at a public Board of which Mr. Neild was a
regular attending member, I saw both the letter and
the bank note, and had no doubt of its being a pious
fraud of the worthy Treasurer; in other words, that
the thousand pounds was a gift from himself."[1]

---

[1] Nichols' Literary History, vol. ii., p. 696.

Mr. Neild died in 1814. A year after, the following incident occurred. A gentleman named Venning was attracted by a Society formed at that period under the presidency of the Duke of Gloucester, and having succeeded in reforming some juvenile offenders at a time when that was judged hardly possible, he resolved to devote his remaining life to the enterprise. Proceeding to St. Petersburg with mercantile views, he found so much room for the exertions of a philanthropist, that he totally surrendered his original pursuits, and gave himself over to the work of ameliorating the national prisons. No personal dangers, and no consideration of ease or wealth, restrained him. He plunged into the receptacles of disease and crime, and by a skilful organization of noblemen of great influence, he was enabled, in a marvellously short time, to correct flagrant abuses. So deep and general was the impression produced by his disinterested consecration, that when he died of a fever contracted in gaol, shortly after completing the thirty-ninth year of his age, Prince Galitzin, in proposing the monument to his memory which now stands in the Smolenskoi Cemetery, said : "While Russia has to show near one frontier the ashes of his contryman who produced the first traces of amelioration in the condition of prisoners and of the sick and suffering, let her show here the monument of a second Howard, a worthy follower and emulator of the good deeds of the first."[1] Mr. John Venning, his relative, sympathized with him. I had the privilege of knowing this gentleman when I was young, and of visiting him

---

[1] Knill's Life of Walter Venning.

whilst occupying a large old house in the city of Norwich. He was well acquainted with the Emperor Alexander, and used to relate how his majesty, when driving through the streets without any parade, would pull up his horses and stop to speak with the English merchant. He was an eminent philanthropist, and liberally supported the Bible Society and other religious institutions.

Upon another man, an eminent Quaker, a French refugee of noble family, Howard's mantle fell. Stephen Grellet was in 1813 led to visit London prisons. First he entered the Compters—now abolished—where offenders were temporarily confined, and was astonished at the number of occupants. In Newgate, accompanied by William Forster, he saw four men under sentence of death, one of them with a wife and two children come for a last dreadful interview. The governor endeavoured to prevent the prison visitor from seeing the women, because they were so riotous and ungovernable. He persisted. " They occupied two long rooms, where they slept in three tiers, one on the floor, and two tiers of hammocks over one another. They had the whole soon rolled up, and all the women came together in one room. When I first entered, the foulness of the air was almost insupportable ; and everything that is base and depraved was so strongly depicted on the faces of the women who stood crowded before me, with looks of effrontery, boldness, and wantonness of expression, that for a while my soul was greatly dismayed ; surely then did I witness that the Lord is a refuge and strength, His truth is a shield and buckler." He spoke to them of Christ's love, they

A A

hung down their heads and began to weep. Then he inquired after the sick, and discovered "a mass of woe and misery, many lying on the bare floor or on some old straw," and several infants, " born in the prison among them, almost naked." [1]

Grellet's Newgate visit was most important, and was followed by memorable consequences. It led to the great mission fulfilled by Elizabeth Fry, Joseph John Gurney, and Thomas Fowell Buxton.

I remember meeting Mrs. Fry in her daughter's house at Kensington, when I felt myself in the presence of an extraordinary person. Her Quaker dress, her muslin cap, her hair parted over her forehead, her beautiful face, her benignant expression, her musical voice, her queen-like dignity, left an impression which forty years have not effaced. That lady, as everybody knows, carried Howard's work to a point it had not reached before. I had heard much of her when I was a boy at Norwich, and visited Earlham, where she had spent her girlhood amidst gaiety not common in the Society of Friends; she had received, through the ministry of a Philadelphia Quaker preacher, William Savory, seeds of grace which ripened into a harvest of spiritual good. Stephen Grellet told this lady, then become a minister of the Gospel in her own communion, of what he had seen and heard within the walls of Newgate; and this inspired her with a wish to share in such visitation. She went, accompanied by a sister of Thomas Fowell Buxton, and found there three hundred women, with their children, crowded together. The

---

[1] Memoirs of S. Grellet, voL i., p. 196.

convicted and untried were in the same apartments, without sufficient clothing, living in rags and filth, sleeping at night on the floor, without bed or bedding, and spending the day in absolute idleness. They were turbulent, profane, intemperate; they clamorously begged of those who came near, and then squandered at the prison tap the alms they had managed to extort. The sight shocked Mrs. Fry. She writes in her journal, "Yesterday we were some hours in Newgate with the poor female felons, attending to their outward necessities; we had been twice previously. Before we went away, dear Anna Buxton uttered a few words in supplication; and very unexpectedly to myself I did also. I heard weeping, and I thought they appeared much tendered; a very solemn quiet was observed; it was a striking scene, the poor people on their knees around us in their deplorable condition."

Four years after her first visit, she attempted a more comprehensive and systematic method. Being left alone for some hours with a number of unhappy women, "she read to them the parable of the Lord of the Vineyard in the 20th chapter of St. Matthew, and made a few observations to them on the eleventh hour, and on Christ having come to save sinners, even those who might be said to have wasted the greater part of their lives estranged from Him. Some asked who Christ was; others feared that their day of salvation was past." She talked to mothers about their children, and thus secured an entrance into their hearts. That key to usefulness she well knew how to turn. She proposed to establish a school for these little ones and desired them to select a governess of their own, impressing this upon them, that without their co-operation she could do nothing. They chose a mistress. She proved herself equal to the hard task. She had stolen a watch, but was now repentant and reformed. Mrs. Fry attended and formally opened the school, installing the young woman in office ; other ladies joined Mrs. Fry in her new work, and it went on successfully.

In 1817 there was formed "an Association for the Improvement of the Female Prisoners in Newgate," with these objects, "to provide for the clothing, the instruction, and the employment of the women ; to introduce them to a knowledge of the Holy Scriptures, and to form in them, as much as possible, those habits of order, sobriety, and industry, which may render them docile and peaceable while in prison and respectable when they leave it." The Lord Mayor, the Sheriffs, and some Aldermen went at a month's end to ascertain the results. One of the ladies read a chapter. The attention of the women was remarkable, their decent dress, quietness, and decorous behaviour excited astonishment and admiration. The magistrates entrusted these humane visitors with a portion of their own authority, to punish refractory individuals by short confinement.

The meetings held were much talked of. Described by the press, they were pictured by artists and engravers. Prints of Mrs. Fry fulfilling her mission, with criminals in front, and the faces of noted Friends and philanthropists at her side were common in shop windows, and began to decorate the walls of Friends, when pictures were rare in their neat abodes. Grandees thought it a favour to be admitted to these gatherings, and royalty itself was glad to see what was being done in Newgate by the queenly Quakeress.

Joseph John Gurney, of Earlham Hall, near Norwich, was a younger brother. He had a dignified presence, a pleasant face, a condescendingly courteous manner, a musical voice, and a flowing utterance, indicative of literary culture. Mrs. Fry and her brother were of one mind in reference to prison discipline; and in their tours for preaching the Gospel, according to the principles of Friends, they steadily persevered in prison visitation. Two memorable journeys they took in the years 1819 and 1828.[1]

In 1819 they visited Scotland and the North of England. "They felt themselves much indebted to the magistrates of the towns and districts through which they passed for the kindness and openness with which they received them. They rejoiced that the views entertained by those gentlemen were correct and benevolent; few evincing any disposition to adhere to the old system, fraught as they had found it to be with accumulated errors and evil consequences. In many places the expediency of erecting prisons on an improved plan was under consideration, and in some they were already in course of building." Thus, after the lapse of more than thirty years, the influence of Howard's visits to

---

[1] "Prison Discipline. Notes of a Visit to some of the Prisons in Scotland and the North of England in Company with Elizabeth Fry, with some Remarks on Prison Discipline," 1819.

"Report addressed to the Marquis Wellesley, Lord Lieutenant of Ireland, by Elizabeth Fry and J. J. Gurney, respecting their late Visit to that Country," 1828.

Scotland, and the spirit he had awakened were producing the desired results.

But in many of the small boroughs, and even at Haddington, Aberdeen, and Glasgow, gaols "were of the worst possible description." Mr. Gurney depicts the prison of Dunbar in terms similar to those employed by Howard in his early researches : "Small rooms," "extreme filth," "a little straw," "a tub for every dirty purpose"—these are the dark colours which he lays on his canvas. Then comes a sketch of Haddington in similar tints : "Miserable cells," "scenes of barbarity," "no clothing allowed," "no medical man, no chaplain,"—these are the wearisome items, sentence after sentence. But there was this happy circumstance, "Many of the prisons in Scotland are without any inhabitant." Special reference is made to the treatment of debtors and lunatics. Owing to peculiarities in Scotch law, the former were kept in "durance vile," like the worst of criminals, and their health was exposed to serious injury; and the latter, though innocent, were placed in prison for want of any other refuge, and treated as if they were felons. "The frequent appeals made by Mrs. Fry in behalf of the insane, and the tenderness with which she treated them when she came in personal contact with those afflicted ones, in prisons or other places, proved how powerfully her heart was touched with compassion for the heaviest of human maladies, 'the worst of evils,' as she once expressed it, 'to the individual and those connected with him, except sin.'" [1]

---

[1] Memoirs of Elizabeth Fry, vol. i., p. 340.

The book produced different impressions. Some contradicted certain statements, being annoyed and irritated because responsible for the evils exposed. Others rejoiced that hidden things of darkness were brought to light, for the unveiling of abuses is one step towards reformation. Best of all, the influence of religion promoted the purpose of these benevolent travellers. Mrs. Fry raised her voice to proclaim, that reformation, not revenge, is the object of punishment, "to be a terror to evil doers, and a praise to them that do well," whilst, in the words of her great Master, she was heard to say, " Neither do I condemn thee : go, and sin no more." [1]

In 1827 the sister and brother visited Ireland. At Dublin they began their inspection of prisons. They found vast crowds of criminals without occupation, without instruction, without provided clothing, therefore half-naked, herded together in great dens. The City Marshalsea was very bad ; the Smithfield Penitentiary was in pretty good order. "While we were visiting," says Mr. Gurney, "the judges, then on the bench of a neighbouring court, heard of us, and sent a message to invite us into their presence." The two visitors, in Quaker garb, entered the hall of justice, and sat by the side of their lordships "in the front of a crowded and inquisitive assembly." [2] Afterwards they went to Kilmainham—so much talked of in our time—and they describe it as "well conducted and superintended," "a contrast to the Dublin Newgate." The prison at Trim, they said, "was once the pride

---

[1] Memoirs of Elizabeth Fry, vol. i., p. 341.
[2] Life of J. J. Gurney, by J. B. Braithwaite, vol. i., p. 325.

of the country, but is now considered one of the worst in Ireland." Such were the fluctuations of prison discipline, showing that a statement in reference to one period is no guide to the judgment respecting another.

The arrival of the travellers at Belfast produced great excitement. Crowds of ladies and gentlemen flocked to meet them ; Presbyterian clergymen, Roman Catholic priests, and Dr. Croly, one of their bishops, were of the number. Mrs. Fry and Mr. Gurney went to the penitentiary, the schools, and the poor-house— a place of refuge well managed. They record facts which show that Ireland then was certainly no better than it is now. At Enniskillen, " a populous town prettily situated on the banks of Lough Erne, we visited the infirmary and a very indifferent gaol, in which were six persons under a charge of desperate murder. This is no uncommon crime in Ireland. Deeply settled revenge is in general the cause ; and it is often attended with awful barbarity. I do not exaggerate when I say that we have seen dozens of murderers during the last week. In Roscommon gaol were ten more, for the murder of a member of our society, a mere nominal Friend, who had a quantity of arms in his house, which were in part the object of pursuit. He defended himself vigorously, but it was all in vain. He was shot by the assailants ; and more desperate characters than they appeared to be, I never beheld. At Sligo there was a prisoner who had roasted a poor woman alive. Nothing can exceed the ferocity into which the unbridled passions of this unhappy people lead them, when party spirit has the sway over them."

As a set-off it should be noticed that in the neigh-bourhood of Lord Enniskillen's Castle, Florence Court, the peasantry, very numerous, were "well dressed, decent, and intelligent." [1]

Again, on their way to Enniskillen, they visited the prison, the lunatic asylum, and infirmary at Lifford, and the prison and infirmary at Omagh. Respecting them Mrs. Fry writes, "We think that in these insti-tutions there is a great spirit of improvement, though some of them remain in a deplorable state. The infirmary we visited to-day was so. I found there a poor patient without any linen, laid between blankets, and in an exceedingly dirty state; but this is not common, some are in beautiful order." [2] There arose light in the darkness.

It is curious to find Mr. Gurney saying of Limerick, "Whilst in that city we could a little understand what the Apostle Paul meant by 'being pressed out of measure;' for the multitudes that came after my dear sister put us to some inconvenience at the prisons." [3] At Carlow there were complaints made by the Catholic priests, that Protestant clergy inter-fered with their prison visitations. They appealed to the Quaker as an umpire. "We happily brought them to terms," he tells us; "and I went afterwards to the Roman Catholic Bishop Doyle, to get the arrangement confirmed." He gave his full sanction to it. The popularity of these visitors was surprising. "We arrived at Wexford, a large town on the sea-coast, early in the evening, and truly it was an evening

---

[1] Life of J. J. Gurney, by J. J. Braithwaite, vol. i., p. 340.
[2] Life of Mrs. Fry, vol. ii., p. 36.   [3] Ibid., p. 347.

of overpowering exertion. Crowds were waiting for us at the gaol, at the entry of the town. It was in vain to attempt to pass by it, though a public meeting was appointed for seven o'clock. We visited it, and my sister formed her committee."[1]

Mr. Gurney was a general philanthropist; but the books he wrote on prison discipline show the especial interest he took in that subject, and how plainly Howard's mantle fell on his shoulders. An anecdote related respecting this trait in his character confirms the impression derived from the publications I have noticed. Not long after the first of them appeared, the Mayor and Corporation of Norwich perambulated the boundaries of the county, Norwich being a county as well as a city, and the boundaries running over much rural scenery. One of the lines approached Earlham Hall; and the hospitable master of the mansion invited the municipal officers and their followers, to the number of 800, to partake of refreshment. Afterwards he made a speech to his guests; and urged upon the Mayor and Corporation the importance of attending to prison affairs, which had been sadly neglected, and had fallen into a very unsatisfactory state. He told them a new gaol was needed; that one much better than that they had at present could be easily erected, since much had been accomplished for the improvement of such edifices; that the whole institution ought to be placed on principles which reformatory investigation had brought to light; and that prisoners should be industrially employed, whilst their morals were watched with a

---

[1] Life of Mrs. Fry., vol. ii., p. 355.

view to their correction. He enforced his appeals by referring to the change recently wrought in Newgate through the exertions of a Ladies' Committee, whose proceedings he described. He promised a donation of one hundred pounds towards the object ; and his speech and example are said to have produced some practical fruit afterwards.

The next prominent name in the succession is that of Sir Thomas Fowell Buxton. It is now between fifty and sixty years ago that I first saw him in the chair at a Bible meeting. In after time his majestic form (he was six feet four)—his thoughtful countenance, his conspicuous spectacles, his measured utterance, and his satisfying judgment on public questions, became familiar. And I can, at this moment, recall a trifling incident illustrative of his readiness. He was advocating slave emancipation, in which cause he caught Wilberforce's mantle, and spoke of negroes becoming our *brothers in law*, which provoked a laugh; in an instant he substituted the words, " in law our brothers." Perhaps his labours as an emancipator of slaves, have thrown into the back-ground his services in promoting prison reform.

He tells us one day, while walking past Newgate with Mr. Samuel Hoare, their conversation turned upon the exertions of their sister-in-law, Mrs. Fry, and her companions, for the improvement of the prisoners within its walls; and this suggested the idea of employing themselves in a similar manner. They soon entered into communication with Mr. William Crawford, Mr. P. Bedford, and other gentlemen, who were anxious to improve the condition, at that time deplorable to the last degree, of English gaols. The exertions of Mrs. Fry and her associates had prepared the way, public attention had been drawn to the subject, and in 1816 the Society for the Reformation of Prison Discipline was formed. In the list of the committee, the name of Buxton stands between those of Dr. Lushington and Lord Suffield. He received a fresh stimulus in this enterprise from a visit to Newgate in 1817. He wrote, " It has made me long much that my life may not pass quite uselessly, but that in some shape or other I may assist in checking and diminishing crime and its consequent misery." In 1817 he published a book on prison discipline. It was noticed and much praised in Parliament; and then, being translated into other languages, it produced beneficial results, not only in England and Ireland, but also in France and Turkey.

In 1817 he visited the Continent, and wrote in his diary full particulars respecting prisons at Ghent and Antwerp. He was struck with the admirable management of the *Maison de Force* in the former town, as Howard had been in 1778 (though with serious modification in 1781); and the new visitor determined to lay an account of it before the Prison Discipline Society in London. He did so, and was requested to publish his report. When he sat down to the task, it grew insensibly in his hands. " It was necessary," he remarks, "to prove that evils and grievances did exist in this country, and to bring home to their causes the increase of corruption and depravity. For this purpose repeated visits to prisons were requisite." Notwithstanding Howard's endeavours after reform, the new inquiries developed a system of folly and wickedness which surpasses belief.

His successful efforts on behalf of the Hottentots who had been enslaved by the Boers—efforts which secured their freedom in 1828—and his untiring exertions in the cause of negro emancipation, so gloriously crowned in 1833, did not wean him from a deep interest in the improvement of prison discipline and criminal law. As it regards the latter subject, he surpassed Howard. In 1821, a speech of his on criminal law excited great interest, " the drift of it was, to prove that the law, as it stood, was at once inhuman and ineffective ; that the severity of the punishment induced judges and jurors to strive for an acquittal; and that the uncertainty of the greater penalty was therefore more readily incurred than the certainty of the lesser one." No less than two hundred and thirty offences were at that time punishable with death. The sanguinary penal code has since been reformed so far, that only eight or nine crimes remain punishable by death in 1848, and now, practically, execution is confined to cases of murder. Sir Fowell's labours contributed largely to this result.

In 1840, he visited Italy ; and it is interesting to place his reports by the side of Howard's account of visits to Roman prisons in the previous century.

"On Thursday," he says, "I finished the prisons by seeing the *San Michele*. This is an asylum for orphans, old men, and old women (several hundreds of each), and a very good one it is. Annexed to it was a female prison, 280 women in it; some imprisoned for life, others for periods from twenty years down to one. It is a wretched place, with next to no instruction; of the 280 prisoners only thirty could read. Why don't they elect me Pope? The army of priests should soon have something to do in the way of Infant Schools, etc."

He also inquired into the state of the Civita Vecchia prison. He found 1,364 desperate criminals He entered a low room with a vaulted ceiling, which, following Howard's plan, he measured. The dimensions were thirty-one yards long, and twenty-one broad. The noise was such as one imagines might be at the entrance of hell. Murderers and bandits were chained to a ring fastened on a platform. A fourth room was worse than any other, damper and darker, the inmates more villanous in appearance. " What are you here, for ? " he asked a heavy-looking fellow lying on his back at the end of the room. He remained silent, but a sharp-featured Italian replied, " He is here for stabbing." " Why is he in this part of the prison ? " the visitor inquired. " Because he is incorrigible," was the answer. " And what are you condemned for ? " " For murder." " Why placed here ? " " Sono incorrigibile." [1]

Leaving the place, the inquirer wrote these words : ' The sight of it has kindled in my mind a very strong desire that the old Prison Discipline Society should make a great effort and visit all the prisons of the world. I had hoped that sound principles of prison discipline had spread themselves more widely ; but I now fear that there are places, and many of them in the world, in which it is horrible that human beings should live, and still more horrible that they should die."

As Howard visited the Pope, so did Buxton. "The

---

[1] Compare this with Howard's prison visits in Italy.

Pope," he says, "is a civil, lively, little gentleman. He gave us an audience of three-quarters of an hour. He was very inquisitive to know what I thought of the Roman prisons." The interpreter said oftener and more strongly than Sir Fowell liked, *contentissimo.* "I praised everything I could," he says, "such as the chancellor of the gaols, the boys' prison, the *San Michele* hospital, and the liberality of the Government in giving me free access and full information ; to all of which, he very gracefully replied, that if gentlemen, from motives of benevolence, took the trouble to visit these institutions, the least he could do was to afford facilities, furnish documents, and listen attentively to every suggestion." When the praise was over, the critic honestly told the Pope that the female prison of the *San Michele* and the gaol of Civita Vecchia needed a through reformation ; and the Pope seemed attentive and well-disposed. I may add, that Sir Fowell mentioned the cruelty of butchers in the treatment of lambs. Some months afterward, he heard that his observations had produced an effect.

He visited debtors in prison, and wished to give them some relief ; but hesitated as to the bestowment of money, lest it might be wasted in drink. It was suggested that he should procure the liberation of some one. He selected a tailor, with a wife and ten children, who was sent to gaol by a malicious creditor for a small debt. "After a most loving and grateful kiss of our hands, away he started, the happiest tailor in the Roman dominions."

In Rome, the traveller found no classification of criminals, except on a small scale with regard to boys. Other prisoners were huddled together, males of all ages and for all sorts of crimes. There was no inspection, no employment for the majority, though convicts sentenced to long periods of imprisonment worked in the streets ; the rest, tried and untried, had nothing whatever to do. There was no gaol delivery. But there were no chains, nor any adoption of the solitary and silent system ; on Sundays there was mass, and the repetition of a creed at nightfall.

He tells a startling story of Italian banditti, and of Gasparoni their chieftain, who combined opposite qualities, like our Robin Hood, only that the latter and his men must not be compared with robbers of the Roman States. No one who travelled from Rome to Naples twenty years ago, could fail to notice between Terracina and Gaeta, ill-looking fellows skulking about, of whose occupation there could be no doubt. Three little towns, perched on rocks, shining like silver, Cora, Norma, and Sermone, attracting the traveller's eye at Appii Forum, were haunts of desperate gangs at a still earlier period ; and tales were told of them not pleasant to travellers, who rode amongst the mountains at night-fall. Gasparoni was seen by Sir Fowell, who asked him, " How many people have you murdered ? " " I cannot exactly recollect," he said ; " somewhere about sixty." It was notorious he had killed twice the number. Yet he accounted himself a religious man, for he never killed anybody on Friday, but fasted that day, saying : "Perche sono della religione della Madonna."[1]

[1] Memoirs of Sir Thomas F. Buxton, Bart., by his Son. That interesting volume is my authority for the facts I have related respecting his work as a prison visitor and reformer.

Buxton's great work was the abolition of slavery, and in that cause he manifested as much firmness and courage as Howard did in another. Well might his daughter say, in a letter written in 1833, " He seems to be devoted to it in a way that renders him insensible to minor influences, and reminds one of the description of Howard in Foster's Essay on 'Decision of Character.' Himself is strangely forgotten ; not subdued or resisted, but genuinely forgotten." [1]

Though I never, to my knowledge, saw Sarah Martin, I seem as if I had been acquainted with her, through the circumstance of my intimate friendship with two gentlemen who were closely connected with her history, and who often spoke to me respecting her. One was a minister [2] who converted her to the service of Christ when she was young, and whose Church she entered " as a member " ; the other was a resident at Yarmouth, [3] to whom she gave many of her manuscripts ; and some of these he showed me, containing hundreds of pages covered over with exuberant versification.

There is a long street, which runs parallel with the Dutch-like quay of Yarmouth. It contains a curious building, now much altered inside, but outside nearly the same as it appeared when I was a boy. A covered wooden staircase in front led up to a small courtroom where the quarter sessions used to be held. The mayor, aldermen, and common council, attending the Recorder, used to march in procession from St. Nicholas' church carrying large bouquets of flowers in their hands, to open in that quaint and ugly edifice

---

Memoirs, p. 330.   [2] Rev. W. Walford.   [3] Mr. Etheridge.

the periodical proceedings of justice in the borough. Beyond and below the court-room was a miserable sort of day provision for debtors and felons; and two dungeons or night rooms were at the end of a ladder in which Howard counted ten steps.

Mr. Neild informs us, that in 1808, there was but one courtyard for all descriptions of prisoners. "One room," he says, "is set apart for the sick, with a large iron grated and glazed window, but no fire-place." In 1805 a recommendation had been made that an adjoining public-house should be purchased and added to the gaol, that the sexes should be separated from each other, and the loathsome cells should be bricked up. But years passed before the recommendation could be carried into effect.

The doors were simply locked, and inside the prisoners prowled about, whiling away time as they pleased—gambling, fighting, swearing in the most fearful manner. That continued a common spectacle sixty years ago. It was the scene of Sarah Martin's toils. Her acquaintance with the place began in 1818, when she entered it to see a woman who had been committed for the cruel usage of her own child. "When I told her the motive of my visit, her guilt, and her need of God's mercy, she burst into tears, and thanked me whilst I read to her the twenty-third chapter of St. Luke—the story of the thief on the cross, who, although suffering justly from man's judgment, sought and found mercy from the Saviour." The incident encouraged the visitor, and she found herself committed to a work which afterwards made her known as the Prison Visitor of Yarmouth.

There was at that period no Sunday worship in the

prison. The first day resembled the other days of the week. She persuaded the inmates to have a service of their own, one reading to all the rest, and she made up her mind to be present as a hearer. " After many changes of readers, the office devolved upon me. That happy privilege, thus graciously opened to me, and embraced from necessity and in much fear, was acceptable to the prisoners, for God made it so, and also an unspeakable advantage and comfort to myself."

She began with reading to the little congregation out of printed books ; at last she preached to them sermons of her own. Many of them are still preserved, and some are printed in the Life of her published by the Religious Tract Society. They are very excellent, plain, judicious, heart-searching,—full of evangelical truth, and breathing much fervour of spirit. Her audience consisted of agricultural labourers, depraved boys who picked up " a precarious livelihood amongst the chances of a seaport town," sailors belonging to Yarmouth and other ports, smugglers (a race of criminals then numerous), a few poachers, and perhaps a few London pickpockets, who had come down to Norfolk to pillage something at a country festival.

This excellent woman agreed with Howard in attributing crime in a large measure to idleness. .She therefore set men, women, boys, and girls to work. To work they went, even with alacrity, and found, after their irksome idleness, amusement in their industrial occupation. Old bronze-faced beachmen took up needle and thread, and began to patch up a quilt ; young folks, with nimble fingers, learned to carve all sorts of things out of big beef bones. Mutton shanks supplied material for cutting out spoons and apple scoops. Straw hats and cloth caps were produced in that busy workshop ; and altogether it became a bee-hive where human bees might be said to fill their dark cells with honey.

Many of the prisoners could neither read nor write. Sarah Martin determined to teach them on week nights. Grandfathers with cramped hands strove to guide a pen, and with empty minds began to use a spelling book, and pick up from lesson boards texts of Scripture. She made herself one of them ; and when she set them to learn and repeat a verse of the Bible, she would do the same exercise herself; and if they said, " It is of no use," she replied, " It is of use to me, and why should it not be so to you ? You have not tried it, but I have."

Once she showed them an etching by Ketzsh. This inspired the emulation of a shoemaker and a bricklayer. Pencil, pen, and paper were given them, and they succeeded in producing a tolerable copy of the original. The etching was selected for a purpose. It represented a chess-player ; it suggested an amusement far superior to that in which they had been accustomed to indulge.

When the term of imprisonment closed, she did not forget them. She would seek suitable lodgings for homeless people, persuade masters to take back old servants, reconcile parents to reformed children, secure employment for industrious youths, get boys and girls into Sunday schools, and encourage sailors to call on her when they returned from a voyage.

Her prison Journal is in the public library at Yar-

mouth. She makes some general remarks, and speci-
fies a number of individual cases. She remarks,—
"I always find the worst of convicts thoughtful before their departure, and softened. The most inaccessible minds then become accessible. Such was the
case with those who departed to-day; and, as usual,
this fresh state of feeling, which was produced and
prevailed before they left the prison walls, was at an
end when they appeared in the street. It was then
subverted by the herd around them, exciting them to
laugh and shout. These were their former companions, the thieves of the place, whose influence was as
a repetition of the death-blow; whilst that evil—the
mad, joyous feeling which they excited in the convicts, reflected back on them—removed all terror
which the example ought to have produced; so that,
instead of being by the sight deterred from crime, a
different effect may be expected."

She relates at length the conduct of several criminals. When she argued with them patiently and
firmly, some of them were convinced and confessed
their faults; one was very obdurate, but at length he
yielded.

"*February* 11. This day I afforded F. J. the opportunity he desired of some private conversation with
me, by asking him to take my Bible up to the gate.
He said he should be sorry to bring up his children
with such views as he had expressed; that he had
reflected, and felt that he had been wrong; he expected to be ridiculed by the other prisoners, but was
determined to adopt a new line of conduct altogether.
There were deep feeling, thoughtfulnesss, and strong
earnestness of manner. He spoke highly of his wife,

I then asked,—‘ Do you love your wife ? ’ ‘ Oh, yes ; and my wife loves me.’ ‘ And do you love your children ? ’ ‘ Oh, yes ; I love my children.’ ‘ And were I or any other to say, “ I hate your wife, I hate your children,” would you like it ? ’ ‘ No ; I should not.’ ‘ And yet you spoke against my God ; and of this holy book you said, “ It is all a pack of nonsense, I do not believe one word of it.” ’ F. J. acknowledged the application with much emotion. He said he had been accustomed to sit from Sunday morning till Saturday night in a public-house, but would attend a place of worship in future, which his wife had formerly advised in vain. He acknowledged that I was justified in leaving him after his having spoken of the Bible and of God as he did.

“After the date, February 11, he seemed a new character, no longer close or sly on the one hand, nor presuming on the other ; but simple, honest, and open. The poor fellow has obtained no work, his children are ill, and his excellent wife, whilst rejoicing at the change in her husband, is cast down by extreme poverty. I gave them an order for some flour.”

And who was this Prison Visitor ? Not a person in circumstances like those of Howard or Neild ; not a lady of the upper class, like Mrs. Fry, but *a poor sempstress*, who earned a few shillings a week, and that for a while “was all her living”; and she would trudge on foot in bad weather from the village of Caistor to the further end of Yarmouth to keep her appointments at the gaol. A relative died, and left her between two and three hundred pounds, and that was really all she had to depend upon when her dress-making failed ; how could that succeed amidst her charitable vocations? Friends helped her; but she was so delicately conscientious, so afraid of being paid for her well-doing, that it was difficult to persuade her to accept what was offered. The corporation proposed to allow a salary for her gaol work; from that she shrunk, and they found it difficult to induce her acceptance of a miserable pittance of twelve pounds a year. One of the magistrates told her, "The business is out of your hands; if we permit you to visit the prison, you must submit on our terms." [1]

"In the full occupation of dress-making," she writes, "I had care with it and anxiety for the future; but as that disappeared care fled also. God, who had called me into the vineyard, had said, 'Whatsoever is right I will give you.' I had learned from the Scriptures of truth that I should be supported. God was my Master, and would not forsake His servant. He was my Father, and could not forget His child. I knew also that sometimes it seemed good in His sight to try the faith and patience of His people, by bestowing upon them very limited means of support, as in the case of Naomi and Ruth, of the widow of Zarephath and Elijah; and my mind, in the contemplation of such trials, seemed exalted by more than human energy, for I had counted the cost, and my mind was made up. If, whilst imparting truth to others, I became exposed to temporal want, the privation, so momentary to an individual, would not admit of comparison with following the Lord, in thus

---

[1] The Memoir of Sarah Martin. I am entirely indebted to this admirable book for the account I give of this excellent woman.

administering to others.　Supported with these views,
I advanced, still meeting increased disclosures of the
Divine goodness."

"Noble woman!" says the *Edinburgh* reviewer.
"A faith so firm and disinterested might have removed
mountains; a self-sacrifice founded upon such principles is amongst the most heroic of human achievements."　Strictly speaking, in later life, she had
no income but the interest on her relative's legacy.
She lived by faith; and friends ministered to her
necessities bountifully.　The friendly hamper never
failed, the grocer's supply reached her week by week.
They were her cruse of oil, her barrel of meal.

In her last days she was greatly afflicted.　She
suffered much, "but in patience possessed her soul."
Twenty minutes before her death, on being told her
end was near, she clapped her hands, exclaiming,—
"Thank God; thank God."　"She slept in Jesus,
October 15, 1843, aged 52 years.　'As we have borne
the image of the earthly, we shall also bear the image
of the heavenly.'"　This is the inscription on her
tombstone.　A stained glass window in the grand
old church of St. Nicholas, Yarmouth, commemorates
her virtues.　Good Dr. Stanley, Bishop of Norwich,
sent his contribution to it with the words, "Could I
canonize Sarah Martin, I would do so."

INDEX.